Duets

**Two brand-new stories in every volume...
twice a month!**

Duets Vol. #65

The holidays are almost here
and we have a delightful duo just for you.
Multipublished author Jacqueline Diamond returns
with a delicious doc and the unexpected twins the
heroine is *clearly* expecting! Making her Duets debut
this month is talented Stephanie Doyle with a
Fran Drescher look-alike character who's definitely
out of her element down on the farm!

Duets Vol. #66

The holiday fun continues with
Harlequin American Romance author Nikki Rivers,
who serves up a quirky, fast-paced romance.
"Ms. Rivers brings her characters to life with a fire
that is magic," says *Affaire de Coeur*. New author
Kathleen O'Reilly will tickle your funny bone with a
warm story about two best buds who suddenly see
each other in a different light at Chistmastime. Enjoy!

Be sure to pick up both Duets volumes today!

The Doc's Double Delivery

"You lied to me!"

"No," he said. "About what?"

"Being so naive and out of it. Like you didn't know your way around." Chelsea put her face into her pillow.

"I *am* naive and out of it." His amused tone might have reassured her, if not for the awkward circumstances. "I spent the past two years on an island in the South Pacific."

"What were you doing on an island?"

"Serving in the Peace Corps. I'm a doctor."

Two years on an island. He'd just returned and immediately gone to a brand-new nightclub known only to savvy locals?

It was also known to Chelsea's employer, who'd asked her to recommend a nightspot for his freshly arrived partner.

"Hank?" she said.

"Hmm?"

"Your name wouldn't be short for Barry Hancock Cantrell, would it?"

He sat upright, nearly knocking her off the bed. "How did you know?"

"Pleased to meet you, Barry. I'm Chelsea Byers, your new receptionist."

For more, turn to page 9

Down-Home Diva

Ross cursed the small interior of the truck.

"Damn, I want you in my bed," he said.

"Me, too," Claudia murmured as she made her way from his lips to his cheek to his neck. Her need was an agony. So much that she actually felt a roaring in her ears. A horn that blasted through her dazed senses. Odd, she thought, most women saw stars.

"I want you naked and writhing, and begging for me."

"Naked, writhing, begging," she repeated in a chant.

"I want to feel your legs wrapped around my waist, holding me inside you."

"Inside you. Yes, that's what I want, too."

"I want—"

"Dad!" A distant shout called to them.

Ross's daughter was a few yards away and coming closer. "Rosa May, go back inside."

"I heard the truck pull up. Then you started beeping the horn and I thought you might be in trouble."

"Oh, the horn!" Claudia flushed, realizing that the sound wasn't coming from inside her.

"Your butt was pressing up against it," Ross accused softly.

For more, turn to page 197

HARLEQUIN DUETS

ISBN 0-373-44131-2

Copyright in the collection:
Copyright © 2001 by Harlequin Books S.A.

The publisher acknowledges the copyright holders
of the individual works as follows:

THE DOC'S DOUBLE DELIVERY
Copyright © 2001 by Jackie Hyman

DOWN-HOME DIVA
Copyright © 2001 by Stephanie Doyle

The Doc's Double Delivery

Jacqueline Diamond

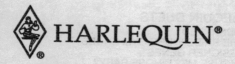

HARLEQUIN®

TORONTO • NEW YORK • LONDON
AMSTERDAM • PARIS • SYDNEY • HAMBURG
STOCKHOLM • ATHENS • TOKYO • MILAN • MADRID
PRAGUE • WARSAW • BUDAPEST • AUCKLAND

Dear Reader,

Barry, the pediatrician returning from two years in the Peace Corps, and Chelsea, the free-spirited receptionist, nearly didn't get their story told. For rectifying that, thanks are due to my editor, Jennifer Tam.

She called while I was working on the book *Surprise, Doc! You're a Daddy!* for Harlequin American Romance, and asked if there were any characters in it who might be bursting for a spin-off romance of their own.

At first I wasn't sure. Barry's so stuffy, he draws up a list of desirable qualities before he goes wife hunting. Chelsea, on the other hand, lives for the moment and rescues castoff pet rodents.

However, opposites attract. And collide. Sometimes they even produce unexpected pregnancies. And thereby hangs a tale....

If you enjoy my story, please write me at P.O. Box 1315, Brea, CA 92822. I promise to answer!

Sincerely,

Jacqueline Diamond

Books by Jacqueline Diamond

HARLEQUIN DUETS
  2—KIDNAPPED?
  8—THE BRIDE WORE GYM SHOES
37—DESIGNER GENES
44—EXCUSE ME? WHOSE BABY?
55—MORE THAN THE DOCTOR ORDERED

HARQUIN LOVE & LAUGHTER
11—PUNCHLINE
32—SANDRA AND THE SCOUNDREL

For my good friend and mother-in-law, Joyce Wilson

1

"THERE WEREN'T ANY GOATS on the plane," said Dr. Barry Hancock Cantrell after emerging from customs.

"Were you surprised?" asked his cousin, Dr. Andrew Menton, who had come to the airport to meet him.

"Pleasantly."

"Good. Then welcome to normality, if you consider Los Angeles normal," said Andrew, and hefted a couple of Barry's suitcases.

After serving two years in the Peace Corps on Prego Prego, a Pacific island formerly colonized by the Italians, Barry was prepared to see goats almost everywhere; they were a mainstay of the island's economy.

They rode in the front seats of cars and slept on living room couches. They had also arrived at his pediatric clinic with their owners claiming to love them like children.

Barry said no to them and to anyone else with an inappropriate request, however tempted he might be to take a goat's temperature just to maintain good public relations. He maintained high standards at his clinic and always, despite the heat, wore a white coat.

Now Barry shrugged aside his stiffness from the

long flight and grabbed the rest of his luggage. "Thanks for picking me up."

"It's the least I could do for my new partner. Believe me, I have a vested interest in making sure you don't get lost," Andrew said as they rode a moving walkway through the huge modern airport.

An image of its counterpart on Prego Prego flashed into Barry's mind. The ramshackle terminal barely provided shelter from tropical rainstorms. Passengers raced across cracked pavement to reach the planes, en route battling monkeys that darted onto the tarmac to snatch at their carry-on luggage.

Inspired by his late mother's idealism, Barry had set out to help save the world after completing his medical residency. Serving on the island had been a worthwhile experience, but boy, was he ready to be back in the U.S.A.

He and his cousin formed a matched set, Barry realized as the two of them stepped off the moving walkway. Although Andrew was seven years older and a few inches shorter, they had similar broad shoulders, moderately muscular builds and dark brown hair.

The family resemblance should make patients feel comfortable, now that Barry was joining Andrew's upscale pediatric practice. He made a mental note to find out where his cousin shopped for those tailored slacks and crisp shirts. His own wardrobe was sadly lacking.

"Your flight was a little late, thank goodness, or you'd have had to wait for me," Andrew said as they skirted a group of camera-laden tourists. "You know how it is, trying to leave early on a Friday afternoon. Kids always get sick on the weekend.

You'd think some of them could at least wait until tomorrow.''

"You work Saturdays?'' When he'd agreed to join the practice, Barry hadn't queried about specifics.

"Yes, for a few hours. I'm giving you this weekend off, though,'' Andrew said. "You can relax until Monday.''

"Thanks.'' Barry hesitated to make his next request, then reminded himself of how urgently he wanted to start his search. "I'm a bit jet-lagged, but I'd like to explore the nightlife. Can you recommend any places to go dancing?''

"Sure. I'll give you that information as soon as I have a free hand,'' Andrew said. "I came prepared because you asked me the same thing in your e-mail last week.''

"I did? I guess I'm a bit overeager,'' Barry admitted. "Well, I'm thirty-one years old. In med school, I wasn't ready to settle down, but boy, has that changed.''

A scratchy touch on Barry's throat reminded him that he was still wearing the island's farewell necklace of seashells and macaroni. He would miss the laid-back island ways, his small patients and his dedicated staff.

He would not miss the absence of a woman in his life. After two years of self-imposed celibacy, he was eager to find the right lady to marry.

The men exited the terminal into a cool early-March breeze. It never got this chilly on Prego Prego. Usually the air steamed in the heat and carried the scents of salt water and blossoms. Los Angeles smelled of exhaust fumes.

Barry hadn't seen this many cars in the entire past two years, he noted, as a long line of vehicles halted to let the two men cross to the parking structure. He liked cars. Seeing so many at once, though, was a little overwhelming.

"What kind of woman are you looking for?" Andrew asked as they entered the parking garage.

"Someone steady and reliable," Barry said, having given the matter due consideration. "Pretty but not flashy. Intelligent."

"Anything else?" His cousin led the way into a garage elevator.

Mentally, Barry searched through the scenarios he'd created during the long, lonely nights on Prego Prego. "She should have a career that matters to her. Of course, she'll have to want children, too."

"Absolutely," said Andrew, who had two kids of his own.

"I guess I'm asking a lot," Barry said.

"On the other hand, you're offering a lot," his cousin commented. "You're a doctor."

"I'm not rich," he pointed out.

"With the proper investments, you'll get there." The elevator door opened, and Andrew led the way between rows of automobiles.

"Here's my car." Stopping behind a Lexus sedan, Andrew set down the suitcases, fished in his pocket and handed Barry a slip of paper. "Before I forget, here's the name and address of a club. Can't vouch for it personally, though. I had to rely on one of my sources."

"That sounds intriguing."

"Apparently this club scene is a complicated business." Andrew opened the trunk. "This is supposed to be the newest, hottest place."

"I'm not sure I'm quite ready for that," Barry admitted.

"Have a drink, and if you don't like the scene, go home," Andrew said. "It's not as if you're going to meet the perfect woman on your first try."

"Besides, faint heart ne'er won fair maiden, right?" Barry said.

"Something like that."

As they piled his luggage into the trunk, his mind skipped ahead to that evening. He pictured a woman sitting at the bar, perhaps with long dark hair like his sister-in-law, Cindi, or maybe short blond locks. Their gazes would meet...

"Cindi arranged for the leasing company to leave your new car in your garage," Andrew added. "It's a sharp little sports number."

"What color?" Barry asked.

"Metallic blue, she said."

"Sounds perfect." Sleek but not loud, that was what he'd requested. And a midpriced American model that wouldn't strain his budget.

On Prego Prego, Barry had lived in a hut made of scrap iron with a roof fashioned from discarded tires. He was looking forward to occupying the new condo he'd bought through an Internet broker.

"Your utilities are turned on, so you're all set," Andrew said. "We're expecting you at my house for dinner Sunday night. Think you can find your way there?"

"Sure." Although he'd grown up in Austin, Texas, Barry and his mother, Meredith, had moved to L.A. when he was seventeen, after she and his father divorced. It had been a painful split, following years of disagreements.

His parents hadn't fought over anything as mundane as money or religion. Both were sixties-era idealists who grew apart over the years. Meredith came to believe the government could solve all problems while his father, Lew, a family doctor in private practice, contended fiercely that the government *was* the problem.

After moving west with Meredith, Barry had visited the Menton family home often while attending college and medical school at UCLA. "I can't wait to see Cindi and Aunt Grace," he said.

His cousin nodded. "They're delighted that you're here."

As he got in the car, Barry reflected that he couldn't wait to find his own version of Cindi— smart, efficient and elegant. Maybe it would happen this evening, if he got very, very lucky.

THE PEDIATRIC waiting room erupted into chaos while Chelsea Byers was on the phone in the reception bay, trying to schedule a child's appointment. The mother, a real estate agent, kept putting her on hold to take other calls.

The trouble started, as far as Chelsea could tell, when three-year-old Laryssa swiped a Lego piece from two-year-old Krystle. Wailing, Krystle threw her doll, missed, and hit four-year-old Tisa, who stumbled against the giant aquarium.

All three girls were children of privilege. Their clothes were probably purchased on Rodeo Drive, their hair was cut and curled at designer salons and one girl had bragged that she drove her motorized minicar through her family's mansion.

They also knew how to act like fishwives.

With a scream of outrage, Tisa flung herself at Krystle. The smaller child dove beneath the Lego table, wiggled out the other end and banged Laryssa on the kneecaps, sending her crashing to the carpet.

"Yo! Stop killing each other!" Wedging the phone between cheek and shoulder, Chelsea waved her hands. Gold sparkles flew from her fingernails.

She could feel her purple-tipped black hair bursting free of its clip, so she set down the phone. A voice squawked on the other end. Chelsea said, "Excuse me," and put the woman on hold.

To her relief, the three girls stopped fighting and stared at her. "You have funny hair," said Tisa.

"Can I see your nails?" asked Laryssa.

"Sure." Chelsea held them out. Poking at the sparkles, the little girl giggled.

Krystle pouted. "Me touch hair!"

"I'm not sure if I should let you." Chelsea looked toward their mothers for permission. The three of them regarded her with varying degrees of exasperation.

"It's no wonder they're restless," said Laryssa's mother. "We've been waiting half an hour."

"I'm sorry. Dr. Withers is the only one in the office this afternoon," Chelsea said. "Dr. Menton went to meet his new partner at the airport. He'll be starting here on Monday."

"His new partner?" asked Tisa's mom.

"He's Dr. Menton's cousin, Dr. Barry Hancock Cantrell." Chelsea ducked out of the reception bay, which was edged by a semicircular counter. Through a door from the inner hallway, she entered the waiting room. "Here." She crouched to let Krystle touch her flamboyantly dyed hair.

"His new partner is a Hancock?" Laryssa's mother sounded impressed.

Benedict Hancock, grandfather of Andrew Menton and Barry Cantrell, had been a legendary pediatrician in Los Angeles. Chelsea wasn't impressed by pedigrees, and from his reputation she expected this Barry person to be a huge stuffed shirt, but the mothers were obviously bedazzled.

"I guess we can put up with a little inconvenience," said Krystle's mother. "For a Hancock."

The three little girls surrounded Chelsea as if she were a new form of entertainment. She found she enjoyed being down here on the floor, away from the demands of the phone.

Let voice mail handle things for a while. As for leaving the real estate lady on hold, turnabout was fair play.

"Anybody want a horsy ride?" she asked.

"Yippee!" The girls piled on.

Chelsea collapsed with an exaggerated groan. "Not all at once."

"Me first!" said Tisa.

"Me!" That was Krystle.

"I want the longest ride," said Laryssa.

None of them got off.

"Make up your minds," said Chelsea.

"I'm thinking," said Tisa.

At close range, Chelsea discovered, the kids were cute. At least, as much of them as she could see from this angle.

She'd never felt comfortable around children. Being a receptionist in a pediatrician's office hadn't been her first choice of job, although she liked it better than the half-dozen positions she'd held previously.

Speaking of positions, this one was cramping her legs. "Somebody has to get off," she said, to no effect.

The nurse, Helen Nguyen, pushed open the internal door. "Laryssa Oglesby," she read from her chart. "Chelsea? What are you doing on the floor?"

"Trying to breathe."

"Having any luck?"

"Not really."

By the time Mrs. Oglesby removed her daughter and Chelsea gave the other two girls their rides, her slacks were covered with carpet lint and her scalp ached from having her hair pulled as reins.

Kids might be cute, but she wondered where their mothers got their patience.

With a sigh, Chelsea went to pick up the calls on hold. It was three-fifteen. In a few hours, she'd be free for the weekend.

Friday night was playtime. She planned to hit the newest, edgiest nightclub, the exciting kind that opened in a converted warehouse without benefit of fire inspections or code enforcement, and would no doubt close as soon as the authorities got wind of it.

Maybe she'd meet a really cool guy, the wilder the better. If not, she'd dance with lots of geeks and have a good time anyway.

BARRY STOOD inside The Slash/Off! Club, trying to take his bearings.

Beams of colored light swept the vast space with

dizzying speed, making the throng of shaggy dancers resemble a herd of stampeding buffalo. Between the so-called music and the stomping of feet, he hadn't heard such loud noise since the last typhoon hit Prego Prego.

"Move it!" came a woman's voice from behind. "You're blocking the way!"

Since she had to scream in his ear to make herself heard, she came close enough to give Barry a whiff of her perfume. It had a sharp, fresh tang that he couldn't identify, definitely not old-fashioned floral.

He moved aside. As the woman brushed by, he got an impression of delicate features set off by black hair tipped in purple. On Prego Prego, she would have been taken for a *strega,* a witch who told fortunes.

A drunken couple weaving toward the door shoved into the woman. When she stumbled, Barry caught her arm to steady her.

The fabric of her blouse felt slinky against his hand. Its indefinable colors shimmered in the shifting light, and its low V-neck gave him an unexpected view of soft, uplifted orbs.

Embarrassed, he released her. Not quickly enough to keep her from noticing where he'd been looking, apparently, because the woman bristled at him.

"Having fun?" she demanded. A lull in the music made her voice carry.

"Not yet. I just got here," Barry said.

Holding her ground against jostling passersby, the woman scrutinized him with narrowed eyes. "How'd you get by the guard in front? I mean, a white suit! You look like a refugee from some safari movie."

Barry had been surprised to find a man posted in front of the club rejecting anyone who wasn't dressed bizarrely enough. He hadn't expected to pass muster, although surely he was due some points for the stubborn wrinkles in his only casual suit. "I told him I was wearing a faux-fur loincloth underneath."

"Are you?" the woman asked.

"That's for me to know and you to find out." Barry stopped, surprised at himself for flirting. This wild-haired woman with the low-cut, bare-midriff blouse was as far from his style as a female could get, regardless of the heat she aroused in his midsection. "Forget I said that."

The noise that passed for music resumed its ear-shattering shriek. The woman drifted into the throng, vanishing from sight almost instantly.

Barry felt a moment's disappointment. She might not be his type, but he would have enjoyed a little more interaction.

After two years of celibacy, he was obviously far too vulnerable, Barry thought. Best to forget her.

To his left, he spotted a bar constructed of raw-looking wood, and headed toward it through drifts of sawdust. Come to think of it, once he disregarded the high-tech gizmos that passed for decor, the entire club resembled a warehouse that had been converted hastily into a nightspot.

What kind of sources did Andrew rely on? Barry couldn't picture his conservative cousin hanging out in a place like this, that was for sure.

He found a stool and tried to catch the attention of the bartender, who was waiting on customers at the other end. In addition to a hefty admission price, the Slash/Off! required a two-drink minimum, which he'd paid for in advance. Barry decided to make one of them nonalcoholic, since he was driving.

People streamed past him. For his taste, the women were by turns too offbeat, too hard-faced, too gaunt. In comparison, the *strega* had been downright conservative.

Jet lag was catching up to him, he realized. Maybe he should forget about the drinks and go home.

"Tough week?" asked the man sitting next to him. Mercifully, the rock music wasn't as loud in this corner, so he could make out the fellow's words.

"Long flight," Barry said.

"It doesn't help that airline service is so lousy." The man had a thin face with a scraggly growth around the chin. His expression was friendly, though. "Hi, I'm Will." He extended his hand.

Barry started to say his name, then thought better of it. Although the guy seemed harmless, he didn't want to give out too much information.

"Hank," he said, shaking Will's hand. Hank had been his nickname in sixth grade, derived from his middle name Hancock. He'd used it because there were two other boys named Barry in the class.

"Save my seat, Hank." Will went to join the knot of people around the bartender. A few minutes later, he returned with two glasses of white wine. "It's the best I could do. The guy had them already poured."

Barry handed over one of his drink receipts. "Thanks."

"No big deal." Will stuffed the piece of paper into his shirt pocket. "How'd you hear about this place, anyway?"

"Through a friend." He took a sip of the wine.

It was odd-tasting stuff, even by Prego Prego standards. "Why?"

"With that white suit, I figured you don't live around here." The man watched him so intently that Barry began to feel uncomfortable.

He'd been ill at ease when he arrived on Prego Prego, too, especially the night a monkey swiped his undershorts and paraded around town in them. Since the bright gold-and-black shorts had "Go, Bruins!" printed on them, there'd been no question about whom they belonged to.

Barry had never felt in any danger on the island, though. He did now, although he couldn't figure out why. His temples hurt, probably from jet lag. His vision was getting foggy, too.

Another sip of wine might clear his head. Barry was lifting the glass when a slender feminine arm reached past him and knocked it away, spilling wine across the counter.

"Hey!" Blearily, he peered at his attacker. It was the woman with black-and-purple hair.

"You idiot!" she said. "You stand out like a sore thumb in that white suit. Don't you know your drink is probably drugged?"

"No, it's not. He..." Barry looked around for Will. "Where'd he go?"

"Back into the hole he crawled out of, I hope," the lady said. "I saw him carrying two glasses and it made me suspicious. Women don't accept drinks from guys at places like this because they spike them."

The room was spinning, not unpleasantly. "How can you spike a drink that's already alcoholic?"

"Boy, are you naive. Where'd you come from, anyway?" she asked. "Outer Mongolia?"

"More or less." Barry realized he couldn't pronounce Prego Prego in his current condition without spitting. "Why would he spike my drink?"

"You'd have awakened in an alley, if you were lucky enough to wake up at all," the woman said. "Minus your wallet and your keys. Your car would be gone and when you got home, so would the contents of your apartment."

Barry felt utterly stupid. Not to mention stupefied. "Nobody warned me."

"I just did," the woman said. "Did you come with somebody? You must not have drunk much, because you're still conscious, but I don't think you should drive."

"Can't drive," Barry agreed. For some reason, he found himself willing to go along with anything she suggested. It must be an effect of the drug.

"You could drive me home," he said.

"I guess I could. I came with my roommate, so I have to find her and tell her." Without hesitation, the woman clambered up a stool and onto the bar, where she stood peering into the maelstrom of dancers.

At this angle, Barry noticed that square-heeled open sandals supported her delicate feet, with the toenails painted midnight blue and studded with ruby-red stones. The shapely length of her legs extended up to the short wrap skirt.

In his present condition, he found blue-and-red toenails utterly fascinating, not to mention the long slender legs and short skirt.

"Anything you can't see from down there?" the woman asked. "I'd hate for you to miss anything."

"You're pretty," Barry said dreamily.

The woman climbed down. "You're smashed."

"Feeling no pain," he agreed.

"You definitely need help. My name's Chelsea, by the way," she said. "I don't see Starshine anywhere."

"Let's go outside and I'll show you," Barry said.

"Starshine is my roommate." Amusement tugged at her lips. "You really are far gone. I barely rescued you in time."

"I like being rescued." She had lovely eyes, he thought, purple with black flecks to match her hair or, at least, in this light that was the color they appeared.

"You didn't tell me your name." Chelsea scrambled to the floor and took his arm.

"Uh..." He thought it started with a *B*, but his lips were too rubbery to pronounce it. "Hank."

"Come on, Hank." She guided him to his feet. Barry discovered that his knees had gone soft. It was an interesting sensation.

In a dreamlike state, he passed through the crowd and out into the crisp night. On the way, he bumped into the guard, who took a long, angry look at his suit. "Hey, bud! You were supposed to strip down to your loincloth."

Barry struggled to marshal the mental resources and verbal agility that had placed him third in his class at medical school. "Huh?" was the best he could do.

"You have your nerve!" Chelsea told the hulking guard. "My client was drugged, right here in this poor pretense for an establishment. You tell your boss he'll be hearing from my firm." Before the man could reply, she hauled Barry out of the building.

"You're a lawyer?" he asked, intrigued, as he wobbled alongside her across the sprawling parking lot. Around it rose the stark rectangular shapes of warehouses.

"No. I didn't want Mr. Jockstrap Mentality to get the idea he was entitled to strip you himself," she said. "Where'd you park?"

"I'm not sure."

It took a while to locate the sports car. Then Barry was fumbling in the glove compartment for his address when Chelsea pointed out that they had to head for her place, not his. "Since it's your car, I'd have no way of getting home. You can sleep on my floor and drive to your place tomorrow."

"Whatever," he said.

"Nice wheels, by the way," said Chelsea, and started the engine. She backed up so quickly that Barry left his stomach in the parking space.

Off they shot into the night. Dazedly, he reflected that he was entrusting his life to a strange woman who drove too fast and had a roommate named Starshine.

He just hoped she didn't keep goats in her apartment.

2

As she drove, Chelsea tried to figure out what on earth had possessed her to pick up Mr. White Suit.

With a name like Hank, he probably hailed from some corn-fed Midwestern town. On second thought, she could swear she'd detected a trace of a Texas twang in his speech, and he had the deep tan a man might get riding the range.

She hadn't even had time to dance after paying that steep admission charge. It didn't make sense for her to leave so early, especially not with some small-town guy from Texas.

On the other hand, the man was like a stray animal who'd been kicked and was too dumb to know it. He needed help. That was Chelsea's problem: She couldn't resist a creature in need.

Besides, Hank was cute. As she edged off the 101 Freeway north of downtown Los Angeles, she sneaked a glance at his profile. More than cute. Beneath the pathetic suit, he had a build on him.

For an instant, she flashed on a similarity to someone she knew. It must be the broad shoulders. But who...?

The thought slid away as she recalled Hank's remark about wearing a loincloth. Dollars to doughnuts he'd made it up. Still, she'd like to see him strike a seminude Tarzan pose, preferably in the vicinity of her bedroom.

Instantly, Chelsea rejected the idea. In the hard-won experience of her younger days, men fell into one of two categories after getting a woman into bed. Either they couldn't run out the door fast enough, or they believed they owned her.

Then there were guys like her former fiancé...but she didn't care to think about him.

Hank the puppy dog could sleep it off on her lumpy couch. In the morning, she would launch him into the wilds of L.A. looking little the worse for wear, since he could hardly cram any more wrinkles into his suit.

She wished he wasn't regarding her with such an engaging smile. Or that he hadn't displayed an unexpected sense of humor. If she didn't watch out, she might start to like him.

Chelsea parked the sports car on the street in front of her place. As she emerged, she heard salsa music blaring from across the way. It bounced off the steep rises atop which sat a row of run-down cottages, mostly converted into apartments.

After a minute, she realized that Hank wasn't getting out. "You okay?"

"My knees are hollow." He didn't act upset about it. "I'll spend the night in the car."

Although Chelsea had no obligation to take care of him, she hated to leave a country yokel unaided, especially when he wasn't in full possession of his senses. Look at how much trouble he'd landed in already.

"I'll help you inside." She came around and opened his door. "You have to stand up."

"This car's really low, isn't it?" He gazed at her from beneath a displaced lock of shaggy hair. Chelsea had forgotten how touchable a man's hair could look when it wasn't hardened with ten layers of gel.

"You should be used to the height," she noted. "It's *your* car."

"Just leased it," he mumbled, and swung his legs out. He hauled himself upright, using the car roof for support.

He looked taller now that they were alone. Not unduly tall, though. Since she was only five foot three, Chelsea appreciated not having to stare at a man's navel.

She locked the vehicle. "Here's your keys."

"Put them in my pocket, please." He stared upward into the night sky.

She dropped them into a pouch in his white jacket. The man radiated heat.

"You can't see the stars," he said.

"What?" Chelsea tilted her head. "Yes, you can." It was a clear night with a three-quarter moon.

"Not many, and they're faint," he said. "What happened to them?"

"You really are from the backwoods," Chelsea said. "It's called light pollution. We're near downtown Los Angeles. See the skyscrapers over there?" She indicated the brightly illuminated structures a mile or so to the east.

"Gee," he said.

"Come on, fuzz-brain. Let's get you inside." She caught his arm. "Think you can climb those steps?"

Hank squinted at the long rise to the house. Chelsea had to admit it was quite a hike, especially since it required an additional effort to get to her second-story unit. "Sure," he said. "Did I ever tell you I once climbed a volcano?"

"I guess you left that out of your life story." With Hank leaning lightly against her shoulder, she began mounting the steps. "I didn't know they had volcanoes in Iowa."

"I'm not from Iowa." His thigh brushed hers. Feminine awareness arrowed into her.

"I meant Texas." She was breathing hard. From the climb, no doubt.

"How did you know I'm from Texas?"

"It's written all over you." For the first time, Chelsea understood why some of her friends thought cowboys were sexy. She could picture Hank riding a horse and swinging a lasso, preferably while wearing nothing but a faux-fur thong.

Grimly, she banished the image. Sweaty men on horses weren't her style.

They barely made it to her apartment entrance without collapsing. Trying to keep Hank from tumbling off the exterior landing, Chelsea wiggled her key in the lock and scraped the door open.

A flick of the switch revealed the shambles that she called home. Formerly a large attic, it featured a sloping roof over a large room subdivided by flimsy walls.

Above the thrift-store furnishings in the main room hung tattered shreds of black-and-orange crepe paper. A large fake web in one corner sported a dusty black spider the size of a plate, while plastic skulls dangled over the kitchenette.

"You *are* a *strega*," Hank said.

"A stray what?"

"*Strega*. Witch. Fortune-teller." His voice had a happy lilt. The man was totally zonked.

"The decorations are left over from Halloween," Chelsea said. "Starshine and her boyfriend had a party and they never got around to cleaning up."

"Halloween was months ago."

"They broke up the next day and she went into a decline. She's just getting over him."

Starshine and—what was her new boyfriend's name? Wiley?—hadn't cleaned up their dinner dishes tonight, either, Chelsea noticed as they wandered into the kitchenette. Wearily, she tossed their paper plates in the trash and cleared away a pan full of congealed baked beans.

"She takes advantage of you." For being smashed, Hank was rather observant.

"She's a nice person," Chelsea said. "Besides, I'm used to disorder. I thrive on it. Usually."

She didn't want to concede that his comment had hit close to home. Starshine still hadn't paid her share of this month's rent, which Chelsea had had to advance.

She expected Hank to slump onto the couch and fall into a doze. Instead, he prowled around examining her possessions. "You have a lot of books." He indicated a long row on the floor, propped at each end by a cinder block.

"I can't resist buying them. One of these days I'm going to get caught up on my reading," she said.

Hank dropped to his knees and selected a volume to examine. Seeing him handle one of her books sent a warm shimmer fleeting across Chelsea's skin, as if he were touching her.

She hadn't gotten close to a man in the year and

a half since her engagement broke off. Hadn't wanted to, either.

Yet tonight, her defenses were tumbling in the presence of this sweet, lost soul. They dropped far enough for her to recognize, as he slanted a grin at her, that a powerful masculine presence had slipped into her apartment in the guise of a helpless puppy.

She ought to throw him out, Chelsea told herself. The tingling that spread into her muscles was pleasant, though. Besides, what harm could he do in his condition?

"My eyes don't seem to focus very well." Putting the book back, he straightened. "Can I fix you something to eat? I'm hungry."

The way he stared at her with his mouth slightly open, he *did* look hungry. But not for food.

"I grabbed a bite after work," Chelsea said.

"Only a bite?" He regarded her slim midsection, exposed by the cropped blouse. "You don't eat much, do you?"

"It seems like a waste of time." This discussion was arousing her appetite—more than one kind.

"I can think of more interesting ways to waste time," Hank said.

"Oh, really?" Nothing was going to happen, Chelsea reminded herself. In his current state, Hank probably couldn't perform even if she were foolish enough to let him try.

The air crackled between them as he studied her. Then his mouth curved ruefully. "I'm afraid I'm not up on the local customs."

"Local customs?"

"The sexual taboos," Hank clarified. Lamplight

raised amber glints in his brown eyes. A woman could get lost in them, Chelsea thought.

"This is Los Angeles. There are no sexual taboos." Realizing that her comment might be taken amiss, she added, "Except the ones I set for myself."

"Of course," Hank said. "That's what I meant. Just tell me what to do. And not do."

"You're very agreeable."

"Not usually." He gave her a frank look. "Enjoy it while you can."

Despite her reservations, Chelsea found herself liking this man. She felt as if they were both on the same side of an equation, working together to figure out the value of X.

"I'll take you up on your offer to cook," she said.

"Done." Hank slowly made his way into the kitchenette and, without asking annoying questions or grousing about the messy cabinets and fridge, proceeded to assemble an omelette.

Chelsea had never before eaten eggs with pineapple bits and water chestnuts. "This is good," she said after she tasted it.

Hank sat across from her at the small battered table, wolfing down his portion. His nose was a little off-center, she noticed, just enough to offset his otherwise classically sculpted bone structure.

"The flavors are intense," he agreed when his food had disappeared.

"That's because you're still high," Chelsea said.

"I'm also je…" He stumbled over the word, and finished thickly, "Jagged."

His word choice puzzled her. "Jagged?"

"You know. I've been flying," Hank said.

"So I noticed. You need to take it easy."

"I don't want to take it easy." His gaze bored into her. "I want to make love to you."

Heat flushed through Chelsea. She wondered how it would feel to kiss this man. To muss that soft, thick hair. To find out whether he was really wearing a jock strap of any persuasion.

"I don't know." *Brilliant, Chelsea. Incisive and definitive!* "I mean, it's been a long time for me."

"Me, too," said Hank. "Two years."

Was that possible? she wondered. There wasn't a place in this country where women could have spent the past two years keeping their hands off a hunk like this, unless he'd been in a monastery. "Did you take vows or something?"

"Only a vow I made to myself," he said.

Desperately, Chelsea tried to get a grip on her self-control. Maybe Hank was manipulating her, pretending to be naive and celibate. Maybe he'd maneuvered her into bringing him home and was right now trying to trick her into bed.

If that was his scheme, it was working.

"I wouldn't want you to break any vows for my sake," she said weakly.

"It won't be a sacrifice, I promise," said Hank, and, sliding off his chair, disappeared under the table.

HE HADN'T MEANT to duck under the table. In his current disoriented state, however, the other paths toward Chelsea struck Barry as clumsy. Going around would take too long. Climbing on top would be messy.

So he went below.

When he hit the linoleum, he considered the possibility of curling up there and going to sleep. He wasn't exactly sleepy, though. He was in a delicious state of suspended reality.

It was about to get even more delicious, if he had anything to say about it.

Down here, he got another close-up of Chelsea's red-stone-studded toenails. Even in the dim light, they glowed like magic orbs.

Her legs were lightly tanned, smooth and slender. Barry ran a hand up one.

"Hey!" Chelsea's face appeared at the bottom edge of the table, turned sideways so she could peer at him. "What are you doing?"

"Making love to you," he said.

"From down there?"

"It seemed like a good idea," Barry said.

She smiled and sat up. "I have to admit, you're original."

Encouraged, he rested his head in her lap. The touch of her fingers in his hair relaxed him. Teased him. Aroused him.

Barry lifted his head and found himself at eye level with her breasts. Tilting his chin so he could see Chelsea's face, he said, "Kiss me."

"I'm not a contortionist."

"I'll help you." Bracing himself on both sides of her chair, he pushed upward. The table edge dug into his back, stopping him short. "Sorry."

"You've earned that kiss." After pushing her chair back, Chelsea stood up. "Let's go somewhere more comfortable."

When Barry rose, he discovered that he had lost patience with halfway measures. His body had achieved a ferocious state of readiness fueled by two years of painful self-control and the nearness of a delectable woman.

"Let's start right here." He caught her in his arms, and made an interesting discovery.

The last time Barry had had a girlfriend, he'd been a socially inept pediatric resident. His amorous efforts had inspired laughter as often as passion.

For two years, he'd worked off his frustrated libido by helping the islanders hoe their crops, dive for shellfish and construct tin-roofed wooden homes to replace ones knocked down by high winds. In his spare time, he'd watched, on video, old movies featuring sophisticated heroes like Cary Grant and Clark Gable.

As a result, he'd developed two things: a powerful body and romantic finesse.

Slipping one arm beneath Chelsea's knees, he scooped her against him horizontally. When her lips parted in astonishment, he pressed his mouth over them.

The tip of her tongue met his, tentatively at first and then with real enthusiasm. Supple and wonderfully curvy, she nestled into his arms. Barry couldn't have invented a more perfect partner for his fantasies.

Holding her easily, he reveled in the softness of her lips, then transferred his attention to the pulse at her throat. He trailed kisses across the vulnerable points where her shoulders met her chest and down the silky open vee of her blouse to the waiting swell of her breasts.

Chelsea gasped. "You're a bold one."

"Let me show you a few more things." Barry

started toward one bedroom, but, feeling her tension, swung toward the other instead. "This one?"

She nodded against his bicep.

As he lowered her onto a patchwork velvet coverlet, the lights of the city sparkled through the flimsy curtains, bathing them both in a half-glow. Barry took a moment to appreciate the shadowed valleys that defined Chelsea's face and figure. "You're beautiful."

"You're not bad yourself." She released a long breath, although whether from admiration or apprehension, Barry wasn't sure.

He shrugged out of his jacket and yanked off his shirt, careless of a few popped buttons. The rope-tied pants slid down easily. His knees still felt wobbly but he ignored them.

"Where's the faux fur?" murmured Chelsea, trailing one hand down the contour of his leg.

"Guess I forgot it." Barry's tight gray underpants were in imminent danger of being split apart as he straddled her. With a couple of tugs, her blouse came open to reveal a tiny wisp of a brassiere.

Chelsea's eyes widened in the semidarkness. "Wait a minute. We were eating omelettes and then...how did I get into this position?"

"I don't quite remember," Barry said honestly, and opened the bra to reveal small, firm breasts. "Shall we try a replay?"

"No need." She moaned as his palms caressed her taut nubs. "There's a...in the drawer. A safe...thing."

He bent to kiss her again, and felt a vibration as their bodies pressed together. "A condom. Yes." With one hand, Barry fumbled for the drawer.

Even in his fuzzy mental state, he remembered about safe sex. He'd lectured the natives and performed numerous demonstrations in village squares, using a banana.

That was nothing like trying to slip this piece of rubberized frustration over himself while his blood seethed and Chelsea shifted rhythmically beneath him. Her skirt had unwrapped itself, and those tiny silken panties disappeared almost as quickly.

The world had tilted off its axis. Only one act would put it right. Determined to save the universe, Barry gave the condom one more well-meaning twitch and, with a great sense of coming home, entered Chelsea.

FOR A YEAR and a half of self-denial, Chelsea had feared this moment, believing that she was partly to blame for her fiancé's problems. That there was something wrong with her.

Yet here was Hank, every manly inch of him filling her with shuddering joy. She had never felt more womanly, more in control of her life or more eager to yield. Against all common sense, she trusted this man.

His movements inside her were long and intense. Yet he never tore his eyes from hers, never stopped drinking her in. He kept them connected in every way.

If this was the kind of men that grew in Texas, maybe she ought to move there, she thought vaguely. On the other hand, she preferred to stay right here.

Hank arched over her, licking the points of her breasts, nuzzling her throat and then kissing her again. She wanted more of him, endlessly, but as the thrusting speeded up, her desire demanded release.

Surrendering the last of her inhibitions, Chelsea caught his hips and urged him along. They were flying. What had he called this sensation...jagged? Yes, it was rough and magnificent.

She couldn't distinguish her cries from his. Maybe there was no difference. They formed one moaning, writhing ball of light, exploding into a shower of brilliant colors and then slipped together into a glimmering, mercurial stream of satisfaction.

Chelsea wrapped her arms around Hank and cuddled against his chest. It was only after a few minutes that she realized he wasn't wearing a condom.

Her throat clamped shut. She never took chances like this. Besides, she'd seen him put it on.

"Hank?" Her voice trembled.

"Hmmm?" He rolled against her, relaxed and sleepy.

"What happened to the safe?"

She could feel his eyelashes flicker against her cheek as his hand fumbled down below, searching for what wasn't there. "I'm not sure."

"You were wearing one, weren't you?"

"I thought I was." He didn't sound alarmed. On the other hand, she recalled, he was still under the influence of whatever drug had been slipped into his drink. "Guess I didn't put it on right."

Chelsea hoped to high heaven that he hadn't put her at risk of catching some kind of weird disease. "I know I'm okay. I haven't been with a man for a year and a half, and I get annual checkups," she said. "Have you... I mean, is there any chance that you've caught something?"

"I thought I had malaria once, but it was the flu," he said.

"Malaria?" Chelsea propped herself on one elbow. "Since when do people catch malaria in Texas?"

In the glow through the window, she saw the ivory glint of his smile. "I haven't been to Texas in years."

Her stomach sank. The man had fooled her all the way around. "You lied to me!"

"No," he said. "About what?"

"Being so naive and out of it. Like you didn't know your way around." She wished she didn't sound so vulnerable. That wasn't the way she pictured herself.

"I *am* naive and out of it." His amused tone might have reassured her, if not for the awkward circumstances. "I spent the past two years on an island in the South Pacific. Behaving myself, if that's what you're worried about."

Her worries refused to be assuaged so easily. "What were you doing on an island?"

"Serving in the Peace Corps," the man said. "I'm a doctor. Believe me, I had every medical test in the book before I came back, so you have no cause for concern."

Two years on an island. He'd just returned and immediately gone to a brand-new nightclub known only to savvy locals?

It was also known to Chelsea's employer, who'd asked her to recommend a nightspot for his freshly arrived partner. "Hank?" she said.

He slid one arm beneath her, pillowing her head on his strong shoulder. A shoulder that she wasn't going to be able to lean on, regardless of what happened, she thought with a twist of regret. "Hmm?"

"Your name wouldn't be short for Hancock, would it?"

Her question had an electric effect on him. He sat upright, nearly knocking her off the bed. "How the heck did you know that?"

"Pleased to meet you." Chelsea sat up and extended one hand. "I'm Chelsea Byers, your new receptionist."

3

THE DRUG that had been lazing through Barry's veins jolted out of his system. In a burst of adrenaline, he saw what a fool he'd made of himself.

His first night back in the States after two years of celibacy, he'd slept with a complete mismatch. The woman might be quick-witted and dynamite in bed, but she wasn't his type and, he suspected, he wasn't hers. Now it turned out that she worked in his office.

"Andrew hired a receptionist with purple hair?" he blurted, then felt even more stupid than before, if that was possible.

"It was pink that week," Chelsea said. "He didn't hire me, though. Sandy did—she's the office manager. Believe it or not, I'm a good receptionist."

"I'm sure you are." Barry rubbed the back of his neck. "I'm sorry about my remark. Your hair color is none of my business, or Andrew's, either."

"Should I call you Hank or do you go by Barry?" Sitting up in bed with her bare breasts peeking over the covers and her lips gently parted, Chelsea looked so irresistible that he wanted to make love to her again.

Resist, you idiot.

"I go by Barry," he said. "Listen, Chelsea, I'm afraid we got off to a bad start."

"I wouldn't call this a bad start." She gestured at the rumpled sheets.

"We have to work together. This is completely unprofessional." Barry finger-combed his hair, more from anxiety than from any expectation of neatening it. He felt alert and confused at the same time. Things had never been this complicated on Prego Prego.

Chelsea hopped out of bed and, retrieving a lavender Chinese-style robe, draped it around herself. "Just pretend there are two of me. The one at the office is a complete stranger."

"I can't do that because..." Barry stopped, unable to complete the thought because he didn't know his own mind.

A part of him balked at giving up this unexpected woman. Yet he didn't want to blunder into a miserable pairing of opposites like his parents.

As he struggled to collect his thoughts, Chelsea strolled toward a ramshackle cinderblock-and-board shelf construction. "There's someone I want you to meet."

"Who is it?" Barry hadn't heard her roommate come into the apartment. In any case, he certainly wasn't in the mood to meet her now.

"This is Smithee." After opening the door of a cage he hadn't noticed before, Chelsea lifted out a small, furry animal.

It hopped onto her shoulder and sat regarding him sharply. The creature was gray, about the size of a squirrel, only more rabbitlike. "What on earth is that?"

"A chinchilla." Indicating a couple of smaller cages, she added, "That's Myrtle, the hamster. The other cage is for Oscar, the mouse, but he escaped last night and I haven't found him yet.''

Barry fought down the urge to check the bed for a furry invader. ''You collect rodents?''

''They were all given away by people who got tired of them,'' Chelsea said. ''If I hadn't taken them in, they'd have been turned loose and fallen victim to a cat.''

Although rodents weren't his first choice for pets, Barry considered it a good sign that Chelsea liked them. If she was that concerned about animals, she probably wanted children, too.

Children. Oh, heavens, how had he missed the obvious? If he hadn't been so off-kilter, it would have struck him much sooner. ''The condom. The one that went astray. Chelsea, you might be pregnant.''

She stared at him for a stunned heartbeat. Then her expression cleared. ''It's okay. Wrong time of the month.''

''You can't be certain,'' he pointed out. ''Ovulation is unpredictable.''

''I hate doctors. They're such know-it-alls.'' She returned Smithee to his cage and put some food inside. ''Take my word for it, okay?''

Barry didn't see that he had much choice. ''If it turns out that you are, you can count on me for help.''

''It won't happen.'' After feeding the other animals, Chelsea swung toward him. In the morning light, he could see that her eyes were blue with brown flecks, not purple and black as they'd looked at the club. ''By the way, I wanted to warn you about the patients' mothers. They're going to fall all over you. A Hancock in their midst!''

"They've already got a Hancock in their midst," he pointed out. "Andrew."

"He's married," she said.

"Aren't they? The mothers, I mean?"

"Not all," Chelsea said. "I could advise you on their personalities, if you're interested."

Studying her face, Barry decided he especially liked her straight, definitive nose. "I don't date patients' mothers. Besides, why should you give me advice on other women? You're the one I'm involved with."

She shook her head. "Obviously, we have to call it quits."

"You don't want to see me again?" Although he'd been thinking the same thing Barry felt as if he'd had the wind knocked out of him. Chelsea might be all wrong for him, but there was a lot to be said for transitional relationships. "I'm not suggesting anything serious. On the other hand, we shouldn't give up too easily."

"It won't work," she said. "Tell me something quick. How do you organize your shirts?"

"By color," he said. "Doesn't everyone?"

She flung open her closet. From where Barry sat, he could see clothes jammed in willy-nilly, some of them dangling partway off the hanger. "I don't organize mine at all. See? We're incompatible."

"I could help you sort them out."

"You try it and I'll sic Myrtle on you," Chelsea said. "She bites."

Reluctant to accept this abrupt end to their affair,

Barry swung out of bed. Usually, he thought better on his feet. This time, he just got dizzy.

It made him realize that he must not be thinking clearly, about the two of them. "I guess you're right," he said. "Where are my clothes?"

"You're standing on them."

"So I am." He bent and picked them up.

It was a good thing she was pushing him away, Barry told himself as he dressed. In addition to being co-workers, they would only make each other miserable if they got involved romantically.

When he married, he wanted harmony. Two people who had the same values, enjoyed the same movies and...bored each other to death? Well, he didn't have to go quite that far.

"All right, I agree to your terms," Barry said.

"What terms?"

"Total surrender," he said wistfully. "Strangers when we meet." He finished dressing and straightened his jacket in the mirror. "I hope we can get along at the office."

"We'll do fine." Chelsea didn't seem to notice that her wrap had fallen open at the neck, baring a lot of cleavage.

"You have a right to be angry." He was a little angry at himself, in fact. "I'm the one who..." He couldn't bring himself to say "took advantage of you," because it seemed ridiculous. "Got carried away."

"I knew you were under the influence. I'm the one who should have said no." Chelsea regarded him from beneath a tangle of colorful hair. "We're grown-ups. We'll get over it."

"Thanks for being such a good sport," he said.

"Is there some coffee? I need a stiff dose of caffeine before I head home."

"In the coffeemaker. I'll reheat it."

Barry waved her back to bed. "I'll drink it cold." That ought to sober him up. "See you Monday," he managed, and went out to the kitchen.

A DOCTOR! Could she have picked anyone worse? Chelsea asked herself a short time later on her way to the shower. She'd waited until she heard his car start on the street.

If she did get pregnant, Hank—make that Barry— would probably try to regulate every bite she put into her mouth. The last thing she needed was some overbearing guy organizing her life like a prison routine.

It wasn't true what she'd said, though, about it being the wrong time of the month. There was no wrong time because Chelsea's periods were spectacularly irregular.

She didn't intend to worry. According to her New Age philosophy, when body and mind were in sync, they supported each other. Since Chelsea's mind rejected the prospect of parenthood, she expected her body to follow suit.

In the bathroom, she removed the robe, which her parents had sent her recently from Singapore. They were fulfilling a longtime dream by sailing around the world for a year, crewing on a movie star's yacht.

As she stepped into the aging shower stall, water streamed over her and spattered against the cracked plastic curtain. Her feet detected a chipped tile and some loosened grout.

It was a good thing Barry hadn't stuck around

long enough to get his patrician feet insulted. Still, Chelsea doubted the plumbing was any better on Prego Prego.

The guy really did have possibilities, if only he weren't about to become one of her bosses. She pictured his dark hair, melting brown eyes and straight eyebrows.

He looked so honest, like the cowboy-type she'd mistaken him for. He was built like an outdoorsman, too.

At close quarters in the shower stall, he would dwarf her. Nearly six feet, she guessed.

Chelsea wished he'd stuck around long enough to take a shower with her. Maybe for breakfast, too, and another roll in the sheets.

Who could understand the man? One minute he was fresh and appealing; the next, stuffy and conventional. Great in bed, but certain to drive her crazy everywhere else.

He certainly wouldn't approve of the mess in her checkbook. Or of the white mouse peeking around the curtain and regarding her warily.

"Gotcha!" She made a dive for it, slipped, and carried the shower curtain with her into a pile on the floor. "Ouch!"

She had the presence of mind to clamp one hand over the fleeing ball of white fluff. Lying there with hot water splashing around her and welts forming on her thighs, Chelsea was glad she didn't have to account to anyone else for her impulsive behavior.

She even liked the bruises. They took her mind off the squeezing in her heart.

In no time at all, it would vanish entirely.

ON SATURDAY MORNING, it rained. Barry spent the day puttering around his new condo, organizing his meager possessions and trying to get used to living with Scandinavian blond furniture instead of driftwood chairs and a tabletop propped on cut-down barrels.

The culture of Prego Prego had been a unique mix of Polynesian and Italian. The national dish, *Pesce Con Cose Pazze,* or Fish With Crazy Things, consisted of fish cooked with coconut and yams, served over spaghetti.

The national anthem was the aria *"Nessun Dorma,"* which translated as "No One's Sleeping." Perhaps it had been chosen because, after eating *Pesce Con Cose Pazze,* no one's stomach allowed him to sleep very well. At least, Barry's hadn't.

Now he was back to the real world. Last night, though, didn't seem very real, more like a hazy dream. He couldn't recall the details, although the overall situation remained painfully clear.

It was hard to believe he'd been so foolish, even in a drugged state, as to sleep with a woman he didn't know. He winced every time he thought about it.

Not that he held anything against Chelsea. As far as he was concerned, this was a case of live and let live. Or, rather, forget and let forget.

Barry forced his thoughts back to his condo. This was the beginning of a new life. He intended to enjoy it.

He'd bought the place based on Internet photographs. It had been expensive, due to its location half a mile from the beach. Thanks to an inheritance left from his mother's trust fund, however, Barry could afford it.

Two stories high and located on a small canal in the Los Angeles suburb of Venice, the place was newly remodeled in shiny white with accents of sea-green and pink. Thick carpets and well-constructed walls kept him from hearing his neighbors on either side in the four-unit building.

Only a few times did Barry yield to the impulse to yank open a closet door and check for scorpions, a habit formed in Prego Prego after he nearly stepped on one while fixing breakfast. He had to admit that he missed, ever so slightly, the drumming of rain on his old tin roof that had turned the daily rainshowers into Caribbean concerts.

The decor was a bit bland, he supposed as he sat in the dining room downing a bagel and watching a beer can float down the canal below his window. Now if Chelsea lived here, she'd throw in some splashes of color.

Barry shuddered. If he lived with a woman as strong-willed and argumentative as she was, the only splashes of color would be blood spatters on the wall.

Better to think about the angelic Ms. Right he'd been visualizing for so long. Sooner or later, he was going to find her. Not at a nightclub, though, he decided.

The ringing of the phone shattered the quiet afternoon. He grabbed the white instrument from its perch on the sideboard.

"Hello, son," came a gravelly voice.

"Hi, Dad." Barry tried to figure out whether today was his birthday or his father's birthday or some other special occasion he'd overlooked. They hadn't talked in months because Dr. Lewis Cantrell hated chitchat. "What's up?"

"I thought I might pay you a visit, now that you're back in the States," said his father. That was quite an offer, since there was no airport in the town of Blink, Colorado, and it was a three-hour drive to Denver.

After the divorce, Lew had departed Austin, declaring that it was becoming too liberal for his tastes. He'd found his new home in a tiny town in the Rockies that was in desperate need of a resident doctor.

"Great. I'll make up the spare bedroom." Barry would enjoy seeing his dad, even though they never knew what to say to each other. Their political views were vastly different and, with Lew Cantrell, almost everything took on a political slant.

Clinging to his sixties idealism, Lew objected to whatever the government did. He opposed spending taxpayers' money for Fourth of July fireworks on the Mall in Washington; he'd thrown so many cream pies at his local city councilmen that, he'd proudly informed Barry, the supermarket had stopped carrying them; he even objected to the Peace Corps, although he hadn't held that against his son.

"I'm looking forward to seeing you. Besides, I haven't been to California since my student days." Lew had studied at UC Berkley, where he'd met Barry's mother.

"Is this a sentimental journey?" Barry asked.

"More or less."

The "less" part bothered him. If Lew wasn't coming West for exclusively sentimental reasons, that meant he was up to something. "What's the government doing now?"

"The city council is trying to tax cats," growled his father.

"Tax cats?" Maybe his father had said "taxi cabs." Barry didn't think Blink was big enough to have cabs, though.

"Anybody that feeds a stray cat in this town is declared to own it, and they're supposed to fork over twenty bucks for a license," he said. "It's rotten."

Barry couldn't agree with his father. "Lots of cities require dog licenses."

"It's not that simple. They're up to their old tricks." Judging by the indignation in his tone, his father was gathering steam. "You know my friend Norman McBride who runs the junkyard?"

Lew had mentioned him before. "He calls the place Best Rust in the West, right?"

"That's him. Well, the place is crawling with cats. They keep the vermin down, and besides, there's no animal shelter in Blink so he takes pity on them," Lew said. "The jerks on the council are always trying to drive him out of business and they've found a new way to do it."

"By taxing his cats," Barry said, seeing the point at last. "That is rotten, but what's it got to do with your visiting me?"

"Nothing," said his father. "You're the one who asked me what the government was doing."

"I meant out here," Barry said. "It occurred to me that you might be combining business with pleasure."

The pause that followed was beginning to concern

him when Lew said, "I assure you, there are no government officials in my sightlines."

That was a relief. "When can I expect you?"

"Around the second week in May. I haven't booked a flight yet."

"It'll be great, Dad," Barry said. Knowing his father's dislike of small talk, he figured they might spend the whole time sitting in front of the TV passing the potato chips, but heck, that was quality time of a sort.

"Super," said his father. "By the way, have you had time to check out the local supermarket?"

"No. There's a service that delivers," Barry said. "Why?"

"I was wondering if they carry cream pies," Lew said. "Look forward to seeing you, son." *Click.*

Cream pies? As he hung up, Barry wished he knew what his father was planning. Not that anything he could say was likely to deter the unstoppable Lewis Cantrell.

Barry decided it was best not to mention his father when he had dinner at his aunt Grace's house tomorrow night. She and her former brother-in-law saw eye-to-eye on almost nothing.

With luck, the two wouldn't run into each other while Lew was in town.

Outside, the rain had stopped and the sun came out. Inspired to explore his new hometown, Barry headed for the beach area.

Bicyclists and skateboarders zoomed past as he walked. Although the palm trees and the smell of salt water stirred pleasant memories of Prego Prego, the neatly organized system of sidewalks, curbs, traffic lights and buildings was a far cry from the island's sprawling chaos.

Everywhere Barry looked, he saw women. Old, middle-aged and, mostly, young. They didn't wear many more clothes here than in the tropics and sometimes, in the case of string bikinis, less.

Women drifted through his line of sight and instantly vanished from his awareness. He found himself watching, subliminally, for a certain lady with audacious hair and plenty of attitude. He didn't see her, of course.

At last, Barry settled at an outdoor café close to the beach and ordered a latte. From here, he could watch the surfers and content himself with the knowledge that, far off, his friends on Prego Prego might be swimming in the same storm-darkened ocean.

He wouldn't see Chelsea again until Monday, he mused. Then they'd have to pretend to be strangers. How was he going to manage?

When he flew home yesterday, Barry had believed he was returning to a land where he knew all the rules. Boy, had he been wrong.

4

"CHELSEA, I'M DESPERATE." Those were strong words, coming from that epitome of societal rectitude, Grace Menton.

Holding the phone to her ear, Chelsea shoved over a pile of her roommate's dirty clothes and flopped onto the lumpy couch. She had to strain to hear over the splashing noises emanating from the kitchen sink. Starshine, who was too cheap to patronize a coin laundry, was spending Sunday afternoon doing her wash, beginning with a week's worth of underwear.

"What's wrong?" Chelsea asked.

"It's Angela." That was Andrew's twelve-year-old daughter, Grace's granddaughter. The whole family lived together in a splendid old mansion in the Hollywood Hills, which Chelsea had visited once when Grace invited her to tea.

Although Chelsea and her boss's mother came from different worlds, Grace's generosity had brought them together. Her passion was the Friends of the Opera and Ballet, better known as FOB.

Eager to win new fans for the arts, she'd invited Chelsea to half a dozen events over the past couple of years. To her own surprise, Chelsea had become an opera and dance buff.

"Angela isn't sick, is she?" Chelsea had attended

the ballet with Grace's granddaughter a few months ago and really liked her. The girl was a talented young dancer in her own right. She'd also been friendly and open, and obviously awed by Chelsea's flamboyant style.

"She might as well be sick!" Grace cried. "It's as if she's caught some disease and we don't know how to treat it."

"What do you mean?"

"Angela wants to give up dancing. Her mother's at her wit's end and so am I." Grace's usually silken voice was frayed. "These last few months, she's hit adolescence and changed so much you wouldn't know her."

"But she loves dancing," Chelsea said. "She told me she wants to be a ballerina when she grows up."

"Since she turned twelve, she hates everything her parents and I approve of," Grace explained. "She cut her beautiful brown hair and spiked it. Now she wants to quit ballet! She's scheduled to dance a solo at a press luncheon we're holding in May to publicize our subscription drive. It's a tremendous honor and she wants to throw it away."

Chelsea would never try to pressure the girl into doing something she disliked. On the other hand, she suspected that if Angela gave up dancing merely to spite her family, she would regret it deeply.

"Maybe she feels stressed-out," she said.

"I don't know." Grace sighed. "I don't understand Angela these days. She used to be so sweet. Now she rolls her eyes at everything I say. But she might listen to you."

"I don't know anything about children," Chelsea said. "Or preteens, either."

"She thinks you're cool," Grace said. "Would you at least talk to her? Maybe you can find out why she's quitting."

"Sure." Chelsea tried to ignore Starshine, who had begun bellowing out the words to the latest Ricky Martin song, off-key and off-tempo. While her roommate might be an aspiring actress, Chelsea hoped she had no delusions of becoming a singer.

"Please come to dinner tonight," Grace said. "I'm afraid she'll act badly in front of her cousin. He's my nephew, Barry, the new doctor you'll be working with. If you're there, she'll behave herself, and I'll make sure you have a chance to talk to her alone."

She sounded at the end of her tether. "Of course," Chelsea said. She owed Grace this much, however uncomfortable it might be.

"Please come at six. Shall we send a car?" The Mentons employed a middle-aged couple who lived on the premises. The wife served as housekeeper and the husband doubled as gardener and chauffeur.

"No need," Chelsea said. "I know the way."

"We'll see you then." Grace cleared her throat. "And, Chelsea, thank you. I can't tell you how much this means."

"I haven't done anything yet."

"If you can't do it, no one can."

The declaration of trust touched her. Chelsea knew, as they said good bye, that she couldn't back out now.

Starshine wandered out of the kitchen, her long blond hair twisted into a chignon and her shimmery, figure-hugging dress clinging damply where it had been splashed. Even while washing clothes in the sink, she'd worn high heels.

How could anyone manage to look so glamorous while washing underwear? Especially when her room, as Chelsea knew, perpetually resembled one of those disaster scenes on the TV news? Then she noticed Starshine looking for a place to hang several wispy, black-and-scarlet bras and panties that were dripping water onto the worn carpet.

"Put them in the bathroom!" she said.

"I can't go in there." Starshine bit her lower lip.

"Why not?"

"On Friday, there was a mouse under the sink." She shivered, her large gray eyes inviting sympathy.

"I caught the mouse Friday night," Chelsea said. "You haven't used the bathroom since then? What have you been doing?"

"The guys next door let me use their potty," Starshine said. "Honestly, couldn't you get a normal pet, like a shih tzu?"

Chelsea liked big dogs but not yappy little ones. On the other hand, an apology was in order. "I'm sorry. You should have told me. I'd have caught him sooner."

"It's not your fault," she said. "I think Wiley let him out."

"Your boyfriend?"

"He took the mouse out of his cage the other night to play with him, and kind of forgot about him," she said. "Anyway, I dumped Wiley. He made fun of my role as a bunny rabbit." Starshine's current job was performing in a children's Easter show that toured day-care centers.

"Go hang up your drippy underwear," Chelsea

said. "Sorry, I didn't realize you were avoiding the bathroom."

"That's okay. The guys next door are kind of cute." Swaying with innate seductiveness atop her high heels, Starshine headed for the bathroom.

"You can hang your clothes in the kitchen, too!" Chelsea called after her. "I'm going out tonight, so I won't be cooking."

"Thanks, but it's already full." Her roommate's voice drifted back.

Oh, yes, dinner at Grace's. Realizing she needed to prepare herself, Chelsea went to pick out what to wear.

It was going to be awkward, encountering Barry again in a social situation. On the other hand, it would be fun to watch him squirm as he tried to pretend they'd never met.

It was going to be an interesting evening.

BARRY'S SPORTS CAR was already here, Chelsea noted as she halted her Honda hatchback in the curved driveway of the Menton home. So was a luxury sedan that belonged to Andrew's brother and former partner, Hugh. He'd been good-natured about Chelsea's many mistakes when she was new in the office, and she'd been sorry when he left to join a research project.

In the fading light, she applied fresh lipstick. Then she swung out of the car, and nearly tripped over the sky-high stacked heels she'd borrowed from Starshine.

They hadn't been the wisest choice of footwear, Chelsea reflected as she limped toward the column-lined portico. She was still sore from Friday night's tumble in the bathroom.

Also, she probably should have worn something more conservative than a bright green halter top and a flowered sarong-style skirt that barely hid the bruises from her fall. The fake emerald in her navel was a nice touch, though, in her opinion.

Besides, she wasn't here to impress Barry. She'd been asked to make contact with Planet Angela. What better way than to dress outrageously?

When she rang the bell, it reverberated through the cavernous house. Inside, the quiet slap of shoes approached, only to be superseded by light, running footsteps.

The door flew open. Standing there, staring out raptly, poised a girl slightly shorter than Chelsea, with dark eyes and short, green-tipped spiked brown hair. Behind her, the butler-chauffeur, Marek, retreated quietly, his gray-haired dignity intact as he yielded his job of answering the door.

"Hi, Angela." Chelsea knew better than to exclaim over how much the girl had changed in the few months since they'd attended the ballet together. Still, it was disconcerting to realize that she'd grown a couple of inches, not to mention chopped off her hair.

"Chelsea! Hey!" The girl grinned at her. Her mother must have chosen the conservative skirt and plain blouse, but Angela had partially unbuttoned the shirt so it gapped open at the top. The necklace of black alligator-shaped beads was, no doubt, her own contribution. "I'm so glad somebody I like is here tonight."

"You mean I'm the only one?" Chelsea teased, slipping inside.

"I guess you can count my Aunt Meg and Uncle Hugh," Angela conceded. "And Uncle Barry."

"Me! Count me!" came a small, high-pitched voice as a red-haired preschooler hurtled into the entryway. Chelsea recognized the new arrival as Hugh and Meg's three-year-old daughter, Dana, who had once been a patient at the office.

"Sure thing, cutie." Angela scooped up the tiny girl. "Come on, Chel, I'll introduce you to my cousin Barry. He's hunky."

He certainly was, Chelsea noted with a catch in her throat as they entered the living room. Standing in profile, talking to his blond cousin Hugh, the man filled the large room with his quiet self-possession. Not even a business suit could disguise that sculpted body, she noted with a twinge of regret that she would likely never see it unclad again.

Before he could notice her, Chelsea heard her name called and turned to greet Grace Menton. Tall and erect, with an energy that belied her sixty-three years, the family matriarch looked relieved to see her guest.

She didn't bat an eye at Chelsea's clothes. Why on earth did Angela imagine her grandmother wasn't cool?

Cindi, a shy brunette with sculpted cheekbones, joined the welcoming committee, along with down-to-earth, red-haired Meg. It was several minutes before Chelsea glanced at Barry again.

He was staring at her with an expression she couldn't read. Alarm? Dismay?

"Cousin Barry, this is Chelsea, and she's absolutely perfect," Angela announced. "You ought to fall in love with her."

"He'd better not." Andrew, who was sitting on one of the couches with his fourteen-year-old son, William, gave his daughter an indulgent smile. "They've got to work together. Office romances are bad news."

"Did you hurt yourself?" Barry's remark at first made no sense. Then Chelsea realized that he, apparently alone of everyone in the room, had noticed her slight limp.

"I had a close encounter with the edge of my shower stall while in pursuit of an escaped felon," she said. "A small, furry one."

"Oh, your mouse," said Barry, and then froze as everyone turned toward him.

"Did I miss something?" asked Andrew. "I didn't realize you two were acquainted."

To Chelsea's relief, Barry recovered quickly. "We met at the nightclub. She introduced herself as one of our staff members."

Chelsea noted a slight narrowing of his eyes, a clear request that she comply with his white lie. Surely he didn't think she was so indiscreet that she would blurt out the truth in front of his family, she thought indignantly.

"I recognized him because he looks so much like you," she told Andrew. "The coloring. Those shoulders. How could I miss the family resemblance?"

She saw Grace's attention fix on a pair of portraits hanging over the fireplace. Her late husband, Frederick Menton, stared solemnly out with the bright green eyes that he'd passed on to Hugh and Andrew.

Next to it hung a picture of Grace's father, the

fabled Benedict Hancock. He was the one from whom Barry had inherited his memorable shoulders and dark hair.

The subjects of the two paintings, who had been medical partners, as well as in-laws, fixed their descendants with nearly identical quelling looks. No wonder the family members felt driven toward high achievement.

Chelsea hadn't grown up with any such demands. Only a few tattered film posters had made the move with her and her parents from one low-rent apartment to another. Clark Gable in *Gone With the Wind* was the closest thing to a patriarch in the Byers family.

Angela squirmed beneath the stern regard of her ancestors, or perhaps from the way her mother was frowning at her half-open blouse. "Come here. I want to show you something," she said, and pulled Chelsea away.

They swept through the dining room, its Victorian table set with exquisite china, and into the den that ran along the back of the house. Through the windows, Chelsea could see the broad lawn lined by banks of flowers, and the swimming pool beyond.

She tried to think of the Menton mansion as a movie set. That made it less intimidating.

Angela plopped onto a couch. "Look at this." She handed Chelsea a flier that said, Join Our Talent Show! It bore the name of the private girls' school that Angela attended. "Doesn't that look like fun?"

"It sure does." Chelsea sat beside her. "Are you going to participate?"

"Mom and Grandma won't let me." The girl flopped against the arm of the couch. "They say dancing at a mere talent show would be an insult to my ballet teacher.''

"I don't see why he should care," she said.

"I don't think he does. I think it's Mom and Grandma that care.'' Angela's face burned with rebellion. "It's so unfair! My friends aren't going to see me dance a solo at the FOB press luncheon in May. I want them to see me at school.''

"Sounds reasonable to me.'' Chelsea decided there was no point in pretending she didn't know what was going on. "Grace tells me you want to quit dancing. I was surprised.''

"I don't want to quit dancing. I want to quit being yanked around like a puppet!'' the girl cried. "Mom drives me to my lessons and then hangs around, watching every move I make. She even picks out my practice clothes. Now she and Grandma won't let me dance for my friends.''

"So you feel like they're trying to run your life.'' Chelsea sympathized. She hadn't received that kind of treatment from her parents because she'd been more responsible than they were, but she'd gotten plenty of it at school. And hated it.

"I knew you'd understand.'' Angela folded her arms defensively. "I just want to dance for myself. Otherwise it's no fun.''

"Maybe I can help,'' Chelsea said. "If you like, I'll talk to them.''

Angela's look of gratitude was more than enough reward.

BARRY HOPED no one noticed his daze as he consumed his dinner of poached salmon, roasted new potatoes and steamed vegetables. Thank goodness for the busy conversation around the table.

He couldn't stop sneaking peeks at Chelsea. Did she have any idea what that emerald in her belly button did to a man? Of course, he couldn't see it over the table, but he knew it was there. Worse, his body knew it was there.

After two years of celibacy, he'd underestimated his needs as a man. As well as his reaction to this particular woman.

When he'd agreed to keep his distance from her, he'd had no idea that she socialized with his family. It was hard to understand. In her bizarre getup and with that hairstyle, she looked as if she'd just dropped in from another universe, although she certainly held her own in a lively discussion about new films.

Apparently she was a friend of Angela's. It seemed odd that his family would encourage such an unlikely relationship, but it wasn't up to Barry to interfere.

Hannah, the housekeeper, served coffee. After she left, Angela said, "Well, Chel? Will you talk to my parents like you promised?"

"Sure," said Chelsea.

Barry wondered why she believed she had the right to intervene between a child and her parents. It seemed presumptuous even for a family friend.

"Talk to us about what?" asked Cindi.

"Giving up ballet," Angela said.

Tensely, Grace stirred cream into her coffee, then stared at it in surprise. His aunt usually drank her coffee black, Barry recalled.

He couldn't drink his coffee at all. Being in the

middle of a family disagreement, however polite, made his muscles stiffen and his jaw ache. He'd endured so many ruined dinners as he was growing up that for years he'd preferred to eat alone.

"You're not going to dance anymore?" Hugh said. "Angie, I love to watch you dance."

"She's not giving it up." Andrew smacked his coffee cup into his saucer, sending drops flying. "This is childish nonsense. She's been taking ballet since she was five and she's the star of her class."

"It's not childish nonsense!" Angela flared. "It's my body and I don't have to move it any way I don't want to!"

"Angela!" gasped her mother. "That was inappropriate and rude."

"As far as you're concerned, everything I do is wrong!" the girl cried. "I'm not even allowed freedom of speech around here!"

"Hey, I thought I was your designated spokesperson." Chelsea's light tone stemmed what, to Barry, looked like a tantrum in the making. "May I speak now?"

Angela nodded. Chelsea gave them all a smile and brushed her hair behind her ears, revealing a mismatched pair of large earrings. The right one featured a tiny dragon in a circle, the other a sunburst.

"Dancing is something Angela wants to do for herself," Chelsea said. "She feels as if other people are trying to control her."

Andrew frowned. "We're doing no such thing."

"For one thing, she wants to select her own workout clothes," Chelsea said.

"She picked a crop top!" Cindi protested. "And

tights with holes already cut in them. It was the ugliest thing.''

"It might be easier if you don't have to look at them,'' Chelsea said quickly. "Marek could drive her to ballet classes.''

"That's my responsibility...'' Cindi's voice trailed off. "I guess it would leave more time for my fund-raising, though.''

"She also wants to dance in her school's talent show,'' said Chelsea. "For her friends.''

"We always invite her friends to her dance recitals,'' Grace said.

"Just my closest friends! I want all the girls to see me,'' Angela said. "And the boys from the Academy, too. It's a joint talent show.''

Cindi opened her mouth to protest, and closed it again without a word. Whatever objection she'd had to seeing her daughter dance at school, it didn't appear to hold up to the scrutiny of this impromptu family council.

"I suppose it wouldn't hurt,'' she said.

"Then I'll do it,'' Angela said.

"Do what?'' Barry couldn't believe the conflict was resolved. In his family, flare-ups between his parents had only increased the sense of ill will.

"What they want me to do,'' said his young cousin. "Dance at the press luncheon that Friends of the Opera and Ballet is holding in May.''

"It's to publicize our subscription drive for the fall and winter season,'' Grace explained. "Angela has a solo. It's a tremendous honor.''

"I'm glad you're going to perform,'' said Hugh's wife, Meg, who'd been quiet until now. "A wonderful gift like yours should be shared with others.''

"So we've got this worked out?" Andrew asked. Everyone nodded. "Good. Hannah, would you please bring in the dessert?"

The apple pastry with whipped cream soothed any leftover hurt feelings. Barry was relieved. It especially surprised him that Chelsea's meddling hadn't made things worse.

Something in the back of his brain nagged at him. Barry tried to focus. May...the press conference...

Lew's visit was planned for May. His father would want to see Angela dance, if he were in town, but that might throw him together with Aunt Grace. They'd never gotten along when they were brother-and sister-in-law, and he doubted they'd see eye-to-eye about much now.

Barry hoped the dates didn't coincide; that would let everyone off the hook.

"I hope I get to dance before that snotty young tenor from New York sings," Angela said. "Otherwise I won't be able to keep a straight face. Have you heard of Fiorello Magnifico, Cousin Barry?"

"He wasn't a big news item on Prego Prego," he admitted.

"Well, his real name's Albert Cork, and someone ought to stick a cork in him for sure," she said vehemently. "He's American. He likes to pretend he's Italian, but I doubt his ancestors ever set foot in Italy."

"He has a beautiful voice," Cindi said. "He's a bit pompous, I suppose, but you have to forgive him."

"You should have seen him walk around with his nose in the air last year, when he was in Rossini's *Cinderella*," Angela said. "He was always hogging the stage, blocking his costar and trying to drown her out.''

Andrew shrugged. ''Opera singers all have big egos.''

''I was backstage one time during a performance. You should see the way he wiggles his rear end when he's getting ready to sing.'' Angela jumped to her feet. ''Like this.'' She turned around and gave an exaggerated bump and grind. ''Then he puffs himself up.'' She faced them and blew up her cheeks. ''I wish there were some way of giving him a mouthful of helium so when he sings, his voice comes out like this.'' She began singing in a high, squeaky voice, then plopped into her chair.

Everyone applauded. ''If you don't want to dance, I think you've got a future as a stand-up comic,'' Meg said.

''I'm surprised he's been invited to perform for the press, if he's so disagreeable,'' Barry said.

''Oh, he's very well-known, always appearing on talk shows,'' Grace said. ''Besides, he's close friends with Werner Waldheim, one of FOB's biggest backers. Werner made a fortune in the computer games business.''

''I heard he was kind of a recluse,'' Meg said.

''He stays behind the scenes,'' Cindi agreed. ''But he's a big political donor with lots of influence. He enjoys having famous friends like Fiorello.''

''If you can imagine that!'' Angela rolled her eyes.

After dinner, Chelsea excused herself. ''I've got to be at work early tomorrow. My boss is a real slave driver.'' She shot Andrew a mischievous look. ''I hope his new associate isn't such an ogre.''

"Barry's worse," Andrew said. "When he was doing his residency, I hear he was such a perfectionist that the interns referred to him as— Was that Simon Legree, or Mussolini?"

"Genghis Khan," said Hugh with a straight face.

"Attila the Hun," joked Barry, enjoying his cousins' teasing. He hadn't really been given any such nicknames, to his knowledge, although he *had* been a stickler for following the rules.

He still was. A doctor couldn't be too careful about adhering to proper procedures.

"Well, good bye until tomorrow," Chelsea said.

Barry got to his feet and shook hands with her. After she left, he breathed a little easier even though the company felt suddenly incomplete.

None of his family appeared to have noticed anything unusual between the two of them. It was a good omen, he hoped.

5

As SHE MADE COFFEE in the office breakroom on Monday morning, Chelsea mentioned to the nurse, Helen Nguyen, that she'd run into Barry at the Mentons' house the previous night. It seemed a simple way of explaining that they'd already met.

"So tell all!" Helen drummed her fingers on the counter. "What's he like?"

"Pleasant. A little stiff." Chelsea didn't want to talk about him, although she could hardly avoid it.

Helen, trim and petite in her white slacks and top, wasn't about to be put off. "Is he handsome? Is he, you know, eligible?"

"Why ask me? You can find out for yourself when he gets here in half an hour." Chelsea, Helen and Sandy, the office manager, arrived early to prepare for the day. "Besides, you're married."

The nurse laughed. "And too old for him. I was thinking about my daughter, April. She's not married yet."

"She's only twenty-two!"

"Old enough." Helen produced a plate of cookies. "She baked these herself. People say the way to a man's heart is through his stomach. Make sure he tries them, will you? The doctors always drift by the receptionist's desk, and I'm sure he'll be hungry."

"I'll be glad to," said Chelsea.

A few minutes later, Sandy Craven arrived. She'd brought a bouquet of roses from her garden, which she arranged in a vase on the reception desk.

Chelsea inhaled the rich fragrance. "These are splendid. What's the occasion?"

"I thought the new doctor might like them," she explained. Fifty and unmarried, Sandy had settled comfortably into a small home in the Palms area of Los Angeles. At her housewarming party the previous year, Chelsea had admired the flower garden, on which its owner lavished great care. "Have you seen him yet? Is he as good-looking as Dr. Menton?"

Sandy had always said she was single by choice. Had she changed her mind? "I ran into him over the weekend. He's fairly attractive, if you like the conservative type."

"Not for me, of course," Sandy said. "I'm interested for my sister, Louise. I mentioned that we had a new doctor arriving, and she's been bugging me to put in a good word. She's thirty-eight and her maternal clock is ticking fast."

"I'm sure Dr. Cantrell would appreciate an introduction," Chelsea said politely, but she had her doubts.

At the house party, the overbearing Louise had prowled among the guests, buttonholing every male between twenty and sixty. She was unlikely to be what Barry wanted, although she might be what he deserved, Chelsea reflected impishly.

Last night, he'd acted standoffish. A few times, he'd looked distinctly disapproving when she spoke up for Angela. To be fair, he had no way of knowing that Grace had requested Chelsea's help with the girl. Still, it wasn't his business to judge her.

Their unsuitability for each other was so obvious, Chelsea couldn't understand why she'd ever succumbed to her attraction. She must have been struck by temporary insanity.

The next staff member to arrive was Josiah Withers, M.D. The 72-year-old retiree, who had been filling in for a few months since Hugh's departure, planned to leave at the end of the week.

He greeted Chelsea warmly. Dr. Withers was popular with the staff and patients due to his fatherly manner and obvious affection for everyone around him.

"Has my new colleague arrived yet?" he asked. "You girls must be all atwitter. A bachelor in our midst!"

"There have been inquiries," Chelsea conceded.

"Naturally, I wish to submit my own bid." The elderly doctor produced a photograph of a woman in her thirties with long maroon hair cut with straight bangs. "My niece, Belinda."

"Very pretty. She's single, I suppose."

He sighed. "I'm afraid so. There've been three divorces. No, four. I can't understand why none of the young men 'took,' so to speak. But five times is a charm, as they say."

"Three times." Noting his confused expression, Chelsea said, "Never mind. I'm sure the new doctor will be interested to hear about her."

"That's what I think." Dr. Withers propped the photo behind Helen's plate of cookies and departed, whistling.

The reception desk now resembled a shrine to marital bliss, Chelsea thought. The only people not trying to corner the eligible doctor were, apparently, her and Andrew.

A couple of patients arrived, and Chelsea checked them in. She handed the first chart to Helen, who summoned a little girl scheduled to see Dr. Withers.

A moment later, Chelsea felt the air sparkle with electricity. Her first impulse was to attribute it to the unstable March weather, until she remembered that the high-rise office building was more or less sealed off from the outer elements.

Then she caught a whiff of tropical aftershave lotion drifting from the back of the suite. Barry had arrived.

Chelsea reached into her purse for a brush and ran it through her hair. She was tempted to check her lipstick, too, but she could hear masculine footsteps heading along the hallway. She switched on the answering machine and began reviewing messages from the weekend.

An appointment was cancelled. Another patient would be fifteen minutes late. A mother couldn't remember when she'd scheduled her baby's checkup.

As she handled matters, Chelsea kept auditory track of Barry's progress. He stopped halfway down the hall, presumably at the office with his name newly painted on the door. She heard the hinges creak and knew he'd gone inside.

A while later, the hairs on the back of her neck prickled again. Barry had emerged and was heading this way.

The nearer he came, the harder Chelsea had to struggle to feign indifference. Yet, she told herself, she didn't need to pretend. She really *was* indifferent.

She was so relaxed, she nearly tipped her chair over by accident. So completely at ease that she chewed on a pencil for several seconds before tasting its bitterness.

"Good morning." His brisk tone sounded impersonal. Professional. Distant.

"Yes?" As she turned, Chelsea fought the impulse to smooth down her blouse. "Oh, Dr. Cantrell. I didn't realize you were here."

"I just arrived." He stood behind her in the bay, with the counter separating them from the waiting room. She could feel his presence enveloping her. "I'm afraid I don't know the routine yet."

"Your first patient isn't scheduled for half an hour," she said, trying not to notice how being seated put her at eye-level with a very personal part of his anatomy. Quickly, Chelsea grabbed the plate of cookies and extended it. "Have some."

Barry took two. "Thanks. It was nice of you to bring them in." She discovered it was impossible to read the expression in his eyes when she dared to meet them. He must be working as hard at his casual attitude as she was at hers.

"I didn't bring them," she said. "They're a gift from Helen's daughter, April. She's single, by the way. I'm supposed to tell you that."

"I see." He glanced at the roses. "Those are a nice touch. I don't suppose you brought them, either?"

She shook her head. "They're from Sandy, the office manager. On behalf of her sister, Louise."

"Is this her?" He lifted the photograph of Belinda.

"That's Dr. Withers' niece," Chelsea said. "He wanted to put her bid in."

Barry set the picture down quickly. "Am I supposed to be up for auction?"

"That's the general impression," she said. "I thought you'd be pleased."

"Why?"

"Well, you did go to a nightclub your first evening in town," she pointed out. "I presume you're interested in establishing a social life."

Before replying, Barry surveyed the waiting room, but by now the second patient had been ushered in to see Dr. Withers, so it was empty. "Listen, Chelsea, I would appreciate your spreading the word that I keep my private life completely separate from the office."

"Of course you do," she said.

He didn't seem satisfied with her answer. "I'd also like to request that you not allow others to use your desk as a dating service. I prefer not to hear about the interest I seem to be generating, however flattering it might be."

Darn it, the man was infuriating! Bossy, cold and full of himself. Chelsea had to restrain herself from kicking him in the shins.

She wasn't afraid of getting fired. Good receptionists were hard to find, even in Los Angeles. Still, she was wearing open-toed shoes and she might hurt her feet.

Verbal abuse seemed more in order. "Do you have any idea what you sound like?" She was about to supply some adjectives, beginning with "arrogant" and leading to "pompous," when Andrew popped in from the hall.

"Morning, cousin!" he said.

"Good morning." Barry managed a trace of a smile. "I was just explaining to Chelsea..."

Andrew took in the cookies, flowers and photograph. "Could those be romantic overtures?"

"Yes," Barry said. "Some of the staff members apparently wish to fix me up with their nearest and dearest."

"Don't let them," Andrew said.

"I have no intention of it."

Andrew clapped his cousin on the shoulder. "Good. I'd hate for them to beat my time. Cindi has a friend she wants you to meet."

He filled in the details as he led Barry down the hall. Chelsea grinned, and then wondered what she was grinning at.

Just because *she* didn't want the know-it-all Dr. Barry Cantrell didn't mean she wanted anyone else to have him, either.

WHILE HE LISTENED with half his attention to Andrew describing the charms of Cindi's friend Philippa, Barry wondered why he'd chewed out Chelsea. After all, he was looking for a wife, so what was wrong with people offering to introduce him around?

What bothered him, he realized, was her complete lack of possessiveness. She considered him nothing more than a casual amusement to be passed along now that she was done with him.

"Yes," he told Andrew.

"Excuse me?"

"I'll go out with her," he said.

"Thank goodness. Cindi would have killed me if

you'd said no." His cousin gave him a rueful look. "You know how it is with wives. Well, no, maybe you don't."

"Explain it to me." Judging by the hall clock, Barry still had twenty minutes before seeing patients, and this sounded interesting.

"Women love to matchmake," his cousin said. "Married women believe true love will bloom the moment they put two single people in a room together."

"Not any two people, surely," Barry said.

"Cindi only knows Philippa through one of her fund-raising groups, but this morning she said, 'You know, I'm sure it will work.' She didn't say why she was so sure." Andrew chuckled. "If a man always fell for the first woman he met, you'd be walking down the aisle with Chelsea. Isn't that a ridiculous idea?"

"Preposterous," muttered Barry. "Now show me around, will you?"

After two years of isolation, he'd been eager to find a wife quickly, he reflected as he noted the locations of the breakroom and lavatory. Now he wondered if that was such a good idea.

Perhaps, though, Philippa would turn out to be exactly what he sought. Getting settled would certainly make his life easier.

CHELSEA WAS bent over the kitchen sink, eyes shut tight, carefully daubing the roots of her hair with black dye when she felt someone reach between her legs and tug open the cabinet. "Hey! Stop that!"

"I've got to finish hiding these Easter eggs," said Starshine. "My friends will be here any minute."

"It won't be Easter for another two weeks!" Chelsea exclaimed.

"It's a bonding experience," Starshine replied.

"A what?"

"We're bonding. You know, the other actors and me. Becoming a family. So when we get out on stage, we won't seem like a bunch of strangers playing parts." Moving around Chelsea's ankles, Starshine stuffed something into an adjacent bottom drawer.

Chelsea felt a strand of long hair working its way loose from its bun. If she got black dye on one of the purple tips, she'd have to bleach the thing and redye it, which would really be a pain. "Watch what you're doing. Those aren't real eggs, are they?"

"Of course they are," her roommate said indignantly, moving away. "Nothing else would create the same experience."

"If you overlook any..."

"We'll find them when they stink," Starshine reassured her. "Oh, come on, look at you. What are you doing on a Saturday evening? Dyeing your hair! You should be thrilled to play host to these artists, these dramatic talents, these tortured souls."

"You're performing in a traveling kids' show about how the Easter Bunny escapes from a killer robot." Chelsea wiped her face and set the timer for ten minutes. "That's hardly high art."

"You left out the key word." On her knees, with a large gold-spangled handbag dangling from her shoulder, Starshine crawled into the living room, careless of the fact that she was wearing a black-silk designer pantsuit. She shopped at secondhand stores that received donations from movie stars.

"What key word?"

Still in view of the kitchen, she stuck an egg under a loose edge of carpet. "The word is *professional*. We're getting paid for this. Not much, but I bought three dozen eggs yesterday and I didn't even use my credit card."

"Because it's maxed out."

"Spoilsport!" Through the doorway, Starshine shot Chelsea a baleful look. Despite her awkward position, she looked ridiculously glamorous with her blond sweep of hair and large gray eyes.

They'd met three years ago, when Chelsea was working in the office of an actors' agent. Starshine, an actress from Florida with a sunny personality and more ambition than talent, had been one of his clients.

She, like the others, had paid for extensive photographs and promotional materials. The agent had promptly disappeared with their money.

Even though Chelsea hadn't known the man was a charlatan and had never received her last paycheck, she'd felt guilty, as well as sorry for the tearful, likable Starshine. So when her then roommate had moved out to get married, Chelsea had invited the would-be actress to move in.

Life with Starshine was like a roller-coaster ride. By comparison, Chelsea felt positively staid.

"Just stay out of my room," she said. "I don't want people searching through my rodents' cages."

"You don't have to convince me! I'll close your door and mark it No Admittance," Starshine said. "You're joining us for dinner, aren't you? After we're done, we're going to chop these up and make egg-salad sandwiches. Or maybe we'll devil some of them. Do you have any mayonnaise?"

"Keep your starving artist buddies out of my food," Chelsea said. "As for dinner, I'm eating out."

Angela had called the day before and begged Chelsea to pick her up so they could go out for dinner. Grandma was treating, she'd said, so apparently Grace wanted the pair to get together.

Chelsea would enjoy seeing Angela and hearing how the talent show was progressing. The discussion might also help get her mind off Barry.

The week had been draining, with the constant need to act as if she didn't notice his powerful masculine presence. Everybody else certainly noticed it. Some of the patients' mothers flirted with him, as did half the women who worked in the building.

Plates of cookies overflowed Chelsea's desk and casseroles arrived regularly at lunchtime. Women's phone numbers, along with a couple of apartment keys, appeared on her desk with whispered pleas to "Just give this to him when he has a free moment, okay?"

She couldn't believe anyone would stoop that low. Barry apparently couldn't believe it, either. At least he'd stopped holding Chelsea responsible for the little gifts that flourished on her desk, and simply accepted them with a resigned nod.

The timer rang. Chelsea rinsed the dye out of her hair and styled it. The purple tips remained intact, thank goodness.

By the time she finished, Starshine's buddies began trooping into the apartment. They were an odd-looking bunch, from the tall, lanky man who played the killer robot to a large-toothed woman who, judging by her flat-footed walk and habit of giving a little hop from time to time, was perfectly cast as the Easter Bunny.

Starshine, who played the ditsy character of Friendly Bunny, fit the role as she scurried through the living room serving hors d'oeuvres. These consisted, alternatively, of squiggles of homogenized cheese and dabs of cream cheese on crackers, Chelsea noted as she swiped a couple.

"I see an egg!" crowed the killer robot, stuffing his mouth with crackers.

"They're not very well hidden," complained the Easter Bunny. "Really, Starshine, you should have consulted me. I'm the expert."

Did these people retain even the remotest contact with reality? Chelsea wondered. Glad for an excuse to leave, she grabbed her purse and went to get Angela.

The girl bounced out of the house as soon as Chelsea's car halted. Now that she'd washed the green spikes out of her hair, Chelsea could see that the short haircut flattered her. Her dark-pink dress with spaghetti straps suited her, too.

"You look great," she said as Angela got into the Honda hatchback. "More grown-up."

"Mom let me pick the dress. Well, she let me pick three, then she made the final cut." The girl smiled. "Things are better now, thanks to you."

"Your mom and dad deserve the credit," Chelsea said. "Not all parents listen to reason."

"Did yours, when you were my age?"

The car started down the circular driveway. "My parents acted like kids themselves." They'd been a lot like Starshine, she realized, which might be why she tolerated her roommate's shenanigans. "I could pretty much do anything I wanted."

"Wow." Angela sighed.

"I also got to cook dinner most nights, take care of the laundry and make sure the bills were paid," Chelsea said. "I could balance a checking account before I learned algebra."

"How do you balance a checking account?" the girl asked. "Never mind, my parents won't let me have one. By the way, we're going to the French Fox. Grandma's arranged with the management to charge it to her. She wouldn't trust me with a credit card."

"The French Fox? I'm impressed." The restaurant, tucked onto a sidestreet off Sunset Boulevard, was famous for its continental cuisine. It seemed fancy for a twelve-year-old. "Did your grandmother choose it?"

"No, I did," said Angela.

"You like French food?"

There was a moment's hesitation before she replied, "A lot of ballet people eat there."

"Speaking of which, how's the talent show going?"

The girl launched into an animated description of the first rehearsal. She went into detail about one boy who performed a magic act.

"Has he asked you out?" Chelsea inquired as they cruised along Sunset, approaching the dazzling brightness of the billboard-laden Sunset Strip.

"Not yet, but I bet he will," the girl said. "Mom probably won't let me go out alone with him. Of course, he's too young to drive, anyway. Marek would have to chauffeur us. That's okay. Marek's cool.''

Angela had gone through a lot of mental arrangements for a date she hadn't even made yet, Chelsea reflected. Much as the girl complained about her mother's tendency to overmanage her life, she had some of the same organizational leanings.

That could be an asset, depending on the circumstances, Chelsea supposed. She herself preferred to let life happen without a lot of planning.

If she'd planned ahead, she might have had a high-stress career instead of a series of interesting, if underpaid, receptionist jobs. She'd also likely have chosen a roommate who paid her rent, but never loaned her any interesting clothes.

''Are you dating anyone in particular?'' Angela asked as Chelsea turned onto a side street.

''No.'' She couldn't resist adding, ''Got someone in mind?''

''I might.''

What kind of adult male would Angela encounter that she'd want to fix up with Chelsea? ''Don't tell me he's a ballet dancer!''

''Certainly not,'' the girl said indignantly. ''Some of them are cute, but they're not your type.''

''What is my type?''

''Opposites attract,'' said Angela.

''Not in my case,'' Chelsea assured her.

''That depends on the guy,'' said her passenger. ''I mean, if he was really, really cute...''

''Don't go there,'' she said, beginning to suspect who her young friend had in mind.

''Okay,'' said Angela. She didn't sound at all convincing.

6

IN FRONT OF the restaurant, a valet collected the car. Chelsea liked the convenience of valets and never worried about her car being damaged. Maybe that was because she knew that if they wanted to go drag racing, they'd take somebody's sports car, not her aging hatchback.

She'd heard about a valet who'd smashed a $170,000 Ferrari into a tree while showing off for his friends. Too bad she hadn't been there to see the expressions on everyone's faces when it happened.

Steps led up to the restaurant entrance. Inside, murals of vineyards festooned the walls. The lobby was small, carpeted and hushed, with several series of small rooms leading away from it.

Angela peered around uncertainly. "You can't see much in here, can you?"

"I think that's the idea," Chelsea said. "It's supposed to feel like a private club."

The girl tapped her foot. "You can't people-watch very well, though."

"You mean in case any movie stars show up?"

"Something like that." The girl marched to the tuxedoed host at the front desk and spoke with him in low tones. They were speaking French, which Angela's school taught beginning in kindergarten.

The man bowed and, after tucking a couple of

menus under his arm, led them through a series of rooms to a slightly larger chamber in the back. En route, Chelsea spotted an actress from one of her favorite sitcoms and a TV newscaster with his family.

She wished she'd worn something dressier than her purple velvet tube top and red sheath skirt. Actually, she didn't own anything dressier, but she could have borrowed an outfit from Starshine.

There were five tables in their chamber, two of them already occupied. Although Chelsea caught a few questioning looks as she and Angela were seated, she held her head high. For all anyone knew, she might be a millionaire following the latest L.A. garbage-fashion trend.

She studied her menu. The entrees cost about thirty dollars, and that didn't include salad or side dishes. Thank goodness Grace was paying.

"Let's pig out," Angela said.

"I don't want to take advantage of your grandmother." Chelsea frowned, trying to figure out the French descriptions. What was all this stuff anyway?

"She said it's good for me to learn how to eat in a nice restaurant," the girl said. "Let's start with appetizers. Then soup. I hear the lobster bisque is out of this world."

"You order," Chelsea said. "I like to live dangerously."

They had just been served one order of baked Brie and another of shrimp salad—Angela had decreed that they should try different dishes and share— when the host brought new arrivals to an empty table.

Directly behind him came a tall, striking woman,

her long hair highlighted with strands of chestnut, brown and copper. A slinky silver evening gown draped her bony figure. She had high, patrician cheekbones, bee-stung lips and a dissatisfied expression.

As she spotted Chelsea and Angela, her nostrils flared in distaste. It seemed like an overreaction to their less-than-elegant clothing. Chelsea wished she'd worn a bone through her nose just to see what kind of reaction that might have provoked.

Then she spotted the man taking a seat opposite Miss Priss. It was Barry, elegant if a bit ill at ease in a dark silk suit.

"Did you know he was going to be here?" Chelsea demanded.

Angela ducked her head. "I heard my mom talking to Philippa on the phone. I can't understand why my parents fixed them up. Philippa's a pain in the neck. I figured he might need rescuing."

So this was why Angela had invited her here tonight. The girl must have some peculiar idea about matchmaking.

By comparison, Starshine's oddball Easter egg hunt wouldn't have been such a bad way to spend the evening, after all.

BARRY'S SOCIAL EFFORTS in Los Angeles seemed doomed to be not just failures but catastrophes. There had been that night with Chelsea a week ago, which he didn't dare think about, and now there was, well, Philippa von Harrigan.

Cindi had given him the impressive resumé by phone. Her friend was a wealthy divorcée eager to have children, she'd assured him. The woman owned a small cosmetics firm and a home in a prestigious area.

He hadn't minded when his date informed him, by e-mail, that he was taking her to an expensive French restaurant. Although it would strain his budget, at least it should give them a chance to get acquainted without disruption.

The evening had not started well, however. Philippa had kept Barry waiting for half an hour in her hotel-size living room while she talked business on the phone. When she finally rang off, she'd gazed with displeasure upon his new suit. He gathered that she had expected him to arrive in a tuxedo.

Outside, faced with his sports car, she'd balked. At first he'd believed she simply disliked the prospect of folding herself into such a low-riding vehicle.

However, she'd disabused him of that notion. ''I couldn't possibly be seen in such a middle-class make of car. You're a doctor. You should be driving a BMW, at least.''

Cindi must not realize how obnoxious Philippa was, he'd thought. Surely she wouldn't have knowingly recommended a woman who instructed her dates on how to transform themselves to suit her taste.

Out of respect for Andrew and Cindi, however, he held his peace and rode with Philippa in her Mercedes coupe. She yakked on her cell phone the whole time she was driving, which was not only rude but dangerous as she wove through traffic with one hand on the wheel.

She must have some redeeming qualities, Barry told himself. Surely they would reveal themselves soon.

At the restaurant, the maître d' fawned over her, since apparently she came here often. A distinguished-looking older couple, who were departing, greeted her warmly, and Philippa switched on the charm. Barry noticed that she emphasized the title "doctor" when she introduced him.

All week, he'd been puzzled by the lavish attention paid to him because of his profession. What if he had some other occupation? Would he be any less interesting or intelligent?

The only woman he was certain had liked him for himself was Chelsea. And she was the one person he absolutely had to put out of his mind.

She was, he acknowledged, an efficient and cheerful receptionist. She was also unconventional and outspoken. Barry had overheard her tell one mother, who'd been harping about having to wait, that it had only been five minutes and she should park her rear end and wait her turn.

Another time, he'd heard Chelsea apologize when the wait ran long due to an emergency. Then she'd gone downstairs and returned with ice-cream cones for all the children, at her own expense.

Since she was on his mind, perhaps it was understandable that, as he followed Philippa into a small chamber, Barry imagined for a moment that a woman across the room resembled Chelsea. His seat faced away from her, however, and he put the woman out of his mind. Being polite to his date was going to take all his resources.

When the waiter arrived, she ordered caviar and a scotch. Barry sighed. He'd have to stick to peanut butter sandwiches for the rest of the month after he paid for this meal.

There was no point in worrying about it. Since he was unlikely to patronize this restaurant again for some time to come, he might as well enjoy himself. He ordered the smoked salmon appetizer.

"I simply don't believe they allowed those two tramps to come in dressed like that." Philippa sniffed.

"Which tramps?" Barry realized she was staring past him at the woman who reminded him of Chelsea and at her companion. He decided against turning around to take a better look. "Just ignore them."

"I try to avoid that sort," Philippa said. "Seeing them in here makes it hard for me to enjoy myself."

"Would you like to switch places with me?" Barry asked.

"I'd still feel their presence. It's like knowing there's a fly buzzing around the room even when you can't hear it."

He gritted his teeth and struggled to control his temper. He was trying to get to know this woman, when apparently the only thing she cared about was whether their fellow diners met her standards.

Maybe it would help if he imagined her to be a member of a bizarre native cult. The rituals and beliefs might be incomprehensible to him, but on Prego Prego Barry had tried hard not to be judgmental. Surely he could extend the same courtesy to Philippa.

"How did you meet Cindi?" he asked, seeking a safe subject.

"We both used to be on the board of FOB." She obviously assumed he knew what the initials stood for. Something to do with the opera and ballet, Barry recalled his aunt saying. "At first I thought she was rather dull, but then I discovered she has a law degree. Did you know that?''

His cousin's wife had practiced until her second child was born, when she'd decided she disliked spending so much time away from her family. ''Yes, I admire her for...''

''She had a position with a very important law firm, I understand,'' Philippa continued. ''I can't imagine why she gave it up.''

Although he'd intended to say that he admired the sacrifice Cindi had made, bringing it up now would only create conflict. Still, Barry *was* curious to know more about his date's desire to start a family. ''I understand you want children.''

''Of course I do.'' Philippa barely glanced at the waiter as he set their appetizers on the table, along with her drink. ''One simply must have children. A girl and boy, like Cindi and Andrew have, don't you think?''

''I didn't realize it was a choice,'' Barry said.

''I'm sure one can arrange such things these days.'' Philippa toyed with her caviar. He wondered if she'd ordered the most expensive hors d'oeuvre on the menu simply on principle.

''Kids take a lot of time and attention,'' he said. ''As a pediatrician, I believe children need strong parental involvement.''

''Yes, well, they can get that from their nanny,'' said Philippa. ''I simply don't believe those two women! They're sharing their appetizers. How tacky!''

''Maybe they'd like to try some of your caviar,'' Barry couldn't resist saying.

''Excuse me?''

"I was joking."

"I should hope so!" She fiddled with her drink, then reached into her purse. "I've got to have a smoke."

"I didn't think that was allowed." Smoking was banned at all indoor restaurants in California.

"In a place like this, who's going to notice?" She took out a cigarette. He wondered if he was expected to play the gentleman and light it, and if so whether that would make him equally culpable. Before he could decide what to do, she lit it herself.

A couple of other diners shot irritated glances in their direction. With luck, Barry thought, they'd summon the maître d' and demand that he and Philippa leave. If he had his way, they'd finish their meal at a Burger King drive-thru.

The waiter, arriving to take their orders for entrées, regarded the cigarette in dismay. "Madame, I'm afraid you'll have to put that out."

"No one minds," Philippa said. "There doesn't need to be a scene unless you make one."

Barry's sympathies lay entirely with the waiter. The man didn't want to antagonize a patron, yet he was required to enforce the law.

Seeing that he wasn't backing off, Philippa gave an exaggerated sigh and snuffed out the cigarette on her plate. "There. Are you satisfied?"

"Thank you, Madame. Now, may I recommend tonight's specials?"

Barry chose a chicken dish. Philippa picked the lobster. After the waiter left, she said, "Don't give him a tip. What an insufferable man!"

"I'll keep that in mind." Mentally, Barry made a note to increase the tip. The man had earned it.

Smoke lingered in the air. A woman nearby began coughing, and she and her husband departed, leaving their desserts unfinished.

After witnessing such inconsideration, Barry knew there was no future for him and Philippa. Because she was a friend of Cindi's, though, he wanted to let her down easy.

"I have to be honest with you," he said. "Although I'm a doctor, I'm not in your league financially."

"You could be," Philippa said. "All you have to do is learn to perform liposuctions and breast implants."

"I'm a pediatrician," Barry said.

"Lots of teenage girls are having plastic surgery," she said.

This was getting them nowhere. "I'm not making myself clear," he said. "I don't think you and I..."

"I don't believe it!" His date stared past him. "That odious girl is coming over here! Don't look, you'll only encourage her."

"What girl?" He'd had the impression there were two women behind them.

"The one who was sharing her food." Philippa stared at the ceiling, pointedly ignoring the young woman who marched past Barry.

He caught only a flash of short brown hair and fluttery pink dress before the girl collapsed to her knees, clutched her chest and announced in dramatic tones, "I can't breathe!"

Uttering a series of coughs worthy of Mimi in *La Boheme*, she feigned a swoon onto the carpet, then popped one eye open and demanded, "Is there a doctor in the house?"

It was Angela, he registered with mingled amusement and annoyance. Apparently he'd been right when he thought he spotted Chelsea earlier. What were the two of them doing here?

While Barry was debating whether to applaud her performance or yank her to her feet, Philippa let out a hiss. "For pity's sake! The riffraff they're letting in these days!"

"Oh, I'm sorry," said Angela, loud enough for everyone in the small room to hear. "I didn't mean to break the rules or inconvenience anyone. On the other hand, if *someone* hadn't smoked a cigarette, I wouldn't be suffocating." She uttered a couple more coughs for good measure.

Two diners chuckled. Philippa's face flushed with anger. "I'll have you arrested!"

"For what?" Angela demanded.

"I'll do worse than that," Barry said. "I'll tell your parents."

"Her parents? Do you know them?"

"Philippa, this is Cindi's daughter, Angela," he said.

His date's furious expression lapsed into confusion. "She's changed so much I didn't recognize her. I don't understand why she's acting like this."

"Neither do I," Barry said.

Angela stared at them awkwardly. Now that her dramatic moment had passed, she was at a loss for words.

"Excuse me." Chelsea's voice from behind sent warm tingles across Barry's skin. "I have to apologize. I had no idea you'd be here, Dr. Cantrell. Angela! Let's go finish our meal."

He didn't like being called Dr. Cantrell away from

the office, Barry discovered. Maybe that was because he wished rather urgently that it was Chelsea sitting across from him instead of Philippa.

When she moved into full view, reaching for Angela's hand, he saw that her tube top and tight skirt were indeed out of place in these surroundings. They were also incredibly alluring.

In contrast to Philippa, Chelsea was bright and spunky and down-to-earth. He doubted she would care who saw her in his midpriced sports car or what kind of suit he wore. Except, Barry reminded himself, he wasn't going to be taking Chelsea on any dates.

"Do you know this woman?" Philippa demanded.

"She's the receptionist in my office," he said.

"Fire her," she said.

Angela looked stricken. "You won't tell Dad, will you?" she asked Barry. "I didn't mean to get Chelsea in trouble." Tears glistened in her eyes.

"Chelsea hasn't done anything wrong," he assured her. "Nobody's getting fired."

"If you were my daughter, I wouldn't let you run around town with a receptionist who dresses like a hooker," snapped Philippa. "I'd see that you were raised properly."

Barry's grip on his temper began to fray. "You'd see that she was raised properly by her nanny," he said. "Isn't that what you told me?"

"You can't be taking her side!"

"You're the one who lit a cigarette," he said. "That caused a lot more distress to the other diners than Miss Menton's little performance. Or her friend's choice of clothing, either."

"Fine!" Philippa smacked her hand on the table,

setting the fine china rattling. "Enjoy your dinner, Doctor. I've lost my appetite." She grabbed her purse and departed.

Barry watched her go without even a twinge of regret. "Would you two mind if I join you?"

Angela let out a whoop, then clapped her hand over her mouth. "I'm sorry," she told the other diners, then added more sedately, "We'd love to have you."

After canceling the order for lobster, Barry enjoyed the rest of his meal at the other table. He and Chelsea kept the conversation general and avoided meeting each other's eyes.

Even so, his body tingled whenever their legs accidentally bumped under the table. They laughed a lot, although later he couldn't remember what they'd said. It was a lovely evening, but not, Barry reminded himself firmly, a date.

Afterward, the pair dropped him off at Philippa's house to get his car. Fortunately, he didn't see the woman around.

Barry drove home with the pleasant sense that the evening hadn't been such a loss after all.

7

"I CAN'T STAND that woman," Angela told Chelsea on the way home. "Barry deserves better than her."

"I hope you weren't trying to fix us up," Chelsea said. "He's my boss."

"I wasn't! Honest!" The innocent facade held for a moment, then crumpled. "Maybe a little."

"Never try that again."

"Okay. I promise. And I'll tell the whole story to Mom myself. Maybe she'll finally realize what a snob Philippa is," Angela said. "Mom tends to see people's good side. Especially when they're big supporters of the arts."

"I'm sure your parents meant well when they arranged the date," Chelsea said.

"Yeah," the girl grumbled. "They always mean well." Then she grinned. "Grandma will get a laugh out of it."

During the next couple of months, Chelsea treasured the memory of that evening. As woman after woman finagled, begged or otherwise snared a date with Barry, she reminded herself of how much more fun he'd had with her and Angela than with that awful Philippa.

Still, she wished him luck with what, she was beginning to realize, was a genuine search for a soul mate. Yet she experienced a stirring of relief each time it became clear that a first date had also been a last date.

Chelsea had no regrets about having called it quits with Barry. Okay, maybe a few. There were lonely nights when she wished she could wrap her arms around him and they could nestle together in bed. Sometimes it was hard to keep her distance in the office, when they would joke together and she'd feel a spark and know that he felt it, too.

But he was so proper. So perfectly starched, so correct in his professional behavior, so critical when he caught her playing horsey with Tisa and Laryssa in the waiting room. Her explanation that the girls had demanded a repeat performance from their last visit had brought only a stern reminder that this was an office, not a playground.

He needed an equally stuffy woman. Someone who would allow him to boss her around or, hard as it was to imagine, who shared his rigid view of life.

At those unguarded moments when Chelsea caught a glimpse of tenderness in his gaze, she reminded herself of how she'd fallen for the same aura of sweetness a few years ago when she agreed to marry Gene. He'd turned out to be a big disappointment.

Although Chelsea hoped someday to meet the right man to marry, she was in no hurry. Since she didn't particularly want children, she had all the time in the world.

Even so, March and April dragged by with little to break the monotony. In early May, Myrtle the hamster escaped from her cage. On her way to the bathroom the following night, Chelsea stepped on something that crunched, and for a terrible moment she believed she'd killed Myrtle.

The victim turned out to be a leftover Easter egg that had rolled out from under a cabinet. The next day, Myrtle turned up in Chelsea's closet, nibbling on an old shoe.

At the office, the cold and flu season slacked off. Thank goodness she didn't have to keep working patients in and throwing off the schedule, Chelsea reflected the Friday before the Friends of the Opera and Ballet press luncheon.

Tomorrow, Angela would perform her solo. Chelsea was as nervous as if she herself were scheduled to dance. For days, her stomach had churned with excitement.

Barry poked his head into the reception bay. "Don't tell me we're actually caught up. Nobody waiting?"

"It's lunchtime," Chelsea said. "I'm afraid I have some bad news, though."

His eyes darkened with concern. "What's wrong?"

"Not a single lady brought you a casserole. Not even a sandwich," she said. "You'll have to provide your own lunch. You can have a stick of my chewing gum, though, if you ask nicely."

He grinned. "I can't believe I've run through the entire female population of the office building that quickly."

"Shall I put up fliers down the block?"

"Spare me." He started to beat a retreat, his usual tactic whenever they had too much fun talking.

The waiting room door opened. Chelsea was about to inform the new arrival that they were closed for lunch, when she saw that the sixtyish gentleman didn't have a child with him.

"Can I help you?" she asked.

"I just wanted to see the place." With his shock of white hair, thin face and scraggly white beard, the man reminded her of Colonel Sanders. Fried chicken, Chelsea thought, that's what she wanted for lunch.

She heard Barry's swift intake of breath. "Dad!" He hurried into the waiting room. "You should have told me when you were arriving!"

"I flew standby. Didn't want to waste your time hanging around the airport." The older man clapped his son on the shoulder. "Man, you look great. Living on that island agreed with you."

Beaming, Barry addressed Chelsea. "Dad's a doctor in Colorado, the old-fashioned kind who treats the whole family and makes house calls. He knows more about kids than most pediatricians."

"And more about mothers and babies, too," announced Barry's father. "Over the years, you develop a sixth sense about what's wrong—or right, as the case may be. Congratulations, young lady."

"On what?" Chelsea asked.

The elder Dr. Cantrell surveyed her knowingly. "On your pregnancy, of course. Who's the lucky father?"

ASTONISHED, Barry stared at Chelsea. Surely Lew must be mistaken. If she were pregnant, she'd have told him.

Judging by the blank expression on her face, this was news to her, too. "I'm not. I mean, I don't think I am."

"There's a glow about you and a kind of hormonal hum in the air. I can sense that sort of thing," said Lew.

"My stomach's been bothering me because of Angela's ballet solo tomorrow," Chelsea said. "I'm sure I'm not...well, almost sure."

"When was your last menstrual period?" asked Lew.

"I don't remember. They're irregular."

"Irregular?" Barry said. "You told me it was the wrong time of..."

He stopped. Too late.

"You're kidding," said his father. "My noble son, the savior of Prego Prego, has been—pardon the expression—boffing the receptionist?"

Chelsea burst into laughter. "It wasn't like that."

"It must have been something like that, or you wouldn't be pregnant," said Lew.

Barry couldn't begin to sort out his reaction. He wanted children. He really liked Chelsea. Yet it wasn't supposed to happen like this. *They* weren't supposed to happen. He didn't want an odd-couple marriage like his parents' twenty-year train-wreck-in-progress.

"You need a pregnancy test." He knew he sounded like an insensitive clod. At a time like this, though, surely such a procedure was the logical way to go.

"I saw an obstetrician's office down the hall," his father said. "We'll go there."

"We?" said Barry.

"I'm not going to miss this." Lew opened the exterior door. "Isn't anyone going to congratulate me?"

"On what?"

"I'm going to be a grandfather!" crowed his father, and ushered them into the hall.

CHELSEA REGARDED the ultrasound image in a blur of disbelief. The obstetrician, Dr. Keller, had not only been willing to see her at once but, in deference to the two anxious physicians accompanying her, had arranged for an immediate sonogram after a quick test confirmed she was pregnant.

"There's definitely two." Dr. Keller pointed to the tiny squirmy black-and-white figures on the TV-type screen. "Active little critters, too."

The pair, in their separate sacs, wiggled and tussled like roughhousing children. Which, Chelsea realized with a start, was exactly what they were.

"Twins?" She could hardly speak through her clogged throat. "I'm having twins?" The last word came out as a squeak.

"Two of them?" added Barry.

"That's what twins usually means," chirped the small, rotund obstetrician. "Unless there's three. Let's take a closer look—no, I don't see a third one."

Chelsea's head swam. What would she have done with three? On the other hand, what was she going to do with two?

"Can you tell the sex yet?" asked Lew.

Although it felt odd to have this complete stranger taking part in the most intimate discovery of her life, Chelsea found the elder Dr. Cantrell's presence a relief. At least he served as a buffer.

She couldn't even imagine what thoughts were

generating those storm clouds in Barry's eyes. Well, she had no sympathy to spare for him.

It was Chelsea, not Barry, who had these cute but intimidating little persons tumbling around in her midsection. She was the one who needed to make the tough decisions. If there had been a way to transfer them to Barry, she'd have voted for that option, but there wasn't.

How could she keep them and raise them alone? Her parents had never been reliable, even with their own daughter, so she couldn't look to them for help.

She didn't want to depend on a man, either. Especially not Barry. He would want to call all the shots. Pick out names like Alphonse and Hermione. Dress them in frills or tiny business suits. Teach them algebra before they were three.

Chelsea wasn't going to let him run her life, and that was that, she thought a few minutes later as she got dressed. Before she knew it, she had made a follow-up appointment and was exiting with an armful of brochures and vitamins.

"Let's go eat lunch!" Lew rubbed his hands together cheerily. "My treat."

Alarmed, Chelsea checked her watch. "We have to get back to work."

"Would you mind bringing us some sandwiches, Dad?" Barry asked. "That would be great."

"Sure thing." His father patted Chelsea on the shoulder. "Welcome to the family, young lady."

After he disappeared down the elevator, she asked Barry, "Does he assume we're getting married?"

"I doubt it. Now let's go talk where it's private." Barry guided her into their suite through the back entrance. There was no one around, although Chelsea could hear Helen and Sandy chatting down the hall.

They scooted into Barry's office. When he closed the door, she realized how small the place was. The diplomas on the walls looked impressive up close, she thought.

So did Barry, tall and broad-shouldered and brooding. With a pang, Chelsea realized how much she missed touching him.

Someone ought to muss that too-perfect dark hair and kiss him fast, then dart away so he would advance and pin her against the wall. When he bent over her to claim another kiss, she ought to unbutton his shirt and run her hands over his firm chest. It would be much more fun than standing here preparing to discuss deep issues when she didn't know what to say.

"What are you going to do?" Barry asked.

"About what?"

"Chelsea!"

"I don't know," she said. "Any suggestions?"

"We could get m..." He seemed to choke on the next word.

"Migraines?" she suggested. "I don't need one. I already have a stomachache."

"I'm surprised you didn't suspect you might be pregnant," he said.

"I guess I was in denial," Chelsea admitted. "Besides, my periods are often irregular. I sometimes skip one entirely when I'm under stress, like when Starshine is late with the rent. She's been doing that a lot recently."

"Well, now that you know, how do you feel about having twins?" Barry asked.

"Not just twins. Kids of any sort," she said. "I didn't plan to."

"You didn't?" He stared at her in dismay. "But you like children. I've seen the way you play with the patients."

"Some of them are cute." Not as cute as the two little figures rollicking around inside her, either. Still, Chelsea had to stick by her convictions, one of which was that if she couldn't keep her rodents from running away, she might have the same problem with her children. "There are a lot of families who desperately want kids. Think of the joy we could spread."

His eyebrows knitted themselves into a fierce line. It was quite a trick. Chelsea wondered how he did it.

"Unlike you, I *do* want children," Barry said, "although I believe they have a right to grow up in a two-parent family if possible."

"So we're in agreement?" she asked.

"About what?"

"Adoption." As she spoke the word aloud, Chelsea wondered how she could go through with it. In principle, she admired birth mothers who gave up babies they weren't prepared to raise. In reality, her heart ached at the prospect.

"I never said that." Barry glared at the door, which someone was knocking on. "Yes?"

Helen stuck her head inside. "We have some patients waiting. Oh, dear. Am I interrupting anything?"

"We were trying to figure out whether to put our children up for adoption," Chelsea said.

"Excuse me?"

From the corner of her eye, she noted that Barry had blanched. It was amazing how pale a man could look under a tan. "I'm pregnant with twins."

"You and Barry have been...are a couple?" The nurse uttered a little gasp. "I was hoping, I mean, Dr. Cantrell, I know you and my daughter didn't fall madly in love on your date, but I thought things might work out in a year or two when she's a little more mature."

"What's going on?" It was Sandy, edging into the doorway beside Helen. When she heard the news, she frowned. "Louise will have a hissy fit. She said she plans to claim you for her groom if she has to hog-tie you and hold a shotgun to your head. I don't know what she'll say about this."

Barry's dismayed look gave way to alarm. "Your sister isn't actually dangerous, is she?"

"Just very determined," the office manager assured him. "I'm certain she didn't mean the part about the shotgun. I'm not so sure about the hog-tying."

"Are we having a conference?" Andrew's voice carried over the intervening bodies, which parted to let him into the doorway.

"It's the babies," Helen said.

"Chelsea's having twins," Sandy added.

"And Barry," said Helen.

"She's having Barry?" Andrew asked.

"I'm afraid she already had him," Sandy said.

Andrew's eyebrows did their own thing, which was to form a peak in the middle like an inverted vee. "Barry?"

He nodded.

Andrew scowled. Chelsea wondered if her boss

was about to chew out his cousin for misbehaving with the office staff.

Instead, Dr. Menton said, "Cindi will be furious. She's got dates lined up for you through July, at least."

It was on the tip of Chelsea's tongue to say that Barry could date anyone he liked. A little thing like a pregnancy didn't have to tie him down, or her, either.

For once in her life, she decided not to blurt out the first thing that came into her mind. It wasn't that she'd suddenly learned discretion.

It was that she heard the front office door opening and inhaled the smell of pastrami sandwiches as Lew's voice called, "Anybody home?"

A mother had to set priorities. Chelsea's was lunch.

ALTHOUGH THE OFFICE didn't schedule regular appointments on the weekend, it opened on Saturday mornings to treat patients who'd fallen ill. Barry arrived at eight and was able to get away by ten o'clock. He hurried home to dress for the press luncheon.

As he struggled to knot his tie, he asked himself for the thousandth time why he hadn't come right out and asked Chelsea to marry him yesterday. He wanted their children, and, quite frankly, he wanted her.

None of the other women he'd dated remotely appealed to him. He'd had no desire to take any of them to bed. Even the few good-night kisses he'd exchanged had been perfunctory.

The memory of that night at Chelsea's apartment

burned in his blood. His body remembered every passionate interchange and reacted with a will of its own every time she came near.

In his heart, though, he knew a marriage between them wouldn't last. Such a volatile relationship would devastate them both and leave their children on shaky ground.

Kids deserved stability. Maybe that meant that they deserved a loving, adoptive home. Yet try as he might, Barry couldn't reconcile himself to giving them up.

He didn't know what to do. It was a humbling feeling.

"Can I give you some advice, son?" asked Lew, appearing in the open bedroom doorway. He wore a black suit with a bolo tie that intensified the resemblance to Colonel Sanders that Chelsea had pointed out earlier.

"Go ahead." Barry knew that his father, who wanted very much to be a grandfather, would probably say something he didn't want to hear. Still, it was only polite to listen.

"Don't eat a man's coconut pie until you know what he plans to do with it."

Barry frowned, trying to find some deep, metaphorical meaning in his father's odd statement. Then he remembered his late-night snack.

"I saw it in the refrigerator," he said. "I figured it was for us both."

"You ate half," Lew pointed out. "That's a lot for one sitting."

"I haven't had a coconut pie in years." An alarming notion occurred to Barry. "You weren't planning to throw it at someone, were you?"

"Who, me?" His father's eyes widened in mock confusion. Barry's mother, Meredith, used to refer to it as his sneaky-fox-pretending-to-be-a-deer-in-the-headlights look.

"There aren't going to be any politicians present today, as far as I know," Barry said. "The event is to publicize the opera and ballet's fall season. Surely you don't object to singing and dancing."

"I'm expected to sing and dance?" Lew joked. "You should have told me. I'd have worn my tap shoes."

The man was impossible. And wonderful. Barry started to give him a hug, then, respecting their habit of keeping a distance, turned it into a clap on the shoulder. "No pie-throwing, Dad."

"I promise." Lew grinned. "I haven't got a pie and, besides, I'm in a good mood today, thanks to you and Chelsea."

"We haven't decided…"

"You'll do the right thing," said his father, and vanished before Barry could respond.

8

THIS WASN'T going to be easy, Chelsea thought as she and Angela drove onto the freeway on Saturday morning. She was glad she had this chance to talk to her young friend alone.

Angela had asked for a ride to the theater, since she had to arrive an hour and a half before the rest of her family. Chelsea had agreed, partly because it would make Angela happy and partly because she wanted to explain the circumstances of her pregnancy before the girl heard the news from someone else.

The problem was, she discovered as she tried to decide how to start, that she didn't want to set a bad example. Although Chelsea treasured her live-and-let-live attitude, she didn't want to give a twelve-year-old the impression that having children outside of marriage was a good idea.

The hard part was to explain why she'd gone to bed with Barry in the first place, besides the obvious fact that he was cute. She was sure there *had* been a good reason, even if she hadn't been consciously aware of it.

Suddenly Chelsea knew what it was.

"I did a foolish thing," she said. "I want to tell you about it because you're going to find out anyway."

"Otherwise you wouldn't tell me?" Her face surrounded by a cloud of hair burnished by the May sunshine, Angela hugged herself protectively.

Chelsea had forgotten how oversensitive an adolescent could be. "I wouldn't have told you because it's embarrassing."

The girl relaxed. "I can't believe you'd be embarrassed about anything!"

"Well, I am." She decided to plunge right in. "Some time ago, I had a bad relationship and it made me doubt myself. I stayed away from men for a long time, which wasn't hard, because most of the guys I meet are creeps."

"I know exactly what you mean." In a few seconds, Angela had gone from vulnerable child to blasé young lady. Chelsea smiled at the transition.

"Then I met a supernice guy and I jumped at the chance to prove something to myself," she said. "I'm afraid I also jumped into bed with him."

"What happened?"

Chelsea took a deep breath. "I got pregnant."

"You're kidding, right?" Angela stared at her. "Is this for real?"

"Not only is it for real, it's twins." She swung past a slowpoke in the middle lane.

"What about the guy?" Angela asked. "Did he turn out to be a jerk?"

"No." Chelsea might as well spill the rest of it. "He turned out to be Barry."

"*My* Barry?"

"The same."

"Good," said Angela. "You two are perfect for each other."

Chelsea's hackles rose. "We are not. You know

how you don't want your family to run your life? Well, I don't want a man to run mine, either.''

"He wouldn't do that," the girl said. "Would he?"

"I like him," Chelsea conceded. "He can be fun to have around. But there's this undercurrent of stuffiness. A place for everything and everything in its place."

"I know what you could do!" Angela said. "You could get married, but live in different houses."

"People don't do that."

"Why not? You'd never be lonely, because you'd each have a baby to play with," the girl said. "I love babies! I'll sit with your kids anytime you want, and I won't charge for it, either."

Chelsea had meant to bring up the subject of adoption, but suddenly she couldn't. What if Angela got so upset she messed up her solo?

"Look! We're almost there." She exited the freeway a block from the theater, grateful to be spared any further conversation.

It occurred to Chelsea, as she parked in the underground garage, that having children of her own meant she would have to set a good example all the time. How on earth did parents manage?

THE CATERED LUNCHEON took place in a large rehearsal hall transformed for the occasion with tables, chairs and a temporary stage. In addition to the press, the attendees included FOB members and their guests. Barry, sitting between Chelsea and Lew, shared a table in back with the Mentons.

From where Barry sat, the reporters appeared to be enjoying their meals of Chinese chicken salad.

The TV crews, however, were too busy setting up to eat, and the newspaper photographers jockeyed for position with the cameras.

Chelsea looked radiant, Barry thought, sneaking a glance at her. She wore her hair upswept, which emphasized the delicacy of her bone structure and the sculpted fullness of her lips.

His father was right, he thought; she did glow. Barry couldn't smell any hormones, however, only exotic perfume mingled with the herbal softness of her shampoo.

Her one-shoulder purple jungle-print dress, made him yearn to slide that strap down her arm. Oh, for a little privacy!

Better not to think in that direction. Indulging his fantasies was how he and Chelsea had landed themselves in this dilemma in the first place.

Barry leaned forward as the current chairman of Friends of the Opera and Ballet mounted the stage. The man spoke a few words about the upcoming season and noted that the details were in the press kits.

"Now we have a treat for you," the man said. "Without further ado, here is the marvelous Fiorello Magnifico, who will star in our holiday gala in December."

To Barry's right, Lew cleared his throat with a low growl. This was not a friendly noise. As the tenor bowed and an accompanist slipped into his seat at the piano, Barry studied Mr. Magnifico for clues to his father's apparent dislike.

Pudgy, of average height, with black hair so thick it was probably augmented, the tenor radiated self-importance. His cavalier's costume, complete with lace-trimmed sleeves and a costume sword strapped across the chest, looked like it had been swiped from a production of *The Three Musketeers*.

"Now I will sing for you," the man said, unnecessarily. He had a strong Italian accent, which was surprising, since he came from New York. In fact, Barry thought he detected a nasal Bronx undertone.

The pianist played a few notes and Fiorello launched into an aria from *Don Giovanni*. The opera had been one of Barry's mother's favorites, so it was familiar, and he could tell that the man sang it well.

However, he didn't like the way Fiorello flirted with every female at the front tables, batting his eyes and wiggling his ample stomach. If he'd been singing the title role of Don Juan, his actions might have made sense, but in this aria, he was supposed to be a devoted suitor declaring that his true love's happiness was his only reason for living.

By the time Fiorello finished to enthusiastic applause, Barry understood why someone might throw a cream pie at the man out of sheer annoyance. He was glad he didn't have one handy to tempt him.

That didn't explain the snarl on Lew's mouth. Barry still didn't know what Fiorello had done to antagonize him.

After one more song, the man left the stage. It was time for the youth ballet.

WHEN ANGELA danced onto the stage, Chelsea thought her heart would break.

The girl looked achingly beautiful. Fragile. Fluid. She floated, drawing all eyes from the other young ballerinas.

Without thinking, Chelsea reached over and took

Barry's hand. She felt as if she had to hold on to someone or she might melt onto the floor.

His large hand enfolded hers protectively. Through their touch, his steadiness calmed her. The dependability, the resoluteness she distrusted so much were suddenly welcome.

Chelsea wasn't sure why she felt shaky, watching Angela strike one graceful position after another. The young dancer managed to capture both the joy of self-discovery and the agony of self-doubt. The sight brought back memories of Chelsea's own adolescence.

From her hairstyles to her study habits, she had insisted on charting her own nonconforming course, despite the taunts of other students and the disapproval of teachers. Sometimes she'd felt as vulnerable, and been as determined, as Angela looked.

Chelsea didn't even notice when the other girls drew back to let her perform solo, because it seemed as if Angela had been alone on stage from the moment she entered. Surely everyone could see that the girl had a rare gift. No wonder tears were pouring down Cindi's cheeks and glittering in Grace's eyes.

As Angela completed a series of leaps and spins, Chelsea's heart constricted. What if this were her child? What if she weren't there for those key moments, the triumphs and tragedies?

She couldn't bear to give birth to a child and never know what happened to him or her. Or, rather, to them.

Not to know whether the twins were crying at night, or laughing at funny stories. Not to watch them grow through all the fearful, magical stages of childhood.

She wanted to be there for moments like this. What else was life about?

When the audience erupted into applause, she discovered she was still holding Barry's hand. For one electric moment, she looked into his face and saw her own longing for their children mirrored there.

This was why a woman might want to tie herself to a strong, self-possessed man like Barry: to share with him the happy and difficult times ahead. To lean on him when she felt overwhelmed, and when the children needed him.

Disgusted with herself, Chelsea yanked her hand away. A woman could certainly come up with some bizarre ideas while under the influence of ballet, she reflected, and began clapping as hard as she could.

BARRY WAS SEIZED by an urge to drag Chelsea aside and demand to know why she'd squeezed his hand, and why she'd then pulled it away. He didn't understand anything about her or, at the moment, himself. In defiance of all logic, he wanted to hang on to her as tightly as she'd just held on to him.

Watching Angela dance had been a transcendent experience, mostly because he'd shared it with Chelsea. His ache for her was both irrational and irresistible.

He couldn't do anything about it at the moment, though. To Barry's intense frustration, he had to sit here for the rest of the press conference or risk embarrassing his relatives.

When the applause subsided, the chairman of the FOB introduced a few celebrity supporters in the audience. Among them was the reclusive billionaire Werner Waldheim, who rarely made public appearances. In his late thirties, slim with graying dark hair, he had a self-possessed air that belied his reputation as a computer geek.

Several reporters asked about Fiorello's upcoming performance schedule, and the tenor strutted back on stage. Barry found it painful to listen to his fake Italian accent with its Bronx underpinnings, but the press lapped up the words.

They kept scribbling as he detailed future engagements in Europe, then added, "And I'm very grateful to Mr. Waldheim for supporting the proposal I discussed on several recent TV shows."

"Could you restate that position, Mr. Magnifico?" called a reporter.

Barry leaned forward. Here, at last, might be a clue to why that coconut pie had appeared in his refrigerator last night.

The tenor drew himself up. "Certainly. It's a national scandal. According to the newspapers, the Army sometimes mistakenly sells items to Army surplus stores and then has to buy them back at inflated prices. I believe it's time we nationalized these stores."

"Why not just demand that the Army be more efficient?" someone called.

"Because these surplus goods belong to the taxpayers. If the Army doesn't need them, it, not the individual storeowners, should profit from the sales directly," said the tenor.

"You've also called for nationalizing junk dealerships," commented another reporter. "What's your justification for that?"

"It's hard to distinguish between the two types of

businesses. Besides, I'm sure junk dealers end up with a lot of government vehicles," said Fiorello.

Next to Barry, his father muttered something under his breath. It sounded like, "My kingdom for a pie."

Aunt Grace, however, was nodding in approval, just as Barry's mother would have done at any suggestion that the government should take charge of private matters. He hoped Lew didn't notice.

"Do you really think you have any chance of succeeding?" asked a TV anchorman.

"Yes, with Werner's support," Fiorello said. "I don't have the pull with politicians, but he does."

"Are you serious about this issue?" someone asked Waldheim.

The billionaire beamed as he spoke into a microphone. "I'm honored to be friends with such a great artist and happy to assist our armed forces."

In his fury, Lew vibrated like a rocket ready for blastoff. It was a relief to Barry when the tenor finally took himself off stage and his father calmed down.

As soon as the press conference ended, Chelsea darted out the door. Instinctively, Barry strode after her through a twisting corridor.

When she took a wrong turn into a no-exit hallway, he cornered her. "I want to know why you grabbed my hand," he said. "You were hanging on to me for dear life."

"It didn't mean anything," Chelsea said defiantly. "I just felt like it. If my chinchilla had been sitting next to me, I'd have held *his* little paw."

"It had something to do with Angela, but there was more to it," Barry said. "We've got to work things out between us. There are two children's futures hanging in the balance.''

''Oh, about that.'' Chelsea gave him a skittish smile. ''I've decided to keep them. Don't worry about it. It isn't your problem.''

''Keeping the children isn't a problem. It *is* an important issue.'' He struggled to maintain an even tone. ''I intend to provide financial support whether you want it or not, and I insist on being involved.''

''Why? To make sure they go to the right schools?'' Chelsea challenged.

Barry winced. He'd had a conversation with Andrew on Friday afternoon about the value of sending children to private schools where they could make worthwhile social connections. Obviously, she'd overheard and gotten her feathers ruffled.

''That's negotiable.'' Barry refused to be dragged into petty squabbling. The two of them sounded too much like his own parents. ''We'll continue this discussion when we've both simmered down. Let's go find the others. I don't want to leave my father alone for too long.''

''Why not?'' Chelsea didn't resist as he caught her elbow and drew her along the passageway.

Barry explained about the coconut pie. ''Now I understand what he's got against this Fiorello character.''

''I agree that the man's an idiot, but why does his stupid campaign concern your father?'' Chelsea asked.

''His best friend owns a junkyard.''

''That's a good reason to throw a pie,'' she said.

''Can you imagine how Aunt Grace would react if my father did such a thing?''

Chelsea gave him an amused look. "She'd get over it."

Barry groaned. "I don't think so."

They found the others chatting in a happy knot near the elevators. "People liked my solo so much that I've been asked to dance at the December gala!" Angela threw her arms around Chelsea. "I'm glad you convinced me to stick with ballet!"

"Yes, thank you," Grace said over her grand-daughter's head.

"She's the one who deserves the credit," Chelsea said.

Barry spotted his father trying to slip off, and caught up with him. "Don't even think about going after that tenor," he told Lew in a low voice. "Pie or no pie, I know you're up to some mischief."

"The man's going to be performing in Europe all summer and fall," his father said. "You can't blame me for trying to take a poke at him before he gets away."

"Physical violence?" Barry asked uneasily.

"Not exactly." From his pocket, Lew produced a dispenser of Silly String. "I figured I could blast him with this gooey stuff. Just to make my protest."

"No," said Barry.

"Spoilsport." Good-naturedly, his father put away the string. Still, Barry knew he'd have to keep an eye on the man until he left town. You could never tell what he might do next.

Any further conversation with Chelsea would have to wait.

tempted, but apparently not Louise. According to
Sandy, trying to have a two-way conversation with her
sister was like talking "to an air-cramming flutter-
bum by standing on your hands and waving your
knees."

"Anyway, he said he would be good for sparring,"
she said cautiously.

"I knew it," said Louise. "I'm clear. I'm—"

9

BY MONDAY, word of the pregnancy had spread
throughout the office building and to various female
friends and relations of co-workers. It amazed Chelsea how many people stopped by or telephoned to
confirm the rumor, as if it were any of their business.

Sandy's sister, Louise, called in midmorning. As
soon as she made sure it was Chelsea on the line,
she said, "Going to bed with him was a fluke, right?
You've always been the carefree type. So I'm clear
to make my moves on the man. Correct?"

Chelsea pictured the large-framed, fast-talking
Louise leaning forward intently at her desk at the
escrow company she owned. A faint tapping, as of
a pen against wood, sounded in the background.

"I'm surprised you'd want to see him again,"
Chelsea said into the phone. "I thought you had him
over for dinner and it didn't work out."

That was putting it tactfully. According to Sandy,
the date had been a bomb. "A plain, old-fashioned
stink bomb."

"That was part of my learning curve," Louise
said. "I was taking the man's measure. I think I
know how to get to him now. Draw him out, ask his
opinions, listen to the answers."

That was what most people did on a date, Chelsea

thought, but apparently not Louise. According to Sandy, trying to have a two-way discussion with her sister was like trying to stop an onrushing freight train by standing on the tracks and waving your hands.

"Listening to him would be good, for starters," she said cautiously.

"I knew you'd agree!" said Louise. "I'm glad I have your permission."

"I didn't..." Before Chelsea could finish the sentence, the phone went dead against her ear. She imagined she could hear a train clicking away along the tracks as Louise lived up to her sister's description.

Shortly before lunchtime, Josiah Withers's niece, Belinda, dropped by. Chelsea recognized her from her photograph.

"No wonder Barry and I didn't hit it off," she said without preamble. "You were undercutting my chances the whole time."

"Please leave me out of it." Chelsea knew that, after taking Belinda to the movies one night, Barry had been ducking her phone calls ever since. "Whatever happened on your date is between you and Dr. Cantrell."

"That's right, it is!" Belinda plopped an apple pie onto the counter. "You're not the marrying kind, but I am, and I made sure he knew it."

Since Belinda had been divorced four times, Chelsea couldn't dispute that she was the marrying type. Besides, they shouldn't argue in front of a roomful of patients and their mothers. "Good luck," was all she said.

"I carved my initials in the crust, so don't give it to him and pretend you baked it!" Belinda said. "You probably can't cook worth a darn anyway."

Chelsea opened her mouth to protest, then closed it again. She doubted Belinda would give her credit for having memorized the phone number of the pizza delivery service.

The woman stalked out. The pie smelled awfully good, Chelsea thought. The crust was flaky and neatly fluted. The pie was so perfect that she couldn't resist picking it up and sneaking a peek at the bottom of the pan.

It was imprinted with the logo of a restaurant famous for its pies. So much for Belinda's domestic talents.

Still, Chelsea didn't want to seem petty. So when Andrew drifted over, drawn by the aroma, she told him that Belinda had left the pie for Barry.

"I'll share it with him," said Dr. Menton, bearing it away. "If there's any left."

A short time later, when the waiting room was almost empty, three secretaries from a neighboring law firm dropped by. "My friends have both gone out with Dr. Cantrell and I'm supposed to be next," said a wispy blonde.

"We wondered if you'd mind if she took her turn," added her tall, thin companion. "Everybody says you're too independent to be tied down."

"No offense, but with that hair and the way you dress, you're obviously not the doctor's wife type," said their buxom friend.

Each of the three women set a dish on the counter.

Tuna-noodle casserole. Potato salad. Bean-and-cheese dip.

"I cried into mine the whole time I was making it," said the blonde. "You can't claim him already. I haven't had my chance yet."

"Dr. Cantrell isn't a ride at Disneyland," Chelsea said. "He's not required to give turns."

"No offense, but you might as well yield now," said the well-endowed lady. "I hear you can't even cook."

"Why does everyone assume that?" Chelsea did recall making such a statement at an office potluck once, when she'd brought fast-food fried chicken. She'd never before realized how fast word spread through the building.

"*Can* you cook?" asked the tall, thin member of the group. The three of them awaited her answer with skeptical frowns.

"With one hand tied behind my back," said Chelsea. It was true. She'd made hot dogs once with her hand behind her back, on a dare.

"What's your specialty?" demanded the buxom one.

She thought quickly. "Eggs. I made an egg dish the other night that was truly unique." It had been unique, all right, squashed flat on the floor en route to the bathroom.

"What's it called?" asked the blonde suspiciously.

"Scalloped egg à la Myrtle," Chelsea improvised.

The three women exchanged disappointed glances. Then they picked up their dishes and beat a hasty retreat.

When they were gone, the mother of the only remaining patient spoke up. "I don't know what this is all about," she told Chelsea, "but if I were you, I'd prove them wrong."

"About what?" she asked, wishing they'd at least left the tuna-noodle casserole, because she was hungry. Then she remembered that the blonde had cried into it, so it was probably too salty.

"I'd make some of that scalloped egg à la Myrtle for Dr. Cantrell," the woman said. "That'll shut them up."

"What if I accidentally poison the doctor?" Chelsea asked.

The woman laughed. "You won't."

All afternoon, Chelsea mulled this advice. She didn't want to bring food into the office as if she were another ditsy female chasing after Barry. On the other hand, it might be fun to surprise him with something at home.

It would be past suppertime before she could cook and get to his condo. Surely he and his father would appreciate a late-night snack, though.

She jotted down Barry's address from the files. On the way home, she stopped at a supermarket.

It had a great deli counter. Really, it would be foolish to cook anything. Chelsea was about to place an order when it struck her that bringing a ready-made dish would miss the point.

"I cooked him dinner last night," she imagined herself saying to the unholy trio from the law firm. "I made it with my own hands and he ate every bite," she would tell Belinda. "Including dessert."

She could do it. Heck, she'd fixed meals for her

parents for years. No need for recipes, either. Chelsea knew how to throw a dinner together and give it her own special touch.

As a teenager, macaroni and cheese with coconut had been one of her favorites. So had peanut-butter-and-maple-syrup sandwiches. They didn't sound fancy enough, however. She wanted to impress Barry.

A bag of chocolate chips in a baking display caught her eye. In a restaurant, Chelsea had once eaten a spicy, chocolate-flavored Mexican chicken dish. Surely she could devise something like that in the microwave.

A green salad went with everything, she decided, making up her menu. It needed a special dressing, of course. Mayonnaise would taste great with a few spices. Garlic and ginger, maybe.

Her enthusiasm rising, Chelsea prowled the aisles, seeking inspiration for dessert. Orange-flavored gelatin was an old favorite, and it would solidify fast if she used ice cubes. She'd throw in a few interesting tidbits, like cheddar cheese bits and whatever chocolate chips were left from the chicken.

This ought to be a meal to remember. Chelsea gave a happy skip as she filled her cart.

CUTTING HIS TRIP short because his patients needed him, Lew flew home on Monday. Father and son exchanged a rare hug at the airport.

As he watched the older man board the plane, Barry was surprised to realize how much he'd enjoyed the visit. When he was younger, he'd viewed his father as a force of nature. Since his mother's death, however, he'd realized Lew wouldn't always be around. He cherished the ties between them more than ever.

Once the plane took off, Barry departed. Only after he was on the freeway did it occur to him that he should have eaten dinner at the terminal before tackling rush-hour traffic.

His condo in Venice lay within a few miles of Los Angeles International Airport. His father, however, had arranged a cheap flight out of Ontario Airport, on the opposite side of the Los Angeles basin. It was after seven o'clock and growing dark by the time Barry reached home.

Chelsea stood on the front steps of his condo, holding an armful of paper bags and poking the doorbell with her only free finger. As Barry approached, he caught a whiff of scents, the most prominent being chocolate. "Hi. What's all this?"

She turned, startled. In the twilight, her speckled eyes shifted into a shade of sorrowful blue-green, mirroring the turquoise of her sweaterdress.

"I did my best," Chelsea said. "The gelatin is kind of loose and I don't know how the Mexicans make their sauce, but I don't think they use chocolate chips. You should see my microwave oven. The chicken practically exploded."

"You cooked dinner?" Barry felt simultaneously flattered and apprehensive. "Good. I'm starved."

"It isn't good." She inched aside to let him open the door. "It would be better if you were really, really full."

"We don't have to eat it," he pointed out. "I'd be happy to buy you dinner."

"I don't believe in wasting food," Chelsea said. "Where's your dad?"

"Eating airplane food," Barry said. "Should I envy him?"

"Probably."

She hadn't exaggerated, he discovered when the food came out of the bags. How could anyone ruin salad? The dressing tasted heavy and oddly spiced, though, and after one bite he gave up on it.

The chicken was worse, a tattered mess covered with brown goo. Even the smell of chocolate, normally an aphrodisiac where Barry was concerned, failed to stir his appetite. The gelatin mold could charitably be placed in the category of organic matter, but not by any stretch of the imagination could he classify it as food.

Barry didn't try to put a good face on it. Chelsea wouldn't appreciate dishonesty and, besides, the disaster was beyond redemption. "What on earth possessed you to cook for me?" he asked, clearing away the bowls she'd brought.

"Everybody said I couldn't. Apparently, they were right." Huddled in her chair at the dining-room table, Chelsea wound a purple-tipped strand of hair around her forefinger. With chocolate smeared on one cheekbone, she resembled a waif out of a Dickens story.

"Everybody who?"

"The women who want to get their hooks into you," she said.

"No generalizations," Barry responded as he marched into the kitchen. "Name names."

"Louise. Belinda. A girl who works in the law firm."

"They hurt your feelings?"

"I don't like people stereotyping me." Her voice drifted after him from the dining room. "I can cook if I want to. Not all experiments work out. Maybe I was trying too hard."

Irrationally, hope spurted inside Barry at the possibility that she'd cooked the meal because she wanted him. They were incompatible in almost every way, certain to drive each other to insanity or at least sword's point. Yet through the kitchen doorway she looked so appealing he wanted to put his arms around her.

As he'd guessed, she made a bright splash in the low-key condo. A ray of sunshine, although Barry hadn't realized until now that he needed one.

From the freezer, he took several packages of Middle Eastern food that he'd bought at a gourmet shop. While waiting for them to heat in the microwave oven, he mentally monitored his response to Chelsea.

Heart rate elevated. Skin prickling. Other virile male reactions taking effect.

He hadn't felt this way about a woman since the night they made love. Despite his better judgment, she stirred him in ways no one else did.

And she was carrying his babies. The two of them needed to find a way to share their parenting and their lives.

What if he simply acted on his feelings? Barry wondered. They were both adults. They didn't have to keep each other at arm's length if they didn't want to.

His chest squeezed at the exhilarating prospect of making love to Chelsea again. He'd be risking the kind of emotional free fall that had followed his parents' bitter breakup. Yet sometimes a guy just had to take a risk.

Soon the Middle Eastern food was ready, with a dip on the side and pita bread to wrap it up. He carried the platter to Chelsea.

She gazed at him in awe. "I can't believe you made this."

"I just heated it," Barry admitted, sitting opposite her.

"Who cares? I love this stuff." She dug in.

Between his own mouthfuls, Barry enjoyed watching Chelsea eat. He loved the eager energy in her movements and her obvious relish. When the woman did something, she put her whole heart into it.

At last she came up for air. "You don't mind that I invited myself over?"

"I'm glad you did." Barry stretched his legs under the table. His trousered knee brushed her bare one.

His whole body sparked with her nearness. How could she just sit there looking so calm while he ached for her with every fiber of his body?

"At the luncheon, you said we needed to talk." Chelsea reached for a wedge of baklava, the honey-drenched pastry that he'd provided for dessert. "About the twins."

"Let's not worry about them tonight," Barry said.

Why on earth had he ever put so much stock in talking?

"Really?" She gazed at him in surprise. "I figured you'd want to nail down the details of our arrangement."

Her blue-green knitted dress clung seductively to her shoulders and bosom, Barry noticed. "Not right now. Middle Eastern food has this druglike effect on me."

"And we all remember what drugs do to you," Chelsea teased.

"We sure do." What a beautifully defined mouth she had. It had been a long two months without her, Barry thought. Unbearably long.

"I want to be clear about one thing," she went on. "I have poor judgment about men." Chelsea rested her chin on one hand. "It's better to keep my distance."

Distance was the last thing Barry intended to keep. "You could make an exception for tonight. Being under the influence of baklava is an alibi accepted in half the world's courts."

She shook her head. "We really need to talk about this."

"Chelsea..."

"I have to tell you something. It's about the guy I nearly married. But it's really about me."

The earnestness in her voice penetrated Barry's haze. Much as he hoped to make love to Chelsea, he wanted even more to understand her and clear away any obstacles between them.

"You must have had a rotten experience to make

you so gun-shy,'' he said. ''Tell me about this fellow.''

''Gene was a director,'' Chelsea said.

''What kind of director?''

''Theater and a little TV,'' she said. ''My parents are actors, so I've always known people in the business.''

Barry didn't know any show business people himself, but he'd heard enough about their serial marriages to consider them poor romantic risks. Apparently Chelsea had discovered that fact for herself. ''He turned out to be a jerk?''

''He seemed absolutely wonderful,'' she said with a touch of defensiveness. ''He was the nicest man. Considerate. Thoughtful. Always taking me places and buying me gifts.''

''What was wrong with him?'' Barry asked.

''He was kind of controlling, and I allowed it. Only he didn't want us to live together before we got married, which made me wonder if he was hiding something.'' Chelsea sounded embarrassed.

''You're so outspoken, I'd expect you would have pinned him down and shaken the truth out of him.''

''I get weird when I'm involved with a man,'' she admitted. ''After having two irresponsible parents, it was a relief to lean on someone. I deferred to his opinions, let him choose where I should work, even what I should wear.''

''He picked your clothes?'' Barry couldn't figure out why a guy would want to do that. ''I'd get bored tagging along to ladies' clothing shops.''

''He'd go shopping for me all by himself, even

for my lingerie," Chelsea said. "His taste was kind of flashy, too. But that wasn't the problem."

"Are we getting to the nitty-gritty here?" Barry asked.

Chelsea looked away from him, and for a minute he thought she wasn't going to say any more. Then she shrugged, took a deep breath and plunged in.

"One morning Gene slept over, while Starshine was out of town. I went out for doughnuts," she said. "I couldn't get my car started so I came back after a few minutes."

Barry tried to imagine what the man had done wrong in a few minutes alone in her apartment. "And?"

Chelsea's face reddened. "He was standing in front of my mirror wearing Starshine's clothes. I mean, he'd wriggled himself into a sequined dress, put on stockings and high heels, even makeup."

Barry managed not to smile at the ridiculous image. Obviously, this had been a painful experience for Chelsea. "So he was a cross-dresser."

"I don't know who was more humiliated, him or me," she said. "He swore up and down that he really loved me. Maybe I should have been more understanding, but I couldn't marry him."

As a doctor, Barry knew that some happily married men had the same eccentricity. Still, he could understand Chelsea's shock.

"The thing was, I wondered if he didn't want us to live together because he liked having access to Starshine's clothes," she said. "Then I worried that he liked me mostly because I gave him an excuse to buy sexy lingerie."

"You don't have to justify breaking up with him," Barry said. "His hobby isn't even the issue, it's the fact that he was secretive about it. I would never hide anything like that from you. I mean, if there was anything to hide, which there isn't. High heels hurt my feet. As for sequins, they don't work with my complexion."

"It's not funny! Oh, all right, maybe it is," Chelsea said, with a small smile. "It doesn't change the fact that, like I said, I have terrible judgment about men."

Barry folded his arms. "Thanks for the compliment. You really know how to make a fellow feel terrific."

Chelsea's eyes flew wide. "I didn't mean you! It's me. I was looking to Gene for the kind of support I never got from my parents. That made me give him too much power over my life."

"And I'm a take-charge kind of guy, so you don't trust your attraction to me?" Barry guessed.

"Something like that." She cleared her throat. "Maybe we should put away the leftovers."

"There aren't any."

She scanned the table. "We ate all that?"

"Leave the dishes. We'll get them later." Barry couldn't understand why a man would want to put on a woman's clothes when all he, personally, could think about was taking them off.

"You're grinning at me," she said.

"Why shouldn't I?"

"Because I'm..." she sighed "...a terrible cook, and a complete failure at relationships. Meanwhile, you've got women for miles around lining up with tuna-noodle casseroles.''

''You're feeling insecure because of an exploding chicken?'' Barry asked.

Chelsea blinked back a sheen of moisture. ''Sometimes I get a bad case of the Norman Rockwells. You know those *Saturday Evening Post* covers with the perfect family sitting down to Thanksgiving dinner? Well, when I get this way, I wish that were me wearing an apron and holding a platter with the perfect turkey on it.''

Barry could scarcely breathe. There really was a sweet, sentimental side to Chelsea. Maybe the woman he wanted would turn out to be the woman he needed after all. ''Let me show you something.''

''What?''

He caught her hand and pulled her to her feet. ''Come on.''

With only a whimper of protest at being rousted after a full meal, Chelsea accompanied him through the living room and up the stairs. On the second floor, three doors opened off a central court. She saw at a glance that two of the bedrooms weren't in use yet, but someday they would be. Maybe soon.

''In here.'' Barry led her into his room. High-ceilinged with a picture window, it overlooked the canal and, beyond it, a maze of older homes, apartments and shops. ''Over there.''

Chelsea followed his gaze to a two-story painting on the side of a building a block away. It showed a Hispanic family eating dinner, with the mother serving tortillas on a platter.

''A billboard?'' she said.

"A mural," Barry corrected.

"Oh, yeah." She studied it. "It's nice. It has the same feeling as the Rockwell painting I was thinking of."

"That's right." He looped one arm around her waist. "You don't have to fix a turkey to have a wonderful family experience."

"Even I can heat up tortillas." She rested her cheek on his shoulder. "If I ever get my microwave clean."

"Mine works just fine," Barry said. "You could move in here. It would save a lot of elbow grease."

"I think you're going a little too fast for me," Chelsea said.

"Let me put it this way." Shifting her in his grasp, Barry brought her close so he could kiss her slowly and deeply. This was one of those times when actions spoke a lot louder than words, and he planned to use his entire vocabulary.

10

CHELSEA DIDN'T UNDERSTAND her eagerness to yield to this man. It must have had something to do with pregnancy hormones.

Or maybe with finally unloading the story about Gene. She hadn't told the whole truth to anyone before, not even Starshine. Especially Starshine, whose clothing had been violated. Chelsea had quietly drycleaned the sequined dress after claiming to have borrowed it herself.

Tonight at dinner, she'd been so torn by conflicting feelings that she hadn't been able to concentrate on Barry. Now, suddenly, she could think of nothing but him.

How firm and steady he felt, pressed against her. How relaxed and open and infinitely masculine.

She wanted to get next to him. Very next to him. And here he was, getting very next to her. She tightened her grip around Barry's neck and resumed kissing him thoroughly.

When he lifted his head, she said, "More."

"Coming right up."

He seemed to think the best position for kissing was lying on the bed, she discovered. Chelsea had to agree with him. Moreover, kissing felt even better when they took their clothes off.

His shirt. Her dress. His slacks. Her...whatever.

Maybe, she decided, as his lips grazed her bare breasts, he really didn't care if she couldn't cook.

WHEN HE WAS with Chelsea, Barry became someone else. Or, perhaps, he became a fresh version of himself.

He simply enjoyed her. The freedom of her. The laughter. The sudden intensity of her response to him. Making love to her was like flying.

Their bodies joined as easily and naturally as two rivers flowing together. Why had he bothered dating other women these past few months? Why had he wasted so much time when they could have been sharing this joyous abandon?

Barry felt Chelsea's thrilled response and quickened his movements, losing control as exhilaration filled him. The climax came urgently, overwhelmingly, for them both.

The fire faded to a warm glow. Holding her close, he allowed himself to visualize the future. And, in a burst of enthusiasm, to verbalize what he saw.

"You can move in here any time you like," he said. "Decorate the spare bedrooms for the babies. Settle your rodents in the utility room. Blow up chickens in the microwave oven."

"Move in?" she asked sleepily.

"I promise not to run your life. I'll just watch over you." Barry pictured himself coming home from work and tussling with each baby in turn. "You and the kids."

THE SCARY THING was that she longed for what he was offering. Not so much for a nesting place, or even to have him share the responsibility of raising the twins, but for Barry himself.

Chelsea could easily fall in love with this endearing man, with his straight, emphatic eyebrows and the boyish grin that tickled her in unexpected places. Every day at the office, she felt a quiver of excitement each time she saw him. The infatuation was ridiculous, even embarrassing, but harmless.

Until now.

She had opened up to Barry. She'd told him her darkest secret, and he'd dispelled the pain.

If she gave herself permission, she would tumble out of herself and into him. Chelsea never did things by half-measures. Maybe she just wasn't grown-up enough yet, cynical enough, experienced enough. She hadn't learned to play it safe by fixing an ordinary meal and she wasn't going to love a man in an ordinary way, either.

What she'd felt for Gene was nothing compared to this cliff-edge teetering she experienced when she was with Barry. One tiny little concession to her susceptibility and she would fall headfirst, with no going back.

The possibility terrified her.

Who would she be if she fell in love with Barry? One frown from him and Chelsea would dye her hair some boring shade of brown. Find new homes for her rodents. Learn to follow a recipe.

She wouldn't be herself anymore. She didn't know who she would be. A shadow, a mirror. A boring woman whom, after a while, even Barry wouldn't be able to love.

"I can't." She sat up.

"Can't what?" He stroked the nearest part of her anatomy, which was her hip.

"I can't move in with you," Chelsea said. "I can't be that close to you. Tonight was a mistake. Well, no, not entirely." As she spoke, she stood and began collecting her clothes. "It was great. You're the best—" Boss? Lover? Pal? None of them worked. "Simply the best. Really."

He propped himself against the headboard and ran one hand through his delightfully mussed hair. "I thought what we just did meant something to you."

Not at all, except for the fact that I'm falling in love with you. "It did. It does. We're going to be parents and it's important that we get along."

"Let's not get along," Barry growled. "Let's fight."

"Over what?"

"Not over what. For what. For our life together, for what we mean to each other. You're scared and you're running away. Well, I won't have it."

Chelsea bristled. "This isn't your decision to make."

Barry threw back the covers and got out of bed. He was magnificent, broad-shouldered, narrow-waisted, rigid with fury. Maybe they could forget all this arguing and jump back under the covers. *No, no, no.*

"I hate conflict," he said. "I've always wanted a perfectly compatible woman so we'd never fight, but I'm willing to fight now. You're an idiot, Chelsea."

"Thank you so much." Where on earth had her bra disappeared to? Or had she forgotten to wear one?

"You and the twins belong with me. Quit arguing and accept it," he said.

She found the bra and put it on. "I admit I'm scared. I don't want to be a doctor's wife, Barry."

"Pretend I'm a plumber."

"That isn't the problem!" Chelsea shot back. "It's me. I let Gene take over, and I'd let you do the same thing or worse."

"I'm not like him."

"I know that! The trouble is, I'm still the same me that I was two years ago. It would be hopeless. I'd hate you and I'd hate myself. I like you too much to live with you. Or marry you. No! Don't even breathe that word!"

Barry stared at her. Apparently he'd forgotten about putting on his clothes, for which she was grateful, because she really enjoyed the sight of him. "Did I understand you correctly? You won't marry me because you like me too much?"

"That's about right." Chelsea wriggled into her sweater dress. "I hope I don't have to change jobs to get away from you. I don't want to get away from you. I just need to be free."

"I'm not an ogre," Barry said. "I won't penalize you at work. Chelsea, I can't believe you'd even think such a thing. Because the way I feel…"

"It wouldn't last," she said. "We'd only hurt each other." And there she'd be, the free spirit, roped and tied like a wild horse she'd seen once on a nature program. Its eyes had been dull and its coat matted as it stood inside a corral, head lowered, quivering and lost.

"Maybe." Barry's breathing seemed constricted. "After all, we're hurting each other now. And that's not good for either of us.'' A shuttered expression dimmed the eagerness on his face.

''What are you doing?'' she asked.

''Excuse me?''

''You just got this turtle look on your face. Like you're withdrawing.''

''Maybe I have to,'' Barry said. ''I've never gone this far out on a limb before. This is *terra incognita* for me.''

''*Terra* what?''

''Unknown land,'' he said. ''A man could fall off the edge of the earth, trying to figure out where he stands with you.''

He was protecting himself against her hard-heartedness, Chelsea thought. It hurt to realize she was driving him away when maybe, just maybe, he was on the point of falling in love with her, too.

''I can't change my mind,'' she said. ''I'd make us both miserable.''

They stood on opposite sides of the bed. Miles apart. ''Are you sure?'' Barry asked.

Chelsea's lungs ached. ''Yes. We need to work out some kind of relationship, though, for the children's sake.''

Barry regarded her tensely. ''I suppose so. But I don't see how we can go on the way we have been, dating other people, pretending to be mere co-workers at the office.''

''We could skip the dating-other-people business.'' She didn't want any of those women to get their hands on Barry, that was for sure. ''We can be...friends.''

''Great.'' He didn't sound like he meant it.

''Oh, come on,'' Chelsea said. ''I'm your worst

nightmare. You were projecting your dreams, imagining that I could be the person you want. But I'm not.''

''My worst nightmare?'' Barry sighed. ''No, Chelsea, you're far from that. But I suppose I was jumping the gun by asking you to move in.''

''Don't tell me you think I'll change, and that you're willing to bide your time!'' She couldn't stand that kind of manipulative attitude.

''No, that would be patronizing.'' Barry glanced down at himself. ''Good Lord. I'm naked.''

''Can I take a picture to remember you by?''

''Go get started on the dishes,'' he said. ''I'll come help you in a minute.''

Chelsea went downstairs, glad that he hadn't blown up at her. Saying no to Barry had been the hardest thing she'd ever done.

Not nearly as hard, she had a feeling, as the next few months were going to be.

BARRY COULDN'T figure out what he'd done wrong. One minute they'd been lying happily in each other's arms, and the next minute Chelsea had gone flying out of bed.

Oh, yes. He'd mentioned moving in together. That had been his crime.

Barry yanked on his clothes, taking out his anger on hapless buttons and zippers. He didn't see anything wrong with what he'd suggested. Chelsea herself had admitted she cared about him.

Okay, she was frightened. Life was scary. So what?

Barry had been intimidated about joining the Peace Corps. Yet he'd wanted to perform a service to mankind, and he'd known that once he got caught up in raising a family and earning a living, he might not find the time.

The experience had been well worth it. The mastodonsize mosquitoes, the monkeys stealing his underwear, the goats appearing at his clinic in the guise of beloved children had all been part of the adventure.

In the process, he'd vaccinated kids against deadly diseases, cured infections, performed minor operations to correct birth defects and helped who-knew-how-many future babies by educating their parents.

Now it was Chelsea's turn to take a risk. He would march downstairs and shout some sense into her, if that's what it took.

She was going to be a mother, for heaven's sake, Barry lectured to an image of her as he went into the bathroom and ran a brush through his hair. It was time to grow up and act like...

Like someone she isn't. He stopped, brush in midair, and stared at himself in the mirror.

Chelsea was right. He was trying to transform her to fit his own ideas. In the process, he was likely to drive her screaming out of his life.

If he didn't back off, she'd leave the office, as she'd threatened. She might shut him out entirely.

Stunned, Barry set down the brush and reached for a notepad he always kept handy. On it, he wrote, "You are Chelsea's friend. You have no right to change her." He tore off the sheet and taped it to the edge of the mirror.

The paper loomed before him like an Eleventh Commandment. It would be as hard to obey as the other ten put together.

Tonight he could finally acknowledge that, on the entire planet, Chelsea was the one woman meant for him. And he, Barry felt certain, was the one man meant for her. Yet, like his parents, they might not be able to get along.

He could only keep her close, ironically, by respecting her space. That was what he intended to do. However much it cost him.

11

Seven months later

AFTER HALTING her car, Chelsea sat for a few minutes listening to the song "Feliz Navidad" on the radio. Its upbeat tempo cheered her and, besides, she had to gather the strength to climb the hill to her apartment.

Only a few weeks short of her delivery date, she was so big that Barry had had to build up the pedals on her car to help her reach them. Dr. Keller had advised her to restrict her activity, but, as usual, Chelsea did what felt right to her.

Today, Saturday, she'd been seized by the impulse to buy baby furniture. It was a task she'd kept putting off, even though Barry had provided plenty of funds for baby-related purchases.

Alarmed at the realization that she was due within three weeks, Chelsea had gone wild at the store. Delivery would be made that very afternoon, the clerk had promised.

Once, she would have saved the delivery charge by hauling the stuff herself, with a little help from some friends. These days, she could hardly even carry groceries up the steep hill to her apartment.

Barry had made it clear, without pressuring, that

she was still welcome to move in with him. Chelsea, however, had clung to her independence even as she grew ever-larger and the twins adopted the habit of playing soccer in her abdomen at night.

Barry had been amazingly supportive these past months—escorting her to checkups, putting up with her cranky moods at the office. He even attended natural childbirth classes with her, which Chelsea had wanted to experience even though she'd probably have a cesarean section.

He'd also made it clear to the other women that he was off-limits. Chelsea wouldn't have insisted, since she was the one who'd called it quits, but she'd been grateful when he quietly informed Louise and Belinda and the law ladies that his attentions belonged exclusively to the mother of his children.

She would never forget the first time Barry had felt the babies move. Oddly, she remembered it even more clearly than the first time, which had been considerably earlier, that she herself had felt a telltale wiggle inside.

Barry had brought Chinese food to the apartment. Chelsea had been resting against him on the couch afterward, with his arms looped around her stomach, when he'd said, "Did that *k'ung pao* chicken disagree with you?"

"No," she'd said. "Why?"

"Because something just kicked me."

"It's them! The kids!"

Through her maternity T-shirt, they'd been able to see the twins rippling against the surface. Barry had kept his hands there, his face bright with wonder, for nearly half an hour until the babies finally nestled down for a nap.

On the radio, the song ended. Chelsea removed her key and lumbered out.

Invigorated by the crisp December air, she reached the first floor of the converted house without strain. As she contemplated the final staircase, the elderly landlady, Liv Olsen, emerged from her ground-floor unit.

"I'm sorry to bother you," said Mrs. Olsen. "It's nearly the middle of the month and I still haven't received the second half of the rent."

"I'm so sorry!" The kindly landlady had allowed Chelsea to pay her half on time, with the understanding that Starshine would pay her share within two weeks. "I thought my roommate had taken care of it."

"I tried to speak to her, but she was with friends and I guess she didn't hear me," Mrs. Olsen said.

Chelsea felt terrible. "If she doesn't have the money, I'll pay you."

"I know." The lady smiled at her. "Now, don't strain yourself. Mothers need to conserve energy."

"I'll be fine." Chelsea didn't have to struggle with the stairs this time. She stormed up them in a fine temper.

Although Starshine always paid eventually, her lateness was annoying. Chelsea supposed that, conditioned by years of looking after her clueless parents, she'd shown more patience than she should have.

As she opened the door, a tortured rock 'n' roll version of "White Christmas" slammed into her ears. At the same time, she gazed in horrified awe at the green-and-red crepe paper draped across the couch, end tables, floor and chairs. It looked as if someone had toilet-papered the place in the holiday spirit.

In one corner, silver tinsel dripped from the world's most pathetic Christmas tree. It appeared to have fallen off a truck and been run over a few times before it was rescued.

What really caught her attention, however, were two inflatable mattresses lying on the living-room floor. They gave her a bad feeling.

"Starshine?" Chelsea called.

"Here!" Her roommate hurried out of the kitchen. "We were just fixing lunch."

"Who's 'we'?"

"Well..."

A scraggly-haired young man and a small redhead popped out behind her. "Yo!" said the man. "We're your new roommates."

"Excuse me?"

Starshine steered Chelsea away from the others. "I figured they could help me make the rent."

"Help you make the rent?" She wished she could go outside, come back in and find the place normal. Please, let this be a bad dream.

Starshine drew herself up defensively. "Well, you're going to have two babies. That makes three of you for only half the rent. Bob and Lucy needed a place to crash, so they can help pay my share of the rent."

Chelsea supposed Starshine did have a point about the twins sharing their apartment, but inviting two strangers to move in seemed cheeky. In any case, Mrs. Olsen still hadn't been paid. "Speaking of rent, your half is overdue."

"Oh, really?"

"You must have collected some money from Bob and Lucy before you let them bring their stuff here, right?" Chelsea asked. "Just give it to Mrs. Olsen."

"Uh, sure." Starshine backed away. "I mean, I'm not good at business, but we'll work this out. Gee, I just remembered, we've got a rehearsal."

"You found work?" That was a hopeful sign.

Since the Easter Bunny show ended, Starshine had worked sporadically as a waitress. She frequently skipped work to attend parties where she hoped to make important contacts, with the result that she was usually unemployed in both fields.

"We got cast in an Equity waiver play," said her roommate. "All three of us. Isn't that great?"

Not in Chelsea's opinion, since Equity waiver theaters didn't pay actors. They put on showcase productions under a special arrangement with the actors' union. "Mrs. Olsen has been more than patient."

"Soon! Hey, guys, time to go!" In a flurry of farewells, Starshine and her two friends cleared out.

Chelsea went into the kitchen. She was not surprised to find her private food cabinet ajar. Someone had opened a can of sardines, which her parents had sent from their latest yacht stop in Spain, and eaten half of it.

Dirty dishes sat in the sink and a half-eaten omelette congealed in a pan on the stove. Chelsea visualized a more modern, pristine kitchen with all the dishes washed, the counter gleaming and the food put away.

It was Barry's kitchen.

The feelings she'd been fighting for seven long months crystallized in one searing moment. True, she was scared of moving in with Barry, but despite the amount of time they'd been spending together, she hadn't let him take over her life. Why worry about that now?

As if she'd been planning the steps for weeks, Chelsea swung into action. She packed her good clothes and left the ratty ones in a heap with a note, For the Poor. She cleared out the bathroom, took her favorite books, gathered her rodents' cages and called the baby store to provide a different address for the furniture delivery.

On Monday, she would forward her mail. Starshine and her roommies could keep Chelsea's meager stock of food. Right now, she just wanted out.

She left a polite note giving her forwarding address and phone number. Downstairs, she knocked on Mrs. Olsen's door and explained about the new arrangements. "You can keep my half of the deposit to pay for the rest of this month's rent. I don't want you to get stuck."

"Give me your address. I'll mail it to you when I collect from Starshine." A steely glint belied the landlady's sweet demeanor. "My son's a lawyer. I'll get Bob and Lucy's signatures on the dotted line and their money in hand, believe me."

Chelsea would have hugged her if not for the fact that, at present, she was so large she could barely get close enough to shake hands. "Thanks for being so understanding," she said, and wrote down the information.

When she reached the car, it occurred to her that she should call Barry before she arrived lock, stock and rodents. She'd never acquired a cell phone, though, and she couldn't face marching up all those stairs to make a call.

It didn't matter. He'd be glad to see her.

"I'M GOING TO CANCEL the newspaper until your father leaves," Andrew told Barry across the Mentons' table. "He and my mother disagree about every item."

"That's a good idea," Barry said. "If he can't get his hands on a paper, maybe he'll break down and stay with me. I don't know why he persists in this idea that Chelsea's going to move in."

"There's no need to talk about me as if I weren't here," Lew said from the other end of the table, where he and Grace had been glaring daggers at each other since the meal began.

The four of them were eating Saturday brunch in the breakfast room, a charming nook with a view of the Mentons' back lawn, flower garden and pool. The rest of the family was out: Cindi had taken Angela to get her hair trimmed for tomorrow's gala, and William was on a trip with his Scout troop.

Two days ago, Lew had arrived without warning. He wanted to see Angela dance again, he'd claimed, denying any nefarious intentions regarding tomorrow night's big event.

Barry hadn't had a decent night's sleep since. He worried that his father, whom the Mentons had generously agreed to house, was driving them crazy. And, when he dozed off, his mind filled with pies flying through the air, smacking a pompous tenor in the kisser as pandemonium erupted at the gala.

Fiorello Magnifico's plan to nationalize sales of Army surplus goods and old government vehicles had gained momentum. Werner Waldheim was reported to have found a congressional sponsor for the Government-Owned Outlets Promotion act, known to its critics as GOOP.

"I just want to make one more comment about an item in this morning's newspaper," Aunt Grace said, ignoring her son's warning glance. "If you don't care about our furry friends, who give us so much love, then you don't have much of a heart."

Her remark, Barry assumed, referred to an article about a luxurious animal shelter with custom exercise equipment and a spa, being built at public expense. She and Lew had been squabbling about it intermittently.

"Because I don't believe in bleeding the taxpayers doesn't mean I don't care about animals," said Lew. "Who do you think persuaded the Blink City Council to back down on taxing cats?"

"How did you manage that?" Barry asked.

"I announced at a council meeting that since the junkyard had to evict its cat population, I would be too busy finding homes for them to hold my usual flu-shot clinic," his father said. "Of course, I would vaccinate people who really need it, but able-bodied adults like our city council would have to take their chances."

Barry smiled. "So they changed their minds?"

"In a New York minute," said Lew.

"If we had socialized medicine, you couldn't pull that kind of blackmail," Grace said.

"Doctors aren't slaves," Lew said. "I could move elsewhere and leave Blink without any physician at all. Let them socialize that!"

Andrew groaned. "I've been listening to this kind of squabbling for two days."

"Dad, come home with me," Barry said.

Lew shook his head. "I don't want to get in the way. That girl's going to come to her senses."

"You hardly know her!"

"Trust me on this one, son," said his father.

"Let him stay here," Grace said suddenly.

The two younger men stared at her in surprise. "Why?" Andrew asked.

"Because if he rides to the gala with us, we can make sure he isn't carrying a pie," she said. "Oh, yes, I know all about your felonious tendencies, Lewis Cantrell. I have my sources."

For once, Barry's father couldn't muster a quick reply. He merely harrumphed and dug into his waffles.

Barry felt as if he'd been watching his father argue with his mother instead of his aunt. Both bullheaded, both certain that their approach was the only one that could save the world. Neither Lew nor Meredith—nor her sister, Grace—would ever willingly admit to not having all the answers.

He'd been like that, too, he supposed, until Chelsea got pregnant and he realized he had to give her free rein or lose her. To his surprise, beneath her flaky exterior, she'd turned out to be a steady person. She never missed a doctor's appointment or a day's work, even when she was experiencing one of her many digestive misadventures.

Still, he was glad she hadn't moved in with him yet. He needed to separate his father from the Mentons. They deserved peace in their own home.

"I can keep an eye on my dad," he said. "Actually, there are fewer places to hide a pie in my condo than in your house."

"True," Grace admitted.

Lew shot his son a wary glance. It occurred to Barry that his father might already have hidden a pie on the premises. In addition to the industrial-size refrigerator in the kitchen, there was a regular one in the pool house. Perhaps some of the family members had small fridges in their rooms, as well.

"I'm going upstairs to pack your bags," he said. "You're coming with me."

"You can't just uproot an old man." Lew was looking guiltier by the minute.

"Sixty is not old," said Grace, who was, if Barry recalled correctly, three years older than his father. "It's the fault of your personality, not your age, that your mental processes have atrophied."

"You two sound like quarreling children," muttered Andrew.

"She said it, not me!" Lew flared.

"Come on, Dad," Barry said. "You're coming home with me now. Chelsea isn't going to change her mind overnight, and besides, I've got two tickets to a UCLA football game this afternoon. I was planning to ask Andrew but..."

"Don't worry about it," his cousin said. "I'll gladly make the sacrifice for my mother's sake."

Lew's jaw thrust forward. Before he could utter another word, however, Barry heard female voices and then Angela darted into the room. "Like it?" she asked, pointing to her softly curled hair.

"You look gorgeous." Lew stood up. "My son's dragging me over to his place."

"Really?" Angela frowned. "But..."

"I'll be there to see you dance," he said. "Maybe I can come backstage and wish you luck beforehand."

The girl brightened. "Okay!"

Barry wondered whether this conversation had a subtext he wasn't grasping. If so, however, he couldn't figure it out.

"I'm glad you're being reasonable, Dad," he said. Grace nodded tightly. Andrew beamed. Even Cindi, who had just arrived, looked relieved. "Let's go."

THE SPACES in front of Barry's condo were occupied by a car that looked like Chelsea's and a panel truck marked Kids' Home Store. "See? She's here," said Lew as they spotted her on the steps, waving at them. "Now take me back to Grace's house. I promise to be nice to the old witch."

What rotten timing, Barry thought. He'd wanted Chelsea to move in, but did it have to be today? "Resign yourself, Dad. You're staying right here."

"Next time I visit L.A., I'm renting a car," his father grumbled. "Then I can go wherever I want."

"Next time you come, Fiorello Magnifico won't be singing at the theater," Barry said. "You won't need to sneak around."

"Hmmph," said Lew.

12

Barry's welcome wasn't exactly what Chelsea had hoped for.

True, he said he was glad to see her. He even showed interest in the furniture, which had arrived earlier than she expected, and helped her put the rodents in the utility room. He also gave her a spare house key without being asked.

Still, those brown eyes seemed darker than Chelsea remembered. Brooding. And Barry's mouth, which usually quirked into a grin at the sight of her, was rimmed by worry lines.

Maybe she'd waited too long to change her mind. Maybe he'd backed off on the come-live-with-me issue because he'd grown satisfied with a low-key relationship.

Chelsea had the baby furniture placed in a single room so she could watch over the twins simultaneously. And so that if, one of these days, she had to move out again, they'd be used to sharing a room.

After the delivery men departed, Barry took her aside in the dining room. "I'm afraid Lew's planning to disrupt the gala tomorrow night," he said in a low voice. "Aunt Grace has done a lot for me. I'd feel personally responsible if anything went wrong."

"I'll keep an eye on him," Chelsea promised.

"He's an appealing old scamp," Barry warned. "He might win you over."

Maybe the old Chelsea, she conceded silently. The new one, pumped with maternal hormones, preferred building a safe nest to thumbing her nose at the world.

A few minutes ago when she saw Barry walk up, recessive cling-to-him instincts had leaped from their hiding places. They must have been lurking deep inside where even DNA researchers couldn't find them.

Now here he stood, the man of her dreams, steady as a knight ready to do battle. Chelsea, who could barely maintain her balance these days, wanted nothing more than to lean on him. She certainly wasn't going to help Lew create problems.

"I'll make sure he doesn't mess up the gala," she said. "I'll threaten to go into labor if he tries anything."

"He's a doctor," Barry said. "He knows you can't control those things by willpower."

"Try me," she said.

Barry's expression warmed. "I'm glad you're here."

"Me, too," she said.

They touched each other, a hand on an arm, a stroke of the cheek. Not getting too close, which would have required advanced engineering techniques or possibly the use of a crane, given Chelsea's girth.

Still, the contact soothed and reassured her. Maybe he cared about her after all.

Or maybe he didn't. Why did these ancient hormonal urges have to make her so darn insecure?

"Help yourself to whatever's in the kitchen," Barry said. "I'm taking Dad to the UCLA game."

He'd invited Chelsea earlier. Unable to picture herself sitting through a football game in her condition, she'd reluctantly declined.

Lew came downstairs. "I'm done unpacking. What's next?"

"I guess we're ready for the game," Barry said.

His father gave Chelsea a kiss on the cheek. "Sure, although I'm surprised you can tear yourself away from this beauty. Gee, I wonder whether the refreshment stands at UCLA sell pies."

"They wouldn't dare," Barry said.

"It was just a thought."

The two departed. Lew was going to spend the entire afternoon teasing his son, Chelsea could see.

She fixed herself lunch and then took a nap on the bed. Barry's scent cushioned her to sleep.

Awake at last, she wandered into the bathroom. While washing her face, she spotted a faded note taped to the mirror.

It said, "You are Chelsea's friend. You have no right to change her."

Her heart thudded. So that's how Barry had held his domineering instincts in check all these months. He'd purposely distanced himself in order to keep her as his friend.

Well, she'd changed. Maybe it was the raging hormones, or the impending birth of a pair of helpless infants, or the insidious work of love. In any case, she wanted more. Much more.

Maybe even to be...a doctor's wife.

To Chelsea's astonishment, the thought failed to send panic shooting through her. So what if she had to sacrifice a bit of independence? Being loved by Barry would be an adventure of a different kind, that was all.

Her fingers touched the note, prepared to remove it. She drew back. It was his note, not hers. Besides, tearing it up wouldn't prove that she'd changed. She needed to do something more substantial to show him that she wanted to be more than a friend.

The image that greeted her in the mirror, from the black-and-purple hair to the maternity T-shirt emblazoned Babies Rock, was better suited to an eighteen-year-old than to a woman who'd turned twenty-seven a few months ago. Chelsea took a deep breath. It was time she changed her appearance.

For Barry. For the gala. For herself.

AFTER THE FOOTBALL GAME, Barry tried to call Chelsea, but the answering machine picked up. "She's probably gone to her apartment to fetch more stuff," said Lew. "Let's have dinner."

Over T-bones and baked potatoes at a steakhouse, they reminisced about Barry's childhood in Austin. He hadn't expected his father to remember so many details. During those early years, Lew had been so busy with patients and political protests that Barry had felt shut out.

Yet his father reminded him of the summer evening they'd eaten a whole watermelon in the backyard, spitting the seeds into Meredith's flower bed, and she'd groused for months about having to weed out melon sprouts. Barry had also forgotten the time he'd thrown up during a class trip to the Capitol building. His father, along as a chaperone, had lauded the act as a symbolic commentary on politicians.

"I didn't know you thought I was tuned out. Is that why you decided to live with your mom after we split up?" Lew asked.

"I didn't figure you'd care," Barry admitted.

"I cared a lot," his father said. "It's my own fault for not telling you. Besides, I was never as nurturing as Meredith. She was a good mother, even if she did have the instincts of a socialist."

"And you have the instincts of an anarchist," Barry couldn't resist saying.

"Something like that."

Before he knew it, several hours had slipped by. He hesitated to call Chelsea again in case she'd gone to sleep.

Sure enough, when they arrived home, she was curled in his bed, forming a large lump beneath the covers. In the darkness, Barry studied the sleeping form of the woman he loved.

When he'd arrived in Los Angeles nearly nine months ago, intending to find a wife, he'd had a list of desirable qualities. Chelsea hadn't appeared to possess any of them. It had taken a long time to accept that, in essence, she was everything he wanted and more.

Love swelled inside him, sweet and painful. It wasn't going to be easy, reconciling their different personalities. All the same, he hoped that her arrival today meant she was willing to try.

He could learn from his parents' mistakes. He would get involved with his children by taking an active part in their day-to-day lives. When there were disagreements, he and Chelsea would talk them over, not just snipe at each other verbally.

When he went into the bathroom, Barry spotted the note he'd left on the mirror. If she'd seen it, she'd probably had a good laugh.

He took it down. He'd memorized it by now anyway.

COOL WINTER sunlight woke Barry the next morning. He lay on his stomach for a few delicious moments, suffused with the happy reflection that Chelsea had come to stay.

He rolled toward her and froze in shock. Oh, good heavens. A blonde.

A woman with long, wavy blond hair had sneaked into his bed. What if Chelsea saw them? She'd never believe he didn't know how it happened. He could scarcely believe it himself.

Barry sat up, discovered he was wearing only his briefs, and snatched the covers over himself. Of all the compromising situations! Was this his father's idea of a joke? But if so, what had he done with Chelsea?

The woman heaved a long sigh and shifted position. A silky purple strap slipped low on her shoulder. She'd had the nerve to put on the negligée he'd given Chelsea for her birthday!

Barry contemplated trying to sneak out. It wasn't going to help if he left, though, as long as this woman was lying here. "Excuse me," he said.

"Mmm?"

"Excuse me? Miss?" He reined in an instinct to give her a light shake. Better not to touch her. "One of us needs to get up."

"Why?" she said. "It's Sunday."

Barry hesitated. That voice had a familiar ring. In fact, the woman sounded like Chelsea.

He leaned over and took a better look. Amazingly, it *was* Chelsea. That straight nose, those full lips, that twin-padded figure.

"What did you do to your hair?" he asked.

"Oh!" Her eyes popped open. "Gee, I hope I didn't startle you."

"Nearly gave me a heart attack," Barry said ruefully. "I thought I'd awakened in a compromising situation."

"You didn't!"

"It's a little embarrassing." He chuckled. "So that's what you were doing when I tried to call you yesterday. I was hoping you'd join us for dinner."

"Shopping and beauty parlor." Chelsea sat up. Pregnancy gave her a glowing sensuality, from her enlarged breasts to the blush in her cheeks. "My natural color is light brown, but I thought this was more flattering."

"You look gorgeous." Black had been a harsh contrast to her delicate features. The cascade of shimmering blond hair emphasized the fairness of her skin and the blue of her irises.

"I bought a new dress, too." Chelsea indicated a black outfit hanging on the back of the door. The dress had a lacy bodice with a long skirt that was slit up one side. "It's big enough to accommodate my stomach, but can be taken in afterward."

"Why the new you?" Barry asked. "Is this in Angela's honor?"

She blinked sleepily. "No, it's for you."

His chest tightened. She must have seen the note

and drawn the conclusion that he was itching to transform her into someone more conventional, only was holding himself back with difficulty.

Well, Barry did like her new appearance, but he'd grown fond of the sense of freedom she'd projected, that element of the unexpected. He'd enjoyed being kept off-balance, although maybe not quite as off-balance as he'd felt waking up next to a blonde.

Still, he wasn't disappointed. No, he was pleased. Definitely pleased.

"Thank you," he said. "I like this makeover and the fact that you've moved in with me."

"I guess I'm finally growing up." Chelsea stretched, thrusting forward her luscious full breasts. Barry ached to run his hands over them, then pull her against him and find a creative position to make love.

Dr. Keller had warned that, during the last trimester, they should refrain. Still, it wasn't easy to ignore his masculinity screaming for fulfillment.

"You've got the weirdest expression on your face," Chelsea said.

"It's lust."

She laughed. "If I'd known you'd react this way, I'd have bleached my hair sooner!"

"You didn't need to bleach your hair," Barry said. "You already did inspire this reaction. How do you think you got pregnant with twins?"

"Dumb luck," she said.

"That, too," said Barry. "For both of us."

SUNDAY EVENING, dressing for the gala, Chelsea put on the necklace and earrings that, in addition to the nightgown, Barry had given her for her birthday in

September. This honey-blond hair was a flattering shade, she decided, regarding herself at various angles as she experimented with a French twist. The cosmopolitan image pleased her, and she pinned it into place.

Since the disastrous relationship with Gene, she'd sworn never again to turn herself inside out for a man. Yet now it felt good. She'd made Barry happy and, frankly, she'd been tired of the retro-hippie look.

"Don't dawdle in there!" came Lew's voice from the hall. "I need time to go backstage and wish Angela luck."

Why? she wondered, remembering Barry's concern about his father. Had he and Angela hatched some plot together? "I want to see her, too. I'll come with you."

There was silence from the hall. As she awaited a response, Chelsea applied a frosted shade of lipstick.

"Great," Lew said at last. His voice lacked enthusiasm.

Chelsea made a note not to leave him alone with Angela. The old scamp was definitely up to no good. She'd make sure he didn't get away with it.

"WHERE'S LEW?" Angela asked, fiddling with her bangs in the dressing-room mirror. She had to half shout to be heard above the chatter of the other dancers.

Brightly lit glass ran along one wall of the long room, above a counter littered with makeup, glitter spray and hair implements. The air was filled with flowery scents and whiffs of aerosols.

"Barry's keeping him under close guard," Chelsea said. "I came in his place."

It was the truth, sort of. She *had* come in his stead, but not at his request.

"Okay." Angela accepted the explanation without question. "You know, I really, really like your hair that way."

"Thanks," Chelsea said.

The girl bent down gracefully and rummaged inside her workout bag. "Here you go."

She pulled out a box. Pie-size. Redolent of lemon.

"Lemon meringue?" Chelsea said.

"They were out of cream pies," Angela explained. "It was the best I could do."

Chelsea stuck the box into her oversize purse. She'd been carrying one on the advice of the childbirth instructor, who suggested taking overnight gear everywhere during the last month because you never knew when you might have to go to the hospital.

"I have to be honest with you," she said. "Lew didn't send me. I came on my own."

Angela's jaw dropped. It took a moment for her to regain her powers of speech. "You're... you're... turning me in?"

"I won't tell your parents," Chelsea said. "I'm going to dispose of it quietly."

"That's not fair!" she said. "It's my pie! Besides, I don't want Lew to think I went back on my word."

"I'll assure him of your loyalty." She winced at the expression of betrayal on the girl's face. "Angela, I know you mean well, but think of what this gala means to everyone else."

"Think of Lew's friend and his junkyard! He gets

all the wrecks from the police department and the city. It's like half his income.''

"There are better ways of defeating a ridiculous bill," Chelsea said. "There's no reason to drag the opera and ballet into this mess.''

"When's the last time those fat-cat politicians listened to little people unless they made a stink?" Angela demanded.

Lew had stayed at her house for two days, and already he'd brainwashed her. Chelsea sighed. "I'm sorry. I can't let you do this.''

Guiltily, she fled the noisy dressing room. Angela's accusing glance followed her.

It bothered Chelsea that she'd misled her young friend. It bothered her even more that she'd probably lost her influence with the girl, who needed all the guidance she could get as she entered adolescence.

Chelsea prowled through the maze of hallways, looking for a trash can. She saw no point in showing the pie to Barry and provoking a battle between father and son. Better to dispose of it and eliminate any chance of its being misused.

Too bad she didn't have a spoon. She really like lemon meringue.

Chelsea wandered into an adjoining hallway. Ahead of her flared bright lights. The sight of a man carrying a shoulder-mounted minicam tipped her off that it must be a TV interview.

Curiosity drew her closer. In a small lounge area stood the reporter, a well-dressed woman with chin-length chestnut hair. "Tell me, Mr. Magnifico. How do you justify trying to put people out of business when they haven't done anything harmful?"

"Oh, please!" The phony Italian accent came

from just outside Chelsea's view. She scooted forward until she could see the man, his thick black hair shining with gel. He wore an old-fashioned brocade smoking jacket and wielded an unlit cigarette in a ridiculously long holder, obviously his latest affectation.

"If Army surplus stores and junkyards can't be nationalized, they should be shut down for aesthetic reasons," he said into the camera. "They're eyesores."

"What about people on a tight budget?" the reporter said.

Fiorello's lip curled into a sneer. "People who shop at tacky places like that are beneath contempt."

The reporter nodded, not exactly agreeing but not challenging him, either. Chelsea slipped away, seething.

She often made the rounds of thrift shops and occasionally picked up an item at an Army surplus store. So Fiorello considered her beneath contempt, did he?

Getting hit by a pie would serve him right. It might also draw press attention to the absurdity of his campaign.

As she recalled, the event was being taped for later broadcast. The incident would be captured on camera.

Chelsea struggled to breathe. She couldn't be contemplating going along with this. She'd given Barry her word. Well, sort of.

She'd promised to keep an eye on Lew, but then, Barry was doing that himself. Nevertheless, she'd assured him she was on his side. It was part of being the new Chelsea, of perhaps becoming a doctor's wife.

Barry's face filled her mind. His strength and tenderness, as always, gave her a thrill. She needed him so much.

The trouble was that if he rejected her for acting on her principles, it meant he loved a woman who wasn't really her. Chelsea might lighten her hair color and wear a conservative dress, but she couldn't let a jerk like Fiorello go unchallenged.

She clenched her fists. If she gave the pie to Lew, she risked driving Barry away forever. On the other hand, it was impossible to build a marriage on a shaky foundation.

Her decision made, Chelsea set off down the corridor, the pie still stowed inside her purse.

13

BARRY HAD NEVER seen his father so restless. Even after the public address system in the lobby announced that it was five minutes to curtain time, he kept insisting he had to go see Angela.

"She's fine," Grace snapped, her nerves wearing as thin as Barry's. "I told you, we saw her half an hour ago and she didn't want to be disturbed."

"Except by me," Lew said. "She promised. I mean, I promised...to give her my best wishes."

"You can do it afterward," said Andrew. "Let's take our seats before the lights go down."

"Where's Chelsea?" asked Meg, who had arrived with Hugh a few minutes earlier. They'd been delayed by freeway construction on their drive from Orange County.

"She went to the ladies' room." Barry frowned at his watch. "Fifteen minutes ago."

"Which one?" Cindi asked. "I'll check on her."

"She didn't say." The theater had a ladies' room on every level. If the main floor facility was crowded, Chelsea might have taken the elevator to a different one.

Fifteen minutes was a long time, though. Suppose she'd started labor? Suppose right now she was doubled over on the floor?

"Here I am! Sorry it took so long." Chelsea materialized from the crowd. Barry wondered why he hadn't seen her coming, since she cut a wide swath, and then realized he hadn't been looking for a blonde.

"Your hair!" Hugh said. "I like it."

"Thanks." She grinned.

The lobby lights flickered. The crowd melted into the seating area. "We'd better get moving." Barry took Chelsea's arm, trying not to show how relieved he was to see her. In hindsight, his worries seemed foolish.

He didn't notice his father heading toward an interior door until Chelsea called, "Lew! Get back here!"

The elder doctor broke stride, hesitated and finally turned. His thin white beard quivered. Now Barry knew for sure that he'd been planning something. "Dad!"

Barry's newly blond companion waddled across the carpet and seized Lew's elbow. "You're sitting next to me. If my waters break, I want a doctor on either side. You're not abandoning me, are you?"

The mention of his incipient grandchildren did the trick. "No, of course not. I'm here if you need me."

There was a crestfallen slump to the man's shoulders, though, that gave Barry a guilty twinge. His father thrived on self-righteous indignation, and they were depriving him of its full expression.

He shook off his sympathy. This wasn't a Blink City Council meeting, it was a theater event in Los Angeles. He was not only preventing a major embarrassment to all concerned, he was probably saving his father from jail.

Barely in time, the Menton-Cantrell party settled

into their fifth row seats, with Lew on the right next to an aisle. Almost immediately, the lights dimmed and the orchestra struck up the overture to *The Marriage of Figaro*.

Chelsea shifted uncomfortably when the music got loud, and Barry realized the twins had started kicking. He stroked her midsection, hoping to distract them, but they thumped about lustily. Wasn't Mozart supposed to be soothing to babies?

The kids turned positively gymnastic during the applause, then settled down as gentle ballet music wafted from the pit. Tchaikovsky was the one with the magic touch, it seemed.

It didn't work on Lew, though. Seated on Chelsea's far side, he kept crossing and recrossing his legs and slumping and straightening in the chair.

He grew still only when Angela pirouetted on stage with the corps de ballet. Even as a member of a group, her elegance and stage presence stood out.

When she danced her solo, the audience seemed to hold its breath. The omnipresent rustle of candy wrappers and light coughing stilled. Everyone sat rapt until she finished, then burst into cheers.

Lew clapped harder than anyone. As the applause continued, Chelsea shifted her purse, which she'd been holding in her arms.

"Would you put this on the floor for me?" she asked Lew. "It's getting heavy."

"I'll handle it." Barry reached for it.

"That's okay." She shoved the purse at his father. "He needs to make himself useful."

With a shrug, Lew accepted the large bag. A puzzled expression crossed his face as he felt the shape of it. "What do you carry in here anyway?"

"Oh, breath mints," Chelsea said. "Would you find them for me?"

"Sure." Lew dug around in the purse. He seemed to be taking a long time, but Barry lost track. The music had resumed and two dancers were performing a brilliant pas de deux.

The dance segment of the gala lasted about forty minutes. There was a short intermission, during which Chelsea declared that she had no intention of stirring from her seat. To Barry's surprise, his father didn't object.

He must realize he'd never be allowed backstage to see Angela during intermission. In any case, he was taking his defeat with good grace, Barry thought.

When the performance resumed, a soprano named Sylvie Bernadis performed a couple of arias. Slim and lively, she wore her chestnut hair upswept above a blue strapless gown that appeared to have been cantilevered into place. Although Barry was no judge of singing, she sounded lovely to him.

At last the true star of the evening emerged from the wings, bowing and smiling. Fiorello Magnifico basked in the applause as he swept to the front of the stage, nearly trampling the soprano, who dodged back.

They proceeded to sing two duets. The splendid music nearly got lost in the unintended comedy as Fiorello's bulk repeatedly eclipsed Sylvie's slender figure. She had to execute a complicated series of steps to remain in public view.

Barry heard titters at one climactic moment when *Il Magnifico* lumbered forward, flung out his arms and came within inches of sweeping his "beloved" into the orchestra pit. The woman glared at the oblivious tenor as she took her bows and exited.

A stir of anticipation ran through the onlookers as the man prepared to sing his arias. Or perhaps, Barry realized, the tension was being transmitted from his father, two seats away.

He glanced at Lew. And couldn't believed what he saw.

His father was holding a pie. Lemon meringue, judging by the smell. Where on earth had it come from?

Barry's gaze fell on Chelsea's large purse. She'd handed the thing to his father, yet surely she hadn't been part of this.

He'd trusted her, and she'd sworn to help. Had she lied?

Chelsea's eyes flicked toward him. "I'm sorry," she whispered. "I just had to."

On stage, Fiorello broke into his signature aria, "La Donna é Mobile" from Verdi's *Rigoletto*. The song's title was translated, Barry recalled, as "Women Are Fickle."

Verdi had gotten that right.

CHELSEA BALLED her hands into fists. She was afraid Barry would tackle his father before he could take action.

Only after Lew stood up and began moving forward did she spot an unforeseen hazard. If he had thrown a pie during the press luncheon, it would have been an easy shot. The theater was a different matter.

Four rows ahead of them, the orchestra pit yawned like the Grand Canyon. It was hard to imagine even an experienced pie-tosser like Lew being able to clear the thing, especially when he hadn't had a chance to practice.

What if he missed? What if he hit the conductor?

Lew didn't appear fazed, however. He planted himself, feet apart and lifted the pie in one hand, carefully taking aim.

When Fiorello spotted him, he forgot to sing the next line. Seizing the opportunity, Lew yelled, "Save the junkyards!" and launched the pie into space.

Over the orchestra it flew. Too high? Too wide?

It smacked into the tenor's forehead, spattering yellow and white goo onto his tuxedo and across the stage. The force of the impact dislodged Fiorello's hair—no, his toupee—which slipped to a rakish angle, revealing sparse clumps of graying hair plastered to a shining pate.

The musicians stopped playing. Time hung suspended for a split second.

Lew bolted for a side door. He didn't make it. A couple of guests, with Werner Waldheim in the lead, pinned him down and shouted for security.

"I can't tell you how disappointed I am," Barry said, close to Chelsea's ear. She could hear the anger in his voice.

Suddenly she didn't feel triumphant. She might have been true to herself, but she'd hurt Barry.

Before she could apologize, a band tightened across her abdominal muscles. At first, she thought she was having a false contraction of the sort that struck occasionally during the last weeks of pregnancy.

The squeezing didn't stop. It went on and on until she wondered if she'd been gripped by a bulldozer.

"I've got to go help my father." Barry stood up.

Chelsea gasped. "I'm in labor!"

"Oh, sure," he muttered. "Let me by."

"I can't." The house lights came up, although most of the audience remained seated. "I'm...it hurts!"

"I'm not going to be made a fool of twice in one evening," Barry growled, then hesitated. "Chelsea? You're kidding, right?"

She could feel sweat breaking out on her forehead. "No!"

"Oh, Lord." Barry turned to his family. "Chelsea's in labor."

"I shouldn't wonder, with all the ruckus," Grace said.

"We've got to get her to a hospital," Barry said.

That was exactly what Chelsea wanted to hear.

IN AN IDEALISTIC part of her brain, Chelsea had been hoping she might be able to give birth the natural way. But an hour of labor while she was rushed to the hospital and prepped for surgery, dispelled any lingering romanticism.

No way were *both* of those babies coming out of *there*. Not if she had anything to say about it. Fortunately, Dr. Keller agreed.

The surgery went more easily than she'd expected. The best part was hearing each twin's lusty cry and seeing the awe on Barry's face. And, of course, cuddling the babies herself as each was wrapped and laid beside her.

They were tiny and fierce and cute. A boy and a

girl. Chelsea hadn't picked names in advance. She'd imagined that when she saw their little faces, names would pop into her mind.

Instead, remembering Lew, all she could think of was the term "tarred and feathered." She didn't think the kids would enjoy being called that.

Watching Barry marvel at them, she knew he would be a devoted father. She wished he could be her husband, too, because she loved him so much.

However, any possibility of marriage had vanished earlier that evening. The right wife for Barry would never have stooped to helping Lew.

"Aiding and abetting." Nope, the kids wouldn't like those names, either, Chelsea reflected as the anesthesiologist injected something into the intravenous tube.

She drifted off to sleep, still trying to think of names.

AFTER CHELSEA was taken to the recovery room, Barry gave the babies a checkup in the nursery. A neonatalogist had already examined them, but it never hurt to make certain. Overjoyed to confirm that they were healthy, Barry then went to post bail for his misbehaving father.

"I'm not going to apologize," Lew said as they left the jail.

"You should. You made a mess of things, although the gala did manage to go on," Barry said.

"Please don't tell me that tenor came back and sang!"

"He certainly did." When Barry had called the Menton house to let everyone know that Chelsea and the babies were fine, he'd learned that the soprano had filled in until Fiorello, head covered by a plumed hat, returned to his devoted audience.

"There's no accounting for taste," Lew said. "Well, I don't know about you, but I'm looking forward to getting some sleep."

"Not so fast."

"It's one o'clock in the morning." His father yawned.

"Andrew assured me that he and Grace are wide-awake and can't wait to see you. We're going by their house," Barry said as they entered the parking lot, and headed for the car. Having gotten his second wind, he was fully alert despite the late hour. Across the roof of his sports car, he watched his father's face register alarm. "You mean I have to face the witch?"

"You're darn right you do."

"Tonight?"

A grim sense of satisfaction gave his words weight. "You're the star of the show, Dad. I wouldn't want you to miss a minute of it."

"Wonderful," Lew grumbled. "Now tell me some good news. Tell me about the babies."

On the drive to the Hollywood Hills, Barry filled him in about Chelsea's delivery. "I'm glad everything went well, but I wish I'd been there," his father said wistfully. "You are going to marry that girl, aren't you?"

"I don't know," Barry said. "She seemed to be growing up, becoming more responsible. Then she pulled a stunt like sneaking you a pie. I'm not sure what to do."

"Wait a minute," his father said. "You're not

going to let a silly thing like a pie-tossing come between you and the mother of your children!''

Around them on the road, headlights softened the darkness. L.A.'s freeways, like New York's subways, never slept.

"You let your differences come between you and Mom,'' Barry said.

Lew took his time before answering. Finally he said, "We both wanted to be in control and we weren't willing to compromise.''

"You still aren't.'' Barry exited the freeway.

"I'm too old to change,'' said his father. "But you're not. Besides, Chelsea isn't afraid of conflict like Meredith was.''

"Mom was afraid of conflict?'' Barry didn't believe it. "That's not what the way she sounded to me.''

"She made lots of cutting remarks,'' Lew said. "She shrank from hashing things out, though. Any hint of real confrontation sent her scurrying into sarcasm. Not that I'm trying to pin the blame on her. I'm a tough guy to live with.''

Thinking back, Barry remembered asking his mother once to talk to a teacher he considered unfair. She'd promised to schedule a meeting, but kept finding excuses for putting it off.

Intuitively, he'd understood her discomfort. After that, when he had a problem with anyone, he'd worked it out for himself.

But some differences couldn't be worked out because they ran too deep. Like the conflict between his parents. And, perhaps, the gap between him and Chelsea.

"When I get married, I don't want to live with

that kind of power struggle in the family," Barry said. "I'm a straight-arrow, like Mom, and Chelsea's off-the-wall, like you. In time, we might start to hate each other."

Lew shook his head. "Chelsea's unconventional, but, unlike me, she's not usually a pain in the butt. As for you, you're stable enough to anchor her and you don't shrink from confrontation. I'd say you two are good for each other."

Barry wished it were true. He'd never loved anyone as much as he'd loved Chelsea tonight, watching her deliver their two precious babies.

On the other hand, she'd made him absolutely furious a few hours earlier. Could he live with such roller-coaster emotions?

They pulled into the Mentons' driveway. "Here we go," Lew said. "Time to face the music and dodge the bullets."

"One thing you can say for Aunt Grace. She's not afraid of conflict."

"You can say that again. But please don't."

Andrew met them at the door and escorted them to the family room. The big-screen TV was tuned to a late-night talk show.

"We're on all the stations!" Grace, looking perky in a fleece pants outfit, was curled at one end of the couch. "Supporters have been calling the FOB all evening pledging donations."

"You've made them famous, Lew." Andrew offered soft drinks all around and Barry accepted one thirstily.

Lew perched on a chair, as far as possible from his former sister-in-law. "You're not angry?"

"I was boiling," Grace admitted. "I've calmed

down, though. Let me show you something I taped on the news.''

With the remote control, she cued the VCR. The image onscreen was replaced by an earlier broadcast of a press conference at the theater.

Fiorello Magnifico, his toupee back in place, stood in a rehearsal room beside Werner Waldheim, facing the glare of lights. Grace fast-forwarded for a few seconds, then let the tape roll at regular speed.

''I don't want any child to suffer the way I did while growing up,'' Fiorello was saying, with no trace of an Italian accent. In the excitement, he'd apparently forgotten about it.

''What do you mean?'' asked a reporter.

''My mother dressed me in Army surplus clothes from the time I was ten until I finished high school,'' Fiorello said. ''Can you imagine what that does to a sensitive artistic temperament like mine?''

''Wait a minute,'' said the billionaire at his side. ''You mean this whole campaign is about the fact that your mother made you wear Army surplus clothes?''

The tenor gulped before replying. ''Of course not. Mostly, I'm angry about the government's wasted money. But you can't know how demeaning it is for a child, having to walk around in camouflage like some kind of nutcase.''

''My father wore camouflage,'' Werner said. ''He was a career Marine. I wouldn't call him a nutcase.''

''Don't tell me your mother wore Army boots, too!'' said Fiorello. ''Sorry. That was a joke.''

''I'm not laughing,'' said his erstwhile friend. ''As a matter of fact, I'm sure she did wear Army boots on duty, if her assignment called for it.''

"Your mother was in the service?" the tenor asked dazedly.

"That's why I was so eager to help you. I thought we were supporting the Armed Forces, not making fun of them!" snapped the executive. "I'm withdrawing my support for the Government Outlet act immediately. And if I were you, I'd drop charges against that pie-throwing fellow. Some people might call him a patriot."

Fiorello babbled a weak objection. Under fire from the reporters, however, he backed down and began treating the entire incident as a joke.

"Hurray!" shouted Lew. "I've struck a blow for little guys everywhere!"

"Please don't strike any more blows of the pie-throwing variety around me," said Grace.

"I know I abused your hospitality," Lew said, "but it was in a good cause."

"All's well that ends well," she conceded. "If you ever do anything like that again, though, I'll hire a thug to break both your arms."

"Mother!" Andrew said.

"I couldn't threaten to shoot him. I believe in gun control," she said.

"Now there's another subject!" Lew said.

"Not tonight. Please." Andrew yawned, and his mother followed suit.

Quickly, Barry bid them good-night and escorted his father out. Lew frothed at the mouth all the way back to the condo, citing friends who had confronted rabid skunks and marauding coyotes and felt safer with protection. Once he got home, however, he went quietly off to bed.

Barry was glad he'd had the presence of mind

earlier to call Dr. Withers and arrange for him to cover at the office tomorrow, as they'd discussed in advance. That meant he could sleep late and then spend time with Chelsea and the twins.

The problem was, he still didn't know what he was going to say to her.

14

ON MONDAY MORNING, the nurse came in early to
roust Chelsea from her sleep. "Time to get up and
move around," said the cheerful R.N., whose name
tag read Ms. Owens.

Chelsea couldn't believe this woman expected her
to leave her bed. "I just had surgery!"

"It's best for you to get moving right away," said
the nurse. "They'll bring your babies in shortly."

"Is my...is Dr. Cantrell here?" Chelsea asked.
She'd nearly slipped and called him her husband.

Last night, she'd made the decision to help Lew
with full awareness that it might drive Barry away.
All the same, she wondered why he hadn't appeared
yet. It was past 7:00 a.m. If Barry didn't arrive soon,
he'd have to start work for the day and she wouldn't
see him for hours.

"He hasn't come by," said the nurse. "I'll crank
up your bed to help you sit. Ready?"

Chelsea wasn't, but she tried to be a good sport.
Somehow, she managed to stand with Ms. Owens's
assistance and shuffled for a few steps. She felt about
a million years old.

Her energy began returning when the twins were
wheeled in, each in a little plastic bassinet. "They're
doing very well," said one of the nursery attendants.
"What are you going to call them?"

Chelsea liked Barry's mother's name, Meredith. She also adored Lew, but she wasn't naming her son after that cantankerous old soul. "The girl's Merry." She spelled it out so it wasn't confused with Mary. "As for the boy..." Inspiration struck. "He's Hank, if Dr. Cantrell doesn't mind."

"Good names." The woman wrote them on stickers, which she attached to the bassinets.

After she left, Ms. Owens returned to give instructions on baby care. Chelsea's milk should come in soon, she said. The hospital encouraged breastfeeding because of the many health benefits.

Then she was gone. The babies, so cute and tiny Chelsea could hardly believe they were real, slept peacefully. The other bed in the semiprivate room remained empty.

An hour later, the babies were taken back to the nursery, to Chelsea's disappointment. Because they were twins and had been born a few weeks early, the neonatalogist had left instructions for extra monitoring during their first few days.

Nine o'clock passed with no sign of Barry. He must have gone to work by now. He hadn't even bothered to stop in.

Chelsea blinked back tears. She'd expected him to be angry. She hadn't expected him to avoid her altogether.

A wave of postpartum blues swept over her. In a dark future, the babies would insist on drinking chocolate milk from bottles and become thoroughly unhealthy, space aliens would invade earth and take over all the receptionist jobs, Barry would return to Prego Prego and Chelsea would have to beg Starshine to let her move back in.

She sank against the pillows in a pool of self-pity. Darn it, she loved that fuddy-duddy doctor. Why did he have to be so stubborn?

In the hall, she heard the rumble of wheels. No doubt some orderly was bringing a cart full of medicines for the nurse to inject into Chelsea's rear end.

The door flew open. Before she could wipe away her tears, Barry shot inside, flailing wildly.

He wore a sweatshirt and jeans instead of his white coat, with a canvas bag looped over one shoulder. And he was—good heavens!—on roller skates.

"What are you doing?" she asked.

"Making a fool of myself." He zoomed past and caromed off a wall, performed an unintended but spectacular twist in the air and landed on the empty bed.

"I give you a 5.5 out of a perfect 6.0," said Chelsea, who often watched ice skating on television. "Your artistic presentation could use work, though."

Dark hair flopped rakishly over Barry's forehead, emphasizing the crazed gleam in his eye. His father's hijinks must have pushed him over the edge, Chelsea thought.

"Sorry I overslept," he said. "Busy night."

He sounded normal, she thought, relieved. "It was a long night for me, too."

"I know. You're the one who worked hard." Sudden joy illuminated his face. "Aren't the kids beautiful? Dad and I were just down at the nursery. We love the names, by the way. He's still there, admiring his grandchildren."

Chelsea basked in the fact that Barry had come to

see her. She was glad that Lew was here, as well. "I'm pleased that they let him out of jail."

"Me, too." Barry began unlacing the skates.

"Where'd you get those?" Chelsea asked.

"Rented them at the beach," he said.

"Mind if I ask why?"

"To surprise you," he said. "Hold on." Setting the skates aside, he took some shoes from his bag and put them on. Then he pulled out a bakery box.

Inside was a lemon meringue pie.

"Uh-oh." Chelsea hoped he didn't plan to loft it her way. If he did, she was a sitting duck.

"Relax. I'm not going to throw it," Barry said. "That pie last night looked so good, I dreamed about it. This morning, we happened to be passing a pie shop and I couldn't resist." He produced a couple of plastic spoons. "Dig in."

The pie tasted sugary, tart and memorable. Barry sat on the edge of the bed, eating from the other side of the pie plate. He kept smiling at Chelsea. It made her feel wonderful.

He looked meltingly handsome, she thought. With his slightly crooked nose and expressive eyebrows, he had the kind of face that only got more appealing with repeated viewings.

Reaching out, Chelsea traced one fingertip along his cheek. Barry leaned forward and his mouth grazed hers.

A long, lemony moment passed between them. When he drew back, Chelsea sighed with pleasure. "Does this mean I'm forgiven?"

"Eat a little more," he said.

Puzzled, she dipped her spoon into the pie, and felt it clunk against something. "What's in here?"

"Scoop it out," he said.

When the spoon emerged, something gold gleamed amid the white meringue. Chelsea wiped it with a tissue.

It was the most beautiful diamond ring she'd ever seen. "Will you marry me?" Barry asked.

She couldn't speak. Words, which had never deserted her before, caught in her throat.

"If you don't like the ring, we can exchange it," he said.

"When did you...?" was all she could say.

"Andrew recommended the jeweler and I bought it this morning," Barry said. "It wasn't primarily the lemon meringue pie I dreamed about. You were in there, too. All night. So this morning, well, I couldn't resist. But if it doesn't suit you—"

"It's beautiful." Her throat clamped shut again. What if he'd only asked her to marry him for the children's sake? she wondered, still not ready to believe her good fortune.

"Are you upset about my reaction last night?" Barry watched her as he spoke. "I was angry. I hope I didn't hurt your feelings."

"I deserved it," Chelsea said. "I don't understand...why..." She indicated the ring.

"This morning, after having a night to sleep on it," Barry said, "I realized that I used to think I loved you in spite of the fact that you're a little weird."

"But you don't?" Her voice squeaked with tension.

"No. Now I realize that I love you *because* you're so unpredictable. You have this freedom, this spontaneity. It makes life exciting."

"You want life exciting?" The ring felt so light in her hand, she feared it might disappear.

"Not *all* the time," Barry said. "Mostly what I want is you, for better, worse or in-between. What do you say?"

"Yes." Immediately, doubts besieged Chelsea. "I mean, no. We're so different. You might get tired of arguing with me."

"Conflicts are okay when they're brought into the open and resolved," Barry said. "It's when they fester, when people snipe at each other and don't deal with the issues, that things go bad."

Chelsea never sniped at people. She didn't know how to snipe. So that was no problem. "I will marry you after all."

"Hurray!" Barry shot one fist into the air. "I'll take best two out of three."

"Two out of three?"

"One no, two yeses. Don't you dare try changing your mind again, either."

"Not in a million years," she said.

BY CHRISTMAS MORNING, four weeks later, Chelsea fit into regular clothes. Not her old zany clothes, but a new, more elegant outfit she'd bought with Barry's encouragement.

After putting on the dark green suit with a festive flowered blouse, she dressed the twins in red-and-white sleepers and newborn-size Santa Claus hats. They blinked up at her like cozy elves.

Barry carried the babies out to the sedan he'd bought to replace the leased sports car, and she carried the gifts for the Mentons. "My only regret is that Dad can't be here," he said as he drove. After all charges were dropped, Lew had gone home to take care of his patients in Blink.

Chelsea yawned. Despite regular naps, she never seemed to get quite enough sleep. It didn't matter. Since becoming a mother, she'd discovered depths of love and patience she'd never known before. "My only regret is that you can't nurse the babies in the middle of the night."

"Was it my imagination, or did I wake up once with Merry under my armpit?" Barry asked with a good-natured grin.

"That was Hank," Chelsea said. "I decided it would be easier to bring the babies into bed with us, and he ended up on your side."

"Is this a permanent development?" he asked.

"You tell me, Doc. How long before they start sleeping through the night?"

He groaned. "A couple of months."

"Okay, so we have bags under our eyes, but the kids are healthy," Chelsea said. "They're a living testament to your skill as a pediatrician."

"My skill has nothing to do with it." He slowed on the freeway to let another car merge ahead of them. Since becoming a father, Barry drove more cautiously, she'd noticed. "You're a natural parent."

"Thank you." Winter sunlight filtering through the windshield warmed Chelsea. So did Barry's approval.

"I do want to ask one thing," she said, "although maybe this isn't the best time."

"Shoot," he said.

"Would you mind terribly if I didn't go back to work right away?" She'd arranged for three months of maternity leave. "I know it's tough at the office with that temporary receptionist. I wouldn't mind if you hired someone full-time."

"You want to stay home?" Barry asked.

"Yes. Maybe when the twins get older, I could go to community college." Chelsea had never been the academic type. Recently, though, she'd begun to think she might enjoy teaching someday. "Meg's been taking classes since Dana started preschool, and she loves it."

"That's a great idea." Barry touched Chelsea's hand lightly before returning his own to the wheel. "One of the best aspects of marriage is that it gives us a chance to grow and change within a safe framework."

"Speaking of marriage," Chelsea said, "shouldn't we start planning our wedding?"

"I thought we decided on March," Barry said.

"That's a month, not an event."

"Whatever you want to do is fine with me," he said.

A mischievous imp inside Chelsea wondered if he really meant that. What if she suggested something outrageous?

Before she could think of anything, they arrived at the Mentons' mansion. From the driveway, she saw a huge Christmas tree in the window, and spotted Hugh and Meg's car already parked.

Inside, they were engulfed in a tide of hugs and exclamations about how fast the babies were growing. Angela immediately took Merry and Hank under her wing.

The young dancer wanted to spend as much time as possible with her tiny new cousins before next summer. At the gala, she'd drawn the attention of a San Francisco ballet company and would be joining its apprentice program in July.

Everyone was also buzzing with Meg's news. She and Hugh were expecting another baby in July, a brother or sister for Dana. "Lots of kids in the family!" Grace proclaimed in delight. "They make me feel young again."

The Cantrells and the Mentons settled down for brunch. At the head of the table, Andrew manned the wafflemaker as per family tradition while Hugh, at the other end, made pancakes. Cindi and Grace had prepared fresh fruit, scrambled eggs and sausages.

Halfway through the meal, Meg asked Chelsea whether she'd made any decision about the wedding, beyond the fact that it was to take place in March. She was about to say no, when an idea popped into her head.

A thoroughly ridiculous idea. She didn't expect to carry it out, but Barry had said that he liked it when she made life exciting.

"We're going to get married on a chinchilla ranch," she said. "We'll have little furry rodents running everywhere. Won't that be cute?"

Dead silence fell over the table. Seated beside Chelsea, Barry choked on a bite of waffles until Andrew whacked him on the back.

"What do you think, honey?" she asked.

He took a swallow of orange juice before speaking. "It's fine with me."

"It is?"

"We'll save money on a bouquet. You can carry a couple of chinchillas instead of flowers," Barry said, straight-faced. "We'll save a bundle on the reception, too. None of the guests will stay to eat."

She burst out laughing. Relieved chuckles sounded around the table as the rest of the family realized she'd been joking.

"Let me propose that you get married in our garden," Grace said. "The roses should be in bloom."

"Thank you. We accept," Chelsea said. "Right, honey?"

"With great relief," said Barry.

THEY WERE FINISHING the meal when the doorbell rang. "Who can that be on Christmas morning?" Cindi asked as she went to answer.

Barry found, to his surprise, that he didn't mind the interruption as he once might have. He was beginning to enjoy the unexpected.

A loud "Ho ho ho!" resounded from the living room, followed by the appearance of a skinny Santa Claus with a natural white beard. "Surprise!" Lew said, and held out a bakery box.

"I'm glad to see you, Dad." Barry went and gave him a hug, careful not to disturb the gift.

"I hope that isn't what I think it is," said Grace. "I wasn't kidding about hiring thugs."

"I hope they like chocolate cake." Setting the box on the table, Lew removed the dessert. "I decided I'd better bring something sweet, seeing as I'm arriving uninvited, and I figured pies were out of the question. I carried it on the plane all the way from Colorado."

"Of course you're invited." The hostess stood and indicated that everyone should scoot over to fit in an extra chair. "You're family."

"In spite of my antisocial tendencies?"

"The opera and ballet are having their best ticket sales ever," she said. "Also, despite his little mishap, Fiorello has consented to give a benefit concert in June. That's one event to which you are *not* invited, by the way."

"As long as he behaves himself, he has nothing to fear from me," said Lew. "I plan to visit as often as possible. Hank and Merry need the stability of an involved grandfather."

"Excuse me, did you use the word stability in connection with yourself?" asked Grace.

"No fighting on Christmas," warned Cindi.

"They're not fighting," said Barry. "They're having fun."

"You got that right." His father beamed. Grace, her eyes alight with merriment, nodded.

"Did anyone tell you, Dad? Chelsea and I are getting married on a chinchilla ranch," Barry said.

"We are not!" She hadn't expected him to resurrect the idea, even though she knew he couldn't be serious.

"I'm disappointed." Barry grinned. "I've grown fond of your little guy, Smithee. Still, a rose garden will probably smell better."

He reached for Chelsea's hand and squeezed it reassuringly. Resting her head on his shoulder, she gazed through the window at the quiet winter garden where, in a few blooming months, she would become Mrs. Stuffy Doctor.

She could hardly wait.

Down-Home Diva
Stephanie Doyle

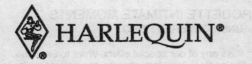

HARLEQUIN®

TORONTO • NEW YORK • LONDON
AMSTERDAM • PARIS • SYDNEY • HAMBURG
STOCKHOLM • ATHENS • TOKYO • MILAN • MADRID
PRAGUE • WARSAW • BUDAPEST • AUCKLAND

Dear Reader,

I have to say that when I wrote this story I laughed and laughed. But of course *I* think I'm funny. The real challenge was finding an editor who agreed with me. Lucky for me, one did!

Do you remember the movie *My Cousin Vinnie*? I loved the idea of a sassy, smart New Yorker who was completely out of her element.

Well, my heroine, Claudia, is certainly out of her element. Plunked down in the middle of a farm, she has to deal with cows who have no respect for Italian shoes, an ornery chicken who could care less about her perfect nails and, oh yeah, a hunky farmer who doesn't know what to do with her, unless of course it's to fall in love with her.

This story asks a question: Do opposites really attract? More important, can they find a way to make a life together? I promise not to spoil the surprise.

I have to thank my sister, Mary Kay, for introducing me to Claire, a true nail artist.

Have fun!

Stephanie Doyle

Books by Stephanie Doyle

SILHOUETTE INTIMATE MOMENTS
792—UNDISCOVERED HERO

Don't miss any of our special offers. Write to us at the following address for information on our newest releases.

Harlequin Reader Service
U.S.: 3010 Walden Ave., P.O. Box 1325, Buffalo, NY 14269
Canadian: P.O. Box 609, Fort Erie, Ont. L2A 5X3

For Carolyn and Jon, a real life romance.
You are my best friends.

Prologue

"I THINK HE'S DEAD."

Claudia Bertucci turned her head and took in her friend's expression. Blank. It didn't surprise her. Antoinette's expression was often blank. But that was appropriate because it matched what was between her ears.

"You got a naked man sitting on three bags of vending machine ice in your bathtub with his eyes wide-open and a round red dot in his forehead, and you *think* he's dead?"

Antoinette shifted her well-distributed weight from one foot to the other and wrung her hands impatiently. "Okay, so he's dead. Whatta we do now?"

Claudia closed her eyes and took in a few deep breaths. Not too deep, however. She didn't want to smell the dead guy. "I assume Rocco did this?" Claudia asked, although she knew that her friend's gangster boyfriend was the only logical choice.

Immediately, Antoinette started shaking her long dyed-blond locks from side to side. "Nooo. Rocco would never do anything like this. He's not a killer."

"He's a gangster!" Claudia exploded. "Of course he could be a killer. He could be the head killer for all you know."

"No, I swear. Rocco just launders some money.
Every once in a while he runs a few numbers. That's
it. Do you think I could be almost engaged to a
killer?"

As far as Claudia was concerned Antoinette could
be almost engaged to Jeffery Dahmer and she'd
never guess. Even after her cat Buffy went missing.
"So who popped this guy? You?"

"Don't be ridiculous, Claude. You know me better than that. I mean we're practically sisters."

It was true. They had grown up together. Like an
older sister, Claudia had been watching over Antoinette as long as she could remember. Currently, she
even employed her as the receptionist at her nail
salon. So what if she mixed up a few appointments
every once in a while. Or even one every day. They
had a history together. Claudia had pulled her out of
every jam she had ever unknowingly gotten herself
into.

This, however, was different. This was a dead guy
in her bathtub. The last time Antoinette had elicited
Claudia's help to deal with something that had died
it had been a pet goldfish. Goldfish she could deal
with. Them, you just flushed down the toilet. She
was pretty sure this guy wasn't going to fit.

Rocco had to be responsible for this. She wouldn't
repeat the sentiment because it would only send Antoinette into another tizzy of defending her almost-
fiancé's innocence. And frankly, she wasn't up for
it. She'd spent all night at the salon doing the books,
which she hated. She'd been hoping to have her one
day off a week to sleep until at least noon. Then
she'd gotten the urgent message from her friend to

come look at the guy in her bathtub. A strange request, but Claudia figured, hey, it had been a while since she'd seen a naked guy. She was expecting some hunky friend of Rocco's to be visiting. She didn't expect that friend to be dead.

"Maybe we should put a blanket over him," Antoinette suggested.

"To do what? Keep him warm? A blanket is not going to have much effect against three bags of vending machine ice, and oh yeah, that's right, he's also dead! Blankets don't work on dead guys!"

Antoinette huffed. "I know he's dead, Claude. But look at his thing. It's all shriveled. I mean if he were alive, he'd probably be really embarrassed that we were standing here staring at his little shriveled thing."

After a silent prayer to her dead mother for patience, Claudia grabbed Antoinette by the shoulders and forced her to meet her stern eyes. "This is important. First, this guy is dead. Second, I don't care about his shriveled thing, and I'm sure he doesn't care about his shriveled thing either, because third, he's dead! He's got bigger problems than a little you-know-what."

Antoinette had the good grace to look sheepish. "So what are we going to do?"

The only thing they could do. "I'm going to call the police."

"Please, no," Antoinette whined. To emphasize her point she pulled on Claudia's arm and jumped up and down like a child. Since Antoinette was dressed in a skintight neon halter top, Claudia was once again reminded that although her friend didn't have brains, Antoinette had everything else. "They'll blame Rocco."

"And this is a problem because…"

"He didn't do it. I know he didn't do it."

"How do you know?" Claudia questioned reasonably. "Did you see the guy who did it?"

"No. When I came home the dead guy was already in the tub," she admitted reluctantly. "But Rocco's got a lot of bad guys above him. There's this one guy Jimmy, who's always smackin' gum. He's got these really beady eyes, and I hear he's been moving up the corporate ladder, so to speak. He probably made the hit."

"Listen Toinette, you're right. Rocco's got a bunch of bad guys more powerful than him in the organization. But the dead guy is in your bathtub. If you don't report it, you're going to look like an accessory."

"A piece of jewelry? Is that a bad thing?" Antoinette asked.

Claudia raised her eyes to heaven once more. This time she would need both her ma and her pop's support. "An accessory to the crime, Toinette. You could go to jail. As it is you're going to have to tell them everything you know about Rocco's business and his friends."

"I won't do it," she muttered stubbornly. "I'll take the Fifth Commandment."

"It's not a commandment, it's an amendment. And you don't take it, you plead it."

"You always have to be such a know-it-all."

"Only because you know nothing! I doubt you even know what pleading the Fifth means."

"Yes, I do," she said snootily. "I see them do it on *NYPD Blue* all the time. And there's also this rule that says I don't have to testify against my husband. I saw that on *The Practice*."

Claudia smirked, "Yeah, and if that bum ever put a ring on your finger that might be an option. But after seven years with Rocco, all you got to show for it is a fake fur in your closet and a dead guy in your bathtub."

"It is not a fake fur! It's real raccoon. And I won't testify. I love Rocco. That's why you're being so mean. You're jealous."

"You're right, Toinette. I want to date a gangster and find dead bodies in my bathtub, too."

"At least I love my boyfriend."

Low blow. Especially since she was trying to help. "I like Marco a whole lot."

"That's why you say no every time he pops the question. Because you like him so much," her employee retorted snootily.

"Listen, now is not the time to be discussing my personal life, okay. Do you have any suggestions?" It was unlikely, but she thought she'd ask considering it was Antoinette's bathtub.

"We could move him," she suggested, but the squeamish look on her face confirmed that she was as unwilling to touch the dead guy as Claudia was. Back to plan A.

"I'm calling the police."

"Who's calling the police?"

Claudia jumped. The loud booming voice was not two feet behind her. *Uh-oh,* she thought, *Rocco.*

When she turned, he was standing in the bathroom doorway, blocking her exit.

"Rocco! Honey, you're home. Come look. There's a dead guy in our bathtub. I told Claudia you didn't do it, but she wants to call the police."

Smooth. Very smooth. Claudia gulped first, then attempted a nonthreatening smile as Rocco filled the already crowded bathroom. He was a short, stodgy guy, who wore cheap suits, cheaper cologne and a fake gold ring on each finger. For the most part he made Claudia want to laugh, he was so pathetic. But he was a member of the mob, and everyone in New York knew that it wasn't wise to mess with mob business.

"Nobody is callin' nobody," Rocco announced. "Show me the stiff, sugarpuff."

Claudia could only assume he wasn't talking to her. She backed off and let Antoinette guide Rocco around the toilet bowl so he could get a good view of the bathtub. Suddenly, there was free access to the door. Claudia didn't wait. A few steps and she was in the hallway. A few steps more and she was in the living room. Almost there.

"Hey, Claudia, where are you goin'?" Antoinette screeched.

That move was even smoother than the last one.

"Hey, get back here!" Rocco shouted. But it was too late. Claudia was out the door and in the elevator before Rocco could catch her. She had to go to the police. Once there she would convince them that Antoinette had nothing to do with any of this. Hopefully, one interview with her should be enough to clear her name. If not, Claudia wondered if there was a defense for the criminally stupid. Probably not, because she had never seen it on *NYPD Blue*.

The elevator dinged. Claudia was about to step out when a man, wearing a baseball cap so low over his eyes she wondered how he could see anything, bumped into her.

"Excuse me?"

"Whatever," he grumbled back.

If she wasn't running for her life, she might have had a thing or two to say about the man's rudeness. Just because this was New York didn't mean everyone had to be mean and nasty. Well, actually, it sort of did, but Claudia had made it her personal crusade to change all that. However, given the circumstances, she decided it was best to keep moving.

She buzzed herself out of the building's front door and was soon sucked up by the city. It was Sunday morning. In any other city or town, the streets might have been quiet except for a few churchgoers. Not in New York. At any time of the day or night the city was crammed with people heading... somewhere.

If Rocco was chasing her, he would never spot her. With her dark hair, pale skin and dark clothes, Claudia blended in with the people walking the streets as if she were related to each and every one of them. In the city she was a chameleon. No one would ever find her.

1

"I NEED A FAVOR."

"Where have I heard those words before?" Ross
Evans wondered aloud as he held the phone to his
ear. He only knew one man who would start a conversation by asking for a favor.

"It's so simple, I can't even believe I'm going to
ask."

"Out with it MacCurdy," Ross growled, "I've
got work to do."

"Actually, it was Frank's idea."

Ross waited.

"We need you to watch a witness for us."

Again, Ross waited.

"She's as harmless as a fly. She's not even really
a witness. She didn't see anything. She just found a
body. But it was mob business, and they didn't like
her going to the cops. Since it happens to involve a
guy we've been looking to snag, we took her under
our wing. The guy isn't the big fish, but we're hoping he's going to lead us to the momma of all fish.
So what do you say?"

"No."

As if MacCurdy hadn't heard the answer, he continued with his pitch. "I don't know why we're going to such lengths for this woman. She's really not

going to do us any good. Two goons attempted a hit, but failed. I can almost guarantee that was the last of it. But you know Frank. Precaution is his middle name. I think he's more worried that someone found out where we stashed her. Actually, if we're going to be specific—''

''Yes, please let's be specific,'' Ross returned coolly.

''They found her twice, but the second time shouldn't count because she hid in the woods, and technically they never did find her. Anyway, since then he's kept her covered by two agents at all times. She's got this employee who happens to be dating our suspect, you know, the little fish who's going to lead us to the big fish. Anyway I think our witness has been calling the friend and giving her location away. How dumb can you get? Right? So what do you say?''

''No.''

Without a second breath the man on the phone continued, ''Frank is worried there might be a leak, but I don't see it. I told him, she's calling the friend. But you know Frank. He told me I needed a place not on the regular list of hideouts, a place as far away from the mob as we could get. Then he comes up with this idea about you probably needing a little excitement in your life. You've been on that farm for years! Frank and I figure you could use a little project to get the old juices flowing again. You were a maniac back in the day, remember Ross? You were probably the most gung ho special agent to ever carry the badge. Now you're Farmer Ted. You've got to be craving action.''

"You're trying to give up smoking again, aren't you?" Ross asked. It was the only explanation for the verbal diarrhea he'd just heard.

"I'm popping Nicorette tablets like they were candy," MacCurdy admitted. "How did you know?"

"Just a guess."

"So what do you say?"

"No."

MacCurdy sighed.

Ross didn't have to explain his reasons. However, this was his ex-partner, he reminded himself. So he owed him something. "I've got Rosa May to consider. I can't put her in jeopardy."

"Who said anything about jeopardy? I'm telling you this is a no-risk situation."

"They found her twice," Ross reminded him. Just because MacCurdy had been running off at the mouth, didn't mean that Ross hadn't been listening.

"Because she called them! I'm telling you it was the friend. This time we've taken precautions. We haven't told her where she is going. As long as you keep her on the farm here in Wisconsin, she won't be able to tell our guy's girlfriend a damn thing. After all, there are a hell of a lot of farms in the U.S."

"Find another farm."

Another sigh. "That's going to be difficult."

"Why?"

"Well, we're driving down your road right now."

Ross cursed, then checked the room for his eleven-year-old daughter. Fortunately, she was nowhere to be seen. "You've got some balls, Mac-Curdy."

"It was Frank's idea. Call him, if you don't want to do it."

Sure, Ross, thought. Call the man who'd saved his butt more times then he could count and tell him that he wouldn't do him this one favor. "You better be right about this, MacCurdy. I smell one whiff of trouble, I'm dumping the girl on the first street corner I find. Deal?"

"Deal," MacCurdy agreed. "Come on outside and welcome us."

Ross heard a click and slammed the phone back on the hook. Damn, he didn't need this right now. He was perfectly content running his farm. Despite what MacCurdy said, he didn't need the action. He didn't miss the action.

Okay, maybe that was a lie. He missed it a little. But he had other responsibilities in his life that took precedence over action. His daughter first. His farm second. This farm was his legacy. It was the last thing his father had ever given him and more important than any job could be.

Beep. Beep.

The sound of the horn echoed through the kitchen. Ross made his way to the back door. He pulled his Green Bay Packers cap off the coatrack and slammed it on his head, pushing the brim low over his eyes to protect them from the strong summer sun.

Rosa May, eager for company, any company, was already standing out front to welcome the visitors. At eleven years old, she was as straight and as willowy as an arrow, with summer wheat hair, like her mother, and a stubborn chin like her father. She was his world, and he would be damned before this witness, whoever she was, put her in any kind of danger. That thought in mind, he would be sure to lay down the law quickly.

"Back up a bit, Rosa May," Ross directed.

"Who are they, Dad?" she asked from her spot at the end of the driveway.

"Old friends." At least part of that was true. He didn't like to lie to his daughter, their relationship was too mature for such childishness. But he also wasn't sure how much he wanted to tell her about their new guest.

Ross watched as the black Ford sedan barreled its way down the driveway. It bumped, it leaped, it jagged, it rocked. Funny, in his pickup, Ross never noticed how many ruts there were in his mile-long driveway. The evil side of him snickered at the state their stomachs must be in currently. Both driver and passengers. Served them right for intruding on his peace.

All Claudia knew was that if they didn't stop rocking, she was going to hurl all over the front seat from her place in the back seat. It wasn't going to be a pretty sight. She had a blindfold on over her eyes and headphones that played some horrible New Age music over her ears. Didn't they know that Verdi, Vivaldi and Madonna were the last of the great composers? She wasn't sure, but she thought the purpose of the music was to dull her into unconsciousness. It wasn't working. In fact, it was only making her irritated. Not that this whole experience, since the day Antoinette found the cursed body in the bathtub, had been anything but an irritation.

First there was the safe house in Jersey. The hit men, because she was sure there was more than one, shot out every window in the house. Somehow, they missed her. Whoever the goons were, they must have been new. Not only did they not hit her, but they never even checked to see if she had been popped. Sloppy. Not that she was complaining.

Next came the log cabin somewhere in Virginia. Again they shot out the windows. They were big on windows. Only this time they shot the special agent in charge in the arm. Claudia had a hell of a time pulling him through the woods. Finally, she found a cave and settled them both in until the coast was clear. Which didn't come a second too soon, what with the special agent acting as if he'd taken one in the gut rather than a flesh wound in the arm. What was it with men and whining?

Damn Antoinette. Damn Rocco. Damn the naked dead guy. She didn't need this. She'd just gotten her salon to the point of actually being an exclusive place to get one's nails done, no easy task in Brooklyn where nail and hair salons were as prevalent as pizza parlors. Only her shop was different. Her nails were custom designed. Women from all over the five boroughs were coming to her salon just to say they had their nails done by Claudia.

Now she was running for her life, and someone was obviously telling Rocco what road she was taking. So the two agents in the front of the car, the government good guys as she liked to call them, were driving her to what felt like East Nowhere. Finally, the car stopped. Her stomach did one last pitch just to remind her that it was not too happy about the ride or the frozen burrito she'd eaten that morning.

"Air," Claudia muttered as she extracted herself from the headphones. "All I need is a little air." She threw open the door and in her excitement to escape ended up tumbling out of the car.

Then it hit her. Full in the face. Like a tidal wave meant to drown her. "Oh. My. God! What is that smell?"

A small giggle came from the corner. A gruff voice told the giggler to hush. Then that same gruff voice informed her. "Farm smell."

Claudia whipped off her blindfold, careful, however, not to mess her hair or her eye makeup. Mascara, after all, didn't look so great once it smudged.

Grass. It surrounded her for endless miles. There were some black-and-white specks off to her far left. Cows, she supposed. To her right there was a house. White, two stories, with a porch that embraced it. She was sure there was some type of architectural word to summarize it, but the only architecture she recognized was a brownstone in Brooklyn or a high-rise in Manhattan. If she had to guess, she'd go with Traditional Farm. Behind it was a barn even taller than the house. Huge! Next to the barn was a long flat building that stretched past both the barn and the house. There was also one of those really tall cylinderlike things that all farms seemed to have. Definite phallic symbol. No surprise to Claudia that most farmers were men.

She'd been dropped onto the set of *Witness*. Was

this Amish country or what? Then she spotted the red pickup near the house and a tractor next to that. Claudia didn't know much about the Amish, but she knew that they didn't drive. So where in hell was she?

"Where in the hell am I?"

Another giggle from the kid. "She said hell, Dad."

Oops. Apparently that was too colorful of an expression for the *Little House on the Prairie* girl.

"I would appreciate it if you wouldn't use that kind of language in front of my daughter." This from Gruff Voice.

Oh, he was going to be a rough crowd. Tall, broad shouldered, massively muscled. This guy would make Arnold Schwarzenegger blink. He was making her eyes flutter. Did they all get this big on these farms?

"I'm sorry. I'm a little rattled that's all."

"If you don't like the smell, maybe you should turn around," the big guy suggested, obviously annoyed that someone would berate his farm.

"I'm sorry. But come on! Who *would* like that smell?" Claudia asked sincerely. She feared she'd ticked him off, but that smell was awful!

"The cows don't seem to mind."

"Well I guess if a couple of cows can take it, so can I." Claudia Bertucci had fended off muggers, gangsters, hit men and Joey Angelucci in the fifth grade who wanted to kiss her with his tongue. She could handle the smell. What she didn't know was if she could handle the big guy.

"She talks funny." Again the girl giggled.

"I'm from Brooklyn not from Mars, sweetheart," Claudia told her and smiled because the girl's laughter was the most normal sound she'd heard in a long time.

That was questionable, Ross thought. She was about as misplaced as an Eskimo in Fiji. A black leather motorcycle jacket was tossed over her shoulders. Underneath he could see skin where her blouse should be and the edges of pink silk that barely covered her breasts. Her legs were encased in the tightest pieces of black lycra that he'd ever seen. Through it every muscle was defined. If she had any flab, he would have spotted it a mile away. She didn't have any flab. Her feet were bare except for some black leather straps attached to three inches of plastic. Hair, sable in color with burgundy highlights, flew out from her head as if she'd just stuck her thumb in an electrical socket. Only Ross was pretty sure that she meant for it to look that way. He couldn't tell if it was her ears or an excessive amount of hair spray that anchored her sunglasses above her hair. And the earrings! Huge gold hoops reached her shoulders. This was not going to work.

"This is not going to work," Ross muttered aloud. So loud she must have heard him because she frowned.

MacCurdy joined them while the other agent switched to the driver's side. He wore a huge, if somewhat insincere grin on his face. "Isn't this great! I think you guys are going to really hit it off."

Ignoring Farmer Ted, Claudia turned her attention to Agent MacCurdy. "Where am I?"

"I told you that is confidential. On a need-to-know basis only."

"Yeah, well I need to know." She needed to know that she was still on the same planet and that one of the roads leading off this farm led back to Brooklyn.

MacCurdy shook his head. "It's for your own safety."

Claudia smirked at him, then turned to the young girl. "Sweetheart."

"Yes?" Rosa May responded.

"Where am I?"

"Sun Prairie, Wisconsin."

"Oh, man!" MacCurdy groaned. "This ruins everything."

"My dad always said I should tell the truth," Rosa May answered plainly.

"Sun what?" Claudia asked, unbelieving that there truly could be such a place. "Are you kidding me?"

"Oh, man!" MacCurdy whined.

She guessed he wasn't kidding.

"Thank you, honey," Claudia told the girl first. Then she turned to the agent with the painful expression on his face. "Relax, all right. I love Antoinette. But the only thing I trust her with is scheduling nail appointments, and then only because I have someone check her work. You think I'm going to trust her with my life?"

At this point MacCurdy had no choice but to hope she wouldn't.

"She won't have access to the phone," Ross told

MacCurdy. "She won't do anything that might jeopardize my daughter's safety." This he said to her.

Recognizing the threat in his voice and his eyes, Claudia did what came naturally to her. She mouthed off. "My name is Claudia or Miss Bertucci, not She, and I have no intentions of jeopardizing anyone. Least of all myself or your pretty little girl here. You on the other hand," she stated pointing in his direction. "You look like you can take care of yourself."

Ross wasn't sure if that was a compliment.

This time the girl had to put her hands over her mouth to stop herself from all out guffawing. Claudia bent down to make eye contact with the girl. "Hey, gigglemeister, what's your name?"

"Rosa May," she said through her hands.

"Rosa May? Rosa…May? What a mouthful. I'm gonna call you Rosie. *Capisce?*"

"Cap… What?"

Claudia smiled. "Is that okay with you?"

She nodded her head.

Claudia nodded in turn. "Rosie, we're going to have to work on your Italian. Now, if that big man over there, who I assume is your pop, will agree to this whole shindig, then I'll take your hand and let you escort me to my room."

"You sure do talk funny," Rosa May said again. But she took Claudia's hand with an acceptance indicative of her age and led her along the path toward the house. After a few steps she turned back. "It is all right, isn't it Dad?"

For a moment Ross was silent. He didn't like it. He didn't like her. The way she spoke, the way she dressed. She would be a bad influence on his daughter. He should stop the whole thing right now before it got out of hand. *My name is Claudia or Miss Bertucci, not She.* Who the hell did she think she was?

He watched while she stood there. His eyes pierced hers while he waited for one more outrageous thing to come out of her mouth. Only she said nothing. And if he wasn't mistaken, those eyes of hers held a measure of vulnerability.

As if she sensed that she was giving herself away, she reached up to pluck her sunglasses off her head to shield her eyes from his scrutiny. Only the frames got caught in a tangle of tease and hair spray, and she ended up leaving them stuck on her head at a lopsided angle.

Ross couldn't suppress his grin. She acted tough, but he guessed that on the inside she was all cream puff. For that matter, so was he. That and a sucker.

"So what's it going to be Ted?" she asked, her pointed chin lifted high.

"My name is Ross, not Ted." Where had she gotten Ted from?

Rolling her eyes, she asked again, "So what's it going to be, Ross?"

"Show her inside, Rosa May. Take her to the third bedroom on the left. I'll bring her things in later."

Her relief was palatable. "Wait," she cried, dropping Rosa May's hand. "I need my bag." Running, if it could be called running in three-inch heels, Claudia stopped in front of the car and reached inside for a purse that was larger than one of his feed bags.

The bag draped over her shoulder, she sashayed

back to where Rosa May was waiting for her and was led into the house. If Ross let his gaze linger a little too long on the sway of her hips, then no one was foolish enough to say anything. Certainly not MacCurdy.

"She's a pistol, isn't she?"

"Yeah, a pistol," he repeated. One that was pointed at his head. "So what's the story. You said she found a dead guy. Who was he?"

MacCurdy slapped his old friend on the back. "That's my Ross. You can take the boy out of Quantico, but you can't take Quantico out of the boy."

"The story," Ross prompted. He didn't have time to stroll down memory lane. Cows needed to be milked.

"The dead guy was a drug runner. Nonunion if you catch my drift. And the mob has their own unique way of dealing with scabs. He was found in Rocco 'The Bull' Capuano's apartment. Rocco is small fish. For all we know he wasn't even the one who pulled the trigger. The real hit man was probably just keeping him on ice, literally, until he could dispose of the body. Anyway, the police couldn't really hold Rocco. No one saw him do anything. He's got fifteen cousins who can testify that they were eating pasta with him down at the local bistro at the time of death. The cops are harassing him, and we're tailing him because we're hoping he's going to lead us to Grotti. Grotti is the big fish in New York these days. Public enemy number one. He runs numbers, blackmails the local shop owners, pimps prostitutes...."

"Deals drugs," Ross finished. Not a pleasant fellow he was sure.

"You got the picture. We're hoping Grotti himself put the icing on this particular cake. So we're keeping a tap on Rocco's phone. Don't know why the girl is such a hot item. Probably just a loose end they want cleaned up. Like I said, they tried twice, failed twice. More than likely they are done trying. Grotti doesn't need the extra attention. The only reason we're taking such precautions by bringing her to an unknown location is because they found her."

"She says she never told the friend," Ross noted.

MacCurdy bunched his shoulders and scrunched his face. "She's not going to admit to being that stupid. Keep her off the phone and no harm will come to you, I promise."

Ross merely nodded, but something in his gut shifted. Claudia appeared to be a lot of things, but stupid was not one of them. Her eyes revealed a quickness of mind.

"So how long is all of this going to take?" Ross had already concluded that it was only going to take a few days for Claudia to throw his life into total chaos.

"Not long. Rocco is pretty close to the edge. A few more days of NYPD Blue heat, and he'll run to Grotti for protection. Then we'll get a tape on him and Grotti. If you want I can have Chuck—" MacCurdy pointed to the other agent in the car "—stay out here."

"No."

Grinning, MacCurdy slapped his friend on the shoulder. "I didn't think so. You always were the lone-wolf type. But it's been a while. Think you're still up for the job?"

Ross didn't change his expression. He did, however, remove MacCurdy's hand from his shoulder. "I'm up for the job. But I mean it, one hint of trouble, and she's gone. If my stomach so much as twitches…"

"You and your gut. They're still legendary down at the Bureau. Trust me. Everything will proceed without a hitch. You have my word."

Ross didn't say it, but he never once knew how far to trust MacCurdy's word.

His ex-partner headed back to his car, popped the trunk with a key, and unloaded some luggage. Ross wasn't paying attention, but when the Ford did a K turn in the driveway and the two men drove away, he was left facing five bags of luggage. Five! Actually four bags, and one trunk. His jaw dropped, and when he heard the *beep, beep* of the car horn, signaling its retreat, he wished all the ruts in the world upon MacCurdy.

Cursing under his breath, freely now because he knew his daughter was nowhere in sight, Ross grimly carried the luggage and the trunk into the house.

And he thought it was going to take a few days for her to throw his life into chaos? It was more like a few hours. As the sweat ran down his back, and he felt the muscles in his arm cramp from the weight of the trunk, Ross definitely decided, that this wasn't going to work.

2

"THIS IS YOUR ROOM," Rosa May said, stepping back as she pointed inside the third room on the left.

Claudia poked her head in first. Then she pulled it back. "Sweetie, you must be mistaken. This must be some kind of upstairs living room."

Rosa May shook her head. "No, this is the right room. Dad said to give you the third bedroom on the left. His is the first. Mine is the second. This is the third. The one across the hall used to be my mom's sewing room."

Arching her brow, Claudia wondered. "Honey, where is your ma?" And why on earth had she ever agreed to let a strange woman into her home? Claudia was going to have to inform her that when one was married to a man who looked like her husband, it was best not to let other women invade her turf. Not that she was tempted by those broad shoulders or that massive chest. Naaah.

"My mom is dead. She died three years ago."

Immediately, Claudia fell to her knees and wrapped the girl in a big bear hug. "I'm so sorry, baby," she wailed.

Rosa May shrugged out of her embrace, her face beet red. "I'm okay. It has been three years."

Claudia stared owlishly at the girl. She seemed so

calm, so in control. "Honey, I lost my mother thirteen years ago, and I'm still not okay. Fathers are important, but nobody can replace a mother."

Rosa May nodded in understanding.

"I mean, who's going to paint your nails for the first time? Who's going to yell at you when you shave your legs too young? Who's going to tell you when you start to put on weight and remind you that you probably don't need that third slice of pizza? Who's going to go to the store with you for the first time when you need to buy feminine...oh never mind."

"My dad, I guess."

"Trust me on this, sweetheart, fathers are good for a lot of things. Intimidating boyfriends you want to scare off, paying for prom gowns, calling you princess. However, painting your fingernails is not one of them."

Rosa May chuckled.

Happy to make the girl smile, especially when she had inadvertently reminded her of such sadness, Claudia poked her head in the room again. "You are sure this is my room?"

Rosa May nodded.

"Oooh, honey, I am in the Presidential Suite. A room this big in Brooklyn could house a ma, a pop, five kids and a grandma." Claudia moved forward into the spacious room. There was a huge queen-size bed that jutted out from the wall. Next to it was a bed stand with a small clock and a lamp with a delicate handmade shade on top of it. There was a dresser located on the opposite wall. Walking to it each morning, Claudia mused, would provide her with all the exercise she needed in a day. In the corner adjacent to the dresser was an old-fashioned rocking chair complete with a quilt.

The chair called to Claudia. "I bet your mother used to rock you in that chair when you were a baby. She wouldn't want to wake your pop, so she brought you to this room and she snuggled into that quilt with you in her arms, just the two of you, and sang to you until you fell asleep."

Rosa May walked over and petted the quilt reverently. "The blanket was my mom's. When it's cold I sleep with it. It still smells like her."

Claudia reached deep into the crevice between her breasts and removed a locket. "This was my ma's." She popped it open and showed Rosa May the tiny picture inside.

"She was so beautiful," Rosa May whispered.

"She was a looker," Claudia admitted proudly. "My pop told me that the angels smiled on him twice in his life. First, the day they made my ma in heaven. Second, the day they introduced her to him."

"Do you really still miss her?" Rosa May asked.

"Yeah. I'll always miss her. But I have her locket. And I have memories. So in a way she's never really left me."

Rosa May hesitated, shuffled her feet, and pinned her eyes to her shoelaces. "I still miss my mom. I just don't like to admit it, you know. I don't want my dad to think I'm sad all the time."

Claudia knelt before her new young friend. "Your daddy is a big boy. A very big boy! He'll understand if sometimes you're sad. Sometimes, I bet, he's sad, too. Those are the times you talk about your ma. You bring the memories back. You bring her back.''

"I'm not sure who you are, or why you're here, but I'm glad you came. Can I call you Claudia?''

"Sure." She ruffled the girl's bangs then smoothed them back into place. They were a little fuller now and highlighted the nice arch in her brow. With a little spritz of hair spray, she'd be good to go all day.

"Come here, Rosie," Claudia motioned for the girl to follow her to the bed. Removing the large bag from her shoulder, she undid the zipper and tilted the bag upside down, dropping its precious contents onto the bedspread.

Rosa May's mouth gaped as lipsticks, hairbrushes, manicure sets, eye pluckers, cuticle scissors and some toothbrushlike item with a comb on one side, came tumbling out of her purse. She wasn't halfway done, either.

More lipsticks, eyeliner pencils, tiny brushes of various thickness. A real toothbrush, a tube of toothpaste, a packet of floss. The contents were neverending.

"Hey, cool. Like Mary Poppins," Rosa May said.

Claudia ignored the reference, too intent in her search. When the bag had given up all of its contents, Claudia shook the bag and muttered to it that it was holding out on her. Finally, she reached her arm deep into the sack, and after a moment of battle, the bag relinquished one small spritz bottle.

Turning to Rosa May, she lifted the girl's chin with her finger, then covered the girl's eyes with her free hand. "Close your eyes, Rosie," Claudia instructed.

Rosa May obeyed without question. A light sprinkling of water hit her forehead, then Claudia teased and tweaked her bangs.

"Perfect," she announced.

Rosa May lifted her eyes high into her head to see the effect, but her bangs were too high for her to spot. Fortunately, a compact mirror was among one of the discarded items that had fallen onto the bed. Claudia watched as Rosa May smiled at her reflection. Her hair was still honey wheat, it was still tied in a braid in the back, but now the bangs were voluminous and mature, where only a minute ago they had been flat and childish.

"Thanks," Rosa May offered. "Dad doesn't let me buy…well, he doesn't think I need, you know, beauty supplies. Hair spray and all that other stuff."

"No hair spray! Ahhh! What kind of monster is he?"

Rosa May just laughed and so did Claudia.

Then she set about returning the discarded contents back to her bag. In explanation of her outburst, Claudia told the girl, "I used to do hair back in the days before I concentrated on nails, so this sort of thing comes naturally to me. I used to fill in for Suzie DeMarco in the hair salon because she was always pregnant and needed to stay off her feet. Only between you, me and the walls, I think she was just fat. I mean who stays pregnant for eleven months straight?"

"I don't know," Rosie shrugged.

"Anyway, I'm out of the hair business for good.

It's too limited. I'm mean how many 'updos' can one girl design? There are only so many ways you can wrap hair around a woman's head. Now it's just nails. Only not just colored nails. I'm talking nail art.''

''So you work in a salon.''

''Not work in, baby, I'm the owner. At least that's what I was in New York. Out here in Wisconsin I don't know what I am.'' The impact of her own words hit her. She'd struggled so long to make her salon a legitimate business, a place where the wealthy would come to have her unique designs painted on to their nails. Without her and her talent there, it was just another one of the masses. She trusted Francesca, the other girl who did manicures with her, to keep the place going, but how long would it take before people began to seek out someone new?

''So what are you doing here?'' Rosa May wondered. ''Not that I'm complaining. So far you're the most interesting person I've ever met in my life. I don't know that many people yet, but I bet even if I meet a hundred people, none of them are going to be as neat as you.''

Neat. Was that still a word? Apparently it was in Sun Prairie. What to tell the kid? No doubt Ted...Ross wanted to keep her shielded from the ugly side of life. It was why he'd left the Bureau, at least that was what MacCurdy told her. He couldn't be a farmer, a proper husband and father if he was always surrounding himself with the wrong element. Whatever the heck that meant.

The way Claudia saw it, protecting a kid from the

"wrong element" was impossible. There were too many threats, too many obstacles, too many bad people out there to shelter a kid forever. The best thing a parent could do was to be on the level and teach a kid that just because bad people were out there, it didn't mean that they were always out there to get you. Necessarily. She would also teach her kid never to mess with mob business. It was a lesson she'd been taught early on, but must have forgotten somewhere along the road.

"I'm here because I'm trying to help the police. And they're trying to help me by hiding me." Simple and to the point.

"Oh," Rosa May breathed. "You're hiding out. Like in the Witness Protection Program? Who are you hiding from? The mob, I bet. I saw this episode of *NYPD Blue* and this guy was ratting on this hit man and he had to go into the Witness Protection Program. Only the bad guy found him and popped him between the eyes."

"Not an encouraging story, honey. Remind me to tell your father that you shouldn't be watching that show. I already know one person that it's corrupted."

"I didn't know she was watching it."

The voice was as large as the man. Low, rough, with a slow drawl to it that wasn't Southern, but was distinctly country.

"Dad it was just that one time. You fell asleep in the chair remember, and I didn't want to turn off the TV because I was afraid I would wake you," Rosa May offered sincerely, her eyes as innocent as an angel.

Claudia began to applaud. "Wooh! That excuse ranks a nine-oh out of a possible ten. You absolutely reeked of sincerity. If only I were young again and could use that excuse. That was priceless, honey."

Unabashedly, Rosa May bowed. "Thank you, thank you, thank you very much."

"Please don't encourage her," Ross warned. "I'm already afraid she's planning to run away to Hollywood. I don't need anyone giving her rave reviews."

Ross smiled down at his still beaming daughter and tried to tousle her bangs. Only his fingers came back sticky with hairspray. "What in the heck…"

"A little poof, you know, for support," Claudia explained as if a "little poof" made all the sense in the world to Ross.

"Yeah, Pop, just a little poof," Rosa May repeated brashly. A stern glance from her father, however, silenced her.

There was love there, Claudia thought. The girl for the father, the father for the girl. It reminded her of the relationship she had had with her own pop and she couldn't help but feel wistful. Boy, she missed him. Almost as much as she missed her ma. For a moment, she tried hard to imagine her almost-boyfriend Marco smiling down at their daughter like that. The image never came.

"I brought your luggage upstairs. And the trunk. It's out in the hall." *Because I couldn't carry it any farther*, Ross finished silently. "What do you have in that trunk?"

"Supplies," she stated, "I never travel without them. Thanks. Can you believe I had to make do with only four bags? I mean jeez, do the Feds expect me to wear the same outfit every day or what? I'm barely squeaking by with what I brought. But you know how it is when you're on the run. You gotta travel light.''

Light? This wasn't going to work. Ross knew it was a recurring thought, but he couldn't seem to shake it. How could they possibly survive living together when she was the antithesis of his wife in every way imaginable? Susan knew how to pack conservatively, dress conservatively and speak conservatively. Ross wondered if this woman knew what the word *conservative* meant.

Not that he was thinking of her as anything other than a guest, but just in case he became a bit tempted by her tiny frame and her pretty face, he made a mental note to quash it. This woman was not for him. That issue settled, Ross knew it was time to get down to business.

''I'm sure you are exhausted after your trip and your uh…adventures.'' No need to mention that she'd been shot at, or Rosa May would have her up on a pedestal before he could blink. ''Why don't you take some time to settle in? When you're ready we'll discuss what your responsibilities are going to be during your stay.''

''Responsibilities?'' Claudia repeated, confused by what he meant. The way she saw it, her only responsibility was to stay alive to make it back to her shop.

''This is a farm. Everyone who lives on the farm must contribute to it. That includes you, Miss Brooklyn.''

Smiling facetiously, Claudia retorted, "You got the wrong girl. Miss Brooklyn was Marie Verdino. She had big you-know-whats, and hair as high as the ceiling, but she came in a disappointing fourth at the Miss New York Pageant."

He didn't even crack a grin.

"What are you-know-whats, Dad?" Rosa May wondered.

Not even then.

But Claudia laughed freely. She never felt a need to stop laughter. Who would? "In a year or two... How old are you again, honey?"

"Practically twelve."

"Eleven," her father answered simultaneously.

"Yep, two more years, and it will all start to make sense."

Ross actually groaned.

Claudia chuckled, pleased to see that he wasn't all bark, bite and brawn. This was going to work just fine. "Now, I believe somebody said something about settling in."

"See you later," Rosa May said, skipping out the door as if it was an everyday occurrence to have strangers from Brooklyn take shelter in her home.

Ross watched his daughter leave, amazed at her ability to adapt to the situation. "She likes you," he said grimly.

"Don't sound so surprised," Claudia retorted. "Many people like me. I'm a likable person. Besides, she's practically a teenager. It appears to me that she is the only girl on this farm. It also appears to me that this farm is the only place for miles and miles around. She probably needs a little feminine companionship.''

''I agree.''

There was a ''but'' in there somewhere. It didn't take a brain surgeon to figure out where it was. ''But you wish that companionship wasn't a girl from Brooklyn on the lam.''

''Yes,'' he answered. He wasn't sure which part bothered him more, though—that she was from Brooklyn and looked it. Or that she could possibly bring danger into his daughter's life.

Claudia felt a stab of disappointment that she couldn't define. Maybe it was because she really liked the kid. Maybe it was because she had already somewhat gotten used to the smell. Or maybe it was because there was something in the stalwart way he stood that seemed to beckon her closer. Like a haven in a storm. Regardless, her next offer was a sincere one. ''I could go. MacCurdy doesn't think there will be any more attempts. And I've got a life waiting for me back in Brooklyn. You didn't ask for this. You more or less got stuck with me.''

More than less. And it seemed she was offering him a way out. Ross couldn't have refused a request from his former employer, even if that relationship was many years old. Frank had saved his life. That debt was unpayable. But she was offering to leave. He certainly couldn't be responsible for the decision a grown woman made....

Stop it, Ross told himself. She was in trouble and she wasn't going anywhere. The mob had made two attempts. If she returned to New York, she'd be nothing more than a sitting duck. Chivalry wasn't

completely dead. Besides, he didn't have the energy
to carry her luggage back downstairs. "You're in
trouble. Whether you realize it or not. You'll be safe
here, so you stay here. You should get settled in.
We'll talk later."

A grin spread across her face. While he crossed
his arms over his fabulous chest like a king who'd
just made a formal proclamation, Claudia realized
that everything he said was in the fashion of an order. She thought it best to clarify her position on
taking orders. But the truth was she was tired, and
she had the feeling that particular conversation was
going to require a great deal of energy. After all,
nobody told her what to do.

"See ya," Claudia said.

Ross nodded and turned to leave. Oddly, he felt
the strangest sensation that her eyes were pinned to
his butt. So much so he was tempted to cover the
body part with his hands. Then he realized he was
being ridiculous. Of course she wasn't staring at his
backside.

Mamma! What a butt. Tight, hard and packaged
in the softest blue jeans imaginable. Her lips were
pursed in the ready stages of a wolf whistle, but
Claudia managed to contain herself until he was
gone. Then she allowed herself a little relief.
"Wheew. I didn't know what I was missing in the
city all those years."

She took a deep breath, then paused.

"Well, I sure as heck wasn't missing that smell.
A back alley on garbage day doesn't even come
close. You're talking to yourself, Claude. Not a wise
move. He might overhear. He'll think you're crazy,

and that is not how you want this relationship to start out. Not that this is a relationship.''

That said, aloud, she collected the rest of her belongings off the bed and returned them to the fifth dimension found deep in the recesses of her bag. Not ready to face the trials of unpacking, Claudia opted for a nap. She removed her coat, hopped up onto the bed and wrapped herself in an afghan she was sure someone's grandmother had made. In minutes she felt herself drifting off to sleep and her last conscious thought was that for the first time in weeks she felt no fear. None.

SETTLING IN over the next couple of days was easier said than done. Crucial issues needed to be addressed. First, she needed a larger mirror in her bedroom. The only mirror in the whole house as far as she could tell was in the bathroom. And even that was only eleven-by-sixteen inches. What happened when Ross and Rosie needed to match their shoes to the rest of their outfit? She wouldn't comment, but she had a sneaking suspicion that they often left the house clashing. Claudia had to resort to sitting on the sink while she lifted her leg high enough into the air to get her pants, blouse and shoes all in the same reflection.

The kid had caught her in that position. It wasn't one of her finest moments.

Second, after unpacking all her bags, she realized she was woefully short on closet space. All her clothes were forced to touch all of her other clothes. Wrinkle city! When she asked the muscle man if she could have an additional closet for her belongings, he snarled at her. When she asked for an iron and ironing board, she was directed to the pantry closest.

And finally, there simply wasn't enough light in her bedroom to accommodate her work. Nail art didn't just happen. Each of her designs were first drawn then practiced on fake enamel nails. Her trunk held a one-piece bench that once unfolded stood at just the right height for her to work without leaning over too far. It also carried a clip device that held the fake nails at the same height and in the same position as a normal hand would be. This way she could anticipate the particular strokes that would cause the most difficulty and might lead to color smudging—a nail artist's worst nightmare. There was only one small window in her bedroom that faced the east, and without sufficient light, she had a difficult time determining if the colors were right. When she asked muscles about adding another window, he mentioned, in a tone even less congenial than before, that she might consider waking up early enough to catch the rising sun. Claudia assumed he was kidding.

After two days however, Claudia was beginning to feel comfortable in the farm home. Which meant it was time to talk to Ross about her...gulp... responsibilities. Checking the clock next to her bed stand, she saw that it was already late afternoon. Too late to start on her responsibilities today, she decided on another nap instead. She would join the two downstairs for dinner and discuss what her options were. That settled, Claudia wrapped herself in her now favorite afghan and once again felt the security of the blanket, the house and the farm overwhelm her.

Later, she woke gradually, enjoying the comfort of the blanket and the soft bed. She could have lingered forever, but her stomach was calling the shots, and it was hungry. Not one to deny her basic human urges, she rolled out of bed. First stop was the ridiculous mirror in the bathroom.

She took a quick peek and decided that her hair was almost unsalvageable. Almost, but not quite. From among the throng of beauty supplies that now filled every ounce of counter space on the small vanity around the sink, Claudia found a can of hair spray. Bending her body in half, her head bobbing upside down between her knees, she proceeded to spray in circular motions. When she lifted her head, she was dizzy, but her hair was back in top shape. The key to beauty was volume. Lesson number one at the Brooklyn Academy of Beauty.

As she made her way down the stairs, she heard voices below and off to the right. They must be in the kitchen. For the most part, Claudia had kept to her room the last two days, but she'd wandered around the house enough to get a feel for the place. There was a living room-slash-family room: very comfortable. A dining room with a formal table and chairs: pretty stuffy. A den with a computer and tons of books: very manly. A homey sort of house overall, she decided.

"I don't want you spending every waking moment with her, that's all."

Ross's voice, Claudia recognized. Not that it was hard to distinguish it from Rosie's. She held her position on the stairs. Something told her they were talking about her. Something also told her it wasn't good.

"But why?" Rosa May protested. "She understands me, even after only knowing me for a few days. We've bonded."

"Bonded," Ross repeated skeptically. "Where do you get that kind of language?"

"Oprah," Rosa May informed him. "She's helping the world get in touch with their inner feelings."

Ross groaned, but quickly recovered. "Miss Bertucci is a guest who will only be staying temporarily. I don't want you to become too attached. More importantly, I don't want her influence rubbing off on you. No more bonding."

"You can't stop bonding, Dad. It just happens. Besides what about you?"

"What about me?"

"Jeez, Dad do I have to spell it out? Claudia may talk funny, but she's awfully pretty. Like her mom. Maybe you could ask her out on a date or something. It has been a while since your last date. And Miss Harkim wasn't your type at all."

"I will not be dating Miss Bertucci."

"Because of her accent? That seems like a petty reason to reject a person."

"Because of her...everything," Ross corrected his daughter. "She is not my type, and you are to get that notion out of your head once and for all. Now I've given you some orders in regards to Miss Bertucci, and I expect them to be followed. Understand?"

"*Capisce,*" Rosa May responded reluctantly.

"It's almost time for bed. Why don't you go upstairs and read for a while?"

He made her sound like she had some kind of contagious disease, Claudia thought. And what did he mean, *Because of her everything?* Who did this guy think he was? She was a catch back in the neighborhood. A beautiful woman with means. He was nothing more than some dumb overinflated farmer. Why, she ought to march down these stairs and punch him in the nose. No, better yet, she'd punch him in the—

"What are you doing Claudia?" Rosa May asked.

Claudia was caught midstairs with her hands balled into fists and her face scrunched up in fury. She hadn't just been thinking of revenge, she'd been acting it out on the stairs.

"Hi sweetie. I was…" Think, think, she commanded her brain. "Exercising?"

Rosa May smiled. "Seven point two. Lacks plausibility. You are on the stairs."

Great, Claudia snorted, she was rubbing off on the girl.

"Don't mind what my dad says. He can be a real dope sometimes. But don't tell him I said so, okay?"

"Okay," she agreed. "You know you're too smart for your age."

"It's the twenty-first century. Children are maturing much quicker these days. It's the adults that are having the difficulty adjusting."

"Yeah. The twenty-first century." Claudia repeated as if that explained everything.

"Good night," Rosa May called out, as she bolted past her up the stairs.

"Good night, sweetie."

Claudia continued her journey in search of food, which ultimately led her down the hallway toward the kitchen. For the first time she noticed the pictures that lined the walls, and couldn't help envying the family scenes. Rosie, as a baby, seemed to be the subject of choice. But there were also pictures of parents and other life events. In one frame Ross stood with a class of very serious-minded-looking men and women. Naturally there were a few wedding pictures. She stopped at one particular portrait.

She was pretty. Not beautiful. Not even striking. Simply pretty. Fair hair, creamy skin, a broad face and a sturdy frame. Not fat, not skinny. Just strong. She was standing in front of the house, her hand acting as a brim over her eyes to shield them from the sun. She wore a cotton housedress, and Keds sneakers on her feet. Her smile was shy, and it was clear she was embarrassed to have her picture taken.

The wife, Claudia surmised. He was right. If this woman was his type, then Claudia was the exact opposite. She didn't know why that should make her feel sad, but it did.

"My wife."

Startled, Claudia jumped. Ross was standing in the doorway to the kitchen. The light was behind him, shadowing his features, but at the same time it emphasized his size. Boy, he was big, Claudia thought each time she saw him. Not bodybuilder big, though. His size was a natural thing, not one he'd purposefully created. Manual labor had built that chest, not weights.

"I could tell. She was very pretty. I'm sorry for

your loss." Claudia shook off the feeling that she'd been caught with her hand in the cookie jar. She'd simply been sizing up the competition...uh...uh...admiring the photograph. That's what she meant.

"We don't talk about her much. My daughter and I. Mostly because we're too busy. But we talked about her over dinner tonight. She says that's thanks to you."

It was hard to tell if he was upset by her interference or not. His face was grim, but she hadn't seen any other expression directed at her since she met him.

"I...uh..."

"Thank you."

"You're welcome," she responded. She stepped a little closer. His voice had been softer, and she wondered if his expression had softened to match it. It hadn't. But his eyes—green like the fields outside—bore into hers, conveying his appreciation in addition to his words. Those eyes! Claudia felt her stomach drop.

"Are you hungry?"

Loaded question. *Don't go there,* Claudia ordered her hormones. You saw the picture of his wife. You heard what he said. You are not his type. And despite his large body, he is not your type. He is Farmer Ted and you are a sophisticated New York nail artist. That decided, it was time to get down to serious business.

"I'm starved," she answered.

Ross moved back into the kitchen, and Claudia followed. She sat at the large oak kitchen table situated in the middle of the room. A hand-embroidered place mat was laid out for her with a fork and knife on opposite sides of the mat. Ross removed a plate from the oven and set it down in front of her.

Mashed potatoes. Fried chicken. Gravy on both. And broccoli. It's what they had last night, too. Leftovers, Claudia assumed and dug in with gusto. While she was eating, Ross sat down at the table with a pad of paper and a pencil in his hand.

"I thought maybe now would be the best time to go over your schedule. I assume you're ready to work."

Her mouth wrapped around a chicken leg, Claudia could only nod.

Taking that as a yes, he continued. "Breakfast is served at 5:30...*a.m.,*" he added in case she didn't understand. "You'll need to eat then. On a farm breakfast is the most important meal of the day because most of the heavy labor is done in the morning."

Heavy labor! Claudia gulped her chicken down in one swallow.

"What chore do you think would best suit you?" Ross asked. He was willing to be magnanimous enough to let her pick her own tasks. After all, she hadn't really asked to be here. But then he didn't ask to have her.

Wiping the gravy from her chin, Claudia considered the question. "I could braid Rosie's hair in the morning."

Ross sighed. She wasn't quite getting the picture.

"Rosa May braids her own hair. And I was thinking more along the lines of a real chore."

A real chore on a farm. Claudia wasn't too sure what that was. "Maybe you could give me a few choices."

"Have you ever milked a cow?"

She shook her head.

"Ridden a horse?"

Again, no.

"Mucked a stall?"

Mucked? Claudia didn't even know what that meant. "Never."

Ross dropped his pad on the table. "Maybe the best thing would be to let you try a lot of different chores tomorrow. Then you can pick which one best suits you."

"Sounds like a plan," Claudia concurred.

"Do you have any clothes…" Ross paused, trying to phrase his question delicately. "More suited for work on a farm?"

"You mean like jeans?"

"Yes, jeans would be all right. Do you have jeans?"

"Sure. Who doesn't have jeans?"

Ross nodded, satisfied that at least that issue was settled. He feared that all her clothes would resemble the ensembles she'd been wearing about the house. Tight pants, high heels, revealing blouses that made him want to reveal more. It didn't do his daughter any good to see her dressed so scantily. It didn't help him, either. Not that he was having a problem controlling his hormones. But a pair of old jeans, and maybe a sweatshirt, would reduce her to the status of any other woman.

"Good. Then I'll see you tomorrow."

Claudia watched as Ross stood and left the room. She heard his heavy footsteps on the stairs above. Finishing the last of her meal, she looked at the clock above the stove. It was only nine, but the house was already asleep. She, on the other hand, wasn't tired at all after her nap.

Hmm, what to do? Maybe she could catch a movie on television. Hopefully a boring one that would put her to sleep. She dropped her plate into the sink and headed off in search of a television. "Oh TV, where are you?" she called.

Wandering about the house, Claudia located it in the living room. It was a huge room that took up most of the bottom floor. Comfortable chairs to ease a man after a hard day's work were spread out about the room. There was a couch that beckoned her, and a TV tucked into an entertainment unit. Quite a change from the days of *Little House on the Prairie,* Claudia mused. A flip of the remote control and she was in business. Immediately, she could see that they had cable, and cable meant they had the shopping channel. A few hits of the remote and she was staring at a one-of-a-kind porcelain cow pitcher, perfect for cream in the morning, and a model that needed a touch-up on her French manicure.

Five hours later the cow made a second appearance. And Claudia was up to see it.

3

"MOO COW. Moo cow. Got to milk the moo cow," she mumbled incoherently.

"Miss Bertucci," Ross said, as he nudged her arm, desperately trying to not laugh at her outrageous mumbling. "Miss Bertucci wake up. Claudia!"

"Whaaat?" Morning never came easy to her. Not even when she was a little girl, and she knew that if she didn't wake up in time she would be late for Sister Mary's first-period class. Sister Mary didn't abide tardiness. Claudia's knuckles had never been the same since. However, even after such stringent conditioning, she'd never quite learned her lesson. Today was no different.

"You're late."

"Fifteen more minutes."

"It's already after five o'clock," Ross told her.

"Five o'clock?" Claudia rolled over and smothered her face in the couch cushions. "Five more hours," she mumbled.

Rosa May joined her father who was sitting on what little couch space Claudia had left. "I don't think she's ready to get up, Dad."

Ross gazed down at the impossibly tiny figure tucked into a ball on his couch. Apparently she'd

fallen asleep watching the shopping network. He felt
no pity. He'd told her when the day began. "She
doesn't have a choice. Now, Claudia, or I get serious," he warned.

"Fifteen more minutes."

The time for games was over. Ross stood and
backed away from the couch. He crouched over his
victim and tucked his arms underneath her. She
mumbled. She grumbled. But she still didn't move.
With little effort he lifted her off the couch and
turned her body so that she was forced to either
stand or collapse into a heap on the floor.

"Heeey!" Claudia protested. One minute she was
asleep on the couch. The next she was standing upright, being held by two of the strongest arms she
could imagine. Then the arms were gone, and Claudia was forced to gain her balance.

"You have exactly thirty minutes to get ready and
get your butt to the kitchen table. No excuses."

Since she was already standing on her feet, it was
pointless to keep her eyes closed. Slowly, she
cracked them open. Then it came back to her that
she was on a farm in Wisconsin, not her beloved
Brooklyn. That it was only five in the morning, still
mostly dark outside. That she was expected to prepare herself for the day in thirty minutes, an impossible task. And shortly after that she would be expected to perform farm chores, a ridiculous concept.

"III waaant to go baaack to beeed," she whined.

Ross grimaced. Her accent was bad enough but
the whining was enough to wish for deafness. He
looked down at her. She was shorter today, and it
took him a minute to realize that she wasn't wearing

any shoes. What a difference three-inch heels made. Her hair was pressed against the side of her head. Her makeup was smeared beneath her eyes. Her red silk blouse was untucked and the tights she seemed to favor were still...tight. Even at her worst, she was a vixen. For a moment he felt a tug deep in the pit of his stomach.

"IIII'mmm stiiiill sleeepyyy!"

The tug was gone. "Upstairs. Take a shower. Join us in—" Ross glanced at his watch, "—twenty-five minutes."

"Again with the orders," she mumbled, but did as she was directed.

It was thirty-five minutes later, after a poor attempt at a makeover and with hair slightly less than full, that Claudia made her appearance.

Sun was now shining through the windows, bouncing off a glass pitcher that held orange juice. Claudia reached on top of her head for her sunglasses only to find that she must have left them in her room. Darn it. She didn't have the energy to make it back up the stairs.

"You call those work jeans," Ross growled. The material was sucked to her body, acting like a second skin. She wore a tight white cotton T-shirt with the words Brooklyn Academy of Beauty written across her breasts. He supposed it was more practical than silk, but it still wasn't a loose-fitting sweatshirt. It wasn't improving his mood, either.

"Whaaat? They're C.K. jeans."

"C.K.?"

"Calvin Klein," Rosa May informed her father. That was good, because cows tended to be impressed by fancy labels, Ross thought facetiously. He noted the time. "You're late."

"I'm here," Claudia warned, not prepared to deal with his mood. "I was up until two last night."

"Watching the shopping channel," Ross quipped disdainfully.

It came back to her. "That's right. There was this adorable porcelain cow pitcher. I wanted to buy it for you, but I couldn't find a phone."

"I've hidden the phone," Ross explained. "There will be no calls unless approved by me. A good thing, since the last thing I need is a porcelain cow."

Claudia bristled, but she didn't have the energy to fight back. Not this early in the morning. So she'd have to remember what he said and get him back for it later.

"Are you ready for breakfast?" Rosa May asked. "Dad made his *special* blueberry pancakes."

There was a note in the girl's voice that made Claudia smile. Obviously, Rosie thought she should feel honored by the feast. Claudia supposed that Ross didn't prepare his *special* pancakes for just everyone. She hated to disappoint the girl, and Ross, too, if he went to the trouble for her, but pancakes at five-thirty in the morning were a bit too much to stomach.

"Thanks honey, but I couldn't. A latte and some dry toast should do the trick."

"A latte?" Rosa May asked.

"A latte?" Ross wondered.

"A latte," Claudia repeated. "You know espresso, steamed milk, maybe a little vanilla syrup if you have it. But if you don't that's okay, I'm not fussy. But, I have to tell you, I've gone two days without one and I'm getting a little antsy."

"We have coffee. That's it. Plain coffee."

She'd been sentenced to hell. That's all there was to it. And the devil was a big dude, who seemed to constantly have a burr in his saddle. "Fine, if you don't have what I need here, maybe you could drive me to the nearest Starbucks." She was willing to compromise.

"Star what?"

Uh-oh. That wasn't a good sign. "Coffee, huh?"

"Coffee. Milk and sugar if you need it."

With a sigh she sat. Rosie plopped two pancakes on her plate, and Ross filled a coffee cup for her. Claudia dropped four sugars into the black froth and hoped that it would do the trick. It didn't. The coffee was horrible. The pancakes sat like lead in her stomach. Her head hurt from lack of sleep, and to top it all off she was having a bad hair day.

"Ready?" Ross asked expectantly.

Trying to keep a stiff upper lip, Claudia smiled big when she answered, "You betchya!"

"Rosa May, why don't you take Miss Bertucci outside and show her around the farm? Start with the barn. I'll be moving the girls in from the field if you need me."

Rosa May leaned over to Claudia. "That's what Dad calls the cows."

"I guessed he wasn't talking about his harem."

Rosa May giggled. "Dad doesn't have a harem. Dad doesn't even date except for Miss Harkim, but that was almost a year ago."

"That's enough," Ross growled.

"He's a little sensitive about the subject," Rosa May continued, much to Claudia's delight. "I tell him the women won't just come to the farm, that he's got to go out and find them. But look, here you are."

Ross didn't like where his daughter's thinking was headed. Claudia was a witness in hiding, not a potential date. He thought he'd made that point clear last night. He would have to talk to her again. "The barn, Rosa May. And mind what I told you last night."

"Yeah, Rosie. Better not stand too close to me, you might catch whatever it is your father thinks I've got." Claudia saw the red creep up his collar, but when she met his eyes they were hard. He refused to be embarrassed. So she refused to feel guilty for eavesdropping.

"What you've got is a big mouth and bigger ears," Ross said candidly. She wasn't supposed to have heard his words to his daughter, but he wasn't cowardly enough to lie about it. "You worry me, Miss Bertucci," he said honestly. It helped him to call her by her last name. It created a certain amount of distance in an impossibly intimate situation. After all, what was more intimate than having someone live in his home with him and his daughter? Only his beloved wife had been given that privilege. "Your attitude, your clothes, your language…these are things I don't want my daughter exposed to."

"Oh, Dad," Rosa May complained, "You're such a stuffed shirt."

That wasn't true. Was it?

"First, I've already apologized for the *H-E* double

L situation. I told you I was rattled and in my neck of the woods it's not the worst thing to pop out of a body's mouth, if you know what I mean.'' The coffee was starting to kick in. ''Second, my clothes come from the finest establishments in the greater New York area. For example, Bloomingdale's. I am a walking picture of what is fashionable, something you, in your jeans and generic chambray shirt would know nothing about.''

What in the world was chambray? Ross wondered.

''And finally, my attitude is pure New York, buddy. Something that over one million other people share. That many people with the same attitude, it can't be all bad. Have I made myself clear?''

''Crystal.'' He tried not to, but he couldn't help but smile. She was a spitfire. And maybe his daughter was right when she called him a stuffed shirt. There was a time, when Ross worked for the FBI, that he used to love traveling the country. He used to anticipate meeting people from all over, and used to enjoy the differences in their mannerisms, speech and dress. But that had been a long time ago.

Susan had convinced him that this farm was his home. His father had helped her. The two of them showed Ross that it was the farm that was truly important. And they were right. In that time he transformed himself into a true farmer. In the process maybe he had become a little intolerant of other people's ways. Ross realized that he wasn't completely thrilled with that change. But he wasn't going to back down to the spitfire. For whatever reason, there seemed to be a line drawn in the sand between them. That line meant war, and war meant no surrender.

"The barn, Rosa May," Ross instructed. He rose from the table with his own plate in hand. He placed it in the sink, spritzed some soap on it and washed it. He frowned when he spotted Claudia's plate from the previous night. "House rules, Miss Bertucci. Everyone cleans their own plate. Whoever cooks sits while the other washes the pans."

"It was a soaker," Claudia asserted.

Rosie giggled. Then under her breath she whispered to Claudia, "Five point six. Lacks originality."

"Always the critic."

"Let's wash our dishes, Claudia, then we can go to the barn together." Rosa May picked up her plate and washed it. Claudia followed suit. Then the two headed through the mudroom where Rosa May packed her tiny feet into some serious rubber boots that rode up to her thighs.

Powder-blue Vans, Claudia's idea of farm shoes, probably weren't much of a defense against whatever was out there.

"Here," Rosa May said, reaching into the mudroom closet. "These were my mom's. They should fit."

They were black, rubber, big and the ugliest foot apparel she'd ever laid eyes on. "What do I do with these?" Other than handing them off to the nearest homeless person who could really use them.

Rosa May giggled. "You wear them, silly. Over your shoes. They're kind of like oversize galoshes."

"Galoshes?" Claudia had a vague memory of

black rubber boots that her mother used to make her wear in the rain. But she gave those up when she found fashion in the fifth grade. Maybe she had one or two more colds as a result of wet feet, but nobody said beauty was painless. Lesson number two at the Brooklyn Academy of Beauty.

Bending down, she pulled on the ugly boots, and finally she was ready for the outdoors. As she followed Rosie outside, she had to adjust her gait. Hard to sway hips when one was plodding.

The barn was a massive building, painted white to match the house and the building beyond. "What's that?" Claudia wondered, pointing to the building beyond the barn.

"It's where we milk the cows. You'll see how that works a little bit later."

If the cows were in the other building, then what was in the barn? Rosa May pulled the two handles in front, and two enormous doors opened wide.

"Oh. My. God! What is *that* smell?"

Rosa May giggled. "Let me introduce you to the horses."

Taking a deep breath, her last of fresh air, Claudia followed Rosa May into the barn. It was dark inside, the only light coming from the open doors. There was a row of stalls on each side of the barn, and a ladder in the front of the barn that led to a loft that was filled almost to the ceiling with hay. To the left was a horse in one of the three stalls that lined the barn. To the right, Claudia couldn't see what was in the stalls, but she heard snorting. She decided not to investigate.

"Ohmygod. Ohmygod," Claudia chanted as she

stepped through the thin layer of hay, fearful of the unseen little creepy crawlies that might lie beneath it. Cockroaches she could handle. Back alley rats didn't scare her. Anything else sent her into fits.

"This is Shannon," Rosa May said, introducing her horse.

She never realized how big they were. They always looked so sweet on television. And the poor horses that pulled the carriages in Central Park always gave her the impression of being worn down and aged. But this animal was a fine, strong, healthy animal. She was a rich brown color with a white star along the length of her nose. Her mane was secured in tight, small braids that created a sophisticated French effect.

"Cool hair," Claudia complimented.

"I braid it," Rosa May proclaimed proudly. Then she opened the stall gate and led Shannon into the middle of the barn. "Here, I'll show you how to groom her."

The horse snorted and some stuff came flying out of her nose. With a screech, Claudia jumped back from the animal. "If you don't mind, I'll just watch."

"Don't be scared. She's sore because Devil is out in the fields."

"Devil?"

"Dad's horse."

"Appropriate," Claudia murmured.

"Horses like company. That's why I got Shannon. Because we have the room, we might actually try to board some more."

"More horses. Fabulous." Claudia stood back

and watched while Rosa May set about a series of chores that seemed as natural as breathing to her. She fed the horse, watered the horse and brushed the horse over and over again.

"Here, come try," Rosa May said, holding out the brush for Claudia to take. It was a large round brush with a handle looped over the top to fit over a hand. The large prongs appeared sharp, but Rosa May assured Claudia that Shannon loved a firm brushing.

She moved the brush in large strokes down the animal's side. Not too bad. She could definitely get into this. After all, grooming was grooming whether it be on people or animals, and nobody knew more about grooming than she did. Claudia moved in front of the horse and began to brush her chest. She bent over to stroke the front of its legs...

"Ooouch!"

She jumped up and immediately gripped her bottom.

Rosa May, who'd been mucking the stable while Claudia brushed Shannon, came running out of the stall, pitchfork in hand. "What happened?"

"She bit me. The ungrateful...never mind."

Rosa May giggled. Shannon snorted. Claudia didn't think it was funny at all.

Still rubbing her bottom in an attempt to ease the pain, Claudia backed away from the offensive horse. "I think I want to try another job."

Rosa May shrugged her shoulders and held out the pitchfork. "You can muck her stable. I'll brush her."

Cautiously, Claudia took the weapon. If it was

possible, it smelled worse than the barn. "What do I do with this?"

"All you have to do is get a block of hay, and pitch it into the stall. I already cleaned it out."

That was good because Claudia didn't think she'd be keen on cleaning up horse doo-doo. While Rosa May saw to Shannon, Claudia searched for a block of hay. There was one already set out for her at the bottom of the ladder. Giving Shannon a wide berth, Claudia made her way back to the front of the barn where the ladder was. The hay was in a large block kept together with some twine. First she tried to lift the hay. It didn't budge. Then she tried to kick the hay. It didn't budge. Then she leaned down and began to pull on the twine, hoping to drag the hay. It budged. A little.

Oh my, this is hard. Claudia lifted her hand to her brow and realized she was sweating. Actually sweating!

"I want to go home," she mumbled to no one in particular. "I don't sweat in New York. Well, only when the air-conditioning unit acts up." Then she leaned over and began to pull on the twine again. And again. And again. Inch by inch the hay slid across the floor.

Ross stood in the open doors of the barn, holding his horse, Devil, who was ready for Rosa May's tender treatment. His guest was mumbling about air-conditioning while she tried to move a block of hay. Her hair was flopping about her face. Her jeans weren't allowing her a great deal of movement, and she kept tripping over her own feet. She didn't have the strength of a flea. Yet, she hadn't given up. She was struggling, with every ounce of strength she had, to move that hay. He watched as she reached Shannon. Standing and eyeing the horse with a sideways glance, while at the same time holding her bottom, Claudia looked for all the world like a woman who'd been nipped by a horse. Ross couldn't say that he blamed the horse; he wouldn't mind taking a nip of that particular piece of her anatomy himself.

Dangerous thinking, Ross warned himself. His daughter in all her youthful innocence reminded him that it had been almost a year since his last date. It had also been almost a year since his last... encounter, to put it mildly. He was frustrated, to put it not so mildly. He'd thought about heading into Madison, visiting one of the local bars and maybe finding some company.

Something about the idea didn't appeal to him. He was getting a little too old for carousing. What he wouldn't mind was finding a nice woman he could bring home to the farm to be a wife to him and a mother to his daughter. In his mind, he envisioned a woman similar to Susan. She was the best combination of strength and softness. She was a helpmate as a well as a friend. The odds of finding someone like her were slim. Which meant he was going to have to compromise, but no compromise could have included Claudia. He didn't need a beauty, he didn't need humor. He needed help.

So no matter how much Claudia's fair face and trim curves appealed to him, she was still the last woman on earth he should get involved with. She couldn't even move a bale of hay without making it look like the most difficult task in the world.

Dropping Devil's reins, Ross moved in to lend a hand. In a smooth movement, he lifted the bale and carried it to Shannon's stall.

"Hi, Dad," Rosa May called. "You're back early."

"Have to get the girls milked. As soon as you're done here, join me in the milking barn."

Claudia watched as Ross climbed up the ladder and dropped another block of hay from the top. He journeyed down the ladder, not missing a step, hefted the hay onto his shoulder and carried it to Devil's stall.

He'd removed his long-sleeved chambray shirt. The morning sun making the extra clothing unnecessary. He was dressed in soft worn jeans, and a light-blue T-shirt that was now dark blue from sweat. There seemed to be a lot of sweating on these farms, Claudia noted. He wore a Green Bay Packers cap with the brim low over his eyes. His favorite, she imagined, as she'd seen him wear it often.

It was June. A month that usually brought with it hot temperatures and heavy humidity in New York. In Sun Prairie, Wisconsin, the sun was strong, as there were few trees to offer shade, but the temperature was fairly mild and the humidity was almost nonexistent. Good weather for nail painting. Humidity always reeked havoc on her polishes, making them sticky and making her detailed work extra tricky. She would have to experiment tonight. If only she could find a place where she could catch the light.

"You're ready," Ross told her, disturbing her creative dreaming.

His arms were at his sides, and Claudia couldn't help but note that his muscles seemed so thick that they forced his arms out to slight angles even at rest. This morning she had felt those arms wrapped around her and knew intimately of their strength. She liked the feeling. Those arms made her feel safe.

Like the house did.

Her almost-boyfriend Marco never made her feel safe. Claudia never would have expected him to make her feel that way. She was far too independent. She lost her ma young. She lost her pop at twenty-one. She was an only child, so in the last seven years she learned to take care of herself with no help from anyone.

Only now she needed help. From the FBI, from Ross. The agent that was with her in the house in Jersey didn't make her feel safe. The agent in Virginia who actually took a shot for her didn't make her feel safe. MacCurdy was too slick to make her feel safe. It wasn't until she saw this house, and she felt Ross's arms, that the tension started to ease.

"More mucking?" she asked, attempting to distract herself from her own thoughts. This house was just another temporary hideout. Nothing more. It was silly to dwell on how it made her feel.

"More mucking."

Claudia took the pitchfork in her delicate hands and moved into the stall, her head as far back on her shoulders as possible to keep her nose as far away from the smell as possible. Ross cut the twine for her, and she was able to break it up with the sharp powerful prongs of the tool she carried. Then she dug the large fork into the hay with the intent to pull some of it out of the pile. Only she dug it in so hard it got stuck, and she couldn't seem to move it. "Oops."

His eyes closed, Ross shook his head. This was going to be a long day. He moved to stand behind Claudia and wrapped his arms around her so that she was imprisoned against his hard chest. His hands were on the pitchfork interspersed between hers. "Pitch and lift," he instructed.

His muscles clenched as he followed his own directions, and Claudia caught her breath. Oh. My. God. He surrounded her. His sweat dampened the back of her shirt, but she didn't mind. His powerful male scent neutralized the smell of the barn, and that she certainly didn't mind. Every nerve in her body was alert and tense, and the only thing she did mind was that she knew there was going to be no release from the tension.

"I'm doing all the work," he growled into her ear.

Was she supposed to have a problem with that? Frankly, she was perfectly content to do this chore all day as long as he was willing to help. She turned her head and saw that his lips were only a whisper away from hers. Full, firm, she couldn't help but wonder how they might taste.

Ross was prepared to reprimand her again for her lack of effort. Then he noted that her focus was on his lips, and that knowledge sent a loud and clear message down below.

Kiss her, the message said. *Steal a taste from her cherry-glossed lips.* In response his head inched lower, almost against his control. Lower. Closer.

Claudia sighed and nestled her shoulders deeper into his embrace, unconsciously rubbing her bottom against his thighs. He was so close she could almost taste his breath.

In an instant, his arms were gone. "I think you get the idea," he said roughly. "Rosa May," Ross called to his daughter who had moved Shannon outside for more grooming room, "Come back in here and watch her. Join me in the barn when she's done."

"But, Dad, that could take forever," Rosa May told him, as she led the horse back to its stall. "No offense or anything," she said, looking at Claudia.

"None taken, sweetie." So she wasn't a quick mucker; there were worse things in life. Shaking off the blast of lust she'd felt, like a dog shaking off a bath, Claudia decided a little hard work might do her overly tense body some good. "Pitch and lift. Pitch and lift," she chanted as she attacked the hay. Only it was difficult to keep the cadence up when bits of hay dust were flying into her mouth. "Phth, phth, this stuff tastes awful."

Nonetheless, she pitched and lifted until her arms ached, and her back was on fire, and blisters had formed on her beautiful little hands. She couldn't even bring herself to check her nails. Surely they were beyond repair. And she had no doubt her hair was little more than a home for wayward hay.

"Finally," Rosa May announced. "Onto the other barn."

Finally, Claudia concurred silently. The next barn had to be easier than the first one. At least she prayed that it was. She only had a little energy left in her body and that was going to have to be reserved for bathing. "Maybe I should take a little rest before I try to tackle the next barn. You know, a power nap."

Rosie was baffled. "A nap?" she asked. "But it's still early."

Claudia checked the slim gold watch attached to her right wrist. She gasped in dismay when she saw that it was only nine o'clock in the morning. She still had eight more hours of this to go. She was never going to make it.

4

SHE WAS NEVER going to make it. Ross watched from one of the stalls as she stopped in the doorway of the barn and clutched a hand over her mouth. To prevent her from vomiting, he assumed. She simply didn't have what it takes to cut it on a farm. He wondered what she was like on her home turf. Something told him she was no doubt invincible. Returning to his work, he let Rosa May handle the instruction.

"Oh. My. God!!! It keeps getting worse!"

"This is as bad as it gets," Rosa May promised. "Well, almost. Come on inside, you'll get used to it."

Claudia doubted it, but she followed Rosa May's lead. "What do we do here again?"

"This is where we milk the cows. You can see they're all lined up in rows," Rosa May pointed to her left displaying the twenty or so cows that were already lined up in their individual cubicles. "The cows' teats are hooked to machines that do all the work. The machines milk the cows then funnel the milk into containers that Dad gives to Robbie, the delivery guy, to take to the factories where they process the milk into cheese."

Okay, so far so good. It sounded like the machines

and Robbie, the delivery guy, did most of the work here. "So what do we have to do?"

"Dad is going to move the cows in and out of the stalls, so all we have to do is take care of the stray girls."

"Stray girls?"

"Some of the cows' teats are too sore for the suction machine."

Claudia had an irrepressible urge to cover her breasts. "Can't say as I blame them." The puzzled expression on the young girl's face amused Claudia. "Give it a few years."

"I know, it will all make sense," Rosa May finished. "Anyway, those cows have to be milked by hand."

She'd seen this done in movies before, and it involved sitting real close to the cows and squeezing their things. She didn't think she'd be any good at squeezing things.

Her expression must have given her away. "You can do it," Rosa May prodded. "It's really easy. Just watch me."

The girl skipped off into a different section of the building. Claudia considered escaping out the barn doors, but New York was a long way away. Instead she followed the kid. There was an area closed off with a fence which contained an open room and several individual stalls. A small stool and large bucket hung on a post next to one of the stalls. Claudia looked on as Rosa May led one of the cows out of the stall and into the outer area. The fence prevented the cow from wandering out of the pen.

Rosa May stilled the large black-and-white animal, then brought the stool close. She placed the bucket under the cow and reached for the cow's udder. Taking a firm grip on a teat, she began to squeeze, steadily dropping the milk directly into the container.

"See," she indicated. "Easy."

It did seem easy. The cow just stood there and let loose with an occasional moo. And she would get to sit while she did it, so it was already an easier chore than mucking. "All right, I'll give it a go."

She moved into the area and closed the fence behind her. Rosa May got up and backed away while Claudia took her seat. Her nose pressed up against the side of the cow, she now understood where the bulk of the smell was emanating from. "Anybody ever tell you a bath would do wonders for that BO?"

"Mooo."

"Just a suggestion. No need to get snippy." Claudia tried to pet the animal as a way to make amends, but the cow started to shuffle away. Lifting her behind, she pulled the stool along with her as she followed the movements of the cow. Once the cow stopped so did she. Only the cow started to move as soon as she was settled. Again, Claudia got up and followed the cow. They made two rotations of the designated area until the animal finally settled down. Thank goodness for the fence or she feared she'd be chasing the darn cow around the whole barn.

Huffing from exertion, Claudia panted, "Are you done yet? I'm exhausted. And if I'm not very careful I'm going to start sweating again. Now let's get this show on the road already."

"Mooo."

"Yeah, mooo, yourself." Irritated by all the chasing, Claudia was ready to milk. Reaching under the cow she found what she was looking for. It was sort of soft, but sort of hard at the same time. It was warm and fleshy and for a minute Claudia wondered if she hadn't caught a boy cow by mistake. But then she yanked, and a steady stream of white milk shot into the bucket. "Okay, cow. Give me some milk."

"Mooo."

"I THINK she's doing good, Dad."

"Well," her father corrected. "And how can you say that? She can barely hold a pitchfork. She blanches at every smell. Thanks to Shannon's nip she's probably afraid of horses. Good thing it wasn't Devil who had her in his sights, or she wouldn't be able to sit for a week. She hasn't even met the chickens or the pigs. You know how Gretchen is with strangers."

"I'll give her my gloves before I send her for eggs," Rosa May noted. "Still, you have to admit that for a city girl she's doing okay. In a few weeks she'll be like an old farm hand. And you do need the help, Dad. Once I go back to school you're going to have to hire someone. If she stays—"

"She's not staying, Rosa May." Ross pulled off his gloves and checked the cows. They still had a few minutes to go. "She's only staying here until it is safe for her to go home. That is the end of the discussion."

The scream bounced off the walls of the barn, sending the cows into a tizzy of mooing. Both Ross and Rosa May dashed back to the milking area.

There they found an outraged Claudia splattered with bits of what suspiciously looked like cow manure. The mound on the ground beside her feet gave credence to their initial thought.

The cow had the good grace to appear guilty.

It happened all the time and certainly wasn't something to get so upset about, but obviously Claudia wasn't aware of that.

"That blasted cow..." She was so offended, so disgusted, she couldn't get the words to form in her mouth. "She—she—" Tears began to pool in her eyes. Before she could stop herself, she was sobbing.

Ross hopped the fence in a smooth motion. Admittedly, it was a lot for a city girl to handle, being pooped on by a cow. "Don't cry," he murmured, as he brushed away her tears.

But the sobbing continued, until he didn't know what to do, so he pulled her into his embrace. "Hush, it's okay."

Ross turned to his daughter. "Rosa May, take the cow out, okay?"

"Right, Dad." Rosa May did as asked, careful to keep the cow from bumping into Claudia.

"No it's nooot," she sobbed. "I was only trying to milk her."

"I know and you were doing a good job," Ross encouraged. Based on the pool of milk that had spilt onto the hay after she knocked over the bucket, he had to say she was doing a fine job.

"I've been shot at," she wailed.

Ross had a feeling these tears went deeper than cow dung. In truth, he'd forgotten how much of a strain this petite woman was under. She was, after all, still being hunted by the mob. But she'd been so tough, so resilient, that it had been easy to push her into something she clearly wasn't ready for.

Strong, Ross admitted silently. She was stronger than she appeared. Not physically, of course, but sometimes mental strength was more important.

"You've been very brave," he murmured circling his arms tighter. She was so small he could shelter two of her in his embrace and still fit a horse between them.

"There was a dead body…in the bathtub. And his thing was shriveled…. And Toinette wanted to wrap him in a towel…"

Her words made no sense to him, but he let her continue flushing the tension out of her system. "Shshsh. It's okay."

"No, it's not! I've been shot at and pooped on!"

Hard to combat that. All he could do was offer his promise. "No one's going to shoot at you here. You're safe." The pooping he wasn't too sure about. It was a farm, after all.

"I feel safe," Claudia hiccupped. "The house makes me feel safe." The house and his arms. They were wonderful arms. Suddenly she realized where she was, and what happened to her. "You shouldn't hold me."

"Why?" It felt damn good to hold a woman in his arms again, especially this woman with her pert breasts and her tiny waist. Even splattered with cow dung she made his pulse race. Although once he was done holding her, he would deny ever enjoying it.

"Because I smell," she squeaked, which launched her into another spasm of sobs.

Ross was grateful she couldn't see his insuppress-ible grin. He didn't want her to think he was laugh-ing at her. Containing his humor, he whispered, "No, you don't. Why don't you go inside and get lunch ready? That way it will be waiting for me and Rosa May. You'll find everything you need for sand-wiches. You can take a shower and get cleaned up. Would you like that?"

"Yes," she murmured against his chest. A chest that was perfect for sobbing on, she thought vaguely. Backing away from this embrace because it was starting to feel a little too good, Claudia made her way to the gate. She turned with soulful eyes and told Ross, "I'm sorry. I tried."

She did try. "I know you did. We'll be by in a little while."

THE WATER WAS HOT, the shower stall was steamy and Claudia reveled in it for about twenty minutes. It took almost every ounce of the scented soap that she had packed to rid herself of the lingering smell of cows. After about fifteen scrubs, she was reason-ably convinced that she was finally clean.

When she was done, she realized that it was close to noon. She had to assume that Ross and Rosie would be hungry, which meant she had no time for her hair. Blowing it dry, only to rid it of the water, Claudia pulled the sable mass into a ponytail high on her head. Since her only pair of jeans were cur-rently in the washing machine, and since jeans seemed to be the order of the day, she would have to improvise.

Wrapped in a towel, she left the bathroom and

found Ross's room. After rooting through his closet she found the smallest pair of jeans he owned. Must have been from his high school days. She pulled them on and then found a belt she was able to cinch tight enough so they were secure around her waist. She trod, barefoot, down to her own room to find another T-shirt. This one was an off-the-shoulder fire-engine red crop top. Checking her appearance in the mirror, she wasn't thrilled, but it would do for lunch. She was clean, and she smelled like lilacs. At this point that was all that mattered.

Ross had been correct when he told her she would find everything she needed. There was a head of lettuce, fresh tomatoes, turkey, cheese and Wonder bread. Ross and Rosa May were walking through the mudroom as she was putting the finishing touches on the sandwiches.

"Wow," Rosa May burst. "These look good!"

"My pop ran a deli in Park Slope. I do great sandwiches," Claudia beamed. She'd finally contributed, and it felt good. She was nobody's freeloader.

"So maybe I could help around the house. I can clean, and I'll have lunch and dinner ready every day for you and Rosie." If she had it her way, the house would smell like roses. Breakfast would be served at a reasonable hour. The meals would be scrumptious, and she would never have to milk a smelly ungrateful cow again.

Susan hated to cook, Ross reflected. She hated being cooped up in the house all day. So they'd always split the chores inside the house. Once again, the differences were glaringly obvious. But were they necessarily bad? The question stayed with him.

As for the answer to her question, it was simple. The help inside the house would prove to be more beneficial than anything she could do for them outside the house which was practically nothing.

"You've got a deal."

"Yeah!" Rosa May shouted. "The only thing Dad knows how to cook is fried chicken, mashed potatoes and broccoli. We have it practically every night."

And she'd gotten sick of it after two, Claudia thought. "Maybe we can shake a few things up around here."

Later, after a satisfying lunch and some freshly squeezed lemonade, Claudia said goodbye to Ross and Rosa May with a broad smile on her face. No more mucking, no more milking. For the respite, she would prepare them a feast.

First, Claudia rooted through all the cupboards. There wasn't much other than some canned vegetables, packages of frozen chicken, a pile of potatoes and three jars of brown gravy.

"Wait. Hold the phone. Stop the bus. And signal the cabbie. Pasta!" There was a box of it behind the vegetables. After a little more rooting, and a few more discoveries, Claudia was set.

Later that evening Ross eyed his plate suspiciously. "What's this?"

"Not a traditional Italian feast, that's for sure. You're going to have to take me into town for some groceries before that feat can be accomplished. This was all I had to work with."

Rosa May dipped her fork into the swirling pasta

and cream sauce. It smelled good. It looked okay. She was willing to give it a try.

Ross was still skeptical. "Where's the chicken?"

Rolling her eyes, Claudia held back a sharp retort. He had been kind enough to spare her from any more milking. The least she could do was be civil. "Eat!"

With a knife and fork in hand, Ross set about cutting up the spaghetti. That is until Claudia screeched.

"What?" he asked. She was looking at him like he had just kicked her cat.

"You don't cut pasta with a knife and fork," Claudia explained as if he were a simple child.

"That's how I eat my spaghetti."

"First," Claudia started.

Uh-oh, Ross thought. She was starting with "first." Not a good sign.

"This is not spaghetti. This is vermicelli."

"Vermin?" Rosa May wondered and put down her fork. "I don't want to eat vermin."

"Patience, Ma. Patience, Pop. I'm going to need a healthy dose of it right now," she requested from the ceiling.

Ross and Rosa May stared at her, after checking to see that her ma and pop weren't actually on the ceiling.

"Not vermin, sweetie, vermicelli. It's thin noodles. You didn't have any linguini, which is more traditional with an Alfredo sauce. Not that this is a true Alfredo sauce. You didn't have fresh Parmesan so I had to use the stuff out of the container. Second…"

He knew there was going to be a second.

"You never, ever, never, ever cut your pasta with a knife and fork." Claudia demonstrated as she continued her lesson. "You plunge your fork into the noodles, then twirl until the noodles form a tight spiral around the fork. Only then can you lift the fork to your mouth. Plunge, twirl and lift. Plunge, twirl and lift."

"Plunge," Rosa May began as she stuck her fork into the middle of her plate. "Twirl and lift," she recited as she watched the noodles do exactly what Claudia said they would do. When she plopped the forkful into her mouth it was a bit much, but it all fit.

"Hey, this is good, Claudia!"

She smiled indulgently at the child, then turned her head to watch Ross follow her instructions. "Plunge, twirl and lift."

He had the plunging part down, but twirling was harder than it looked. Every time he lifted he ended up with half of his plate of spag— vermicelli on his fork. He eyed the mass disdainfully.

"Would you like me to stand behind you and help?" Claudia offered.

He knew she was being facetious, but he couldn't stop the image of her pert breasts pressed against his back as they had been pressed against his chest earlier today. If a mirror had been in front of his face, he would have seen his nostrils flare like that of his stallion's when Shannon was close.

It wasn't the fact that she smelled like lilacs. He wasn't the type to respond to a flowery smelling woman. It wasn't even her body. Truth be told, she was a little too much on the skinny side for his tastes. It was her. It had to be. The essence of her flipped certain switches in his body. That essence, or whatever the hell he wanted to call it, had flipped his switch from the moment he saw her. And the light inside had been burning slowly and steadily ever since. He didn't understand it.

She didn't act like his wife, or laugh like his wife, or even cook like his wife. And he'd loved his wife. So his feelings for this stranger had to be the opposite. Didn't they?

Don't be such a fool, Ross chastised himself. This wasn't about feelings. This was about lust. Wasn't it?

Ross filled his mouth with the noodles covered in the tasty cream sauce. It was different than his usual fare, but he grudgingly had to accept that it was delicious. She couldn't groom. She couldn't muck. She couldn't milk.

Okay, so she could cook.

"Well?" Claudia prompted, waiting for his response. She wasn't modest. The food was excellent, and he had to know it. Since everything else she'd done today had been an abject failure, a little praise would go a long way toward restoring her ego.

"It's all right."

The jerk. His lips quirked and his eyes held a twinkle of mischief. He was teasing her, and Claudia couldn't stop the bubble of mirth that rippled through her. He was forgiven.

After the meal was over, after Rosa May's final oohs and ahhs, Claudia willingly took responsibility for the cleanup. Just one more step in her attempt to save herself from the stables.

"You haven't given up on the farm completely, have you Claudia?" Rosa May queried.

Given up. She didn't think she'd ever taken it on.

"Because you still have to meet the chickens, and the pigs, and Prowler the cat, and—"

Ross interrupted, sparing Claudia further trauma. By the expression on her face, one would have thought that Rosa May was listing various poisons to swallow.

"I think Claudia has had enough for one day. You can introduce her to the pigs tomorrow. For now you can watch some television until bed, munchkin."

"Dad," Rosa May chastised. "Not in front of company." Then she headed for the living room.

Smiling, Claudia turned back to the dishes. She filled the sink with hot water and suds, and plunged her hands into the froth.

"Ouch!"

Ross stood and moved behind her. "What's the matter?" He could see the expression of pain in her eyes. He didn't like it.

Reaching down, he pulled her hands out of the water.

"It's nothing. Just some blisters," she muttered. His strong hands were wrapped around her wet soapy ones and brushed against the sensitive skin, causing a strange melting sensation to occur in her knees.

Unaware of the havoc he was causing in his patient's legs, Ross lifted the hands for closer inspection. Large ugly white blisters marred her otherwise soft fingers. He didn't like them, either.

Befuddled by his attention, although she didn't know why, Claudia tried to tug her hands away from his grip. He was standing too close, that was it. So close she could smell his scent, the same one that had enraptured her that morning. So close she could feel the puff of his breath rustling her hair, sending tingles down her neck. The whole experience was making her unreasonably edgy.

He was just a man, she told herself. *Yeah right!* her subconscious whispered back.

"You should have stopped when your hands started hurting. I didn't mean to work you to the bone like this."

Claudia finally succeeded in gaining freedom for her hands. Only it didn't help because he was still too close for comfort. She met his eyes, those green sultry eyes, and part of her wanted to give in to the craving to melt at his feet. The other part of her refused to sacrifice her pride. So she had a slight crush on him. One that she knew would not be reciprocated. That didn't mean she had to quiver at his slightest touch.

Her voice as steady as she could make it, Claudia tried to laugh off the blisters. "It was my fault. I should have known to wear gloves. Hey, it's no big deal. I used to get blisters like these after cutting hair for eight hours straight."

Ross sincerely doubted it, but he accepted her answer. He couldn't help but be grudgingly proud of her toughness. He didn't know why, but subconsciously he was rooting for her even though he knew ultimately she would fail on this farm.

"How—how about some coffee?" she asked on a slight stutter. He was still too close, and if he didn't back off soon she'd find herself in his arms again, only this time she wouldn't waste the opportunity crying like a sissy.

"Sure," he answered. She was telling him to back off. It was in her body language. She was pressed against the kitchen counter as if it were her only escape, and belatedly, Ross realized that it had been. He'd all but pinned her against the sink.

Distance, he told himself. He needed to keep it.

Alone together in the kitchen with the sun shining its last ray of light, Ross realized he was suddenly desperate to make conversation. Something, anything that would relieve the tension that had filled the room the moment he touched her hands.

"Rosa May told me you gave up 'updos.' Not that I have any idea what that is, but I know it relates to hair. Does that mean you don't cut hair any more?"

A safe topic, Claudia decided and gave points to Ross for shifting the mood. Nine point three. A subtle move and completely unsexual in nature.

As she prepared the coffee, the plain, dull ordinary coffee, and brought it to the kitchen table where he sat, she explained, "Nope. Not anymore. Now my focus is nails, but not just your ordinary manicures, I'm talking custom-designed nails."

"The trunk," Ross remembered. "You said it was filled with supplies. There is no way that nail polish can possibly be that heavy."

Claudia laughed at his outraged expression. She

wouldn't tell him that the trunk held over two hundred different types and colors of polish and that the polish alone could be quite heavy. "Actually, it also carries my workbench, my stool, all my brushes and tools and a nail dryer."

"Isn't that a lot of stuff just to paint some nails?" Ross queried.

"Like I said, I don't just polish them," Claudia reminded him haughtily. "I create designs. See."

She held up her hands for inspection, and Ross stared at her fingertips. The nails were chipped now, but on some of them he could make out tiny perfectly drawn flowers. The detail was amazing. Like little works of art drawn onto something as small as a fingernail.

"Roses," she explained staring down at her pitiful hands. "I painted a rose on each nail, in a progression of blooming. Now they're nothing more than chips of red enamel. That's one of the downfalls. My creations don't last very long."

"Rosa May told me you have your own place."

"Yep. It's all mine. It took me five years to get it off the ground, but now it's hopping. Very trendy and very exclusive. Mostly because my designs are so unique. And of course it didn't hurt to win first prize at the National Nail Expo."

"Nail Expo?"

"It was in Florida this year. Thousands of nail artists from all over the country competed in a five-day nail extravaganza."

"A nail competition. Unbelievable."

"Not just any competition, either," Claudia informed him, "let me tell you, this thing is fierce. I barely beat out last year's reigning champion, Margaret Stone. She used special neon lights to create this fireworks effect... I won't bore you with the details.''

Please don't, Ross urged silently. He already knew more about fingernail painting than he wanted to. However, there was something contagious about her enthusiasm. He found himself interested despite the subject matter.

"Anyway, I did world-famous skyscrapers which by itself might not have put me over the top, but on my Empire State Building I did a little miniature King Kong with a little miniature lady in his hand. I hate to brag but, I must say it was impressive.''

"I bet. So now your store is a success.''

"Salon,'' Claudia corrected. "I don't like to say success because that sounds like I made it, and if you think that for one second, that's when your customers start to walk away. There can be no complacency in the nail art world. Customers can be fickle. My being away for a few weeks might be enough to send them searching for someone new, which could tank the business.''

"It must be driving you crazy to be stuck out here,'' Ross sympathized. "I know I couldn't leave the farm for any length of time without it causing irreparable harm.''

"Well, it's a little different. If you left, your cows might die or something. My cows will just find another nail artist. If you know what I mean.''

He laughed at that. "I guess you're right.''

"So how did it happen that you became a farmer?

I mean you were an FBI agent right? That's a pretty big leap.''

''Actually, not so big. I was raised on this farm. Then my father died and left it to me.''

''I'm sorry about your pop.''

''I was, too. He was a good man.''

''You could have turned it down,'' Claudia pointed out.

Ross just shook his head. ''No, I couldn't have. This farm was my father's gift to me, and it will be my gift to Rosa May. It's been here forever and will continue to be here forever. There's something special about being part of something that is so constant. Susan grew up on a farm not too far from here, and she loved the life as much as I did. I think it scared her to leave. We were married after I finished college and she followed me to Virginia when I was accepted into the FBI academy. Never complained once. When my dad died, though, we knew it was time to come home. We both knew this was the right choice for us and for Rosa May. Don't get me wrong. I did love being an agent. And every once in a while I miss the action. Then MacCurdy calls me up and asks me for a favor and the next thing I know I'm playing host to a lady on the run from the mob.''

''So I brought excitement to the farm. That's a good thing, right?''

She sure as heck brought excitement; whether or not that was a good thing remained to be seen. ''I guess,'' he replied noncommittally.

''I think it's great that you love this place,'' Claudia mused. ''So many people where I live don't really care about what they do. They're just in it for the paycheck. They never understood why I sacrificed so much to have my own place, when I could have made better money working at one of the fancier salons in Manhattan.''

"Because the salon is yours. More importantly, it is you," Ross concluded easily.

"Yes," Claudia acknowledged. She couldn't say why, but the fact that he understood that, that he understood her, this man who was supposed to be so different from her, shifted something inside her heart. For the first time since her parents died, she felt like someone understood her. That it should be Farmer Ted amazed her.

"Just like the farm is yours and you all at the same time," she whispered back in recognition of their mutual understanding.

"Yes."

Time seemed to stop as their eyes met across the table. Neither could say why the tension was suddenly so thick, but it existed like an entity between them. They weren't supposed to relate to each other. They weren't supposed to have anything in common. They were supposed to be strangers, opposites, maybe even enemies. Only they weren't.

"It's a pretty chunk of land," Claudia finally blurted out in an attempt to break the tension.

"Thanks."

"But it smells."

He exploded in laughter. And in that minute, Claudia knew that the slight shifting she had felt in her heart before was just a precursor to the sensation of feeling herself fall in love.

5

"I DO NOT love him."

Claudia stared at herself in the mirror. It had been a few days since she realized her feelings for Ross and she had decided to take action.

"I do not love him." It sounded so calm, so rational. So sane. So she said it again. "I do not *love* him. I do *not* love him. I. Do. Not. Love. Him. I won't love him today. I won't love him tomorrow. I won't love him on the moon. I won't love him on the sun. Who am I kidding? I'm so done!"

"Huh?" Rosa May asked.

She jumped three feet in the air. High enough that she could catch a glimpse of her shoes in the mirror. A good day for that to happen because it was possible that her purple heels clashed with her red shorts. "What are you doing sneaking up on me? You could have given me a heart attack. My uncle Mickey died a similar way when Aunt Estella caught him in the closet you-know-whatting."

"No," Rosa May admitted. "I don't know whatting he was doing. I never do."

"And it's a good thing, too, an innocent girl like you. Back to the original question. What were you doing sneaking up on me?"

"I wasn't sneaking. I heard you talking to yourself again and—"

"What do you mean again? I don't talk to myself."

Rosa May chuckled. "Sure you do. You do it all the time when you think Dad and I aren't around. And you sing, too. Some kind of opera stuff. No offense or anything but you're not that good. You should stick to nails."

"Always the critic," Claudia murmured, only slightly embarrassed that she'd been caught singing. She was more concerned with what she'd been caught saying. "So what did you hear? And how much is it going to cost me?"

"Honestly," Rosa May said, "all I heard was you quoting something that sounded like Dr. Seuss, but I don't think you got it right. If you want I can get you the book from the Sun Prairie Library."

"Are you sure that's all you heard?"

Rosa May considered the question for a moment. "Well, I heard all that stuff about you not being in love with my dad, but I don't get why you had to say it in the mirror. Adults can be so confusing. I've decided that in cases such as these it's best to let you guys work it out between yourselves."

She had been lifting her foot high enough into the air to get another glimpse of her shoes in the mirror to determine if the colors truly didn't match, so she missed Rosa May's admission and instead continued with her own warning. "Because if you think you heard anything else you're wrong. I wasn't saying anything in this bathroom that anyone needed to hear or to repeat. *Capisce?*" Claudia dropped her foot.

The shoes could stay. After all they were Prada. And Prada went with everything.

"Capisce," Rosie replied, happy to use her new favorite word. "I came up here to tell you that Dad says not to forget to put ointment on your chicken pecks or else they'll get infected, and that we're leaving for town in twenty minutes."

"And thank you for bringing up that painful memory," Claudia said sarcastically.

Rosa May giggled and darted out the door.

Claudia surveyed her damaged hands and cringed. Since her hands were her living, she felt that it was important to lead by example. After all, who would trust their nails to a nail artist who couldn't even take care of her own hands? No one, that's who. Lesson number three at the Brooklyn Academy of Beauty.

"It's a good thing they can't see me back in the academy today," Claudia confirmed. Naturally, she'd done her nails. She had decided on a black-and-white theme with cows and horses interspersed on each finger. She figured it would be a good way to blend in with the other locals she was going to meet today. Sort of a sign of farm solidarity.

The rest of her hands, however, were a mess and no amount of creams was going to fix them. The blisters from her adventures in mucking were healing, but they were leaving blotchy red marks. They didn't compare, however, to the chicken pecks.

"Gretchen," she whispered to an empty room in a lethal tone. If that chicken thought she had seen the last of Claudia Bertucci, she was kidding herself. Revenge ran hot in her Italian blood, and someway, somehow she would have it. Feather by feather, if that's what it took.

It happened two days ago.

All she wanted were some eggs. They weren't even for her. The Cholesterol King and his Princess ordered eggs for breakfast. "Omelettes," they'd proclaimed. "We want omelettes."

When Claudia announced that they were out of eggs, the two of them laughed.

"This is a farm," the King said. "We raise our own chickens. You do understand where eggs come from, don't you?"

She was a New Yorker, she wasn't dense. Eggs came from chickens. Then nice unknown people, to whom the world obviously owed a great debt, collected and stuffed them into clean safe cardboard containers, which miraculously made it to aisle four of her corner market back in Brooklyn. That day she, Claudia Bertucci, New York miniature nail artist extraordinaire, became one of the unknown egg collectors. Life sure took some funny turns.

She marched through Smelly Barn Number One, as she referred to it, which she could actually do without covering her nose these days, to the chicken coop located outside the back door of the barn. Sheltered in their own minibarn, several chickens were perched on stands covered with hay. The temperature was toasty, but the girls, like Claudia, were a little cranky after having been awoken at such an ungodly hour.

"I know girls," she commiserated. "No rest for the weary. If you hand over your eggs, I'll be out of here before you can cock-a-doodle-doo."

No such luck. So Claudia strolled down the row of chickens stopping in front of the fattest chicken in the coop. Her assumption was that the fattest chicken would fork over the most eggs, allowing her to end the tedious task as soon as possible. But when Claudia reached under the chicken's belly for her precious cargo, the chicken raised all kinds of chaos.

Squawking and spitting, she pecked Claudia's hands and wrists and would have pecked her eyes out if she could have reached. In the struggle, Claudia managed to wrap her hand around one precious egg and refused to let go. She would not be beaten by a chicken. She had a reputation to maintain, after all.

Her mission only barely accomplished, Claudia rescued herself from the chicken coop and sprinted back to the kitchen—no easy task in thigh-high galoshes—just in case the chicken had decided to pursue her. Once inside, she was greeted by the sound of more laughter, as the Cholesterol King and his Princess amused themselves at her expense.

"You've got chicken feathers in your hair," the Princess announced joyfully. "I guess you met Gretchen. We meant to warn you. She doesn't like strangers."

"Did you get the eggs?" the King wanted to know.

"Oh, I got the egg," Claudia informed him, huffing and puffing as she struggled for her breath. She then proceeded to crack the egg over his head, dumping the precious contents into his thick brown hair. Flicking her feather-ridden hair back over her shoulder, her chin held high, Claudia had filled the sink with ice and had plunged her hands into the frigid bath until the pain subsided.

That was the day she met Gretchen.

Two days later and her hands had somewhat recovered. So much so that Claudia decided to forgo the ointment. After all, this was her first trip into town. They were bound to run into neighbors and she didn't want to greet any of Ross's friends with white gunk all over her hands.

"There you go again," she told herself. "You're thinking about him too much." Verbally denying her feelings had become a daily ritual. She had performed it every day since the day she realized that her stomach wasn't flopping about inside her body because of nerves. And her pulse wasn't racing because of exercise. And her blood wasn't heated because of overexposure to the sun. She knew this because these physical reactions only occurred when Farmer Ted was in the vicinity.

When they'd talked in the kitchen about her salon and his land, Claudia had felt something shift deep inside. As she listened to him speak, she'd heard the strangest sounds in her head. They were words that Ross didn't say, but she heard them anyway. They spoke of his commitment to his father, his wife and his daughter. She began to understand that leaving the FBI hadn't been as easy for him as he proclaimed; it was simply that in his mind there was no real choice. This farm was his home. More than that, it was his future.

In some ways, by coming to understand his deep devotion to the land, she had come to understand the farm better herself. It no longer seemed like Mars to her. Now it was just the moon. Not that she was an unofficial cowhand yet. But she was learning. Ross was teaching her. Which was both a good thing and a bad thing. The more time she spent with him the more she knew that he was unlike anyone she had ever known before.

Oh, yeah; and he had a really great behind! It didn't hurt.

"Don't look at me like that," Claudia told the mirror. Her conscience was telling her to wipe that gooey-ooey expression off her face and to erase that lovey-dovey gaze from her eyes.

Just because she was attracted to the big brute didn't mean that he returned her feelings. It was a good bet that his only thought regarding her was wondering when she was going to be able to leave. Okay, maybe he lingered a little bit at the dinner table to have a cup of coffee with her at the end of the day, and maybe she could see him staring at her when he didn't think she was paying attention. But that wasn't love. He'd loved his late wife, and Claudia was about as different from her as they come.

And maybe it wasn't even love. Who fell in love in a few days? She'd known Marco all her life, and she'd never fallen in love with him. Claudia had always chalked up her heartless heart to stubbornness. She was too independent to make the compromises a person needed to make to be in love. Yet somehow, Ross had sneaked by the defenses she had built to keep the weak-hearted away.

Sneaked? No, more like bulldozed. He was too big to sneak.

Regardless, the whole emotion was pointless.

Most of the time he looked at her like the cows looked at her. Like she could walk around naked in front of their eyes and they wouldn't care. It wasn't a pleasant look. From either Ross or the cows.

"Claudia!" he bellowed from below.

At least he'd ceased to use her last name all the time.

"Whaaat?"

Ross never could decide if it was her accent or her unique voice in particular that caused the windows to rattle every time she shouted. He decided it had to be uniquely Claudia or else no one living in the city of New York would have any windows in their homes.

"Come on. We're going to be late." He wanted to run his errands in town, catch a quick lunch and be back before sundown so he could repair one of the back fences. But he was learning that it was best not to rush Claudia. The harder he pushed the slower she became. She denied it, of course; but it seemed intrinsic in her nature to defy him.

He rose his head when he heard the familiar *click click* of her heels on the wooden steps. White legs stretched forever until the very tips of her thighs disappeared behind outrageously tight red cotton shorts. A short black cotton shirt with a mock neck—he actually knew what a mock neck referred to now—teased him with glimpses of her belly button every time she moved. Her hair as usual was filled to capacity with hairspray, and if he wasn't mistaken, she had silver dolphins hanging from her ears.

When she finally stood before him, she was only

a few inches shorter. When he glanced at her feet he knew why. "Are you going into town dressed like that?"

"Why do you always say that like it's a bad thing?" she countered. "I planned for hours to put this outfit together." Oops, she thought. No need to share that tidbit with him. Lesson number four at the Brooklyn Academy of Beauty: beauty should appear effortless.

Which was a crock as far as Claudia was concerned. No one could ever mistake her hair as effortless.

"Don't you like my outfit?" she grilled.

Like was a difficult description. When she dressed like this, which was all the time unless she was out in the pastures, several contradicting opinions entered Ross's mind. First—oh no, now she had him doing it—he thought about how much he liked the look of her lean shapely legs and her soft white tummy. So pale, she almost seemed to glow, but rather than appear unhealthy, she accomplished luminescence. He thought about what that skin would feel like under his rough brown hands. More times than not it kept him up at night, wondering about it, obsessing about it.

During the day he caught himself brushing against her accidentally just to get a hint of her scent on his clothes and feel the brush of her body against his. At the sink washing dishes. At the table reaching for the salad bowl. At night on the couch when his weight dipped the cushions so low that she rolled into him.

Then he remembered the second thought that always came to mind when he saw her. She wasn't Susan. She wasn't close to Susan. Her loud voice, weak arms and outrageously inappropriate clothes, should have irritated him. The fact that they didn't, irritated him. As a rule he favored one type of woman, and if that type had an opposite her name was Claudia.

So why did he find himself anxious at the end of the day to see her? Why did he always stay for that extra cup of coffee after dinner? Why did he anticipate her late arrival to the kitchen each morning, hoping that she'd oversleep so he could have the fun of waking her and watching her fight the morning?

Trouble. All of it. His feelings. His sleepless nights. His lust. All because of her and there was no getting rid of her. He was stuck with her until MacCurdy nailed Rocco and Grotti. Which according to the last update from Frank wasn't going to be as soon as MacCurdy had indicated. Just his luck.

"You don't have time to change, so we might as well go," Ross told her gruffly. It wasn't much of an answer to her question, but it was all she was going to get. If he started confessing that he liked her skimpy clothes, the next thing he knew he'd be telling her how much he liked her, and how glad he was that she'd come to his corner of the world, if only for a brief time.

"Mr. Charming step back, you've got nothing on Ross Evans," she said aloud in her uniquely sarcastic way.

Ross merely grunted and led her out the front door. Rosa May was already seated in the cab of the truck.

"What's she so excited about?" Claudia wondered. "All we're doing is going grocery shopping."

"I told her we could stop at Friendly's for lunch."

"Oh. Friendly's, huh?"

"Yeah, why? You've got a problem with Friendly's?"

Claudia sighed as she sashayed her way to the pickup. Ross opened the passenger door and gave her a boost up as she was unable to lift herself into the pickup. He took the driver's seat and started the engine. "If you don't want to go to Friendly's, I'm sure we can find something else," he told her as they drove down the driveway.

Rosa May actually gasped. "Not go to Friendly's! But it's the friendliest place in the world."

Claudia grinned, then ruffled the girl's bangs. As she reached for her purse in pursuit of her hair spray bottle, she explained, "I don't have a problem with Friendly's. I just thought in a place called Sun Prairie, there'd be one Main Street with a Sun Prairie drugstore and a Sun Prairie hardware store. And a diner on the corner with a cranky old lady behind the counter, where everyone goes to get the best coffee and the best gossip in town."

"This is Wisconsin, not the Old West," Ross informed her.

Rosa May closed her eyes obediently as Claudia spritzed her hair and teased her bangs.

"Friendly's is the best place in town for gossip. You'll see," Rosa May promised.

Ross was right. Sun Prairie wasn't the Old West. It was the New West she supposed. Shopping malls instead of Main Street. Fast food restaurants instead of diners. A popular hardware store chain. A popular drugstore chain. There was a Main Street, but it was busy with Saturday afternoon traffic. Not exactly what she pictured.

"Look, Claudia there's my new school! I'm going to junior high next year. Boy, Dad, you sure will be lonely on the farm when I go back to school. You know in a few years I'll be going to high school, then off to college. You'll really be lonely then."

"Enough, Rosa May," Ross growled seeing through his daughter's act. "I managed just fine when you were at school last year, and the year before that, and the year before that. Somehow I'll muddle through this year as well. As for college, I think I have a few years before I have to start worrying about that."

"I just think maybe it's about time you considered settling down. You know you can't be a bachelor forever. Maybe you should think about dating Miss Harkim, again," Rosa May suggested.

Reverse psychology. Eight point nine, Claudia mused. "Ah, the infamous Miss Harkim. I have to say I'm slightly curious about this woman. What made you stop calling her, anyway?"

"She was too much of a city girl. Milwaukee," he said pithily.

"Milwaukee is actually considered a city?" Claudia asked with a smirk, his hidden meaning not so hidden.

"Here we are," he announced as they pulled into the supermarket parking lot. And in the nick of time, he added silently. The crew piled out of the truck and sought out an appropriate shopping cart.

Not surprising, Claudia made as much of a production of choosing the right shopping cart as she
did of actually shopping. One cart was too tight, the
other too loose. One's wheels wobbled, and one she
found offensively dirty. After ten minutes they finally found perfection. Rosa May pushed, while
Claudia selected items off her shopping list, half of
which Ross couldn't even identify.

After a period of time he gave up trying. "Here
take the checkbook. I've signed a blank check for
you. Don't go overboard," he warned. "I'm heading
to the hardware store. I'll meet you back at the
truck."

"Have fun."

"I'm just going to look at a few tools. It's not
what I would consider fun."

"Oh, please. A man, a farmer no less, in a hardware store. The testosterone levels in those places
are enough to get you high."

Shaking his head, he walked off. If nothing else
a visit to the hardware store would restore his sanity.
A man could go crazy being around a woman like
Claudia for too long. And it had definitely been too
long.

A little less than an hour later, Ross finally spotted
Claudia and Rosa May departing the grocery store.
He'd been waiting by the pickup for what felt like
forever. "What were you two doing in there, growing the food yourselves?"

"Ha, ha," Claudia said sarcastically. "No, but I
was trying to find the ingredients for my special
gravy. Not an easy task in your neighborhood mar-

ket. Back in Brooklyn this wouldn't have been a problem.''

"Back in Brooklyn, the last thing you'd be worrying about is gravy," he returned, reminding her why she was here in the first place.

"Very true."

"Now can we go to Friendly's?" The girl was on the verge of becoming a teenager, but in many ways was still just a kid at heart who lived for ice cream. Ross began to think that maybe Rosa May wasn't influenced by their mature visitor.

Then he saw what could only be considered a pout. Fat bottom lip and all. So much for not being influenced by their visitor. "Yes, now we can go to Friendly's."

The pout instantly vanished and was replaced by a gorgeous smile. That was the one good thing about pouting, Ross reflected—it was so much fun to make it go away.

The threesome strolled across the busy street to the restaurant on the corner. They walked in and immediately Ross felt all eyes upon them. No, that wasn't true. All eyes were on Claudia.

"Dad, how come everyone is staring at Claudia?"

"It's because she's new in town, honey. You know how folks around here are with strangers." What he didn't say was that folks around this neighborhood were sometimes intolerant of strangers. Surely, Claudia's hair and her chic, tight-fitting clothes would spark the gossipmongers' attention.

"Why are they staring at me?" Claudia whispered.

Ross moved closer to her as a clear message to

the town that she was with him. He didn't like the
women's disapproving glances or the men's out-and-
out drooling. "Don't worry about it," he told her
under his breath so that only she could hear. "They
don't know what to make of you, that's all."

"I know what to make of them," Claudia whispered back.

He had been hoping to shield her from their un-
pleasantness, but clearly she understood what was
going on.

"It's obvious they're jealous."

Okay, maybe she didn't understand what was going on. Jealous? How did she figure that? "How do
you figure that?" Ross asked incredulously.

"Well, look at them. I've never seen a more pa-
thetically dressed group of people in my life! That
woman over there actually has rollers in her hair. I
haven't seen a painted nail yet. And their clothes
look like something that came out of the *Farmer's
Almanac* mail-order catalog. Ten years ago. Good
grief have these people never heard of fashion!"

"Can I help you?" a young girl asked.

Claudia took in the Friendly's uniform and grudgingly admitted that she couldn't blame this girl for
her lack of taste. After all, it was a uniform. But the
mousy brown hair had to go. "Tell me something
honey, have you ever considered blond highlights?"

"Uh, no. Did you need a seat for three?"

"You've got a lot of natural highlights that just
need a boost," Claudia continued, unperturbed by
the girl's expression of shock. She was on a mission
of mercy and wouldn't be deterred. "A little diluted
peroxide with some lemon and you'd be a babe."

"Would you like smoking or nonsmoking?" the girl asked. "A babe?"

"A babe," Claudia reiterated. "Listen, I don't really do this sort of thing anymore, I specialize in nails now." As proof, she flashed her bovine and equine themed nails. "But for you, I'm willing to make an exception. Before I leave, I'll write down some instructions for you. I want you to follow them to the letter. What's your name, honey?"

The girl thrust out her right breast with name tag attached. "Shelby."

"Shelby, you give us the best table the house has to offer and I'll throw in tips on how to condition your hair with mayonnaise."

"Okay," she said happily. Then she showed the mock family to a large booth.

A booth that happened to be situated directly across from a table where the two worst gossips with the two most disapproving frowns sat. "Hello, Ms. Pritchet. Mrs. Harkim. How are you today?"

"Just fine Ross, and yourself?" the older Mrs. Harkim asked in an insincerely sweet voice.

"Wonderful," he lied boldly.

"Are you going to introduce us to your new friend?" Ms. Pritchet, the sixth-grade schoolteacher, asked politely but with a thread of steel running through the request, which made it sound more like an order.

"Howdy," Claudia responded, as she waved her hand to the old broads. "I'm just an old friend from…the Bureau. Special Agent and stuff. I'm only visiting. No hanky-panky or anything." She was trying to help, but the resigned look of desperation on

Ross's face told her she wasn't doing such a terrific job. So much for defusing the gossip. "So who does your hair? You've got some nice silver highlights," she complimented the older woman.

Mrs. Harkim huffed and grabbed at her head. "I don't know what you're talking about. My hair color is completely natural."

Claudia laughed boldly. "You go, girl. You stick to that story!"

The two huffed and turned their faces away from Claudia. Ross ran his hands down his face. He couldn't help but ask, "Do you always approach strangers and comment on their highlights?"

"Only the ones that have highlights," Claudia answered cheekily.

"Here comes our waitress. Maybe you could leave her alone," Ross suggested.

"Maybe."

But when Claudia saw the state of that poor woman's hands she almost swooned. Before their meal was over Claudia had explained to the woman in detail about the merits of soaking her hands in aloe every night. When the nails were soft, that was the best time to cut and shape them. The woman, skeptical at first, couldn't help but be drawn in by Claudia's openness and sincerity.

By the time they left, Claudia had done her part in the war against the fashionless and the beauty deprived, and Rosa May got to pick out a free half gallon of Friendly's ice cream on the behalf of the grateful staff.

"You are outrageous, you know that," Ross commented as they walked back to the pickup.

"Whaaat? All I did was offer a little advice. And did you see the way those two old broads came around when I mentioned my cure for those little tiny wrinkles over the mouth? They know a good thing when they hear it. Even Mrs. Harkim, who had to hate me on principle."

He hoped she hadn't noted the one woman's last name. He'd stirred enough gossip by bringing Claudia to town and was going to take enough heat from his friends and neighbors because of it. He didn't need to take heat from her at home as well. He and Hannah had been nothing more than friends. Despite what Mrs. Harkim and Claudia believed.

Still, it hadn't been as bad as he thought. For a town notorious for its wariness of strangers, the group at Friendly's had taken to Claudia relatively quickly. In the course of a lunch and just because of a few beauty tips, Claudia had gone from town hussy to town beauty consultant.

"Did you know that there is only one beauty salon in Sun Prairie? And it's one of those chains. No wonder these people are a mess. You can't really give your clients quality time when you are trying to deal in volume."

"How horrible," Ross mocked.

"Laugh all you want, but if someone opened a real salon here they could make a fortune."

"Sometimes I forget that you're a business-woman."

"Actually, I like to consider myself an artist first, a businesswoman second. But no one ever said that you couldn't mix beauty and business."

"Hey, Dad look at this," Rosa May screeched.

She reached the pickup first and pulled a flyer out from underneath the windshield wiper. "They're having a real old-fashioned barn dance at the high school next Saturday night. Everyone's supposed to dress up like cowboys and cowgirls. And it's for adults only. That's you and Claudia!"

Ross all but ripped the flyer out of his daughter's hands. He didn't want to be rude, but the last thing he intended to do was attend a dance at the school. A dance where he would be expected to invite Claudia. A dance where he would be expected to hold Claudia.

"A dance, huh?" Claudia asked over the hood of the truck, her on one side, Ross on the other, Rosa May already in the cab.

"I'm not much of a dancer," he said. "I wouldn't be any fun at a dance."

"Yeah, you're probably right. I mean if you were to ask me to a dance, what would people think? Besides, you'd probably spend the whole night crushing my toes and tripping over your own two feet. That wouldn't be much fun. Not fun at all."

Irritated, because he knew she was deliberately trying to draw him in, but he couldn't seem to stop himself, he said, "I didn't say I couldn't dance. I said I wasn't much of a dancer. There's a big difference. Besides, what would a city girl like you know about a barn dance? I doubt you know how to two-step."

"Of course I do! I've seen *Urban Cowboy*. John Travolta. Debra Winger. It's one of my favorites."

There was no way out. He might as well face the inevitable and get it over with. He only wished he wasn't as excited by the proposition of holding her in his arms all night as he was.

"Claudia?"

"Yes, Ross?"

"Would you like to attend the barn dance with me next Saturday?"

"I don't know. I'll have to check my schedule." With that Claudia hoisted herself into the pickup with a little help from Rosa May pulling on her arms. "Let this be a lesson to you kid, never say yes to a man the first time he asks you on a date. It smacks of desperation."

6

"NO. NAH. NOPE. No way. Uh-uh."

"This is harder than it looks," Rosa May muttered under her breath. They'd been searching through Claudia's clothes for hours in a vain effort to find the perfect outfit for the dance that night. So far no luck.

"What can I say? I did not come prepared for a barn dance. Every other contingency I was ready for. Elegant dinners, informal parties, but somehow barn dances eluded me." They were shoved in the bathroom together, desperately trying to gauge the appropriateness of each outfit in the tiny mirror. Claudia pressed dress after dress up against her body. Strapless, spaghetti straps, scoop necks. Nothing seemed quite right. Nothing said cowgirl.

"Hey, I know!" Rosa May chirped. "You could wear one of my mom's old outfits. She had lots of stuff you could use. We still have everything in boxes in her closet."

Claudia hesitated. She wasn't so sure about wearing Susan's clothes. Susan. She'd come to think of her as a real person even though she'd never met the woman, and was never going to meet her. She still seemed to occupy such a large part of the farm and the house, and Ross's heart. But that wasn't necessarily a bad thing.

At night, wrapped up tight in the afghan Susan's mother had knitted, she sometimes felt the woman's presence. It was a comforting feeling. She imagined that Susan could see her doing Rosie's nails, or fighting with Ross over the remote control, or struggling to move a cow into the barn. She wondered if she understood that despite the fact that she was only on this farm to hide out temporarily, she yearned to feel included. Even a little needed.

Yes, Claudia was certain that if Susan were alive they would probably get along despite their differences. After all they both cared for Ross, didn't they? Which made the thought of borrowing her clothes a little weird. It was one thing to make the moves on a dead woman's husband, it was another thing all together to do it in her clothes.

But Rosa May was insistent. "Come on," she urged, pulling Claudia out of the bathroom and dragging her to Ross's room.

Unaware of her older friend's reluctance, Rosa May started extracting skirts and blouses from boxes. She dug deep into the box and pulled out a pair of red cowboy boots. "See. These are perfect."

Wary, Claudia stammered, "I—I don't know. I don't think your pop would appreciate me going through your ma's things. Clothes are very personal."

"Not to her they weren't."

"Ross!" Claudia turned at the sound of his voice and found him in the doorway of his bedroom. His white T-shirt was plastered against his thick chest,

damp from hard work. At the V, she could see tufts
of hair escaping the cloth. The thought of running
her hands through those tufts made her mouth go
dry. No man had ever made her mouth go dry.

He stared at her from his position and saw her
eyes cloud over with desire. Instantly, his body responded to the knowledge that she wanted him and
couldn't seem to hide that fact. Then he saw the
boots she held in her hands and tried to remind himself why he shouldn't want anything to do with her.
It was getting harder and harder to do just that.
Maybe if she was dressed head to toe in Susan's
clothes it would show just how unlike Susan she was
and would make it easier.

"You can wear them. She wasn't the clotheshorse
you are. To her clothes were just things she had to
wear so that she could walk about the farm without
shocking the animals. But she did have some nice
things. She wouldn't have minded someone borrowing them."

*Even if that someone was me? A woman who was
hot for her husband?* Claudia didn't ask the question, she merely gathered up the clothes. "They're
pretty."

Again Ross nodded. He tried to imagine how she
might look in his wife's clothes, but the image
wouldn't come. No doubt that she would wear them
in such a way as to abolish any likeness she might
have to his late wife. Maybe she'd choose the short
skirts Susan avoided. Susan hated to show her knees.
She said they were bumpy. He smiled at the memory.

Then he saw Claudia watching him intently. She

was worried about his reaction. He could tell by the way she stood so stiffly and the way her hands clenched and unclenched around the boots.

"I'm sure I can find something of my own. I didn't really look that hard."

"We looked for hours and hours," Rosa May groaned. "And I'm sure Mom wouldn't have minded."

Claudia turned from father to daughter and back to father. "If you're sure."

"I am. Are you?"

She sensed that the question went a little deeper, but she was too rattled to analyze it. "No," she answered adamantly. "But that never stopped me before. I've got to go and get dressed or we're going to be late."

"The dance starts in less than an hour. We're definitely going to be late," Ross said. He knew it was going to take longer than that to get her hair "just so." And Claudia's hair had to be "just so" before she would stick her big toe out the door.

"I meant more than fashionably late, dummy. Heavens, I would never consider arriving to a dance on time. The embarrassment."

"And the shame, I know. Go get ready."

It took less than thirty minutes for Ross to shower, shave and dress for the dance. He wore his cleanest jeans, a white-collared shirt with a slim black tie, and cowboy boots of course. He even agreed to wear the cowboy hat that his daughter had given him the year before on his birthday. He felt a little silly in it, but Rosa May said he looked better than Garth Brooks. When he caught his expression in the small mirror above the sink, he grunted. It was the best he was ever going to look.

Then the waiting began. He didn't anticipate that Claudia would be ready in anything less than an hour. It gave him time for a relaxing beer and for some small talk with Betty, the girl he hired to watch Rosa May for the night. "I don't think we'll be late," he told the girl.

"Whenever. I've spent more than one night on a stranger's couch."

She was sixteen. Ross wasn't too sure how to interpret that statement. In the end, because he wasn't going to be getting anyone else at this late hour, he decided to accept it at face value.

"So, Mr. Evans do you know what Claudia's schedule is like for next Monday?" Betty asked him.

"Her schedule?" Ross repeated having no idea what the girl was referring to.

"Um, she's pretty booked," Rosa May interjected. She shook her head quickly in the direction of the baby-sitter.

"Booked with what?" Ross wanted to know as well why his daughter was making subtle slashing motions against her neck.

"You know, Dad. Cooking and cleaning and the chores and stuff. Claudia does a lot in a day. And now that she's not afraid of the horses anymore, she's grooming Shannon and Devil."

That was fine, but why did Betty care about all of that and what did that have to do with next Monday? It was pointless to pursue it with his daughter. He would just wait for Claudia to come down for an explanation. He began to watch the clock. After an hour and a half, he began to pace. Finally, unable to wait any longer he opened his mouth to bellow for Claudia.

He closed his mouth abruptly. She was already at the bottom of the steps. Before he could contain his reaction his jaw dropped.

"Whaaat?"

It was amazing. A transformation. Her hair was pulled into a loose ponytail, with wisps of tendrils that framed her soft face. She wore only a hint of lip gloss, and for the first time he realized the natural color of her lips was a muted mauve. Without the benefit of eyeliner and eye shadow her eyes were soft. Only the deep blue color in her irises drew his attention. She wore a blue chambray shirt, his, he suspected, that she had tied off at the waist in the shape of a bow. Below the shirt she wore a matching jean skirt that flowed about the ankles. Ankles that were covered by shiny red boots. She was, for all intents and purposes, a cowgirl.

"You seem different," he told her.

"I wanted to fit in," she explained.

And she would. She would indeed resemble a number of other women there, and strangely the idea bothered him. "Come on. We're late."

"We're always late."

"No, you're always late."

Claudia rolled her eyes as a retort. They were too late for an argument.

"Goodbye, kids," Rosa May chimed from her position on the couch, waving to the couple as they departed. "Hold the door for her, Dad. And make sure her punch glass is always filled. Dance with her

for the first dance of the night. Don't worry about
coming home late. Stay out as late as you want.''

''Thanks,'' Ross stated, shaking his head at his
daughter's obvious attempt at matchmaking. He was
really going to have to talk to her.

As he escorted Claudia out of the house, he could
have sworn he heard his daughter tell Betty that he
and Claudia made a great couple. Couple! What
nonsense.

THE THEME WAS definitely country. The school gym
was decorated with lofts of hay and the tables were
covered with red gingham tablecloths. Fake stars
glittered from the ceiling. For a moment Ross felt as
if he was back at his senior prom. He'd taken Susan,
of course. They'd dated from the very beginning of
time it seemed. She'd worn pink chiffon and his cor-
sage, and when he'd danced with her that night, he'd
known she was his future.

This night was going to be vastly different. He
certainly couldn't dance with Claudia and see the
future. He'd never been able to see beyond the next
day as far as she was concerned.

''Would you like some punch?'' So far he'd
opened all the doors for her, so punch was his next
task of the night.

''Okay. Make sure it's laced with something,
though.'' She was going to need it. For some bizarre
reason she felt like a schoolgirl at her first dance
with a boy. She'd purposefully dressed to mesh, just
for him, but he didn't seem to appreciate her efforts.
She probably reminded him too much of his wife.

He was probably regretting that he brought her. But she couldn't regret that she had come.

Her unreasonable feelings for him led her to this point, prodding him to take her to this dance. She should be mortified. He was probably counting the minutes until they could leave, until they could call a halt to this sham of a date. Why had he let her pressure him into this? Because he was a sweet man, with a kind spirit. Or because he was a sadistic bastard who enjoyed yanking her emotions about on a string he controlled. Either way she felt like an idiot.

He returned with the punch, but rather than hand her a glass, he set both glasses on the table beside them. The music was playing. "Our first song. This is a dance," he said in explanation. "Shall we?"

"I don't know if this is such a good idea. Maybe we should just call it quits right now."

"Afraid you're going to step on my toes?" He smirked, and she couldn't stop her lips from twitching in return.

"Just remember you asked for it."

She was warning him, but he didn't foresee danger. The bottom line, however, was that despite all his reservations about this night, he had looked forward to one thing: holding her in his arms. Over the weeks she'd lived on the farm, he'd touched her. Sometimes accidentally. Sometimes not so accidentally. Sometimes out of necessity in regard to work. Sometimes out of necessity in regard to lust. But tonight, he was going to hold her.

Quickly, he moved her into the midst of the crowd. Couples pushed back and forth to the music. Some rhythmically. Some not so rhythmically. For the first few minutes they vied for position amongst dancers who were invading their space. Then a small spot opened up for them.

Awkwardly at first, they tried to fit their arms together. Hers up, his down. Then his up and hers down. Finally, Ross took matters into his own hands, literally. He secured Claudia about the waist. Then he linked his right hand with her left hand. She had no other place for her right hand to go but around his waist.

They were holding each other. When Ross started to move to the music they were dancing. Intellectually, Claudia knew these things. It helped to calm her down. This was a dance. They were in a gym with tacky glow-in-the-dark stars over their heads, watered-down punch and people dressed in what she prayed were costumes.

She was not in another universe. Or in another dimension. Or on another spiritual plane. It might have felt like a place where the world stopped spinning and the starlight burst through cement and brick to rain down on her. But it wasn't. It was a gym in Wisconsin. Certainly not a place to be so ridiculously happy. Or so excited at the same time. They were only dancing after all.

He wasn't wrong about his skill. He was a fair dancer. His brute strength allowed him the luxury to lead effortlessly. All she had to do was hang on, and he could carry her across the dance floor if need be. Claudia barely managed to keep up with him without having her feet actually leave the ground.

"You do know the two-step," he said in mild surprise.

"And the Tush Push and the Electric Slide," she added, beaming up at him with pride.

Ross didn't know what she smiling about. He hadn't heard anything beyond "tush." It was only inches away from his hand. Waiting for him like a ripe melon. Actually, two ripe melons that he wanted to squeeze and test for resiliency. The temptation was killing him. It took all his considerable will-power to keep his hands above the belt.

And her tush wasn't the only temptation. As talented as she was at the dance, there was no need for her to study her own two feet. So instead she studied him. Their eyes linked almost as solidly as their hands did. He could see so much in her naked eyes. Uncertainty. Anticipation. Desire.

True, he didn't know if he saw it simply because he wished to see it, but in his mind it was there. It pulled at him and lured him in against his better judgment. A woman's desire was a siren's song. Compelling. Powerful. Irresistible.

The music changed, one song into the next, and the tempo slowed considerably. The quick steps were gone, replaced by slow shuffles. As couples pressed closer together, the area around Ross and Claudia seemed to clear. They were alone in a circle, unbothered by the rest of the town.

Ross raised his hand from her waist to touch the curled tendrils that framed her face. He wanted to say something witty, something sarcastic that might take the edge off the sudden tension he was feeling. But when he opened his mouth, all that came out was, "Pretty. So pretty."

Her heart pounded against her rib cage. It was a

simple compliment, but it moved her like no other had. He thought she was pretty. Without her hairspray. Without her makeup. Without her trendy clothes. Not that this sudden revelation was going to have her tossing away her makeup kit. Heck, no! After all, fashion was fashion.

The point was that Ross looked at her as though she was beautiful all the time. In the mornings when she pranced around the kitchen whipping up breakfast, when his resistance was low due to early-morning fatigue and he couldn't seem to keep his eyes off her, or when she had his jeans rolled up as far as they could go, topped with a skimpy T-shirt when she was working in the barn. He found her pretty in her clothes, his clothes and in cowgirl clothes. He found her pretty. Not her face. Not her body. But her soul.

She wanted to kiss him. Not in gratitude, but in love. She wanted to run her hands through his hair, caress his rough jaw and gently stroke the soft skin over his full bottom lip. She wanted to wrap her hands around his massive body and hold on until she couldn't hold on anymore.

Vividly, she remembered the day in the cow barn when he held her against his chest and rocked her until her sobs subsided. She'd wanted to kiss him then too, but he'd been a stranger. A farmer. Now, he was Ross. Her friend. Her...

Claudia pressed her hand against the hand that cupped her cheek. She could feel his calluses on her petal-soft skin and it forced a shiver down her spine. Inside her body she felt liquefied.

''Claudia,'' he whispered gruffly.

"Ross," she sighed.

"Well, hello there, Ross," Mrs. Harkim interrupted. "Look who I brought with me for you to dance the next dance with."

Reluctantly, the couple separated. Ross gritted his teeth, but did the polite thing. "Hello, Hannah. How are you?"

"Good, Ross." Her face was beet red, and he knew that she suffering from the scene. Her mother had a way of humiliating her daughter all in the name of finding a husband. "We haven't met," she said as she turned to Claudia. "I'm—"

"Miss Harkim," Claudia finished for her. "I'm Claudia. An old friend." She stared at the woman who Ross had once dated, and who Rosa May had said wasn't his type. Rosa May was wrong. She was exactly his type. Strong, sturdy, with white-blond hair that spoke of a Nordic heritage. She was built to live and toil on a farm. No doubt if Susan had to approve her replacement it would be this woman. For the first time in a very long time Claudia felt woefully inadequate.

If she were the weepy type, or if she hadn't already met her crying quotient for the year, she would have broken down right there on the gym floor. But of course she couldn't. What she could do was step back and realize what a fool she'd been making of herself by pining after Ross. He wasn't for her. This woman was.

Doing the noble deed, Claudia announced, "Ross why don't you dance with Hannah? I'm going to snag some more punch."

She took a few steps backward before his hand

caught her about the soft flesh of her upper arm. His hand was so big it practically wrapped around her whole arm. With no muscle to speak of, she could hardly break away. "We were dancing. We'll finish it," he ordered. "Hannah, I...uh..."

"You don't have to explain Ross," she smiled sweetly.

Ross nodded in gratitude. They shared a smile and Ross instantly understood that Hannah was no more interested in him than he was in her. Perhaps for the same reason. They were almost too similar, and they shared absolutely no chemistry.

Hannah turned to leave, but paused. Glancing down at her nails, then back up at Claudia she asked, "I know this may sound presumptuous, but I saw the flower scene you did for Dorothy on her nails. Do you think?"

Claudia was at a loss. On the one hand, she hated this woman for being everything she wasn't. On the other hand, Claudia could begrudge no woman decent nails. "I'm pretty booked Monday, but I should be able to squeeze a half hour in after one."

"Thanks," she offered and quickly parted.

Alone, although they were still surrounded by couples, Claudia turned on Ross. "Why didn't you dance with her?" she grilled. "She was crushed." Maybe not crushed, but surely the girl had to be disappointed. The closest thing she'd ever felt to heaven was the strength and security of Ross's arms.

"Booked. You're booked on Monday. That's what Betty meant. Are you turning my house into a nail salon?" Ross had visions of lines of women stretching down his driveway, anxiously awaiting a smidgen of advice from the Beauty Guru.

"Can we stick to one topic here?" Claudia stomped her red cowboy boot in a huff. "That girl was perfect for you. You should have danced with her. Rosie's right you know, we're not going to be around forever. What are you going to do when we leave?"

Claudia leaving. He didn't like it. "I'll tell you what I'm not going to do. I'm not going to be keeping your Monday morning appointments!"

"Oh! You are impossible. I'm talking about your future, and your talking about ten or fifteen women with perfect nails."

"Fifteen!" Ross shouted. "Are you forgetting why you are here in the first place? You're supposed to be in hiding, not starting up your own business."

"I can't help it. These women need me. And I highly doubt any of the women from Sun Prairie are really New York hit men in disguise. But I don't want to talk about that now. We were talking about you and your future and Hannah."

"I don't want to talk about my future. Or Hannah. Besides what right do you have to plan my future? You're nothing but a guest. That's it. Here today and gone tomorrow. Right?"

If he'd slapped her across the mouth it wouldn't have hurt any worse. With a sudden surge of muscle, Claudia managed to pry her arm free. She left the dance floor in steady strides, careful not to bump into people, careful not to make a scene. She didn't need to add fuel to old lady Harkim's fire. A fire that she instinctively knew was a blaze by now.

A guest. Nothing more. She didn't know why it should hurt so much when, intellectually, she knew that he was right. She was a temporary guest. Any day MacCurdy could call and tell her that it was safe to return to her beloved New York. Her city. Her people. Her salon. It's where she'd been born and raised. Where she went to school. Where she'd met her first boyfriend, and her last, both being Marco. In New York she fit in. In New York she knew the places to go, the people to see and the smells to avoid.

The mere thought of her home should have comforted her. The thought of returning to it should have thrilled her. But there were two things that New York didn't have that Sun Prairie, Wisconsin did: Ross and Rosie.

It wasn't fair that they both had come to mean so much to her in such a short time. It wasn't fair that even if she could bear the thought of never returning to the city again, Ross wouldn't want her. Here today. Gone tomorrow. More than likely he'd be glad of it.

Of course there would be no one to add a spoonful of salsa to his scrambled eggs to give them a little kick. No one to turn his traditional chicken dishes into Italian feasts. No one to make sure his pillows were plumped, his shirts were ironed and his books were dusted. No one to tell him that he was being unreasonable when it came to Rosa May and lip gloss. No one to directly disobey his orders.

Helpful Hannah wouldn't do that. She'd go along meekly with every order he issued. Every proclamation he proclaimed. Every command he uttered.

It would certainly make for a boring marriage. Claudia was mad enough at him to hope that he did marry the girl, and that one day he would come to realize how colorless his life was without her in it.

By the time she'd finished cursing him to a life with Hannah, Claudia realized that she was outside the school. Despite the summer month, tonight the air held a chill. She wrapped her arms around herself and went in search of the pickup. She didn't know what she was going to do when she got there, but it seemed like a plan.

"Hey there, cowgirl."

Claudia started at the low voice. Her first thought was that Ross had followed her. Her second thought, after she turned around, was that she was in trouble.

He was a big dude, with a big belly, and a ten-gallon hat. He stood ten feet away from her, but she could smell his alcohol-laced breath from where she stood. His belly was rolling over the top of his jeans, his thumbs were tucked into his pockets, and he oozed arrogance.

"Look buddy, you don't want to mess with me tonight," she warned.

"Now is that any way to talk to a cowboy, cowgirl?" The cowboy moved in with a swagger. "I saw you in the gym and thought maybe you and me could two-step."

"You thought wrong." Claudia backed up a few paces but the cowboy persisted.

"Come on sweetheart, you and me would be a great couple. Let me show you." The drunk shuffled forward with his hands raised in an attempt to grab hold of her.

Claudia shook her head. "You asked for it." She was a woman who'd been born and raised on the streets of New York. She'd dealt with muggers, drunks and Marco when he'd gotten out of hand. She could take the big guy.

The cowboy reached for her, leaving his body completely open for attack. Claudia slammed a well-placed knee into the man's groin. When he buckled over with pain, she took advantage of his vulnerable position. She managed to grab hold of a thumb and twisted it so that the cowboy's arm was around his back, his thumb at a backward angle to his body.

"Say uncle," she commanded.

"Let go of my arm," the man moaned.

Feeling slightly vicious after the night she just suffered, Claudia smiled evilly and repeated her order. "Say uncle."

There was a pause, then a whimper.

Claudia tightened her hold. "Uncle," she taunted.

"Uncle," the man murmured. As soon as the word escaped his mouth he was released. Claudia wasn't one to renege on a promise.

"Now get the hell out of here before I really get mad."

The man scuffled to his feet and took off as fast as he could. Claudia watched his big butt as he rambled away. That's when she heard the clapping. She turned to find Ross leaning against the pickup she'd gone in search of. His legs were crossed at the ankles and he wore a large grin. Enthusiastically, he applauded her performance.

She amazed him. "For a woman who still can't

move a bale of hay, you sure handled him easily enough.''

''It's all in the moves,'' she explained.

''Remind me never to tick you off,'' he teased.

''You already ticked me off.''

''Again,'' Ross corrected himself.

Determined not to forgive him, she marched forward, waited until he unlocked the doors, then tried to hoist herself up into the cab. Her anger gave her the strength to lift herself into the truck without his help. When he situated himself in the driver's seat he asked, ''I'm surprised you didn't take the truck and leave.''

''Don't think I wouldn't have. If only...''

''If only what?''

''If only I had the key and...I knew how to drive,'' she admitted grudgingly. Now was not the best time to admit her weaknesses. Not when she needed to be strong.

''You don't know how to drive?'' he asked, astonished. ''No wonder you're making the women of Sun Prairie come to the house. We're going to have to change that.''

''What do you mean 'we?' I have no need to learn how to drive. In a few days I'll be back in New York. I don't need a license there. And that is what you're waiting for isn't it? For me to go back to New York so you can run off with Helpful Hannah.''

''Hey, you were the one who told me to dance with her. You said I needed someone to keep me company after you leave.''

''And you just listened to every word I said, didn't you?'' Claudia accused irrationally. ''Fine.

Marry her and move on with your life. Just leave me alone.''

"Maybe I don't want to leave you alone," he growled. That said he slid along the bench seat of the truck and pinned her against the passenger door.

Claudia was so surprised by the move, she barely caught her breath before he was swooping down to capture her mouth with his own. So surprised that she couldn't think, couldn't act, couldn't shout. What she could do was kiss him back. So that was exactly what she did.

7

"OH, ROSS," she breathed. When he let her come up for air, which wasn't often, she desperately tried to gain control of her emotions. But it was impossible. His kiss wasn't subtle. It wasn't tender. It wasn't soft or romantic.

It was fire. Molten lava that he spilled over her body, numbing her, forcing her to submit to his wicked will. Which was okay by her.

His tongue teased her own, his teeth nipped at her lips causing them to swell, and his hot musky breath pushed into her mouth, increasing the heat and the intimacy. It was like no kiss she had ever known. Every sense was occupied, every nerve was on alert. She felt simultaneously alive and numb. A long way away from Joey Angelucci in the fifth grade.

He held her head in the grip of his two powerful hands, while his mouth ravaged her. Claudia clutched at his shoulders, but didn't have the strength to hold on, so she let her arms flop about her sides while Ross held her securely. She trusted him not to let go.

But then he did.

Her head hit the window with a jolt, but no real pain. She was too shell-shocked for any pain to register.

"We're still in the parking lot," he said as he started the car's engine. "We can't do this here." Roughly, he threw the gearshift into drive and peeled out of the parking lot.

Claudia remained mute, but the questions flew inside her head. He said they couldn't do it there. Did that mean they were going somewhere else to do it? And do what precisely? They were too old to play like teenagers and make out under the stars in a parked car. But they were the perfect age to make love under the stars. Is that what she wanted?

Yes! her heart shouted freely. Her fire-ridden body willingly agreed.

But there was her mind. Her stubborn, highly rational mind. It always had to put its two cents in. What if they did make love? What would happen after that? It was still painfully clear that Claudia didn't belong on the farm. It was also clear that Ross was searching for someone vastly different from herself. Someone like Susan. Like Hannah.

So what would happen after? The passion would subside. Awkwardness would set in. They would struggle for their clothes, embarrassed that they'd seen each other naked. He would mumble some apology about how it never should have happened. Claudia would agree, but inside her heart would break. The next several days would be excessively uncomfortable, then she would leave, never to see him again.

But she had to consider the flip side. A night of pure passion. A night like she had never experienced before in the arms of a man she unfortunately believed she was in love with. A memory that she could take with her for the rest of her life.

The car stopped shortly and Claudia was jerked out of her thoughts. She turned to Ross, realizing they hadn't said a word the entire drive home. He must have been answering some of his own questions.

"Where are we?" she wondered. They seemed to be stopped in the middle of nowhere. Some trees looked familiar as did the telephone pole. "We're stopped on your driveway." About halfway down as far as she could tell.

"Betty is inside the house with Rosa May. We can't very well go inside like this."

She wanted to ask like what, but she imagined that her hair was all over the place, not a truly unusual style for her, but probably suspicious under these circumstances. As for Ross, he seemed unscathed by their little tumble, except for the taught lines of his body and the grim expression on his face.

"Okay. We'll wait out here for a while."

"We can't do that, either.

"Why?" she wondered.

"Because if we don't exit this car in about two seconds you're going to find yourself in my lap, and it won't be to tell me your Christmas wish."

Oh, Santa! Claudia supposed he issued the threat to make her bolt out of the car. But the threat was going to have to be a lot more…threatening for her to do that. Instead she sat with her hands folded primly in her lap.

"You're not leaving," he said.

"You're not leaving, either," she returned.

"Do you want this to happen? Because it will happen. I've been thinking about it too long for it not to happen." And after that kiss, he understood that she wasn't getting off his farm until she had gotten into his bed. He'd never felt such heat before. He heard guys all his life talk about hot women and steamy sex. He'd always believed they were exaggerating for the sake of the story. But what he felt now was urgent. It was more than lust or desire or want. It was need.

He turned to Claudia to gauge her reaction. She had a dreamy smile plastered to her lips. "What?" he asked.

"You've been thinking about me," she crooned happily.

Damn, he shouldn't have admitted as much. They were still on opposite sides of the line drawn in the sand. And in war one didn't reveal a weakness to the enemy. "Let's get back to the topic at hand...."

"Absolutely," was her answer.

"Absolutely what?"

What a dope. Slowly this time, so he understood, "Ab...so...lut...ely."

Lost, Ross wondered if he hadn't destroyed some of his brain cells back there in the school parking lot.

She huffed, then tried again. Turning to her right, she very obviously locked the passenger door. Her message was clear. She wasn't going anywhere.

Ross wasn't thrilled with the location, but beggars couldn't be choosers. In a swift move he lifted her off her seat, over the gearshift and settled her weight onto his lap, her knees on either side of his hips. She was tiny enough to fit, but it was tight. He was sure the steering wheel was pressed into her back, forcing her to press herself against his chest. Which was all right with him, but he didn't know how comfortable it was for her.

Oh, my gracious, she thought. His chest. His wonderful gloriously thick chest. She held onto the headrest above his head, allowing her breasts full contact with his hard muscles. She actually moaned.

"Are you in pain?" *Damn that steering wheel,* he thought.

"Oh, yeah, agony." She lifted herself against him, then slid down his body once more.

This time Ross groaned. "I want your mouth."

"Me, too," she uttered, not knowing if she made sense or not.

Tentatively, tauntingly, teasingly, she brushed her lips against his, then pulled away. She licked the tip of his nose then retreated. She gently bit his earlobe then escaped. His hands were cupping her bottom, so she doubted he would release that treat to force the kiss. She had all the power and she reveled in it.

She had all the power, he thought, because he'd be damned before he moved his hands. He'd waited weeks to squeeze this precious part of her anatomy, and he wasn't letting go now. Besides, he could take any torment she could dish out.

A nip of his neck. A drag on his ear. A suckling of his bottom lip. Anything. He could take anything. Then she dragged her hands down his chest, and began to unbutton the buttons, starting with the bottom and moving up. Still, he was in control, but when all the buttons were undone, she pushed her hands inside the fabric. Her lengthy nails kneaded his flesh like dough. Then they began to scrape against his tight nipples. A jolt shot down his chest, through his stomach and to his groin. It was like no other sensation he'd ever felt before. He never knew how sensitive his nipples were. Never associated them with sex before. Not until Claudia. It was driving him delightfully nuts.

Maybe a year, she counted hazily. If she touched and kneaded his chest for a year straight she might be satisfied. Anything less than that would leave her wanting. She couldn't say what it was that so enthralled her. But there was a male essence that hovered about Ross that humbled her. Something that Marco did not possess. Simultaneously that essence made her weak and strong. Weak with desire. Strong in the knowledge that she was desired.

Claudia lifted her head from his expansive chest and she noted the color of his eyes. Dark, hazy, they spoke of a powerful lust. In that instant the game changed. This wasn't about teasing and touching anymore.

She clutched his face in her hands and bent her head to capture his lips. The kiss was intense. It spoke of fulfillment instead of arousal.

Ross recognized the change instantly. Releasing her bottom, he burrowed one hand under her shirt, and captured her breast. It was encased in a lace that both thrilled him and irritated him. He wanted to feel her soft flesh. He wanted to feel her nipple pucker into a tight bead of desire.

"Damn, I want you in my bed," he cursed, longing for the room and the time he would need to fully experience her.

"Me, too," she murmured as she made her way from his lips, to his cheek, to his neck. Her need was an agony. So much that she actually felt a roaring in her ears. A horn that blasted through her dazed senses. Odd, she thought, most women saw stars when they made powerful love.

"I want you naked and writhing, and begging for me to come into you."

"Naked, writhing, begging," she repeated in a chant.

"I want to feel your legs wrapped around my waist, holding me inside you."

"Inside you. Yes, that's what I want, too."

"I want…"

"Dad!" a distant shout called to them. "Are you guys okay?"

A beam of light from the flashlight that Rosa May carried hit him square in the face. She was a few yards away and coming closer.

"Stop," he ordered, halting Rosa May in her tracks. "We're fine."

Still in his lap, her face a portrait in guilt, Claudia whispered, "Oh. My. God."

In one smooth motion Ross lifted Claudia up and off his lap. "Ow!"

"What?"

"I hit my head on the roof of the truck."

"Are you sure you guys are okay?" Rosa May called out again.

"Worry about your head later, button up your

shirt now!'' he instructed Claudia. To his daughter he shouted, ''What are you still doing up?''

''I heard the truck pull up, but it stopped. Then you started beeping the horn I thought you might be in trouble or something.''

''Oh, the horn,'' Claudia concluded realizing that the sound wasn't coming from inside her.

''Your butt was pressing up against it,'' Ross accused softly as he finished with the buttons on his shirt.

''No,'' Claudia corrected as she, too, finished redressing herself, ''my butt was pressing against your hand, which was pressing against the horn. This is your fault!''

''My fault,'' he roared. ''If you hadn't...'' he stopped.

''What?''

If she hadn't aroused him to a feverish pitch, was what he was going to say, but he managed to bite his tongue. Obviously, she couldn't be held responsible. Still, knowing that all amorous activities had been suspended for the night left him in a bear of a mood. A mood he was willing to share with everyone who crossed his path.

''Rosa May, go back inside. We'll be in shortly. We were just talking,'' he called to his daughter.

''Six point two, Dad. Lacks both believability and originality,'' Rosa May said laughing.

''Rosa May,'' he threatened.

''I'm going. I'm going.'' The light receded and they were left alone again.

Claudia unlocked her door and was about to get out when she noticed Ross wasn't moving. ''Well,'' she wondered. "Are you coming inside with me to face the music?"

"I'm not going anywhere for a few minutes," he snarled.

For a moment she was confused, but then her gaze shifted and she caught a quick peek at his lap. Oops. He wasn't going anywhere for a few minutes. Claudia had the nerve to giggle.

"Don't you dare laugh," he warned. "There is nothing funny about this situation."

Claudia begged to differ. Like a couple of teenagers they were caught red-handed making whoopee in his pickup truck by his eleven-year-old daughter. It was a little funny. However, she didn't feel now was the time to share her mirth. Instead, she took a more practical approach.

"Look at it this way," she began, "at least we spared ourselves the awkward phase."

His features were knife sharp in the moonlight. When he turned and pinned his gaze on her, Claudia sucked in her breath. "What the hell are you talking about?"

Fearless, almost, she trod forward. "We both know that this would have been a huge mistake. After it was over we both would have been mortified. We spared ourselves that."

"You think it would have been a mistake?" His tone was neutral, so it was hard to gauge the intent of his question. Was he angry or in agreement?

"Don't you? We're clearly wrong for each other."

"Are we?" he asked.

"Aren't we?" she asked back.

"You've been adjusting rather well to this place. You can actually walk around the farm without me or Rosa May being right there next to you. Shannon likes you."

"Shannon likes having cool hair."

"You can touch the cows now without having to put gloves on first."

"Yeah, but I puked up my guts when I found out that the piglets' names weren't jokes."

Ross twitched his lips. Ham and Bacon had endeared themselves to Claudia. She thought they were pets. When she found out they were food, she had tossed her cookies into the hay, marched out to where he'd been repairing some fence, and called him a list of vile names, beginning and ending with pig murderer.

Maybe she was right. She couldn't handle farm life, which meant she couldn't stay. If she couldn't stay what made him think that making love to her would have been a good idea? *His hormones,* he answered. Hormones, however, should never outrank brains.

Claudia continued with her list of reasons in case one wasn't enough. "You could never make it in New York, either. You don't dress well enough. Rosie would be stuck in an apartment all day. No. No. It's all wrong for us to be together."

"What if we were together for the time you had left? Would that be so wrong?" he wondered.

No, she thought. *Yes,* she thought. Before she had been able to talk herself into a short, mutually pleasurable affair. One where she walked away with good memories and no regrets. Unfortunately, that had been her hormones talking. Vicious little devils. Somehow they had managed to short-circuit her brain and convince her heart that she would feel no pain. Now that she had them under control, she could honestly admit that she'd been lying to herself. Leaving Ross would hurt.

She wasn't the brief affair type. And she would walk away with a pierced and bleeding heart, if she had Ross for a time, then was forced to give him up. Besides, he didn't really want her. Oh, he *wanted* her, but not all the way. If they made love, would he even ask her to stay? The answer was too easy: he wouldn't.

"Yes. It would be," she said sadly, answering his question.

Ross sighed. She was right. He couldn't very well conduct an affair under the nose of his daughter. An affair that would never end in marriage. What kind of example would that set for Rosa May?

So ask her to stay.

Ross dismissed the idea as soon as he had it. Of course she wouldn't stay. She had a business, friends and a life back in New York. For her to give all that up to stay, she would have to love him.

Starting the engine, Ross pulled the pickup farther up the driveway. He and Claudia were silent as they walked toward the house. They found Betty asleep on the couch and Rosa May crouched halfway up the stairs, hoping to catch a good-night kiss.

"To bed, Rosa May. The show is over," Ross called to her.

"Oh, Dad. I miss all the fun!" There were a few stomps then nothing.

Claudia waited a beat. "No good, kid. It's at least five stomps to your door from the steps. I only heard three."

"Oh, man!" This time the stomps were real.

Ross smiled, as did Claudia. It was a shared moment of recognition over a wonderful child. Suddenly, the air was thick around them. It was almost as if they were a family. Almost. But Ross and Rosa May would never be hers. She didn't know why that should make her so sad, but it did.

Together they woke Betty and paid the groggy baby-sitter. Claudia handed her a mug of coffee to keep her awake during her drive home. After she left, the two stood in the living room wondering what should happen next.

"I guess I'll go to bed," Claudia announced first. It was the best course of action. Out of sight, out of mind. *Out of mind was right!* She was out of her mind if she thought she was going to be able to stop thinking about him for a full minute.

"That would be good," Ross agreed. "Tomorrow, we'll start over like none of this ever happened."

Claudia nodded and started for the stairs. She had climbed the first two when she stopped. Sprinting, she returned to where Ross stood rooted in the living room. As quickly as she could, she leaned up and pecked his cheek.

"I just wanted to say thank you for tonight. You know, before we start over." She sprinted back to the stairs and took them two at a time.

Ross stared at her back as she left him. "Stay," he whispered to an empty room. But nobody heard him.

"Is IT OKAY if I go to Suzanne's house today?" Rosa May asked. "Her dad just built an outside pool and he invited me over to go swimming."

Claudia placed the waffles on the table and waited for Ross's answer. If his reply was negative she fully intended to lend her support. The way she saw it, Rosie did far too much work around the place. A girl her age should be swimming in a pool with a friend. Not mucking stables and milking recalcitrant cows all summer.

"You've earned it. You've worked hard this week, Rosa May. Don't think I haven't appreciated your help. Do you need a ride?"

Claudia turned her back from the table with a goofy smile on her face. For as different as they were, they were often on the same wavelength. *Don't go there,* she told herself. After a restless, sleepless, agonizing night, she'd come to the decision to bury any and all feelings she might have for the farmer.

"No, Mr. Davis is going to pick me up. I just have to call. But I need to use the phone." Rosa May blushed a bit with embarrassment when Ross paused. He indicated for Rosa May to come closer and then whispered in her ear. After a few seconds, Rosa May hightailed it upstairs.

"Oh, come on," Claudia shouted. "I will not give my location away! You think I want Rocco and his goons to come after me? Give me a little credit."

"It's not that I don't trust you," he explained.

Claudia poured herself a cup of coffee, winced at the bland flavor and lack of foam, and sat down across from him. "For the last time, it's called an espresso machine," she mumbled, then returned to the matter at hand. "I know. It's just that you don't trust the world. Spare me the lecture. My father gave me the same one when he said I couldn't date Vito Camarari in the eleventh grade. He drove a motorcycle."

"It's for the best this way. Now, there will be no doubt if another leak occurs."

"I understand that, but I miss my friend. I'm all she's got besides that goon, Rocco. She's never had to go this long without speaking to me. In a lot of ways I'm more like her mother than her best friend. How would you feel if you couldn't get in touch with Rosie?"

An answer wasn't necessary. Regardless, she still wasn't getting the phone. "Listen, we have other priorities today."

Uh-oh. Rosie was gone. Chores still had to be done. It was back to the barns for her, she just knew it. "Okay, here's the deal," she started before he could say anything. "First, I will feed the chickens and gather the eggs, except for Gretchen's of course. Second, I will pitch hay, but I will not muck. My days of hand milking are over, that you know. But I can herd the girls into the barn. And I refuse to feed the piglets, thereby contributing to their extinction and your next breakfast. Agreed?"

He chuckled in response. "Agreed. But that wasn't what I was referring to."

"Oh."

"You need to learn how to drive."

"Huh?"

"Drive. As in a car. As in case there is an emergency and I'm out in the fields. You need to be able to get to me, or to the nearest neighbor for help. If I'd known you couldn't drive before, I would have begun your instruction earlier. It's ridiculous that a woman your age doesn't know how to drive a car."

"First," she snapped, "a woman my age is still considered a very young woman. Second, I don't need to drive in New York. Not when there are professional cabbies to do the job for me."

Ross had ridden in a New York cab back during his days with the FBI. He breathed a sigh of relief that she was still alive. "You have no choice. Your life is in danger, and you need to take precautions. It's either a car or a horse. Take your pick."

Like she was going to pick the horse.

THE SUN WAS LOW over the farm, hailing the end of the day within the next few hours. Rosa May had been invited to spend the night at her friend's and had accepted the invitation, leaving Ross and Claudia to themselves. Claudia would have been worried about being alone with him after last night if it wasn't for one critical fact: at the moment she hated his guts.

"I said reverse. Reverse. As in backward!" he shouted.

"For the last time, stop yelling at me!" she shouted back. "I'm trying."

The pickup pitched forward, stalled, the gears ground together in a symphony that would make

Ross's mechanic a very rich man, and after all that they hadn't moved backward.

Inhaling as large a breath as he could to calm himself, Ross began again. "Let's start over."

"Nooo," she whined. "Not again."

Gritting his teeth against her whining and steeling himself against the power of her pout, he placed her hand over the gearshift, his own on top of hers. "This is first gear," he said as he moved the stick in the correct direction. "This is second. This is third. This is fourth. This is reverse."

"I don't understand why you need four gears to go forward and only one gear to go back. Forward, back. That's all any car has to do."

Apparently his lecture on engines, power and speed had gone unheard. "Your gas is on the far right, your brake is next to that. Your clutch is next to your brake. You have to shift and clutch at the same time. Shift and clutch."

Claudia looked down at her feet and the three pedals on the floor. She wasn't stupid, but for whatever reason she was having difficulty grasping the basic concepts. Maybe it was the vocabulary. "Clutch," she mentioned. "Clutch makes me think of pulling. That's why I want to pull this thing over here when I shift."

Patiently, Ross corrected her. "And that would be right. If that were the clutch and not the emergency brake."

"Emergency brake. Regular brake. What's the difference?" she asked testily.

"One you use in an emergency and after you have parked the car," he answered slowly. "Maybe it would help with a little hands-on training. Switch seats with me.''

In a practiced move, Ross lifted Claudia on his lap and then pushed her off to the side. Then he moved behind the wheel, and pushed the seat back as far as it would go. "Okay, now come here." He pulled her close and again lifted her into his lap settling her between his legs so that his feet were on either side of hers. It should have been a reminder of the position they were in last night only they were both so irritated with the other that they failed to notice. "Now watch. I clutch and shift at the same time.''

Claudia felt his arms push against her own. One hand held her own to the steering wheel. The other pinned her right hand against the gearshift forcing her to mimic his motions. His legs hugged hers, and his feet pressed hers into the pedals.

"Hey, watch it," she cried. "You're ruining my good leather sandals with your icky work boots.''

Ross glanced down at said "icky" work boots, ready to contradict her insult and keep her mind on the task at hand. The words froze in his throat when he spotted her milky white legs. Today her shorts were white. A snowy white that emphasized the little sun she'd received during her stay on the farm. They rode so high up on her thighs and clung so tightly to her body that he couldn't imagine where she found the room for panties. The idea stirred his imagination and other parts of his anatomy as well. He shifted his weight a bit. She wore a white crop top to match her shorts and Ross discovered that from his position he could peer into the depths of her meager yet satisfying cleavage.

It must have been the puff of breath that hit her neck and stirred the sensitive hairs there that alerted her to his change in mood. It wasn't an irritated sigh or an angry huff. It was sensual. Hot. Arousing. It reminded her that she was surrounded by him. Encompassed by his heat and his hardness.

The fighting stopped. The bickering ended. Conversation came to a halt altogether. Claudia didn't dare move. Any shift, any sigh, any deep breath would have pressed her body more firmly into his. If a match had been lit the spark alone would have ignited the whole inside of the truck.

Time passed. So much time that it was apparent what was happening to both of them. If someone didn't say or do something quickly, there would be nothing to stop what they both decided was so wrong last night.

"Maybe I should give the horse-riding thing a try," Claudia announced.

8

"GOOD IDEA!"

Ross almost fell out of the car, he was so quick to escape. The two of them, a jumble of legs and arms, tumbled out of the pickup onto the dirt below. Unable to defuse the tension, they bolted to the stables in search of a horse.

The smell, Claudia mused, was enough to get anybody out of the mood. She stood in the doorway of the barn while Ross escorted Shannon toward her.

A little saner, a little less aroused, she reconsidered, "Maybe this wasn't such a good idea."

Slowly, the horse plodded toward her, pushing her backward. Ross carried a saddle over his shoulder. With quick efficient movements, he buckled the saddle around the horse's belly, pulling the leather straps tighter than Claudia believed was comfortable.

"It's a saddle, not a girdle," she reminded him.

"Shannon is a trickster," he explained. "She takes a breath of air while she's being saddled to keep the straps loose. I wouldn't want you falling off on your first ride."

"She-devil," Claudia muttered. It wasn't enough that the horse had bit her butt, now it seemed she wanted to drop her on it.

Once the horse was ready, Ross turned toward

Claudia. "Take off your shoes. I don't want you hurting Shannon with those spikes."

"Me hurt Shannon? What about Shannon hurting me?"

A flick of his wrist sent the reins looping over the horse's head. Ignoring her reluctance, and her apparent fear, Ross instructed her patiently. "Hold the reins tightly in your left hand. But don't pull too hard or you will bruise her mouth. Put your left foot into the stirrup and your right hand on the pommel."

"The whattell?" she asked as she moved closer to the horse, patting its hide to show that she'd come in peace.

"The knob sticking up on the front of the saddle."

Claudia obeyed, but when she finally got her foot into the triangle rung, the damn horse moved way, pulling her along while hopping on one foot. When she was finally able to release her foot she toppled over and fell flat on her butt. "I can see where this is going," she mumbled.

"Come on, try again. This time I'll help you hold Shannon steady."

"What a pal."

Leading the horse back to her, Ross wiped clean any smirk he might have been sporting. "Try using her neck for leverage. Put both your hands on her neck, your left foot in the stirrup. Now heave."

Heave. Come on, Claudia told herself, *heave!*

"Are you heaving?" Ross asked. He moved around the horse to stand behind her.

"I'm heaving," she grunted. She just wasn't getting anywhere. It was like trying to do a chin-up in high school. Her arms then, her arms now, simply didn't have what it took to lift even her meager weight.

"You're lifting too much with the arms," he told her. "Use your left leg to boost you up."

That was an idea. Claudia started to straighten her knee, but instead of lifting her up, she was being pushed out. Then the dreaded horse started to shuffle, and Claudia could sense she was about to fall before she did.

This time Sir Galahad had the decency to attempt to catch her, but he was too late. She went flying off the horse, and before he could get a decent grip on her, she flew into his arms. The two of them stumbled over each other and onto the ground, leaving Ross pinned to the dirt and Claudia sprawled on top of him.

Puffing out breaths of air, she said, "Maybe I could learn to run real fast."

He chuckled. Ross reached up and brushed a smudge of dirt from her cheek. She didn't know it yet, but her pure white outfit was now pure brown. He could almost hear the screeching that would take place when she finally saw her reflection. That was his Claudia.

"Hmm."

"Whaaat?" she wondered.

"No hair spray. I can run my fingers through your mane rather easily today."

"I'm running low," she offered in explanation. "And I refuse to buy generic, over-the-counter at a grocery store, hair spray. I was thinking maybe, if

I'm still here in a few weeks, I could have my favorite salon deliver me some supplies.''

"If you're still here."

"If I'm still here."

What was left unsaid was the alternative.

It was the alternative that seemed to erase the doubts in both their minds. What had been so wrong last night, seemed ridiculously right in the light of day. Time was limited and since the inevitable was…inevitable, there was no sense in wasting precious minutes.

Ross made no effort to remove her weight. Claudia made no offer to do it herself. In fact, she was quite comfortable with his big body sheltering her from the ground. If he didn't protest, she would be more than willing to remain in this position until she did have to leave.

"Claudia?"

"Hmmm?"

"Rosa May is gone for the night." Ross moved both hands into her hair, loving the feel of its rich texture as it slid through his fingers.

Claudia traced his cheekbones with the tip of her finger. "So she is."

In return he kneaded the back of her neck with his strong fingers, loosening the muscles, loosening her. "So what are we having for dinner?"

"I was thinking eggplant Parmesan," she replied, while she brushed soft kisses across his forehead, over his eyes and his cheekbones that she never realized were so spectacular.

Hands wandered down her back, seemingly out of

his control until they cupped her buttocks firmly. "I hate eggplant."

For that, she nipped the bottom of his earlobe. "Tough," she blew into his ear.

"Claudia?"

"Hmmm."

"Have you ever done it in a barn, on a bale of hay?"

At that she lifted her head, levering herself off of him with both of her arms. "No way, Jose. And if you think I'm going to start now, you're crazy. I want a nice, soft, freshly scented bed!"

Laughing, he lifted her off him and stood. He saw to the horse first. Then in the tradition of all great heroes before him, he swept her off her feet and carried her inside. He took the stairs two at a time while Claudia showered him with kisses on his face and neck. He reached his room and dropped her on the bed. Then took a moment to just enjoy the sight.

"What are you looking at?"

"You in my bed. I'm trying to decide if it's real this time or another dream."

To prove to him that it wasn't a dream Claudia reached up and circled her hands around his neck. She didn't have the strength to pull herself up on a horse, but she had no problem pulling Ross down to her for another kiss. No doubt because this particular animal was cooperating.

Ross released himself from her hold for a moment to get rid of his shirt. Her mouth practically watered. In the light of a dying afternoon, he was a bronzed god. Those muscles she'd felt last night under her fingers were now hers to gaze upon. Hers to kiss.

She lifted herself and traced the outlines of his chest with her nose and tongue.

Ross dipped his head back and sighed in sheer pleasure. "Your turn," he muttered. Leaning down, he pulled at the white cotton shirt until it ripped into two pieces.

"That was a designer T-shirt," Claudia accused, but not too harshly.

"Now it's a dust rag," Ross returned unashamed. His mission accomplished, he stared at her breasts which were now exposed to his eyes except for the tiny bit of lace and engineering she wore over them. He reached down to rip that offensive garment off as well, but Claudia stopped him.

"Wait! It's my favorite WonderBra," she announced. Then gently she undid the catch in the back and removed the bra before he could destroy it.

Naked under his gaze, she leaned back on the bed. For a while he just stared at her, and she couldn't help but feel self-conscious.

"I'm too small," she admitted, hoping he would disagree.

"You're perfect," he contradicted. Proving it, he bent down to capture a ripe nipple between his lips. He sucked the morsel into his mouth and worried it with his teeth and tongue. Although he wasn't the sort to romanticize, he swore he tasted cream laced with lilacs.

"Sweet," he moaned.

"It's my scent of lilac lotion," she explained, while her fingers explored the chest she had come to worship.

"It's you," he corrected her.

Moved, she stared into his eyes. "No one has ever made me feel this way. No one has ever come close. I don't understand how this is possible when we're so wrong for each other."

"Don't think," he ordered. Mostly, because he didn't want to think himself, about her feelings or his own. He wanted to feel. He wanted to lose himself inside her, and for once know what true passion was. "Touch me."

Her fingers were knotted in his chest hair, her nails were raking over his nipples. "I am."

"Lower," he commanded, his voice rougher than gravel.

"Again with orders," she reprimanded, but willingly obeyed. Following the line of fur that ran down his belly and dived deep into his jeans, Claudia found it necessary to undo his belt, unbutton his pants and unzip his zipper in order to continue her journey.

She found him hard and hot against her hand, and she squeezed him the way she had squeezed the cow, but instead of mooing, he moaned deep in his throat.

"Now," he uttered. "I can't wait."

Briskly, he removed her shorts. His callused hands scraped against the soft flesh of her thighs, the backs of her knees, her ankles, until the shorts were history. All that remained was a scrap of white lace panties that Ross considered pulling off with his teeth. But he had a better idea.

"What kind are these?"

Peeking down at her own lingerie, Claudia squeaked, "Victoria's Secret. Let me guess, another dust cloth."

"More like a hanky," he teased. Then with a jerk of his wrist, the cloth separated beneath his onslaught. He kicked his own boots off, and tossed his jeans and briefs on top of them. Naked he flattened her against the bed, until every part of their bodies was touching.

"Too much," she cried, as her system went into overload. Her nerves simply couldn't process all the feelings. His hair-roughened thighs against her soft ones, his hard shaft pressed to her belly, his nipples spiking into her tight breasts.

Her insides were having trouble adjusting to his onslaught as well. Her heart pounded heavily in her chest. It beat to a rhythm of emotion. This man, this wonderfully strong, honest, humorous man, was on top of her, forcing her to acknowledge that she was in love with him. When his thick fingers pushed inside her giving wetness, she felt more than physical pleasure. She felt unity. He'd given her a brief glimpse of what it was like to be joined, and she wanted more of it. She wanted all of it.

"Please," she asked, as the tears left her eyes and traveled to the pillow beneath her head. "I want to know...."

"Yes," he answered, because he wanted to know, too. Shifting his weight, he pressed open her legs with the power of his own. Taking her hand, he pressed it against his needy flesh, silently asking for her to join him in the taking of her own body.

Eagerly, she guided him to her until she could feel the press of his sex against her heat. There was a tightness, a fullness that caused her to gasp, then a giving and a filling that left her breathless. She tightened her hands over his taut buttocks, buttocks that she once had to admire from a distance, and concentrated on the power of each thrust.

He was touching her, deep inside, a place in her soul that she'd almost given up on. It was so right to do this, she thought vaguely. So right to open herself to his invasion of her heart, her mind and her spirit. Her body sang out, tightening and gripping, clutching and holding. It knew, as she did, that it didn't want to let him go. It didn't want to release him…ever.

But release was unavoidable. And Ross knew it. He pushed and pushed deeper, forcing her to feel a pleasure she'd never experienced before. "Yes," he told her. "Come with me," he pleaded.

His hand moved between their sweat-slicked bodies and stroked the plump bud he'd uncovered. He felt the thrust of Claudia's breasts against his chest, heard her desperate cry for release, sensed that her back was bowed into a full arch, and knew as her legs locked around his waist that she was lost. Lost like he was. With one last heave he let himself go, releasing himself inside her, feeling as if he'd been absorbed into the pores of her skin.

Exhausted, sated, he fell on top of her, his head next to hers. The slide of her fingers through his hair relaxed him, as she massaged his scalp and crooned to him with her lasting sobs of pleasure.

Only one thought managed to penetrate the pleasure-induced fog around his brain.

Stay.

9

"Ross!" Claudia screeched, as she was flopped over onto her belly like one of Ross's special blueberry pancakes.

"Whaaat?" he mimicked with his best attempt at a Brooklyn accent. He kept his hands pressed against her buttocks forcing her to lie still on her stomach. He'd waited to have her in just such a position for weeks, and he planned to take the opportunity that had been so eagerly presented to him.

It was early morning. Predawn, actually. They'd spent the whole night rotating sleep and sex. Rosa May was scheduled to return after breakfast, so the way Ross saw it, he only had a few precious hours left to gorge himself on Claudia. He hoped that the memories would be enough to last him a lifetime. If not beyond.

With tiny nibbles he worked his way up her calves, massaging the muscles, soothing away the bites with his lips. He paid special attention to the sensitive skin behind her knees, but tempted beyond control he moved up and up.

Claudia stretched out her arms and tugged the pillow beneath her head. She bit into the downy cushion to stop herself from begging for release. Her body felt like an instrument that he had tuned to perfection. At his will he plucked whichever string he chose, creating a song inside her.

"Yikes!" she squeaked when he landed a nip on her bottom.

Then he was pulling on her hips, lifting her onto her knees. His arms wrapped around her until his hands cupped her breasts, and he held her tight against his chest. When he slipped inside her from behind, she wondered how she'd gone so long without having him inside her body. She pushed against him accepting his thrusts, teasing him with her soft buttocks that rubbed against his furred belly. The tension built, but Claudia relished it, knowing there would be release.

And there was. A beautiful explosion of feeling. She closed her eyes and let her head drop back against his shoulder.

I love you. The words bubbled in her mind, but she wouldn't voice them. He had given her this night, and it was all she could ask of him. In a few days, she would leave. Perhaps even before Mac-Curdy gave her the okay. Living on the farm, loving on the farm, made her want to stay longer. And it wasn't a choice. Even if Ross did ask, she would have to say no.

He needed someone more capable than her. Someone less concerned with fashion and more concerned with...milk. He needed someone who could muck stables and ride horses and do all the chores that he needed help with. Together they might sizzle, but it wouldn't last. He would resent her failings, and she simply couldn't change.

You could take the girl out of Brooklyn, but you

couldn't take the Brooklyn out of the girl and replace it with Sun Prairie. It would never work.

Tears squeezed out of her closed eyes. Ross released her and turned her so that she lay back on the pillow. He'd seen the tears before, but knew they were tears of pleasure, of joy. These tears, however, bothered him.

"Claudia?"

"Oh, damn! My eyes are going to get all red and swollen. I hate to cry. I never cry."

"You cry all the time," Ross noted.

Claudia lifted her head, a ferocious gleam in her red swollen eyes. "I do not cry all the time."

"You cried when the cow pooped on you. You cried after I made love to you the first time. And the second time. And the third time..."

"I get the point."

"I understood those tears." Ross reached down and swiped away a drop that rested on her cheek. "But these tears are different. What's wrong?"

She shook her head, unwilling to speak. Afraid she might say too much. Afraid of how he would respond.

"You'll tell me when you're ready," Ross concluded. They'd become too intimate in the course of a night to attempt to keep secrets from each other. "I hate to say it, but the sun is up."

Which meant the night was over. Time for them both to return to their respective roles. "I'll go down and fix breakfast."

"No. Stay and sleep for a while. I can grab something. Just make sure you're up before Rosa May comes home. I don't want her to see..."

He didn't want his daughter to know that they had become lovers. He didn't want his daughter to know that two people could make love to each other and separate when it was over. He was right. Something as intimate as sex should be shared by two people who were willing to commit to each other. They weren't those two people. Her eyes sprang another leak, but this time Claudia turned her head into the pillow before he could see her face.

Ross bounced off the bed and strolled naked out of the room. Claudia heard the shower spring to life and she tried not to dwell on what he might look like, naked under a spray of hot water. Her heart leaped, then crashed when she realized that she might never see his beautiful naked chest again.

She'd been such a fool to think that she wasn't going to suffer horribly for the decision she made. But she also knew she would have been a fool to think that last night wasn't going to happen.

"Think of the memories," she commanded her subconscious. "Then think of New York. Think of your salon. Think of Antoinette. Think of your next nail design. Think about anything. Just don't think about him. Don't think about this farm, or Rosie, or the pigs, or the cows..."

Ring. Ring.

Distracted from her pity party, Claudia tried to isolate the sound.

Ring. Ring.

It sounded like a muffled telephone ringing. Wrapping the sheet that they had tugged loose from the bed around her, Claudia followed the sound to his closet. Once there it was easy enough to spot the cord that ran along the floor and disappeared into the closet.

"Not the most original hiding place, Ross." She opened the doors and spotted the phone on the top shelf. It was still ringing.

Of course she knew she wasn't supposed to use the phone. But it could be an emergency. It could be Rosie trying to reach them. There could have been an accident, an illness, any number of bad things.

"Oh, just answer the darn thing," she told herself.

Lifting the receiver off the hook, she pulled it against her ear. "Hello?"

"Claudia!" A familiar voice rang out.

"Antoinette!"

"I've missed you so much. And I have so much news to tell you. You are never going to believe—"

For a minute Claudia allowed herself the pleasure of hearing her friend's voice again. Then she abruptly interrupted her. "Antoinette, how did you get this number? Nobody is supposed to know where I am."

"Oh. Well, Rocco told me where you were. He wants to help you. I'm calling because he told me to. See, I told you he was a really terrific guy, but you wouldn't listen. Oh no, Claudia, no man is never good enough for you or for me. Your problem is you are too picky—"

Claudia struggled for patience. "Antoinette! How did Rocco get this number? What do you mean he's trying to help me?"

"That's right, he's trying to help you," Antoinette exclaimed. "You see he didn't pop that guy in the bathtub. That guy Jimmy, you know the one with beady eyes who's always chewing gum, he popped him. And he's the one who wants to ice you for going to the police. Anyway, he knows where you are, but he doesn't want to do the hit himself. So he told Rocco to sic the Caravacci brothers on you."

"The Caravacci brothers? Never heard of them."

"They're new. They're trying to build a reputation. You know how that is."

"Yeah, it's tough breaking into any new business," Claudia agreed. Then she slapped her hand against her head. Here she was talking calmly about two hit men who wanted her dead. "Can we forget the commentary, Toinette. Get to the punch line."

"Huh?"

"What happened next?" she asked slowly.

"Oh. Anyways, Rocco says that he's not siccing anybody on his future wife's friend. Get it? Wife! He finally proposed! I've got a real diamond and everything. Can you believe it?"

"I would really love to be excited for you, Toinette. But there's this slight hitch. You see, people are trying to kill me!" Claudia shouted hoping to make her fear known.

"You know Claudia, not everything is always about you. You could spare a minute to at least congratulate me," Antoinette said in a haughty tone.

"You're right, Antoinette. Congratulations. I hope I live to be a bridesmaid in your wedding. Now can we get to the rest of the story, please."

"That's pretty much it. I mean Rocco said he wouldn't do it. So Jimmy said he'd call the Caravacci brothers himself. Then Rocco overheard

Jimmy telling the boys where you were. So he told me to call you and tell you that they're on their way. We're in Wisconsin now, but Rocco doesn't think we'll get there in time to stop them. So he said you should hightail it out of there, right now.''

They were on their way. For all Claudia knew, the Caravacci brothers could be outside this minute. Outside where Ross worked and Rosa May played. She couldn't leave. If they didn't find her there was no telling what they might do to Ross and Rosa May to make them talk.

''Listen, Antoinette, I've got to go.'' She hung up the phone, her mind suddenly numb with fear. She couldn't think of what she needed to do next.

''You called her. You called that woman.''

Ross. Claudia turned and saw him standing in the doorway, a towel wrapped around his waist. Under normal circumstances she would have taken the time to admire his extremely fine physique, but now was not a normal circumstance.

''I can't believe you called her,'' he accused. ''Do you have any idea the danger you could be bringing down on your head, not to mention Rosa May's?''

''I didn't call her.''

His hard expression and pressed lips told her that he didn't believe her.

''I didn't!'' she protested. ''She called me. She got the number from some guy named Jimmy. This guy Jimmy is the one who's been after me. He's sending the Caravacci brothers. We have to get Rosie and get out of here now!''

Ross saw the fear in her eyes, heard the tremor in her voice. He wanted to believe that this wasn't an act to cover up what she'd done. "You promise me, you're telling the truth?"

"I promise. Do you honestly think I would risk your life after what we shared last night? And Rosie, do you think I would let anyone hurt her? I love her. I love...this place. That's why we have to leave. Please believe me."

He did. It was that easy. He knew the moment he met her that she wasn't stupid. And he knew after last night that she cared deeply for him. She wouldn't jeopardize him or his daughter. Which meant someone had leaked their location. Someone who knew where she was. It wasn't a large list of people.

"You said this guy who is after you—his name is Jimmy?"

Nodding, she answered, "That's what Antoinette calls him. Says he's always chewing gum. He's the one who shot the naked guy."

Ross didn't ask her to explain. Instead, he bolted into action. He dressed in seconds. Then he went to the closet to search for a metal box he'd put away a long time ago. It was right where he'd left it. The key that he kept in a secret compartment underneath the box was also in place. He used it and lifted the lid.

Claudia thought she was going to puke. "It's a gun. What do we need a gun for? All we have to do is get Rosie and leave."

"And go where, Claudia?" he asked sharply. "What are the three of us going to do, run forever? I'm not leaving this farm. Call Rosa May—the number is in the phone book downstairs. Tell her to stay put. Then I'm going to put you in the car and—''

''I don't know how to drive, remember,'' she shouted, jumping up and down in a fit of panic, wishing she'd been a better study. Not that it mattered. Stubbornly, she decided that this was going to end here. ''I'm not leaving. They came here for me. If I go with them, they'll leave you alone.''

''You are not going with them,'' he stated firmly. ''Go call Rosa May.'' Ross lifted the .38 Special from the case and loaded it. He filled his pockets with the extra bullets and shoved the gun deep into his jeans. It wasn't an automatic, which was what he would probably be facing, if not worse. But it was the only defense they had.

Claudia bolted back to her room and threw on the first thing she found in her closet. This was no time for matching. What *was* important was that she be dressed. If she was going to be murdered, she was not going to die naked. She knew from firsthand experience how humiliating that could be. Once dressed, she sprinted down the steps and found the phone book with the number for Rosa May's friend. She bolted up stairs and stopped short when Ross came out of the bedroom, the handle of the revolver sticking out of his jeans.

It made her sick with worry to think that he was going to confront two mob hit men. Not that she didn't trust his expertise, but he was one man with one gun. More than likely the Caravacci brothers would come loaded with an arsenal of weapons.

She wanted to plead with him again to run away with her, but the intense look in his eyes told her not to bother. His protective instincts had been alerted, and he wasn't going to budge. Claudia moved around him and made the call. She didn't talk to Rosa May as she was still asleep, but the friend's mother understood the urgency of Claudia's request. She would keep Rosa May with her until she heard otherwise.

Racing down to join Ross, Claudia found him shutting the curtains. For every curtain he pulled, he first checked outside for any signs of trouble.

"Do you see anything?" she asked.

"Get down," he ordered.

Without thinking, Claudia dropped to her stomach. She'd been through this routine before at the house in New Jersey and the cabin in Virginia. But now it was much more frightening. Now she had Ross to consider. She couldn't let anything happen to him, but he wasn't letting her do anything to help.

"No sign of them yet. It will be hard for them to approach the house. Too much open space. More than likely they'll ditch the car and come on foot. If we're lucky they'll run into some of the electrically charged fence we use to keep the cows in their sections."

Claudia was familiar with the thin white bands that sectioned off parts of the farm. Thinking it harmless, she had attempted to lift it over her head so she could duck under the fence and had been treated to a jolting shock. Ross and Rosa May had found the whole situation hysterical. Just one more episode in the TV sitcom that was her life, appropriately titled *Claudia: Down on the Farm.*

"Shouldn't we call the police for backup?"

Ross sighed and bowed his head. "I've considered that option. Freddy's just a kid they elected sheriff because his dad held the office before him. He passes out speeding tickets and breaks up bar brawls. I don't think he's prepared to handle the mob."

"So what do we do?"

"We wait. Let them come to us."

"OH, MAN, what is this stuff?" Donald asked his brother as he pulled his leather loafer out of a pile of brown goop.

Irving noted the goop and the smell. "Trust me, you don't want to know."

"They were Italian!"

"Will you stop worrying about your shoes," Irving ordered. "We're here to make a hit."

Donald lowered his head, but grumbled under his breath, "If you ask me, we never should have taken this job."

"Yeah, well, nobody asked you."

Irving had really good ears. "But Wisconsin? It's not like we're going to attract a lot of attention out here, Irving. If we want the big contracts, we've got to build our reputation in New York. And so far Claudia has been bad luck."

Irving progressed slowly, carefully choosing his steps. He turned back to his partner, "That's why we're here. We muffed the first two hits. So we've got to finish the job. Didn't you learn anything from Ma? She always told us—"

"You gotta finish the job," Donald finished. He understood, but Ma wasn't out here plodding through cow manure. Donald glanced up to judge the remaining distance to the house. It was about a quarter of a mile away with what looked to be a million cows between them and the front porch. His Italian shoes were never going to make it.

"Hey, Donald. Come here and hold this rope up while I crawl under it." Irving pointed to the thin white band that was stretched between two poles.

"Not much of a fence," Donald snorted. He handed his brother his gun then bent down to lift the band up. It was the shock of his life.

"Ooow!"

Inside the house, they heard the scream. Ross looked over his shoulder to where Claudia was still belly-down on the floor. "They found the fence."

"But it won't knock them unconscious," Claudia recalled. It had only left her mildly stunned with really full hair for the rest of the day. No hair spray necessary. "Ross, I'm scared." She army-crawled to where he stood watch by the window. "Please duck." She yanked on his pant leg until he complied.

He crouched low and took her into his arms. "We're going to be fine." He didn't know how much he believed that, but as long as Claudia was reassured, that was all that mattered. After a minute he released her, then stood again to check the window. He hated waiting. Even as an agent he'd never been any good at it. These men were on his farm. Here to attack his loved ones, and all he could do was sit and wait.

No, that wasn't all he could do. "Claudia, I want you to stay here."

"Ooohhh," she whined. "The hero always says that right before he leaves the girl to go and do something stupid."

Ross smiled gently. "It won't be that stupid. I promise." He left the living room and headed for the kitchen and the back door beyond. Crouched low, his gun poised in the ready position, he sprinted from the house to the barn. Once inside he searched the area for potential weapons. All he saw were the animals.

"OH, MAN, my hair is still sticking up," Donald complained.

"It was just a small shock, get over it."

Again, under his breath, Donald muttered about his brother not getting the shock so how would he know how big or small it was. All of that was interspersed with a few choice four-letter words intended for his brother to hear.

"Move cow," Irving ordered as they were in the midst of cow central. The large bovines didn't seem to mind the strangers. They went about their daily activities undisturbed. So oblivious they were, they didn't seem to watch where they were going.

Irving and Donald were bumped about like pinballs in a pinball game.

"Ooof. Ouch. Hey, watch it you dumb animal."

"Mooo."

Donald gave one speckled cow a hefty shove. "Moo yourself. I told you this was a bad idea, Irving. We don't know nothing about making no hit on no farm.''

"Stop your yapping," Irving growled. "We're almost there. Just one more fence to go.''

"I am not holding this one up!''

ROSS CROUCHED behind the barn door. He waited until he saw the two hit men clear the fence. Once they were in the yard he raised his pistol over his head and fired a shot that blasted through the barn. Since all the barn and stable doors had been opened, the animals did the natural thing and bolted. Ross pushed himself up against the door and out of the way of Devil, Shannon, the pigs and a cat as they all charged out of the barn.

It was almost enough to make Ross smile. He peeked around the door to witness the effects of his plan. The two goons stood in the middle of the yard, stunned by the sound of a gun. When they looked up, they saw that they were about to be stampeded by a menagerie of animals.

The horses got to them first. Shannon sniffed the air around them, bumping them with her backside, while Devil lifted his two legs high into the air and issued a warning cry. The one goon hit the dirt and startled to wrestle with the pigs, while the other tried to keep his balance, enough to aim the automatic in his hand. Gretchen was pecking at his leg making it difficult for him, but the goon was able to shake her off. He aimed at Devil as if to shoot, but Ross wasn't about to let that happen.

His two fingers between his lips, he whistled to the horses, calling them back. They trotted off, giving Ross a clean shot. Patiently, he took aim, knowing he had to make each shot count. He fired once at the man standing. Instantly, the man clutched his hand as his gun went sailing into the air.

The other one had apparently already lost his gun in his tussle with Ham and Bacon.

"Freeze," Ross called authoritatively. Slowly, he left the safety of the barn, his one hand wrapped around the gun, the other holding his wrist steady. "Arms high."

The two hit men did as they were told.

"On your bellies. Arms stretched out wide in front of you. If either of you goes for your backup, you're dead." Ross moved forward as the two stretched out on their stomachs.

"Is it over?" Claudia asked as she carefully made her way into the yard, a large frying pan held high above her head.

"Get back inside!" he commanded.

"All right, already. No need to get grumpy. I'm going to call the police." But as Claudia turned she realized that she vaguely recognized one of the men lying on the ground. Moving closer, she tilted her head side to side to get a closer look at their profiles.

"Irving? Donald?"

"Hi, Claudia."

"Hi, Claude." They reluctantly greeted her.

Flabbergasted, Ross questioned. "You know these guys?"

"Yeah," she informed him, irritated that two old high school buddies would attempt a hit on her of all people. "Only their name isn't Caravacci. It's Schultz. Irving and Donald Schultz."

"Caravacci had a better ring to it. You know...meaner. More Italian," Irving explained.

Shaking her head, Claudia tapped her foot maternally, "Donald?"

"Yes, Claudia?" His tone was satisfactorily contrite.

"You asked me to the prom!"

"Yeah, and you turned me down. I've never forgotten," he defended himself as if the ten-year-old jilt was still fresh in his mind.

"I attended the Brooklyn Academy of Beauty with your sister!" They were practically family. The nerve of some people. "How is Ingrid, by the way?"

"Good. You know she got promoted from head washer to stylist," Donald said proudly.

Ross had been warped to another dimension. It was the only explanation for the conversation that was taking place between the girl with the frying pan and the two hit men lying belly-down in the dirt. "Are you finished?" Ross directed his question toward Claudia. "Or perhaps you'd like to relive your high school graduation party?"

She grimaced at his facetiousness. "Yes, I'm done," she obliged. But she couldn't help but add, "Excuse me for being a little shocked that my two very good friends from high school turned out to be two hit men who wanted to kill me."

"You didn't really like us in high school, Claudia. You called us geeks," Irving reminded her.

"Only because you guys still dressed alike in the twelfth grade. You're not even identical twins."

"Our Ma made us do it," Donald muttered.

Ross rolled his eyes in disgust. "I'm calling the

police. Then I'm calling Frank. I think I figured out who our infamous Jimmy is.''

Smack. Smack. MacCurdy popped another Nicorette tablet into his mouth and chewed ferociously. He stood behind the couple, a gun pointed at their backs. ''You always were the best, Ross. A legend.''

10

"MacCurdy," Ross greeted, a grim smile on his lips.

"MacCurdy?" Claudia repeated, not sure she knew what was happening.

"Didn't you catch his full name?" Ross asked Claudia. "Allow me to introduce James MacCurdy III. Or as he is more commonly known in mob circles, Jimmy."

"Antoinette was right," Claudia noted. "You do have beady eyes."

He smirked and wiggled his brows for effect. "So you figured it out, Ross? I suppose it was that infamous gut of yours."

"It wasn't hard to put it together. Rocco found Claudia. Only you, me and Frank knew where she was. I know I didn't tell Rocco."

"And good old Frank certainly wouldn't have turned out to be the leak," MacCurdy returned, apparently repeating a familiar refrain.

"Frank is an honest man. You… Let's just say I always had my suspicions."

His face mocked surprise. "Me? Really? But I was clean when we were partners. I didn't get into this whole gig until a few years ago."

Time. Ross needed it to plan his escape. He'd

been forced to drop his gun, and the Cara—Schultz brothers were collecting theirs and shuffling back to stand behind MacCurdy. All too soon it would be three guns to none. "Exactly what kind of gig is this, MacCurdy? A little moonlighting as a contracted hit man?"

Seemingly anxious to confess, MacCurdy shook his head. "Not at first. I started out just providing some inside information every once in a while. But you know how it goes. You do a good job, you work really hard and you get promoted."

"Why was he naked?" Claudia wondered.

Ross didn't see that information as pertinent, but what the hell, the more time they bought the better.

"I popped him in the shower. What you don't know is that the naked guy lived in the apartment above Rocco's. I was trying to take his body someplace to send the appropriate message to someone when some cops pulled up to the building. Rocco's door was closer, so I hid inside, dumped the body in the bathtub, threw some bags of ice that Rocco had in the freezer on the guy so he wouldn't stink up the joint, and left. I figured Rocco would keep his mouth shut until I could come back for him. What I didn't figure on was his girlfriend and you finding the body and squealing to the police. You know you bumped into me that day on your way out the door. I knew then that I had to take you out. As a precaution, you understand."

"Sure. A precaution," she agreed as if that made all the sense in the world. Claudia tried to recall that day and the people she'd seen, but she'd been rattled by the dead guy and was too busy trying to escape from Rocco to pay much attention to her surroundings. "But why bring me out here?"

"By the time I got to you the FBI was already involved. I couldn't take you out with a bunch of agents around you at every turn."

"Sorry for not making myself an easier target," Claudia tossed out sarcastically.

"Was it the money?" Ross prodded. He glanced toward the barn. The doors were still open. If he could shove Claudia aside, maybe she could reach the safety of the barn while he charged MacCurdy. Too far, he recognized at once. She'd never make it. He needed another plan.

Just keep talking, MacCurdy. Tell me what a smart guy you are.

"That corrupted me?" MacCurdy clarified. "Is there any other reason? I was going nowhere quick living in your shadow. Everybody figured I'd been riding your coattails. I got tired of trying to prove myself. So I found a job where I could shine. My aim is accurate. And I know how to dispose of evidence."

"Not very well," Ross reminded him. "You missed Claudia, twice."

"Yeah!" she cheered, backing up her man.

MacCurdy snorted. "I didn't miss. These two idiots missed." MacCurdy pointed his thumb over his shoulder in the direction of the twins. "It's a good thing I didn't leave anything to chance this time. Enough talk. I've got a lot to do today. These guys will make the hit. I'll call Rocco's number from your phone. Frank will think that Claudia once again gave her location away, and Rocco will go to jail in my place. See, neat as can be." MacCurdy turned his head. "Okay guys, let them have it."

"Are you going to stand there and take orders from a guy who just called you idiots? Really, Donald. Really, Irving. You can do much better than this loser." Claudia looked over the shoulder of MacCurdy straight into the eyes of the Schultz brothers.

"Do it," MacCurdy ordered. "Now."

"Don't do it. Think of the prom we might have gone to together. Do you really want to murder the girl who could have been your senior prom date?" Six point one, Claudia judged. Absolutely lacking any teeth. But she was desperate. "And think of Ingrid. You know she would have failed coloring if it hadn't been for me. And then where would she be? Washing hair for the rest of her life, that's for sure."

Ross couldn't believe it. The Schultz brothers actually appeared to be undecided. It was time to make his move, but MacCurdy still had a gun pinned on him. He needed a distraction.

Beeep! Beeep!

"Yo! Claudia! It's me. Your for-real engaged friend and employee!"

"Antoinette!"

A large black Cadillac was tumbling over the ruts in Ross's extended driveway. Ross couldn't help but keep his eye trained on the big-breasted, dyed blond temptress that was hanging out the passenger window. With flailing arms and a voice that ricocheted off every cow on the farm, she demanded everyone's attention.

Including MacCurdy's.

Ross was quick to react. Smoothly he twisted his

body, simultaneously landing a hard fist to Mac-Curdy's jaw while his other reached for the gun. By the time the rest of the cast remembered that they were in a standoff and turned their attention back to the matter at hand, Ross was standing over an unconscious MacCurdy, armed.

"How did you do that?" Claudia gasped. Her mouth gaped as she tried to assimilate the fact that they were going to live after all. And she hadn't even been watching.

Ross didn't comment, but instead took aim against the Schultz brothers. "Well, what's it going to be?"

The brothers looked down at their fully automatic 9mm guns, then considered Ross's lone gun. It was still two against one.

"Nobody is shootin' nobody."

Rocco swaggered hip-first up to the gathered crowd. "Donald, Irving, put your guns away. You mo-mos."

The twins did as they were told. Ross lowered his weapon, but kept it clenched tightly in his fist. The short guy may have had pull with the Schultz boys, but his orders carried no weight with him.

"Rocco, I presume?" Ross held out his empty hand in offering.

The smaller man took the hand and crunched it between his beefy fingers. Ross kept his expression neutral, but inwardly grimaced at the unnecessary clench.

"Yeah. Who are you?"

"Ross Evans. I own the farm."

"Like the sausage, right?" Antoinette blurted.

Claudia shook her head in resignation. "No,

honey. That's *Bob Evans*. This is Ross. He's been hiding me for the last few weeks.''

"Oh.'' Antoinette openly ran her eyes over Ross, stopping for a moment at some of his more interesting body parts. "Ooohhh.''

The laughter erupted from Claudia as the blush encompassed Ross's whole face. He lowered his eyes, and Claudia would have bet that he was fighting the urge to cover his lap with his hands.

"And exactly *where* has he been hiding you?'' Antoinette wanted to know.

"Down girl,'' Claudia warned. "Now is not the time or place.'' Especially since she was going to start blushing herself any minute. She turned to Ross, who as far as she could tell was the only sane person left on this farm. Other than herself, of course. "So now what?''

"I'll call Frank and let him deal with this mess.''

"Nobody's callin' nobody.'' Rocco hitched up his faux silk slacks over his protruding belly.

Claudia rolled her eyes.

Ross looked bored.

Antoinette beamed proudly at her man.

The Schultz boys shuffled over to stand behind Rocco.

And MacCurdy let out a groan.

Logically, Ross pointed out, "Rocco, I've got a bad agent who has got to be turned in. But the way I see it, that's all the FBI has to know. MacCurdy will get pinned with the murder of the naked guy, as I've fondly come to know him, and you are free to leave.''

It didn't take a rocket scientist to see that Ross's plan was the best for all concerned.

Rocco was no rocket scientist. "So you're saying all I gotta do is...go?"

"That's right. Take the twins with you."

"They did try to kill me, Ross," Claudia whispered. "Maybe we shouldn't let them off so lightly."

"Trust me," Ross whispered back. "I'm not worried about the population at large. If these two stay on the same career path it won't be long until they find themselves sharing a cell. Then they can dress alike forever."

It took a minute. Rocco rocked back on his heels, his thumbs tucked into the waistband of his pants in a distorted Napoleon pose. If Ross had to guess, he would say that he was attempting to think. And it seemed that Antoinette was doing her level best to help him by staring at him intently. It was as if it required their combined brain power to reach a decision.

"Yeah," Rocco nodded. "I'll do that. Sugarpuff, get your buns in the car. You mo-mos, the back seat. Evans, you're an okay guy. And you," Rocco pointed to Claudia, his eyes fierce and his mouth tight, "see what happens when you mess with mob business? Next time, leave the dead naked guys lying in the bathtubs on bags of ice to me. *Capisce?*"

"*Capisce.*" Next time, Claudia cringed. There had better not be a next time.

"See ya, Claudia." Antoinette attempted to walk backward to the car as she said farewell, only she kept tripping in her three-inch heels. "Don't forget, when you get back we got to go shopping for gowns and stuff.''

Visions of pink chiffon lace with fake flowers sewn across the bust and along the hemline danced in front of Claudia's eyes. "I'll call you."

The doors of the Cadillac closed and the engine started up. In a cloud of dust, the car took off down the road, weaving and bumping the whole way.

"I've got to do something about that road," Ross muttered.

"No, you've got to do something about our beady-eyed friend. He's coming around."

He moaned on cue and cracked his eyes open.

"I can fix that." Ross leaned down and clipped him neatly on the jaw. Before MacCurdy's eyes had a chance to completely open, they were closed again. "That's for trying to hurt Claudia."

"My hero," she crooned. As he stood she reached out to him, wrapping her arms around his neck. "You know the hero always gets to kiss the girl after he saves the day."

"The hero is a sucker then." Ross lifted Claudia into his embrace cupping her buttocks in his palms. "I'm getting a hell of a lot more than a kiss for my efforts."

"So what happened then?" Rosa May was perched on her chair, excited beyond reason by the events that had taken place in her very own backyard.

Ross and Claudia shared a secret smile. The version of the story they told Rosa May would have to be rated PG. "We tied MacCurdy up and left him outside, then called your pop's old boss to come pick him up. After he was gone we uh...we...took a nap. It had been a rough day. You understand.''

Her expression was one of pure disgust. "You took a nap. Geesh! What are you guys, like eighty years old or something?''

"Or something," Ross answered slyly. Claudia had left a considerable chunk out of the story. For which he was grateful. But there was another piece of the story she was also omitting that had Ross wondering.

Frank had flown out on the first flight and had arrived at the farm three hours after Rocco's departure. He took MacCurdy away in handcuffs, and cheerfully thanked Ross for his aid. He'd told them both that he suspected James for some time and was looking for a way to trip him up. He knew that if he sent Claudia to Ross's farm, she'd be safe and MacCurdy would be forced to show his hand if any attack was made. Ross had told him that he didn't like the idea of the Bureau using Claudia to trap one of their own, but Frank had shrugged off the complaint behind the excuse that he'd only been serving justice.

Frank commented that at one time that was all Ross had ever wanted to do, too. But Ross honestly admitted that those days were over for him. He wouldn't deny that he missed the action from time to time. He'd forgotten what it felt like to have adrenaline pump pure and clean through his system, exhilarating him. But he'd also forgotten that when his adrenaline was pumping, it was usually because somebody else was in danger. This time it had been his loved ones that were at risk. While Ross dealt with the threat at hand, he couldn't for a minute forget that Rosa May and Claudia were counting on him. He didn't know what he would have done if anything had happened to them.

That fear had illuminated a truth. Rosa May and Claudia were linked in his mind. He viewed them both as his family. That revelation confirmed the obvious fact that he was in love with Claudia. It shouldn't have surprised him. After the other night, he knew that what he felt for her was more powerful than lust. That level of intimacy, that kind of intense communication, could only be achieved between two people who cared deeply.

Which is why it disturbed him so when Frank told Claudia that he would return for her tomorrow after he dealt with MacCurdy.

Claudia said nothing. She didn't correct Frank. She didn't turn to him for confirmation. She just stood there, in the middle of his driveway and nodded. When she turned back to him she wore a large smile that he didn't for a minute believe was sincere. But she said nothing, so Ross said nothing.

Did she want to stay? How could she, Ross thought dismally. She hated the farm. Didn't she? Sure, maybe she didn't flinch as much when she had to retrieve eggs from the chicken coop. Maybe she even liked to feed the horses with the organic oats she discovered. She did deal with the horses much better than she had, and Ross was convinced that in another few months he could get her back into the milking barn.

If he thought about it, there was no reason why she wouldn't want to stay. She loved the house. She had turned it back into a home in the short time she'd been here. Now it was filled with the smells of good Italian cooking and her perfume.

Added to that, she had practically started up her own business. His den had been transformed into her temporary shop with hundreds of different-colored nail polishes, lotions and strange-shaped instruments that she said were for making nails more beautiful but he believed were some kind of torture devices. Apparently the women didn't mind the torture if the fact that Claudia was completely booked for next Monday was any indication.

More important than any of that was that he had something to give her: love. Family.

The question was, was it enough? Everything had happened so quickly he doubted he could persuade her that it was for real. Then again, he could be stubborn when he needed to be. His heart had been so stubborn it had done exactly what his brain had told him not to do. He'd gone and fallen in love with the damn woman. His feelings weren't fleeting. And maybe that scared him more than anything. If she did leave, he'd be lost. Where could he ever find her equal?

Ask her to stay.

But what if she stayed because of the way she felt now and realized down the road that she couldn't live the rest of her life here? What would that do to Rosa May if she left? It would be like losing a mother all over again. Ross couldn't let that happen. Not for his daughter. Not for himself

He couldn't ask.

CLAUDIA WRAPPED HERSELF into her afghan that night and inhaled deeply. She was trying to muffle her sobs with little success. Finally, she gave in and pulled the covers over her head and turned her face into the pillow and let loose.

After a few minutes, exhaustion finally set in and Claudia was forced to either stop bawling or literally drown in her own tears. Ross was right. She did cry a lot. Only when she had good reason to, though. And tonight she had the best reason of all.

He didn't ask her to stay.

Not that she could have stayed even if he had asked. She'd already decided that she wasn't the right woman for him to marry. However, she at least wanted the chance to prove how selfless and noble she could be by telling him that she had to leave for his own good. That chance never came.

"Why?" she asked in hushed tones to an empty room. Why hadn't he asked her to stay? Why couldn't she be the right person for him? Why did she fall in love with him when she knew it was all so hopeless?

No answers came. Not that she was surprised. Life, Claudia found, held many questions and few answers. Her only option was to leave with Frank in the morning. She would say her goodbyes as emotionlessly as possible, walk stoically down the driveway to Frank's waiting car, and she wouldn't look back. Not once.

MORNING CAME EARLY. Earlier than usual since she'd been up most of the night crying. Gingerly, she cracked her eyes open as her brain registered that there was sunlight in her room. *How pathetic was that?* she thought. She was even conditioned to wake up with the sun.

When she turned her head on the pillow, her mouth stretched in a huge yawn, she saw him standing in the doorway with his arms crossed over his sculpted chest.

His chest, she sighed inwardly. She'd never touch it again.

Tears started to spurt, but ruthlessly she stopped them. All crying jags had to be postponed until she was safely on the plane back to New York. It wouldn't do anybody any good to see her as an emotional wreck. For the time being she had to be strong.

For a moment they stared at each other; words were unnecessary. He was remembering, she knew, all the other mornings he'd been forced to practically drag her out of bed by her hair. And she was remembering all the times she purposefully stayed in bed just so she could feel his arms around her when he inevitably had to lift her out of the bed. She smiled, and he smiled back. Their thoughts were synonymous.

Ask me to stay.

Ask her to stay.

Clamping down on the overwhelming urge to utter the words, Ross paused before he spoke. "Time to get up. Because this is your last morning, Rosa May and I made you breakfast. We wanted to thank you for all you've done for us."

Claudia nodded, but said nothing. Because if she had said anything it would have been something like: *First, don't thank me. I did what I did out of love for you and Rosie. Second, I can't believe you are not going to ask me to stay, you lily-livered coward!*

It was a hunch she had—perhaps Ross wasn't asking her to stay because he didn't know what her answer would be. She'd often grumbled about the farm. And just as often praised New York City. And there was her salon, which she had worked so hard to make a success. Maybe he thought she wanted to go. Didn't he know that the women of Sun Prairie were going to need touch-ups?

"Ross," she called just as he started to walk away.

He moved back into the doorway, "Yes?"

"I—I—"

"Claudia tongue-tied. That's a first," he teased.

She smiled lamely, then swallowed and tried again. "I've had a really good time."

This time he nodded, but said nothing. Then he just walked away.

Obviously, that hunch had been wrong. Okay, now she was getting angry. She practically came right out and said that she loved his smelly old farm and he still didn't ask her to stay. What did she have to do send up smoke signals? Paint it in lipstick on her forehead? Revved with a fire fueled by her anger, Claudia hopped out of bed. She stepped into the outfit she had set aside last night while packing. It was a killer. Leather pants with a lime-green scooped neck top. She wore high-heeled sandals and made sure her hair was at its all-time fullest. If he was going to let her go, he was going to regret it every minute of the rest of his life.

Downstairs, Rosa May was trying hard to be brave, but her cheeks were flushed and her eyes were swollen with tears. Claudia's heart ached for the girl as well as for herself. This girl needed a woman in her life, and Claudia needed her. It wasn't right that they should have to separate just because Ross was being stubborn. One more thing to be angry about.

"I made pancakes," he said from across the room. She wanted to tell him that he looked silly with her apron on, but she was too furious to speak. She marched over to the kitchen table and took her seat, then reached out for Rosa May's hand and gripped it tightly in her own.

"It's going to be okay, sweetie," Claudia comforted.

"No, it's not," Rosa May wailed. "You're leaving and I don't know when I'll ever see you again."

Claudia said nothing, but she glanced over her shoulder in Ross's direction to see the impact Rosa May's words had on him. Apparently none, because he was still flipping pancakes.

"That's enough, Rosa May. Claudia doesn't want to see your tears." *And neither do I,* he added silently. It was bad enough to deal with his own pain, but he couldn't cope with his daughter's as well. "Why don't you go outside and wait for Uncle Frank? I think I hear his car now."

This was it. Frank was here. Ross still hadn't asked her to stay and so she was going to have to go. It felt like sand slipping through her fingers. No matter how hard she clenched her fingers together she still couldn't stop it. The overwhelming sense of hopelessness plunged her into a place that she hadn't been since her mother died.

"Hey, Ross," Frank called out from the back door. He entered the house and the two men shook hands in greeting. He was an older man, but in very good shape, Claudia noticed. He carried himself ramrod straight, wore his gray hair army short and sported a strong, if weathered, face. He reminded her of what Ross might look like in another twenty years. Only she wouldn't be around to know if she was right.

"Good morning, Miss Bertucci. Are you ready for your trip back to civilization?" He was trying to be funny, but she couldn't laugh, not even politely.

"Yes."

Frank immediately ended his small talk. A perceptive man, she thought. He guessed immediately that this wasn't going to be a happy send-off.

"I'll go get your things," Ross announced, not knowing what else to do.

"Excuse me, Frank." Claudia left the kitchen and went out back in search of Rosa May. She found her sitting on a tree stump not far from the barn, swinging a stick back and forth across the grass.

When she heard Claudia's footsteps she lifted her head. "Is it time?"

"Don't make it sound like I'm going to the electric chair. It's just New York. Although people have made that comparison in the past."

Rosie didn't crack a smile. Claudia understood. "You know you can come visit me whenever you want. Maybe next summer break…"

"I don't understand why you won't stay. Don't you love us? I thought you did. I mean you and Dad..." The girl waved her hands in the air to indicate that there was something there between them that she didn't know how to verbalize.

"It's not that simple. You know I love you."

"Is it the farm?" Rosa May asked.

"No."

"Is it the fact that we don't have an espresso machine? Because I saw one in a catalog for real cheap."

"No. Although no home really should be without one."

"Then what is it?"

Claudia shrugged her shoulders. How did she explain to the girl what she herself didn't understand. "I—"

"We're ready." Ross stood next to Frank's blue sedan. Frank was loading the last piece of luggage into the trunk and the two men were shaking hands.

Claudia stood and called back, "I have to get my bag." Slowly, with the sound of a requiem ringing through her ears, she walked back to the house and retrieved her bag from the couch in the living room. She looked around one last time and tried desperately not to dwell on the fact that it could have all been hers if only Ross had asked her to stay. She did love this farm. It protected her and made her feel secure in a time during her life when she needed it most. If nothing else she would always remember that.

Shoulders back. Chin up. Claudia marched out the front door and down the porch steps toward Frank's car. She needed this to be as quick and painless as possible. No turning back. Not a peek. Not a glance. Nothing. She knew Ross and Rosa May stood together farther down the driveway, but she would not look at them, could not look at them.

But as she walked closer to the car, her steps slowed. So slow she stopped completely.

"What are you doing?" she asked herself out loud. "Walk over to that car and get in. Do it now!" Her body refused to obey.

Ross stood a distance away watching Claudia. She was stopped halfway to Frank's car and it appeared that she was talking to herself. Her head was bobbing, her arms were flailing and Frank was looking at her as though she had just lost her mind.

Then it happened. She turned around in a flash and came storming down the driveway directly toward him.

"First," she shouted.

Ross beamed.

"I can't believe you were going to let me get in that car and drive away when you know you want me to stay. Second."

The joy burst inside him.

"You never once gave me the chance to prove how noble I could be, by telling you that I couldn't stay even if you did ask because you needed someone better than me to run this smelly farm with you. Third."

Ross moved forward and wrapped his arms about her waist, pulling her up against his chest. The perfect place for her.

"Third," she repeated, a little calmer now that she

was where she was always meant to be
is for the birds. I may not be the best h
I do love you. And I will make you a spectacula
wife.''

Rosa May jumped up and down, little squeals
erupting from her mouth.

"Fourth," Ross finished. "I love you, too. Desperately. Which makes you the best helpmate I could ever have."

"I am going to want to start up my own nail salon in town."

"Does that mean I get my living room back on Mondays?"

"Yes, but we're going to have to get an espresso machine," she warned him.

"And you're going to have to learn to milk a cow," he promised.

A decent compromise. To seal the bargain they kissed on it.

Claudia felt the blush spread across her shoulders, up her neck and over her face to the very tip of her head. She was absolutely positive she was glowing. Lesson number five at the Brooklyn Academy of Beauty: Love is the ultimate cosmetic!

CALL THE ONES YOU LOVE OVER THE HOLIDAYS!

Save $25 off future book purchases when you buy any four Harlequin® or Silhouette® books in October, November and December 2001,

PLUS

receive a phone card good for 15 minutes of long-distance calls to anyone you want in North America!

WHAT AN INCREDIBLE DEAL!

Just fill out this form and attach 4 proofs of purchase (cash register receipts) from October, November and December 2001 books, and Harlequin Books will send you a coupon booklet worth a total savings of $25 off future purchases of Harlequin® and Silhouette® books, AND a 15-minute phone card to call the ones you love, anywhere in North America.

Please send this form, along with your cash register receipts as proofs of purchase, to:
In the USA: Harlequin Books, P.O. Box 9057, Buffalo, NY 14269-9057
In Canada: Harlequin Books, P.O. Box 622, Fort Erie, Ontario L2A 5X3
Cash register receipts must be dated no later than December 31, 2001.
Limit of 1 coupon booklet and phone card per household.
Please allow 4-6 weeks for delivery.

I accept your offer! Enclosed are 4 proofs of purchase. Please send me my coupon booklet and a 15-minute phone card:

Name: _____

Address: _____ City: _____

State/Prov.: _____ Zip/Postal Code: _____

Account Number (if available): _____

097 KJB DAGL
PHQ4013

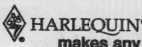